John Ashton Nicholls, Sarah Ashton Nicholls

In Memoriam

A Selection from the Letters of the Late John Ashton Nicholls

John Ashton Nicholls, Sarah Ashton Nicholls

In Memoriam
A Selection from the Letters of the Late John Ashton Nicholls

ISBN/EAN: 9783337145941

Printed in Europe, USA, Canada, Australia, Japan

Cover: Foto ©Raphael Reischuk / pixelio.de

More available books at **www.hansebooks.com**

A SELECTION

FROM

THE LETTERS

OF THE LATE

JOHN ASHTON NICHOLLS, F.R.A.S.

In Memoriam.

A SELECTION

FROM

THE LETTERS

OF THE LATE

JOHN ASHTON NICHOLLS, F.R.A.S., &c.

EDITED BY HIS MOTHER.

Printed for Private Circulation only.

1862.

CONTENTS.

IN presenting this volume of Letters, it will be understood that, with two exceptions, they were written without the least view to publication, and mostly during the hurry of travel. What, if he had been spared, my dear Son might have done with the facts and information which they contain, I cannot say ; but in their present form they certainly would not have appeared in print. They do so now in compliance with the wish of many friends, who were especially desirous to read the American portion of them.

The work of copying them out for the press has furnished sad, but at the same time sweet occupation for many solitary hours, and helped to bring into felt and living communion with the spirit that has passed into another world, the one that has been left for a little while longer in this.

Let me take this opportunity of acknowledging, with sincere gratitude, the numerous evidences which my husband and myself received, in our deep and abiding affliction, of the kind sympathy of friends whose letters, though they might be at the time unanswered, were highly prized, and will be preserved among our most cherished possessions.

SARAH NICHOLLS.

Eagley House, Ardwick,
  Manchester, 1862.

Private Letters.

PRIVATE LETTERS.

MANCHESTER, *June 28th*, 1844.

MY DEAR MISS D——,

I RECEIVED your kind letter in due course, for which I was much obliged. You would have been answered sooner, but my occupations have been very considerable, since my connection with the Ancoats Lyceum, as one of its directors, compels me to give much time to it, particularly at the present juncture, as we are thinking of removing to a larger building until we can raise one of our own. The only thing that deters us from going at once is the expense of removal, which will be considerable, and will oblige us to canvass our kind friends for assistance. I do not doubt of success, especially as the object we have in view is good, and conducive to the best interests of a large and important class of persons, forming, as they do, the bulk of the population of our great factory district.

Our Lyceum affords the advantages of a Mechanics' Institute at a cheaper rate, and is thus within the reach of numbers; for it is evident that there are many desirous of education, and its attendant mental and moral advantages, who, though unable to subscribe a pound a year, can yet well afford eight shillings, which is the amount of the subscription to our Institution. No fact shows the importance of our Lyceum more than this,— that of all the 1,100 members of the Manchester Mechanics' Institution, there are only about 16 connected with cotton and cotton factories, the majority being from warehouses and shops.

Where we are at present we have no lecture-room; in fact, no accommodation whatever. The premises we have in view were once a large corn warehouse—consequently strongly built and commodious,—where we shall have room to grow. I intend calling on some friends to try and raise a little of *the needful*. * * *

So the small dog is a proper piece of mischief;— I am much indebted to you for taking care of it so long: I shall claim it shortly. Mamma and I are going to Cork next month, and on our return we will call for it.

Your opinions coincide with mine about our Chapels' Bill; and although we cannot help praising Sir R. Peel for bringing it on, and giving it his support, still we must remember that it was only a matter of duty, of strict justice, and as such he ought, of course, to support it. The fact really is, that amongst the higher classes there is a great deal of sympathy for Unitarians and Unitarianism. Very many must see that the time will come, when sentiments very much akin to ours must be general. * * * But whenever higher thoughts and better motives seek to exert their sway, *expediency, that fell destroyer of many a good and well-formed scheme,* steps in and ruins the whole, and again submits the neck to the iron yoke. * * * Let our influence be felt in every Institution in the country; and let the spirit of our simple worship go forth, like the spirit of our great Master, into the world, and diffuse its gladsome smiles, and no longer be shut up in the cold selfishness of a fancied superiority, in expectation that all men must come up to us, without our reaching down a helping hand to raise them from the low abiding-place of mental debasement.

Yours, &c.

JOHN ASHTON NICHOLLS.

Ancoats Crescent, *September* 19*th*, 1844.

My dear Miss D——,

I am glad you approve of the subject of my lectures for the winter. I shall do my best to make them interesting and instructive; but as to entering into any very minute details, such as pointing out those gradual shadings off, till the darkness of the middle ages became the morning dawn of our own day, would be impossible; since my auditory would groan over a discussion on Anglo-Norman, and go to sleep over the Monkish records, and the semibarbarous Latin they contain. No; my object is to sink all display, and strive rather to infuse a taste for sound knowledge and right principles, into the minds of a class possessing small general information, and little if any refinement: and though I say they have no refinement, still I am not blind to the fact that there is springing up in the minds and homes of the working classes, an indefinable craving after something they don't yet possess,—a something for which they cannot find a name; in fact the idea of beauty, which must in the end triumph, is struggling in their breasts, and seeking to cast off the veil of coarseness and vulgarity which has so long covered its fair proportions, and shrouded them from public view.

The best proof of this is the now acknowledged

truth, that working-men and women seek in music saloons and picture galleries, a means of gratifying this passion, which the nakedness of their own hearths will not allow. What a pity it is that these places should be conducted in the manner they are! However *we must hope*, and in the meantime do all we can to forward whatever in this world is good, and true, and right, casting aside mere selfish considerations, or as I may say, Miss-G—— notions —*don't tell them*—about the poor; remembering that they with us are fellow-travellers, starting from the same point, journeying to the same end, with the same stake at issue, and with these facts before them, that there is but one Judge and one judgment by which all men must be tried—God and conscience.

Yours, &c.

JOHN ASHTON NICHOLLS.

ANCOATS CRESCENT, *December 5th*, 1844.

MY DEAR MISS D——,

You must allow me to apologize for not writing sooner, but I have been so much occupied with one thing and another, that I really have not had time to devote to my private correspondence.

We are going to have a Soirée in connection with our Lyceum, in January; we had fixed the 23rd of this month, but cannot make our arrangements for then. All the management of it has devolved upon me; and letters! letters!! letters!!! have been my work for some time past. The 23rd however, after all my scribbling, had to be abandoned, because all we wished to come were engaged, so that I have just got my work to begin again. We had one of our smaller tea parties on Tuesday evening last, at which I presided, which passed off very well indeed.

You can't think what a hubbub has been created about our asking Lord J. Manners to be our patron; Cobden and the League, *in private character*, have given it us prettily, and even in the leading article of the *Guardian*, there is an implied cut at us,— " these Institutions should not look to property for protection." This is said in connection with the name of Young England, *alias* Lord J. Manners,— however, I flatter myself I have disarmed Cobden's prejudice in a great measure. I have been thrown a good deal in contact with him lately, and I have been very much struck with him indeed. He is a noble fellow, somewhat hasty in judgment, but a man that speaks what he feels;—*he at least is sincere*. Would that I could say so of every member of the Lower House, or Upper either!

I trust we shall get up a Soirée in January, not of course on the scale of the Athenæum, but one suitable to our means and Institution.

Yours, &c.

JOHN ASHTON NICHOLLS.

LYCEUM, ANCOATS,

Manchester, December 11th, 1847.

DEAR SIR,

I HOPE you are improving in health; I do
trust we shall meet one of these days. I shall get
down on Monday night to the Lyceum : if I see
you there, it will be just five weeks since I had
that pleasure before. What would the world say of
an Institution whose Treasurer and Secretary have
not seen one another for five weeks? It would
either say it was on the *canine* highway, or else
that it was in such trim, as to be able to hold on its
course without much supervision. I think the
latter solution is correct; but if I see you on
Monday, we can talk it all over on the spot: I suppose we are not bankrupt yet, are we? I have
given up the " *Chimney Removal Bill,*" at all events
at present. I am sorry you cannot get G. Dawson.
By the way, that reminds me, £8. 8s. 6d. to pay
next week. Oh, dear a' me, receiving is one thing,
paying another; but if we receive plenty, I don't
mind forking it out a bit. The school is doing
wonders for us. £5. 10s. a week is a moderate
income : certainly our preliminary expenses have
been great, but we soon shall be fully repaid.

I wish H———s would send their short-
timers, then we should do: they have 60 to 80,
so that 40 more, morning and afternoon, we could

do with. Our present staff is enough, except perhaps an outlay of 10s. per week. I am always
scheming.

> DEAR SIR,
>> Faithfully Yours,
>>> JOHN ASHTON NICHOLLS.

F. RICHMOND, Esq.

MANCHESTER, *January* 21st, 1848.

MY DEAR MISS D——,

    *   *   *   I HAVE been proposed as a Mem-
ber of the Literary and Philosophical Society,—a
Society so long ornamented by the Presidency of
John Dalton;—a name which will go down to
future ages, radiant with the brightest glory,
clothed in the most innocent simplicity—a man
without guile. To-night they will decide my fate
—for the ballot takes place this evening. If I am
elected, I shall deem it a high honour; if not, I
must only strive to make myself worthy at some
future period.

I told you some time ago I was going to give
some lectures on Literature, but the Directors of
the Lyceum thought the subject too difficult for the
people to understand; so instead I am to give
four on Astronomy, illustrated by the Phantasma-...

goria, of which I will take care to send you a syllabus in due course.

Am I not an inveterate Leaguer? There is a meeting to-morrow in the Free Trade Hall, and I have distributed 140 tickets myself.

Yours, &c.

JOHN ASHTON NICHOLLS.

MANCHESTER, *August 24th*, 1848.

MY DEAR MISS D——,

* * * I AM going to enter the lecturing world again this winter.. The Directors of the Salford Mechanics' Institute wish me to give them my course on Physiology, which I have already repeated twice. The lectures are written, so I shall have but little trouble with them.

I am commencing writing a new course for the Ancoats Lyceum, on the Literature of England from the earliest period to the time of Shakspeare, which will take me some time to complete. I give them in November and December, and sometime I shall bring the course down to the present period.

You must excuse this being a short note, on the score of press of business. I hope soon to hear from you.

Yours, &c.

JOHN ASHTON NICHOLLS.

ARDWICK, *August 24th*, 1848.

MY DEAR SIR,

    * * .* * I HAVE however placed those subjects in the hands of P. W. Holland, the Secretary to the Health of Town's Association, himself a medical man. As yet I have not heard from him. You may remember he promised us a lecture some time ago; so I do hope to be able to carry out the original plan of our lectures.

I am perfectly sure that some sound information generally diffused, would do more good in allaying the often needless alarms of the ignorant, than what are generally called Boards of Health. I do not say that it is possible to popularize the science of medicine, so that every man may be his own Doctor, but I do think several cautions might be given, impressing the need of attention to certain simple rules, not as a means of cure when disease has set in, or become chronic, but simply as a preventive; and I do not think at the same time, that the Lyceum could engage in a nobler work, than an attempt to lessen human suffering, pain, death, and ruin, to hundreds, consequent upon the loss of natural supporters and friends. * * *

I purpose writing to the Committee of Privy Council this week, or beginning of next, enclosing the agreement. I shall at the same time ask them if any arrangements have yet been

made about publishing good and approved text-books for teachers and pupil teachers also; and whether it would be possible to make any arrangement with their Lordships, for obtaining some grants in aid of good evening schools.—You understand the drift of this. I quite agree with your remarks about Mr. H——, and as no doubt some proposal will emanate from him when next we meet, I shall not say anything on that head.   *   *
I hope to see our mill this week, but this dreadful weather keeps me in. I fear for our harvest, and our future prospects in general, what with wet weather and potato rot, so prevalent throughout the country. If I revolutionize, it must be but small: I have no Chartist *itch*.

I thank you for all your good wishes and hints, and believe me,

Dear Sir,

Ever your faithful Friend,

JOHN A. NICHOLLS.

F. Richmond, Esq.

Chapel Street Mill, *May 20th*, 1849.

My Dear Sir,

I received your note yesterday. I have looked at the Minute Book, and seen what had been done at the Meeting on Monday evening last.

I think it will be a good plan to call a meeting of members, and discuss our prospects together, and see what can be done to increase the number of members, and also the question of opening the news room to the public at one penny each. I think the Directors are quite right to hold it some time in June. I do think that we are approaching a crisis, and nothing but strenuous efforts will keep us on our legs. I do not mean the effort that would expend itself in one day's exertion, as a Ball or Soirée, or some piece of absurdity like what the Athenæum has so long depended upon; but that quieter effort which will continue over a longer period, and embrace the legitimate objects of the institution in its results. I know that it would be possible to relieve our present necessities by an appeal, and an excitement of some kind or other; but I always admit the force of the natural law, that "action and reaction are always equal and opposite," and that the discontinuance of the excitement would leave us in a worse position than we are at present. We must depend on the elaboration of those principles on which the Lyceum was originally founded, and I should rather wish to see the working classes themselves making the requisite exertions, than have it done for them. Now, with the exception of you and me, all the Directors are working men, and I should feel very anxious to leave in their hands, as far as practicable, the operation of the need of increased effort on their own part, and the class they represent. The apathy and indifference of the factory population towards education, is something painful as well as fearful to contemplate. I would that it were otherwise. We have put our shoulders to the wheel, and cannot, nay must not, draw back; and with an agreeable Directory, as we at present have, I hope we may ultimately succeed in our plans.

At the meeting of the Lancasterian School Committee (the annual meeting), Mr. F. said that the education of the factory children was a dead failure. Mr. M. was much vexed at this speech, and has been asking my opinion about the progress made at the Lyceum school. I told him that he might contradict Mr. F.'s statement *in toto*, at least so far as we are concerned. I said the boys of our educating had passed the examination for pupil teachers. This of course satisfied him, but I could see the insult thrown by Mr. F. had rankled in his breast a good deal. Mr. Alderman Neild called upon me the other day, to act on the Lancasterian School Committee, but I declined, telling him that the Lyceum had the first and greatest claim upon me; Mr. R. N. Philips also asked me, but I declined for the same reason:—better do one thing properly than half-a-dozen ill. * * * * * * * * * Now what are you up to in talking about offending people, and hurting feelings, and all the rest of it, —not mine I hope, at all events, and then I don't care. I hope I have not done anything very wrong, have I? Let me know your ideas on this truly important subject, as well as on the other I have alluded to. I always receive your opinions with respect and deference, as the opinions of one I esteem most highly, and whom I know to be actuated by the best and kindest motives, as well as being the opinions of one older than myself, to which I ought therefore to pay every respect. Let me hear from you soon,

And believe me, Dear Sir,

Ever yours Faithfully,

J. A. NICHOLLS.

F. Richmond, Esq.

Chapel Street Mill, *March 4th*, 1856.

Dear Sir,

I am going to give a lecture in the Mather Street Room, to-morrow evening, at eight o'clock precisely, on Strikes: will you favour me by coming? I don't know whether it will be requisite to appoint a Chairman; but, if so, will you kindly act in that capacity?

Most truly Yours,

JOHN A. NICHOLLS.

F. Richmond, Esq.

CHAPEL STREET MILL, *March 5th,* 1856.

DEAR SIR,

YOUR quiet rebuke I must reply to. I most certainly intend to keep my promise, and give a lecture at Cavendish Street; but my considerations were just these,—Am I likely to do more good by lecturing on an abstruse subject to an intelligent audience, or; at this moment of transition from a state of excitement to one of rest, by exposing popular errors and fallacies, and telling the uneducated some plain truths? I weighed the two in my own mental balance, and decided, I think rightly, in favour of the latter. Both at this moment I could not undertake. The subject of my lecture to-night has long occupied my thoughts. I have hesitated and doubted: I even now cannot say how my effort will be received.—If well, I shall be deeply gratified: if ill, I can only console myself with the thought that I have done what my conscience told me was a duty. I expect blame from two parties,—the class of inconsiderate, selfish employers, and the Union Committees.

It is no light undertaking—it is one full of serious responsibility. You must tell the truth to both, and not only that, but the *whole truth.* However, I have undertaken a certain course in life. I would fain, with God's blessing, do what little good

B

I can; and I will not turn aside because I may meet with some obloquy. I cannot always please, no man can do that; but at least I can satisfy my own conscience. This is enough for the best of us, and surely sufficient for one with so many faults as myself.

Now I know you will excuse me for apparently not keeping my promise. I do not repudiate, I only delay.

Most sincerely Yours,

JOHN A. NICHOLLS.

F. RICHMOND, Esq.

Letters from the Continent.

Vienna, *March 19th*, 1851.

Dear Mama,

I shall devote the remainder of this evening to you. I received your very welcome letter on Sunday. Thanks for all your chat and gossip, which was very agreeable to me indeed. I had just returned from dining with Count B——. Very grand, very stiff; no one but himself and his three sons, five grand servants, and a *great big beadle* or *porter*, at the door, in crimson and gold. We dined at half-past four, and I left at half-past seven. Count Augustus wished me to go with him to one of their castles on the Danube, to shoot roebuck,— *don't smile.* We smoked a cigar in his divan, which is filled with pictures. He is a very fine young man.

I think I have told you all up to last Friday. Next day I visited a few places of interest, among them the Capuchin Church and Vaults, where the bodies of the Imperial Family are buried, their hearts being preserved in silver urns, in the Loretto Chapel (St. Augustine). The most splendid sarcophagus is that of Maria Theresa; perhaps the

most interesting, the plain copper coffin of the
Duc de Reichstadt, Napoleon's son.   In one corner
lie the remains of the Countess F——, the beloved
governess of Maria Theresa.   This is the only
coffin containing other than the members of the
Royal House.   I was shown through the church
and vaults by one of the monks, in his long gown
of coarse stuff, with rosary at belt.   He took with
him a small lamp, like in form to those used by the
Romans.   Very funereal was the light it gave.   One
portion of the vaults is quite dark; the other is
sufficiently lighted from a large window.   From the
vaults I went to St. Stephen's, and mounted the
tower, which is very high; but I was well rewarded
by the splendid view from the top.   Here a man is
stationed day and night, to give notice of any fires
which may break out either in the town or country
round.   He has a small telescope, which fits in
either of the four windows of the room.   This instrument is mounted with circles, by which he can
tell exactly where the fire is, and then writes down
on a paper the particulars.   This he encloses in a
brass ball, and drops it down a tube, whence it is
carried to the fire office.   He pointed out to me
the battle fields of Napoleon,—Wagram, Aspern,
Essling, the island of Lobau, in the Danube.   I
had also a fine view of the Carpathian mountains.   *   *   *   *

On Sunday Mr. F—— took us to the Prater, the
Hyde Park of Vienna ;—the race course, and thence

to Schönbrunn, a sort of Versailles, but not so magnificent. The palace is not shown—this is not the time of the year for gardens; but the green-houses well repaid a visit. We dined at the hotel, and saw a true picture of Vienna life. The saloon was magnificently decorated; and one of the first bands in Vienna played all the time we dined. We got plenty of invitations from perfect strangers. One gentleman, who was alone, would take one of us in his cab back to Vienna; and I can assure you the day passed very pleasantly.

On Monday I called on H——, to whom Count Augustus gave me a letter. He was unwell, and could not go with me to the Geological Museum, of which he is a director, but sent for a gentleman to take me there. In the meantime, we had a long talk. He it was that arranged Mr. Allen's cabinet, and drew out the catalogue, which cabinet is now Mr. G——'s :—he was very glad to hear something about the collection. Mr. H—— then came, and we visited the geological cabinet, which is very fine. He then went with me to the Palace, where there is a splendid collection of aerolites, and introduced me to Mr. P——, who has written a good deal on meteoric stones. He then took me to the Museum of Antiquities: introduced me to a director, who very politely showed me many curious things,— remains, both Grecian and Roman, not usually exhibited; Maria Theresa's watch, made out of a single emerald; a bouquet of flowers made for her;

precious stones; and an opal, the largest in the world, worth about £8,000. In the evening we visited the Karl Theatre, which is the handsomest in Vienna. They had an Englishman in the play, and they really made a fine fellow of him; but, of course, very stolid, cold, phlegmatic.

Kohn does not much care about scientific museums, but he went with me to the Ambras Museum, which contains a very fine collection of armour; you will easily believe that I was pleased—covetous at the same time. I thought how well some of it would look in a little room I wot of * * * There were many suits of the Austrian and German Emperors, among them Charles V., Maximilian, &c. The French stole four suits in 1805—that of Godfrey of Bouillon, the Constable de Bourbon, and two others. We then visited the Belvidere, which would have delighted you. In the Church of St. Augustine is a master-piece of Canova, the Monument of the Arch-Duchess Christina. I took Kohn to the Observatory, and introduced myself as an F.R.A.S. Mr. Littson, the Astronomer, was very polite. The building is very unsuitable for the requirements of an Observatory, but Mr. Littson hopes soon to have something better. Last evening I sent for my passport, and was told I must go for it myself, which I thought strange, as Kohn's was sent without personal attendance; but I found when at the office, it arose from an order from the English Government, to know the number of

English on the Continent, for the census of the population of Great Britain, which is to be taken this year. To-morrow, Thursday, we leave for Trieste; and, if possible, shall visit in our way the quicksilver mines of Idria, and the Cavern of Adelsberg,—the Count having given me an introduction to the director of mines, of which department he is minister. * * *

TRIESTE, *March 22nd*, 1851.

DEAR MAMA,

* * * * ON Thursday morning we made our last turn about Vienna; and in the evening, at seven, left for here, by railway. The line is only open as far as Glocknitz, where it meets the last outlying hills of the Alpine chain, which we crossed in an eilwagen. The hill—for it is hardly a mountain—we then travelled on, was called the Semmering Pass. The scenery was very fine, for although night, after ten o'clock, the moon lighted up the snowy peaks, making them prominent, and leaving the rest in still deeper shadow by the contrast. After passing the mountain, we again proceeded by railway. I kept sleeping and awaking until about six in the morning, and found that we were entering a true Alpine valley. The rocks immediately surrounding not very high; but in

the distance the snow-covered summits reared themselves majestically in the air. Out of the main valley many others opened on various sides. For a long way we ran by the side of a river, I think the Mur, on which were numerous small timber rafts; in fact, until four in the afternoon, we had one long succession of splendid views, the whole terminating in a fine open plain, in which Laybach, where the railway ends, is situated. Here we arrived at five o'clock on Friday afternoon; and at six, left by an eilwagen for Trieste, which place we reached at ten o'clock on this Saturday morning; a journey of about thirty-nine hours. On the road, we were passed by the Imperial travelling carriage :—the Emperor is also visiting Trieste. When it became daylight, we found we were toiling up hills, over a most barren country, covered with large lime-stone walls. At last, a column on the road-side gave notice that we were at the top. It had been raining, in fact has rained all day, hence it was cloudy; had it been otherwise, the view must have been beyond measure grand! At our feet lay Trieste, with its ships, mole, and harbour, seeming as if we could step down upon it, and yet the descent took us about an hour, so winding is this mountain road; the blue waters of the Adriatic; the mountains of Illyria even to Istria; and those along the head of this fine sea. Had it been clear, we might have seen to Venice, which I can hardly believe is only ten hours' sail from here. We are in the

Hotel National, where too is staying the great Austrian General, Marshal Radetzky. As soon as the Emperor arrived, he paid the Marshal a visit; and just as we returned from a walk we met the Marshal in the hotel hall. He is a fine old man, 86 years of age; a little bent: and seems to suffer from weak eyes. I was, indeed, glad to see him— the Austrian Wellington.

We heard the Opera House was to be illuminated, and as all the seats were taken, went early, and got good standing places. Just before the play began the Emperor came, attended by his brother, and the Governor of Trieste. I felt pleased that I had not missed him. After all, it was rather curious that he should thus follow us to Trieste, especially as I regretted not having seen him in Vienna. The theatre was very full, and most brilliantly illuminated. All wax lights, near 700 in number. The opera was the *Huguenot*. I only staid two acts, for I felt very tired with so long a journey, and having to stand all the time.

The pavement here is very good, all large stones, I may say flags; but then they have few horses, mostly cattle with those sulky faces you noticed in Cologne. Manchester calicoes seem to be in great demand; the shops are full of them.   *   *   *

March 24th.—The weather is so wet that we have to give up our visit to the Cave of Adelsberg, which is seven miles from Trieste. Owing to the heavy rain, the bad roads would be impassable. I am very sorry; but under the circumstances it would be foolish to go there. The quicksilver mines of Idria are too far; we could not possibly accomplish them. To-morrow I leave for Venice: Kohn, having business here, will follow me in a day or two. He is a very nice travelling companion, and we get on very well together. Having seen all there is to be seen, it would only be wasting time to remain here any longer.   *   *   *   *

I know many that are dear to me will not forget that to-morrow is my birth-day, and only the second one I have ever spent from home. I cannot mark it better than by seeing on that day, for the first time, the ancient " Queen of the Seas." Yesterday the town was all afloat, because the Emperor intended to visit one of the ships of war in the harbour. A large crowd collected by the stairs leading to the barge intended for His Majesty and suite. We waited a good while, and as he did not make his appearance, went back to our hotel, where Radetzky was holding a kind of levée. All the officers, both army and navy, the town authorities, and many others were there. Some of the uniforms were very splendid, more especially the Hungarian hussars. After this we took a boat and went to one of the war steamers, which the officer allowed us to see;—the engines were English. We then returned a little way, and met the Emperor, who went on the steamer we had just left. We remained in our boat close to the ship, and saw all that passed. The men went through a few manœuvres, but not with the alacrity of English tars. The vessel was dirty; a deal of noise; want of neatness; not to be compared with our English war steamers. Just then, during the exercise, an English brig came into port, and certainly looked very well. I was glad to see again the old Union jack: it looked like a little bit of home. The Emperor did not stay long on board, and when he left, we followed, and went home to dinner. One circumstance has struck me here very forcibly,—the silence with which His Majesty is everywhere received. He is quite a young man, about 21. His mother is the real governor of the state.

This letter is determined to be one of odds and ends, and little scraps, &c. Yesterday afternoon, we took a long walk, and had some fine views over the Adriatic. We also saw many curious costumes. Greek sailors, Greek merchants, Turks, Albanians; in fact, Trieste seems to be an *omnium gatherum* of all nations. Many of the streets are steep and narrow; houses high. The Cathedral has nothing very remarkable, except its age, having been partly built in the 5th century. It is in the circular or Greek style, and very dingy.

All the people we meet are going to London, and ask a thousand questions, chiefly about hotel expenses. Heaven help those who cannot speak English! * * *

VENICE, *March* 30*th*, 1851.

DEAR MAMA,

THIS place is so entrancing that I can hardly find time to do anything but wonder what kind of people the ancient Venetians must have been; but my pen points homewards, and reminds me that I must not forget my duties.——In my last letter, I said that I should leave Trieste on the 25th; but on that day it again rained heavily, so I did not start, for I dreaded having my first impressions of Venice spoiled; therefore, I put that day down as a lost one. Wednesday morning was fine, so I got up at a quarter-past four—the boat sails at six—got comfortably on board, and away we went across the blue waters of the Adriatic. The day was glorious; and about two o'clock, we came in sight of Venice, of which we could only see the domes and Campanile rising above a low bank, which separates the Lagoon from the open sea.—— The entrance from the port is difficult; and we went winding along between islands until, at one turn, the whole frontage of the city was before us. The boat stopped opposite the Lion of St. Mark. Gondolas came all round and about. I got one; and was soon at the Albergo dell' Europa, which was formerly the Giustiniani Palace. The halls are paved with marble; stairs also of marble. Every

good house has two entrances; one into a narrow
street or lane; the other, from the canal. I was
not long before I issued out on an exploration; and
passing through the street door, a few turns
brought me under a piazza, in the Square of St.
Mark, which square far surpassed my expectations.
It is not so large. A piazza runs round it on three
sides, of marble; the fronts of the building being of
the same material, of course much blackened by
age. The nearest idea I can give you of it is, the
Palais Royal, in Paris, with this exception, that the
square is paved all over. Under the piazzas are
shops and cafès, drinking houses, and a palace. The
fourth side is occupied with the Church of St.
Mark, built in the Eastern style, like a mosque; all
marble. The front is beautifully ornamented with
mosaics, and much gilt. The interior is rather
gloomy, owing to the small size of the windows; but
contains a great deal of splendid mosaic work: the
floor all marble, beautifully inlaid; and some very
curious figures and patterns of different colours,
also in mosaic. Before the church stand the three
great masts, on which the gonfalons of the Republic
formerly floated.

The Doge's Palace is built in the form of a
quadrangle, surrounding a large court yard. Entering by the Giant's staircase, on the top of which
the Doges were crowned, I went first to the hall of
council, a noble room, containing very fine pictures,
mostly of an historical character. The pictures have

been taken out of the ceiling, on account of the bombardment of Venice, lest any stray balls should fall through them, and have not yet been replaced. Round the room is the celebrated frieze of portraits of the seventy-two Doges, with a black curtain covering the space which should have been occupied by the portrait of Marino Falierio. The views from the windows and balconies are very fine, looking either towards the Lagoon, or on the open space in which the two pillars stand, on one of which is the Winged Lion; on the other, the figure of St. Theodore, the first patron saint of Venice. The Lion was taken to Paris, but has been restored. I saw also the well-known Lion's Mouth, in which the secret accusations were dropped; and afterwards went into the dungeons, which are something serious. There are not any instruments of torture there, although the dungeons of the Venetian Inquisition. Of course I went on to the "Bridge of Sighs," leading from the palace to the prison. There is not much to see in the palace, except pictures; and it is useless only giving you a mere catalogue of them. It is more a feeling of veneration for departed glory—for historic reminiscences—than for what is actually before you as a mere show; and so it is throughout Venice, which, while it gives you the greatest pleasure, affects the mind with melancholy.

The palaces of marble are in decay:—not sixty of the real old families in existence; and their dwelling places, once most princely, are now crowded by a squalid, filthy population; else converted into barracks for Austrian troops, or into hotels, and so forth. The Canale Grande, spanned by the noble Rialto, is lined with these palaces. On some, rank weeds are running over wall and roof; whereas, a few—a very few—are in good order. The Duc de Bordeaux and his mother, the Duchess de Berri, are living in one; Taglioni owns five; and, to her credit be it said, is restoring them as well as she can. The new buildings are all brick and plaster, and join up to those of more costly materials, giving the effect of a fine garment patched with coarse stuff. The streets are, indeed, narrow, they would delight you—for in some of the most crowded, in the part called Merceria, where the best shops are, if you stretch out your arms you touch both walls. Then you are constantly crossing little bridges over small canals, and hearing the cry of the gondoliers to warn one another at the turns.

The gondolas are ugly things; a long boat with a covered place in the middle, for all the world like an English country hearse. They are all painted black, and the central cabin is covered with coarse black cloth, and has little crape bows and bobs over it;—the dexterity of the men is wonderful.

I have seen many churches, but will not trouble you with these visits, beyond saying that the Jesuit's

C

is the finest. The interior is white Carrara marble, inlaid with verd antique. We went to the Church of the Scalzi, built A.D. 1680, in which several of the wealthiest families of Venice contended together who should erect the handsomest altars of the purest marbles; and splendid indeed they all are. The Church of the Frari contains the monuments of Canova and Titian : poor Foscari is buried there. There are many more very singular monuments; but I would rather tell you what I see more characteristic of the people. The day after I arrived here, his Imperial Majesty followed, and this ancient city was decorated in the old-fashioned manner—carpets, tapestry, silk, and velvet hanging from the windows; —the vessels all dressed out in flags, for it was known that the Emperor intended to restore the Franco Porto, or charter of free port to Venice, the deprivation of which has reduced it most terribly; its trade gone—its merchants migrated to Genoa. * * * *

When the steamer came into port she was saluted by all the forts, and then the ships of war, gunboats and floating batteries, took it up. The sight from my bed-room window was very fine. I then went into the Grand Square, where the Emperor, followed by a brilliant staff, was reviewing the troops—the band playing "God save the Emperor." In the evening, and every evening since, the Square of St. Mark has been illuminated. The next day Kohn rejoined me from Trieste ; he is delighted with Venice. The morning after we took a gondola, and went round to the Churches I have alluded to, finishing our day's work at the Opera. The ballet was beautiful, taken from Goethe's "Faust"; it has had a great run in Rome,—I enjoyed it very much. We could not have seen Venice to greater advantage—all gaiety. I can hardly describe what I have witnessed to-day. It is what is called a Corso on the Grand Canal. Every gondola was engaged; we had one; and about two o'clock they all flocked to the Grand Canal, and commenced rowing up to the Rialto, where there was a military band. Many of the gondolas were much decorated, especially those belonging to private families. Some of the gondoliers were dressed in fancy dresses—many of them old-fashioned.

The Emperor was there, and as soon as he turned down, all the boats set off as fast as they could drive down the canal, in number perhaps a thousand, and formed quite an exciting scene; the men all so good-tempered with one another, and yet all trying to pass the rest. Some had flags flying on the bows, some with one rower, some with two, three, four, and even six or eight. At one time we were running close by the side of the Duc de Bordeaux, (Henry V. of France, if he can get the crown), with him his mother, the Duchess de Berri; then by the side of the Emperor's brother; next by one of the Infants of Spain—a very handsome young man; then by the Arch-Duchess

Sophia, mother of the Emperor, and a whole host of other great people, whose names I cannot remember. The Papal Ambassador was there, with the tiara and keys on his flag; the Russian with his one-headed eagle, and the Podesta of Venice— (I am glad they preserve the old name of Podesta) —in fact there has not been seen a Corso for several years, and we esteem ourselves fortunate to have been here at such a time.

I am glad my letters interest you. I try to make them as clear an account of what I see, or rather the chief of what I see, as I can, but must really acknowledge that I do not possess my Mama's descriptive powers. Your enquiry about beds is amusing. The best I have yet had is here in Venice. Throughout Italy they are now using iron bedsteads, and do away with the traveller's delight as much as possible. They are a dirty people, and therefore idle. I now understand *dolce-far-niente*. The men lie about on marble steps, sleep all day and night too;—a very little money keeps them a long time; when it is done they work for a little more, and then are idle again. We had a nice instance this evening. We were taking an ice in the Square, and saw opposite to us a little boy, who wrapped himself up in his jacket, and sat on a step. I called him and gave him a kreutzer; he came for it, took off his cap, bowed his head, and went back again. Then he began talking to us, but as we could not understand what he said, he repeated his words several times, but always from his seat; still we did not know what he said. At last, with a sigh, he got up and came to us to tell it; it was such an exertion for him to rise. Kohn gave him another kreutzer; then we saw him putting his money in all forms, perfectly happy. Some have such Murillo faces, and eyes that seem to express everything without language. Among the lower orders we meet with the finest faces, but the old women are ugly. * * *

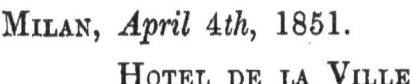

MILAN, *April 4th,* 1851.
HOTEL DE LA VILLE.

DEAR MAMA,

* * * * THE next day, Tuesday, we left Venice at ten in the morning, by rail to Verona. The country is very flat, but particularly fertile. The almond and peach trees in blossom; the trees budding forth;—and the whole has all the appearance of spring. The railroad crosses the Lagune, to the mainland, on arches; and you see Venice behind you in the sea. The effect is very fine. Looming in the distance were the Alps, covered with snow; and on the other hand the outlines of the Appennines.

We arrived at Verona at two : finding a diligence at nine in the evening, we determined to take that, and have a few hours in the town. We first went to the Roman Amphitheatre which, in the interior, is still as perfect as when erected by the Romans in the year 71,—near 1800 years ago. The seats are all there, the stairs to them ; the galleries below giving access to different parts of the building ; but the row of arches round the top is nearly all destroyed by an earthquake : it will hold 80,000 persons. The works are of immense strength, and except that the coating of cement is knocked off the walls, are for the most part perfect. There are still remaining the ticket offices, actors' rooms, and the great den under ground where the wild beasts were kept, and let into the vast arena, where no doubt many of the early Christians met a fearful death.

You may be sure I looked with great reverence upon this majestic work ;—the first large building constructed by the former masters of the world I ever saw. I think it would not be possible to commence with a finer example. Verona contains many remains of Roman antiquities, large arches, but of course the Amphitheatre absorbs the greatest amount of interest. I also could not forget that Verona was the scene of Romeo and Juliet; I saw the house of Romeo, and also that of the Capulets. Juliet's tomb no longer exists, but they show you a well, and call that the tomb. I did not go to see

it. Near an old Church, Santa Maria l' Antica,
are some curious tombs of the Scaligeri family,
about eight in number, surrounded by a very beautiful palisade iron railing or trellis work, consisting
of open *quatre-foils.* * * * We then dined,
and at a quarter past nine left by diligence for
Milan. They go so slowly that it was really tiresome, we reached Treviglio at two next afternoon.
There we joined the railway, our diligence was put
on a truck and so on to Milan, where we arrived at
four o'clock. After the passports, Douane, &c., we
went to our hotel. The custom-house officers
asked for money; about eightpence each prevented
any examination.

Kohn did not want to dine at the *table d'hôte,*
but I would insist on it; he is a good-natured
fellow, so we hurried and went. Now I am going
to surprise you. In the room we saw some
American friends, who left Venice by the same
train, and who we knew would be at the hotel.
I spoke to them, and was sitting down, when a
gentleman jumped up, " Nicholls, how are you?
Oh, how astonished I am to see you here ! " Who
do you think it was? Westphal, with his wife, on
their wedding-tour! They are, indeed, a handsome
couple : he 20, his wife 17, just married a fortnight : he was delighted to see me, and I to see
him, and we had a deal of talk. The next day
they went to Monza, and we did not meet till
dinner time. In the evening we had a walk toge-

ther. Westphal is more manly in face and figure than when you saw him. He made many inquiries about you and Papa, and desired to be remembered to you. They left to-day for Venice. Yesterday morning I set out for the Palace of the Brera, where I found Frisiani lived, as Secretary to the Imperial Society of Science. I went to a door with his name on, and then he came up from some other place; I knew him again in an instant; of course he did not know me until I gave him my card and told him who I was, and then I really thought he would have wept over me, he was so truly glad to see me, and then we had a long talk about all in Manchester. Many were the inquiries about our family, and was very sorry to hear that grandpapa was dead. He wished me to come and stay with him, but I told him I had a friend with me. I went over the Observatory, and made an appointment for the next day. I then met Kohn, and we went to the Cathedral, which I cannot justly describe, it is so really magnificent. Here we found the American family, who went with us into the vaults of the Church, to see the tomb of Saint Carlo Borromeo, which is a room entirely surrounded with silver mouldings and pillars, and in the intervals with gold tissue cloth. The sarcophagus is solid silver; by a machine, the front is made to descend, and disclose the body of the saint. The priest who showed it, first lighted eight wax lights, and put on his cope. The coffin is silver, with panes of pure rock crystal, through which you see the mummy, dressed in full pontificals, with mitre, pastoral staff, and gloves, and over his head hangs a gold crown, richly studded with jewels, and an emerald cross, once belonging to Maria Theresa, of great value; but all the gorgeous trappings serve but to mock the poor dried black skeleton that peers from out of them. * * We then ascended to the roof, and had a very grand and extensive view. We saw the whole line of the Alps, from Mont Blanc, 165 miles distant, Monte Rosa, St. Gothard, St. Bernard, with the passes of the Simplon and Splugen, the Jung Frau, and all on that side,—of course at a very great distance.

The roof of the Church is quite as interesting as the interior, covered with pinnacles, each surmounted by a statue; it is really wonderful. We walked all over, through galleries, up and down stairs of the most beautiful construction. It took us several hours to see it. We then visited Sant Ambrogio and Santa Maria delle Grazie.

Milan is a fine town, the streets are bustling, but things look bad, it will not be long before a revolution breaks out; the Austrians are hated, no one will speak to an officer, indeed they dare hardly go alone, and only Austrians go to the Theatre. The whole city seems in a state similar to a lulled volcano.

This morning I took Kohn and the Americans

to the Brera, and saw through the picture galleries. Frisiani is giving me a letter of introduction to Father Rosa, a Jesuit priest in Rome, at the Observatory there, in the Collegio Romano. * * * I must now write to Aunt Staley.   * * * To-morrow we leave for Genoa.   * * *

FLORENCE, *April 11th*, 1851.

DEAR MAMA,

I TAKE the first opportunity of writing since leaving Milan. On the Saturday morning Frisiani called with the letter, and, after packing up, we set off at one o'clock by the courier, for Genoa. The first part of our journey was through a flat but fertile country, with the vines festooned on larger trees, not yet in leaf. We see but the skeleton of the beautiful Italian scenery. About four we reached Pavia, and crossed the Ticino by a wooden bridge, roofed in with tiles. A miserable bridge of boats led us over another branch of the same river, where our passports were *visèd*—hence a few miles, and we came to the last Austrian outpost, which marks the frontier of the extensive empire which has taken us so long to travel through—crossing the Po by a bridge of boats, we

were on the frontier of Sardinia. The river is very
broad, in fact, a noble stream, and quite disgraced
by the bridge which crossed it. At this point all
the luggage was taken down, and really examined,
passports *visèd*, and then we were allowed to continue our journey. Night soon came on; as usual,
I composed myself to sleep, and did sleep soundly,
from half-past eight till five the next morning.
Kohn really envies me the power of falling rapidly
into the arms of Morpheus. When I awoke on
Sunday morning it was quite fine and clear, and
we were ascending among bold hills, not to be
called mountains. On the summit we had a fine
view over Genoa, something similar to the first
view of Trieste, except from this road you do not
see the whole town at once. At the gates, passports again. About nine o'clock we reached our
hotel, and after dressing, breakfast, &c., we engaged
a *valet-de-place*, and sallied forth to see the lions.
The Cathedral is nothing particular, but curious—
some of the pillars being black and white marble,
in alternate squares, a style of building of which
I have now seen several examples. Here is kept
the celebrated Sacro Catino, which is locked up
with the greatest care—one key being kept by the
town authorities, the other by the church—hence
two fees. This is one of the doubtful treasures of
the Romish Church, so strongly commented upon by
Lady Wortley. The church says it is a single
emerald, formed into a dish, perhaps 14 or 16

inches in diameter, given by Queen Sheba to Solomon—that it was the vessel which held the Paschal Lamb at the Last Supper, and that Joseph of Arimathea caught in it the blood which flowed from the side of our Saviour, when pierced on the cross. The French say that it is a piece of glass, but undoubtedly very old. We also pronounced it glass, for you can distinctly see your fingers through it, which would not be the case with a real emerald. The Ducal Palace contains some fine marble halls and floors, but is nothing like so interesting as that in Venice.

I may say marble no longer excites our attention as it did. In our hotel,—Hotel Feder,—formerly the Palace of the Admiralty, we had a noble bedroom with a vaulted ceiling, painted with beautiful frescos, marble balconies, marble door and window frames, &c. At Sant Ambrogio or di Gesù service was going on; this is a magnificent church, rich in gilding and painting; it is built entirely and is still supported by the Pallavacini family, whose Palazzo in the Strada Carlo Felice is still kept up in the olden style of furnishing.

In the Palazzo Durazza is the most elegant marble staircase I ever remember to have seen.

The Palazzo Reale was in a manner re-furnished for the late King Charles Albert, the state-rooms are tastefully decorated, and it possesses a fine gallery of pictures; as the rooms are high up, there is a hoist connected with one room, so that His

Majesty can be saved the trouble of walking up
and down stairs, but is wound up and down like a
tin of cops or a bundle of yarn in a Lancashire
cotton mill.

After seeing the gardens we took a boat, and for
the first time floated on the waters of the Mediterranean. The view of Genoa from the sea is fine,
houses rise in terraces above houses, and the tops
of all the hills are crowned with forts—it deserves
its name Genoa la Superba. The streets, especially the aristocratic quarters of the Strada Balba,
Nuova, Nuovissima, are indeed streets lined with
noble palaces. The women wear a sort of scarf,
the poorer class of coloured print with the gayest
pattern; it is thrown over the head, brought under
the chin, and falls flowing over the shoulders. The
better class wear white muslin—this dress is peculiar to Genoa.

The Sardinian soldiers are little, dirty, shabby-
looking fellows. In the evening we went on board
the Capri steamer, and at eight sailed for Leghorn,
where we arrived the next morning, between eight
and nine. The sea was smooth, and to my surprise and his own too, Kohn was not ill. Our
luggage was overhauled, more particularly to see
that we did not carry arms,—for now in the Grand
Duchy of Tuscany, all the towns are full of Austrian soldiers to prevent revolutions. Passports are
becoming really troublesome and expensive.   *   *

I called on my old schoolfellow, David Moro,

who was very glad to see me, and did his best for us in the way of sight-seeing, &c.—Left the next morning by rail for Pisa, where we arrived in half an hour. Before leaving Leghorn, luggage again examined, and sealed with lead,—a paper was given to us, but my name was put out and in its place, Signior W. S. Leather.—I said, "this is not my name;" the man said it was on the portmanteau: then I found that he had *written* me down as War-ranted Solid Leather. We had a good laugh, for they are very stupid.

In Pisa we visited first the Campo Santo or Cemetery, in which no interments now take place, except by permission. Next the Baptistry, and then to the Cathedral, containing the usual quan-tity of pictures, altars, &c. It was here the lamp hanging from the roof first suggested to Galileo the idea of the pendulum. The Campanile, or Leaning Tower, now claimed our attention. These four, the only objects of any attraction in Pisa, being close together, constitute a very fine group of buildings. The Tower is most extraordinary in its effect. It is fifteen feet out of the perpen-dicular; and when on the top, you just feel as if about to slide off. The ascent is by 330 steps, and not so very easy : to confess the truth, I did not think so much of it as I did before seeing it.

We passed a palace of the Medici, with the well-known crest of balls. At four we went by rail to Florence, arriving here about seven, and came

to our hotel pretty well tired. Next morning we
sallied forth ;—first the Cathedral, which is constructed of variegated marble ; the front still unfinished. The Church of the Annunziata is very
magnificent. The altars and Chapel of the Annunziata are crammed full of wax legs, arms, &c.,
the offerings of those who have been cured by
miraculous agency. I then called upon the Baron
S——, and found the Baroness at home. She
invited me to come in the evening. I told her I
had a companion, and hoped I might present him.
So in the evening we both went, and spent two
hours very pleasantly. The Baroness is a Russian,
the Baron a German. Between my morning and
evening visits, they had intelligence of the death of
her father, which obliges them to return to St.
Petersburg.

Now come our failures. The great galleries of
the Uffizi and the Pitti Palace, are closed till after
the Holy Week. Thus far though we have tried
all we can—shall not be able to see the Venus de
Medici, and the other treasures of art they contain.
This is a real disappointment, the most serious we
have met with. We have wandered over half the
town to find the director of museums, to try and
get a special order which he will not grant. Only
been able to see the curious Museum of Natural
History in the Pitti Palace, and the wax anatomical
models, which are truly beautiful ; and also, to
my delight, the Salon erected to the memory of

Galileo; here are his instruments, and here his great triumph—the first telescope ever made,—a noble statue of the great philosopher, and in a glass vase the first finger of his right hand. Some of the instruments are very curious, both in design and construction. We then visited the church of Santa Croce, containing the monuments and tombs of Galileo, Dante, Michael Angelo, Alfieri, Machiavelli, the wife and child of Joseph Buonaparte, and many others belonging to the noble families of Tuscany,—it is their Westminster Abbey. We have also seen the Convent of St. Mark, dirty enough for anything, and if ever in my life I connected any idea of a romantic character with convents or monks they are for ever disenchanted. There are Dominican monks in white dresses, coarse, fat, lazy, hypocritical-looking fellows, too idle to work; they enter the Church and rot in their cloisters. We have seen plenty of Franciscan friars in brown serge cloaks and sandal-shoon, and all look as if clean water were unknown to them: all have the same slouching gait, and all seem equally averse to labour. As for priests one is really tired of seeing them,—they literally swarm over the land.

The fine Medicean Chapel, in the Church of San Lorenzo, was intended for the reception of the Holy Sepulchre, which, however, was not obtained. It is a lofty chapel, surmounted with a cupola; round the inner surface of the vaults are some very fine paintings; the walls are entirely covered with different-coloured marbles, with porphyry, chalcedony, jaspar, agate, lapis lazuli, mother-of-pearl, and other precious stones, worked into roses and groups of flowers, composing the Florentine mosaic of *pietre commesse*. Round the base are the armorial bearings of the cities and states of Tuscany. It is a fine town, but not so fine as I expected to see. No doubt not seeing the galleries has had a bad effect on our general impression. The Arno, yellow with mud, is crossed by several bridges; one, the oldest, is very singular, as it is, except in the middle, a street of shops, something like the Rialto at Venice.

Beggars swarm—too lazy to get up even to beg, but with their eyes shut, snoozing in the sun, ask for alms. In Pisa we were much amused; a beggar woman asked charity of us; we shook our heads—she said "Non, non," then slowly pointed one finger up to heaven, shook it—then turned it down, and pointed the other way, as much as to say she, a poor woman, would go to heaven, and we, who refused alms to her, would go to another nameless place.   *   *   *

ROME, *April* 18*th*, 1851.

DEAR MAMA,

I REALLY date this letter from the Eternal City, but I must not anticipate.

Saturday, we *looked* Florence over again. Baron S—— called, and gave me a letter of introduction here, which I have not yet delivered. In the afternoon we went to the Observatory, but did not meet with Father Antinoi, the astronomer. Sunday, visited Fiesole, and had some fine views of Florence and the surrounding country. * * * * . * * On Monday morning, up at half-past five, in time for the diligence; and now for a day of adventures. We were taken to the railway, and had tickets given us for Siena, whence the journey to Rome is performed in a diligence. We were told the conductor would look after us in every way. Kohn, I, an English clergyman, his wife, and a young lady, were the passengers from Florence. We had been talking together for a long time; and noticing we were passing some stations we had seen on the way from Leghorn, enquired from the guard if it was a Siena train. "Oh, you ought to have got out at Empoli." Here was a fix; we had passed the station. Well, we went on to Pontedera, where there is a telegraph station, and told the station-master. Though the telegraph is only for the use of Government and the railway, he politely allowed us the use of it : we sent a message to Siena, telling them the diligence must wait for us. Got an answer that it could not, and would start at one o'clock. As no train could get to Siena till near nine at night, we sent them another message, that if they would wait till four, we could get an express engine. No, they would not wait. We then sent them word to send back our luggage and passports, which were in the hands of the conductor : we should hold him responsible. We then set off back to Florence. The clergyman would have it, it was all a trick, a cheat. At Empoli got a third answer ;—all would be sent back. Pleasant this, after paying our fare to Rome. At Florence we found some difficulty in getting in to the town, not having any passports; a small bribe did that for us. We went to the diligence office, and told our tale. The master listened till we had had our say, and then said, " Well, gentlemen, it is clearly the fault of the conductor ; you must go back to Siena to night. I will send a clerk with you, and if the diligence has gone on, will forward you by post direct." This gave us every satisfaction ; we then got some dinner. The master came again, and said he had received a dispatch—the diligence was waiting for us. At half-past five we retraced our steps ; the conductor met us at Siena, where he had waited eight hours. Of course he was not to blame ; it was the railway guard : however we were all pleased with the termination, and off we set. The next morning early we reached the Tuscan frontier, on a fine hill commanding an immense prospect. A little further on we crossed, or rather went through a stream, and were in the Papal States. The road is very hilly, scenery lovely on all sides. We sometimes had in addition eight horses, and two or even four bullocks, where the passes were very difficult. Each step we took showed us a more beautiful country, and a more wretched population. The late appearance of the diligence at the different stations, caused great excitement, and over and over again the same tale had to be told. We met plenty of carriages attended by soldiers, but no *brigands*.

At the Tuscan frontier we had a little bad coffee; a boy priest was the waiter, and I saw him trying if the beverage was warm, by putting his dirty fingers in the can.

At Acquapendente, where we arrived at noon, we had a *déjeûner à la fourchette*, after which we travelled on all day. The conductor would not stop again, as he did not like to pass some places in the dark.

We passed the beautiful lake of Bolsena, the shores of which are fertile, but the malaria prevents those who till the soil living near it. Another beautiful moonlight night, and about half-past five I caught a view of Rome. The approach gives you no idea of your proximity to the great Capital.

Desolate roads, a few old towers, a few tombs, you cross the Tiber by the Ponte Molle, through a straggling suburb, and then reach the Porta del Popolo, and you are in Rome. At the Custom House, a few pauls saved us any trouble. Then for an hotel : we wandered about for two hours— could not get rooms any where. Here we are at last in furnished apartments, fourth story, looking into the Corso. We afterwards got some breakfast at a café, and then called upon Mr. K——, who gave us tickets for Lent Sunday at St. Peter's. After this visit we proceeded to St. Peter's, crossed the bridge opposite St. Angelo, which frowns over it with its vast round keep ; and turning to our left, were soon before the noble façade of the chief Catholic Temple in Europe. To enter it, and not feel its grandeur is impossible ; but to say that I was as impressed with it as Cologne, or York, or Westminster, I certainly was not. Dickens, in his " Letters from Italy," is quite right about it. There is nothing in it to give you any impression of a religious nature. Its very vastness destroys this effect, and yet it is truly noble in its proportions.

I have been in it now several times, and think that it rather grows upon you. The monuments are not many, but are fine. I will talk about them another time. At three o'clock, after returning to our lodgings to dress, we visited the Sistine Chapel to hear the Miserere, and found ourselves in the midst of a fashionable crowd, chiefly English; and had full time to admire the Swiss Guard, in their quaint dress. The doors opened, and we all rushed in, and the chapel was soon full—2,000 people trying to get into a place that holds 500 only. I got close to the front railing, which separates the priests from the people. At a quarter-past five it began: a little before that, the Cardinals came in and took their seats, dressed in purple robes, scarlet stockings. I counted fifteen of them, each attended by his servant in orders, who unswathed him as he stood, *and let down his petticoats.* Antonelli, the Cardinal Secretary of State, an intelligent-looking Jesuit, was conspicuous amongst them; though there were several very fine old men. They now brought fifteen candles, on a triangular frame—all lighted; then a wooden cross. And now the Pope, in a splendid scarlet embroidered mantle, and a mitre on his head; he was conducted to a seat under a canopy, and then the Penitential Psalms began. Gradually all the lights, except one, which was carried behind the altar, were extinguished; this lasted two hours, and was particularly tiresome; then the Miserere commenced, wild, wailing, unearthly voices, that seemed tones of some instrument, swelling and falling in a really touching and impressive manner. After this, a great knocking of sticks, the light was brought from behind the altar, and all was over. I was very glad, for 46 hours' travelling, and standing in the chapel near six, had wearied us quite out. This chapel, as you know, is decorated with the frescoes of Michael Angelo, which are very fine, but much discoloured; it did not come up to my expectations. The next day the Pope blessed the people, and washed the feet of the pilgrims; we contented ourselves with the last exhibition, not being able to *do* both, so we went into the chapel, filled with people—(seats for the ladies, all of whom are obliged to be veiled in black)—foreign ambassadors, French officers, and, in a box, the ex-King of Bavaria (Lola Montes' friend) and the Grand Duke of Saxony. I got close to a barrier by which the Pope passed, and had a good view of him; he has a cunning look, but withal shrewd, but such a pious demeanour. As he passed he blessed us, and we all bent to him,—preceded by the Noble Guard, consisting of young men of the first Italian families. He then took his seat; the thirteen pilgrims, who had previously entered, were perched up in full view, each attended by a Cardinal—such a set they looked!—one old man had a fine white beard; they were placed just under a picture of the Last Supper, and one was not unlike the Judas above; they were of all nations, one Chinese, one Cingalese.

The attendants took off the Pope's mitre and robe, and wrapped a towel round him, one holding a basin, another a towel; then he went to the first in order, sprinkled a little water on his foot *(all their feet had been well washed)*, wiped it with a

towel, and then kissed it; so on to all. His Holiness got through as quickly as possible.   *   *   *
The first evening we arrived here, we went to the Colisæum, to see it first by moonlight; and here I cannot describe the impression—I felt it was old Rome !

There was that arena in which so much blood had been spilt; there, the walls that had resounded with the cries of people excited by the most barbarous sports; and there was the placid sky, and the moon casting the arched shadows where they have fallen for 1800 years ! It was a scene I can never forget;—one of those hallowed spots in memory which nothing can efface ! In the centre is erected a cross triumphant, where early Christians perished.

There were many people there, talking and laughing; but we stayed till all was still, and then you feel the place and the hour.—Surrounded by all that was great in the world : close at hand the arches of Constantine and Titus : the palace of the Cæsars, spreading its vast ruins over one of the seven hills; temples, fountains, columns,—all, all in ruins ! Modern Rome is dirty and wretched, with a miserable people, priest-ridden to the last degree,—a mere stye to what the ancients have left grand in decay and desolation. Up this morning at half-past six : at the Sistine Chapel at half-past eight, to hear pontifical high mass, which begins at ten. Another squeeze ; very hot, and very unpleasant.

The cardinals came in again; in broad daylight they are a set of fat, snuffy, dirty-looking fellows. Then the Pope and the service began, which is very beautiful indeed,—they chaunted a chapter from the New Testament, the crucifixion of Christ. Then they uncovered the cross and figure of our Saviour, which is veiled during Lent; it was laid on a cushion, the Pope knelt before it, adored it, and kissed it; after him, all the cardinals, chief officers, and inferior clergy. Then a grand procession : the Pope went to fetch the consecrated elements from the Pauline Chapel: shortly returned under a canopy, with a large silk umbrella over his head,—the vessels in his hands under his robe. At half-past twelve it was over.

After all, these ceremonies of the Holy Week are rather tiresome.   *   *   *   *

You must look at this Letter as a sketch only.

ROME, *April 22nd,* 1851.

DEAR MAMA,

    *   *   *   * FIRST, I suppose, you must receive my absolution in full, concerning what you alluded to in your letter—for now, having been so often blessed by the Pope, some virtue must have

descended upon me, and gives me the power to absolve.

In Florence, for the first time, one moonlight evening, I really felt myself in another climate ; the clearness of the soft night falling round the deeper shadows, by contrast, and the mild air, all contributed to the effect. In Rome we have met with the deep blue sky for which we have been longing. It is getting very warm, but as yet not too hot to prevent our taking plenty of exercise ; the multitude of stairs we have to climb giving us plenty of that.

When I first went into St. Peter's, there were a great many pilgrims in the church, with their staffs and wallets, and olive-coloured faces ; they all kissed the toe of St. Peter, which figure is a large one of metal, quite black, seated in a white marble chair. The toes on the right foot are nearly kissed away— I saw one pious individual carefully wipe it with his pocket handkerchief before kissing it.

I am glad the holy week is over; it is the hardest work in the world to attend the ceremonies ; there are no seats, and you have to stand for hours in a dense hot crowd. * * * * On Saturday we went to St. John Lateran, which is a magnificent church, being the chief or head Catholic church in the world. Here the popes are crowned. Service was going on, being a consecration service of priests, the chief cardinals conducting it. Here we were shown many Catholic relics,—a portion of the table on which Christ eat the last supper with the Apostles; it is religiously preserved, in a gilt frame, with a lamp before it; also the pillar of the Temple of Jerusalem, which fell when the Temple was rent in twain, at the Crucifixion; two pillars of Pilate's house; and the well at which our Saviour met the woman of Samaria. These are kept in the cloisters. In the church is a fine chapel, and monuments of the Torlonia family, rich bankers in Rome. Near this church is another building, containing the sacred stairs, up which many penitents were painfully toiling on their kness, at each step a prayer is said, then the penitent kissed the step, and so on to the top. I saw that the most knowing ones crept up close by the wall, which helped them up a little. The finest thing is a statue of Constantine, outside the church, under a portico.   *   *   *   *

Sunday; up at six, and off to St. Peter's, where pontifical high mass was celebrated by the Pope. It began a little after ten. Again a dreadful crowd and crush near the altar. The centre of the church was kept open by a line of soldiers on each side. The procession enters. First, the acolytes and incense bearers, crosses, &c.; then, priests and cardinals, and lastly the Pope, seated in his chair, carried by men, with the canopy over his head, the fan-bearers on each side. His dress was white, magnificently embroidered with gold, and on his head the tiara; before him were carried mitres, and another tiara. He blessed the people as he passed; and close to me he extended his hand, and blessed: I was not a yard from him. He had a smile on his face, and looked to much better advantage than when I saw him before. He seems a benevolent, kindish man; but cramped on all sides by those odious priests. He was conducted to his seat; and then he began to chaunt the service, of which little could be heard. The most imposing part was the elevation of the host; when, having taken off the tiara, he (the Pope) first held up the consecrated wafer, and then the cup of wine, over which prayers had been constantly said since Thursday evening. At that moment all knelt, the soldiers' swords clattering on the ground, and then all silent; it was really imposing. By the altar is the shrine of St. Peter, with the hundred red lamps burning before it. Ere the service was over, all rushed out to see the benediction of the people. We got near, under the gallery or balcony, but that is only in the square. The sight was very fine. About 4000 soldiers, drawn out in order, a vast throng of people completely filling it. The Pope appeared, pronounced the benediction (which we could just hear), with outstretched arms, the cannon fired, and all was over:—so ended the Holy Week!

On Sunday afternoon we set off along the ancient Appian way, and visited first the Baths of Caracalla, which are of vast extent; some portions of mosaic pavement yet remaining, but all one mass of ruin. In fact, I may say once for all, that the

Roman ruins but show how great and vast was the
scale on which everything was erected. Of the de-
signs, the divisions of buildings, you can make little
out now; the marbles are gone, statues removed, a few
shattered walls alone remain. We then went to the
tomb of the Scipios, which is a singular excavation
in the rock, of great extent. Scipio Africanus is
not, however, buried here. From there to the
Columbaria, the most curious place I have yet
seen; a small one-storied building; you open a door
and descend a deep flight of steps, excavated in
the rock. The walls are perforated with small
holes, like pigeon holes, hence its name. In small
holes at the bottom of these pigeon holes, were
deposited the ashes of the dead, after the burning
of the bodies. They are thus : ⌒ ⌒ ⌒ ⌒ [0 0 / bottom]
so each one would hold the ashes of two bodies;
the holes being covered with earthenware lids. In
many of them were fragments of bone. Out of one
I took a small bone, which is the last bone but one
of the vertebræ, hence I know it to be human. It
has been burnt, and from the inscription, it was one
of the Freedmen of Domitian. There were three
of these very interesting tombs.

In the evening we went to see the great sight,
the illumination of St. Peter's. When we arrived
there they were lighting it up, rows of lamps from
the earth to the top of the cupola; so that, as it
got darker, the whole architecture of the vast temple

stood out in lines of light—pillars and windows,
dome and cross. A little after eight a bell sounded;
at the first stroke, light issued from the top of the
dome, and on it hundreds of torches were blazing
out all over it. The cloisters in front of the building seemed one vast fiery erection.

It was a sight impossible to describe, for so much
of the effect was produced by the sudden transition
to intense brilliancy. We left it still burning.
From the bridge of St. Angelo the fiery cross, high
in air, looked splendid.

Monday morning; first visited the Quirinal, in
which are the two fine horses, one by Phidias, the
other by Praxiteles, the works of the best days of
Greece. The palace contains some fine rooms.
Here the Pope lived before the revolution, and is
again going to reside there in the summer. His
bedroom is very plain, steel bedstead; next to this—
what? a billiard-room—*it must be a good game.*
Then we went to St. Maria Maggiore, which is a
noble church, with its great nave supported by
Ionic pillars of white marble; the chapel of Pope
Sixtus V. is very handsome. Then to the Cata-
combs of St. Sebastian; a monk took us in, and,
with lighted tapers, we solemnly marched after
him—such passages! I no longer wonder that
people have lost themselves therein. We saw many
under excavations, in which the early Christian
martyrs were interred, their secret chapel, and
other places of great interest: the tombs of St.

Cecilia and St. Marcella, they are merely shelves scooped in the rock, and have been walled up again. We then visited the Circus of Romulus, son of Maxentius, which is very large, though only the foundations point out the site; hence to the celebrated tomb of Cæcilia Metella, the wife of Crassus, which is a large round tower, the walls 25 feet thick; it was used as a robber chieftain's castle in the middle ages, and although war, pillage, plague, and every other evil has passed over it, it is in many respects perfect, and from its massiveness bids fair to be eternal. Next, the Palace of the Cæsars, gardens high up cover its fallen ruins; few rooms remain; one they call Seneca's room, and his bath adjoining, also the Emperor's room and library—the wild weed growing, and a thousand years press on it now; those of its halls that remain are used for farm purposes. How are the mighty fallen—an empire's dust is there, and better so than desecrated as so many remains are. After a visit to the pyramidical tomb of Caius Cestius, went to the Cloaca Maxima, the great sewer of Rome; it was constructed by Tarquinius Priscus, 800 years before Christ, and is still the main sewer of Rome. *It is also one of those buildings erected for eternity.* The vast stones are put together without any cement, like those in the Colisæum, but fit exactly. Near here is the Arch of Titus. In the evening the fireworks concluded the festivities. Upon our arrival at the Piazza del Popolo, it began to rain a little, but this soon cleared away, and at a quarter-past nine the cannon fired, and then a vast erection of scaffolding, covered with fireworks, blazed out in most beautiful colours; then a girandole of hundreds of rockets burst into the air, like a vast volcano, covering the sky with a canopy of fire of all colours. Bouquets of flowers, wheels, serpents, crackers, and cannon. The most beautiful was a representation of a waterfall. Streams of fire fell from the upper part, and appeared to pour down into the square red and green fire: the whole ended with a tremendous discharge of rockets. It was a most brilliant sight; in fact, I never saw such a display of fire-works before: it lasted twenty-five minutes; and must have cost a deal of money. We have been fortunate in seeing all places to the greatest advantage.

To-day we have been to the Barberini, Borghese, and Doria-Pamfili Palaces. In the first is the picture of Beatrice Cenci, very beautiful indeed, a soft melancholy countenance, full of expression. In the other palaces are magnificent galleries of pictures, many of them of not much value. In the Rospigliosi Palace we saw the Aurora of Guido Reni.

This afternoon we went to a theatre in the open air. The play was Romeo and Juliet, not quite the same as the English Romeo and Juliet. This theatre was once, or rather the building, the tomb of the mighty Augustus, now turned into an amphitheatre. The arches of Titus, erected to commemorate the conquest of Jerusalem, and of Septimus Severus, are fine indeed.

We visit the Vatican to-morrow. On Friday we have made a party,—ourselves, H——, an Italian, an American from Philadelphia, a converted Quaker now a Catholic,—to go to Tivoli. We shall take a coach, and perhaps be two days away.

We are tired of churches, having seen so many. Except the four Basilicas, they are not particularly interesting.

I enclose a short note for Dr. B——. I cannot undertake any writing whilst I am away from home. One gets too jaded to write much, except to you; and I am glad you think me a good correspondent: it cheers me up, and makes me still more wishful to please you both. Fathers Zecchi and Rosa, of the Observatory, in Rome, have been very polite: they both take snuff, and look very dirty indeed. A great comfort—they speak English!

NAPLES, *May 3rd*, 1851.

DEAR MAMA,

FOR the first time, eleven days without writing to you!—owing, you may be sure, to circumstances over which I had no control. * * *

Well, I must resume. The 23rd—the day after

E

I wrote last—we went to the Capitol, and saw the pictures and gallery of statues.; among the latter are many very fine antique busts of celebrated personages, including philosophers and statesmen, as well as emperors. In the Farnese Palace nothing particular—a few painted ceilings.

In the Palazzo Spada is the noble statue of Pompey, at the feet of which Julius Cæsar fell, when mortally wounded by his assassins. This I was indeed glad to see; it absorbed all my attention there so much, that the pictures did not receive their fair share of notice.

We then passed the Tarpeian Rock, and visited the celebrated Mamertine Prisons, the state prisons of ancient Rome, consisting of two dungeons; the only access to the lower one was by lowering the criminal by means of a rope, and then leaving him to perish : now there is a staircase. Tradition says St. Peter and St. Paul were imprisoned here, and from all considerations and circumstances I think there can be little doubt it would be a most likely place for incarceration. The fountain is still there, full up to a certain height, which arose at the Apostles' command, for the purpose of baptizing the faithful converts to Christianity. Not many good pictures in the Gallery of St. Lucca. As a matter of course, among so many galleries there are many fine paintings, but also much rubbish, of Saints, Madonnas, and Crucifixions; so much repetition is rather tiresome.

Next day tried the Vatican again; still closed.
Some Grand Duke going through. Five times
we were unsuccessful, and did not see this famous
gallery until our last day. This being a broken day,
we only saw the Pantheon, and the St. Pietro-in-
Vincoli. The former is the Roman Temple of that
name, exactly as it was in ancient times, and converted into a Church. It is lighted by a large open
aperture in the roof, and as it was wet (it can rain
in Italy) the rain poured down in torrents through
the opening. Here Raphael was buried. The
Pietro-in-Vincoli is a handsome church: we did
not see the chains which bound the Chief Apostle;
—the Pope keeps the keys. The next morning,
in company with a Frenchman, H—— and the
American, we went to Tivoli—eleven miles from
Rome—and spent a most delightful day. Our first
duty at Tivoli was to order dinner at the inn. Then
taking a guide, set off to the Cavern or Grotto of
Neptune, where the water has worn the rocks in a
most wonderful manner. A great portion fell some
years ago, which spoiled the Grotto. The old fall of
the Romans has been altered by the last Pope, and
its direction changed. We then went down and
saw the smaller fall from another point of view,
till it fell into a deep dark chasm, called the
Grotto of the Sirens. We then took donkeys, and
mounted up a steep hill, until we came to the
new falls, which were thundering down to a great
depth. We had some other views of the falls, which

everywhere are beautiful. The country round is really lovely. I cannot describe it. We were among the hills, and before us an immense plain, extending to Rome, which place was marked by the stupendous dome of St. Peter's, the size of which you do not appreciate until you see it from a considerable distance.

We returned, and dined in the ancient temple of the Sibyl, which is in the hotel grounds, and commands a fine prospect. On one side we had the site of the villas of the poets Horace and Catullus, with that of the rich Mecænas. After dinner we returned by Hadrian's villa, and saw gigantic ruins of palaces, which in size and splendour must have far exceeded anything in the world. Here were found most of the finest statuary and marbles in Rome, mosaics also. The country round is volcanic in structure; we crossed a sulphur stream so strong, that we could smell the sulphur more than two miles off.

Next day, again unfortunate at the Vatican;— visited the manufactory of mosaics; these are made of little pieces of coloured composite, not unlike glass, but harder, each piece has to be fitted in separately, and to complete a picture, say the likeness of the Pope, then in hand, will take an artist eight or nine years; they are then polished, and at a distance look like a painting. In St. Peter's, all the altar pieces are mosaics, and must have taken an immense amount of time and labour to complete, to say nothing of those in the dome. Those I saw were all intended for St. Peter's.

Sunday, we went to Frascati, twelve miles from Rome; our carriage held representatives of six nations,—I, Kohn, an American, a Frenchman, a Russian, and the driver, an Italian. We again mounted miserable donkeys, and went to the ruins of the Theatre, then to the celebrated villa of Cicero, which commands a noble view,—on one side the Castle of Gondolfa Ricca di Papa, and the valley sweeping down into the plain, with St. Peter's again visible; the Villa Borghese, which is also well situated. Prince Borghese married for his first wife a daughter of the Earl of Shrewsbury. In the chapel is a statue of her as an angel, holding the shell for the holy water.

Next day, successful at the Vatican, and well we were repaid; such galleries of rich statues, busts, basso and alto-relievos; everything that is grand and noble. The real Apollo Belvidere, the Laocoon, the Torso, Perseus, Head of Medusa—wonder after wonder till you become quite bewildered amidst such a concourse of all that is celebrated in art. We wandered about, I may say quite lost in astonishment—but we saw everything, *that* I can say. We only regretted not being able to go again, for that night we left for Naples. The picture gallery is not large, not more than fifty pictures, but all good.

* * * *

In company with four others we left Rome at

one o'clock, for Naples, in a post carriage, holding six, stopping when and where we liked. Throughout the whole day we travelled through a beautiful country, past orchards of oranges and lemons, all ripe, or ripening on the trees, and bought them fresh gathered for us; palm trees and cactuses, all in the open air. We passed the celebrated Pontine Marshes, which quite disappointed me; I expected to see something much worse than Chat Moss, instead of which it is one mass of rich vegetation. Our road lay through a grand avenue of trees the whole day,—I did not feel any malaria *(so don't believe in it.)*

The last Papal town is Fundi, and soon after we entered through a gate into the States of Naples. Passports looked at, we had to spell the names of the places we had passed through, so stupid were they. Next place, the luggage taken down, but not examined; they at once asked you for money—made no bones about it. At half-past five on Tuesday afternoon we arrived at Molo-Gaeta, near where the Pope stayed when exiled, and as we could not pass through Capua after a certain time of the night, we dined here, and remained until eleven. Before dinner we took a boat, and sailed in the bay, orange trees hang over the sea, everything different to what we had seen before. The scenery of the bay is very fine indeed.

Start off again, and at nine next morning are at the Hotel de Genève, at Naples.

After breakfast first went to the Museum, which
contains the relics of Herculaneum and Pompeii.
Here were the lamps that were found in these
cities, which must have been lighted every night
when our Saviour was on the earth. Cooking
utensils, pans, stoves, paste-moulds, locks, keys,
arms and armour, ladies' toilet apparatus, even the
rouge still in the pots; jars of fruit and wine,
bread left in the oven, and burnt quite black, with
the maker's name on it; rings, seals, jewels, articles
in glass, in earthenware; statues, bronzes, inscription papers.; in short, the whole contents of a house
that will not perish. Of course hardly any wood-
work, if any, unless we may reckon a few things in
ivory under that head. Stocks for the prisoners'
feet, skeletons, and a few mummies; it is, indeed,
a wonderful collection. The bay surpasses my
expectations. Vesuvius is quiet, only a slight smoke
hanging on the summit; it is not *quite* so high as I
expected to see, but it looks, knowing what it is,
very *volcanic* indeed. Went to bed early, tired after
two nights' travelling.

Next day, in the afternoon, went by railway to
Pompeii. I hardly know how to begin: a city of
silence—the pavement as good as when laid down;
good footpaths of party-coloured stones, the ruts
still there, worn by the traffic of 2,000 years ago.
The fronts and most of the walls of the houses are
standing, and only require roofs and furniture to
make it again a city fit for life. The wine shops,

with great earthen jars fixed in the marble counters, just as now in this town; the former with its pillars and tribune. The temples, theatres, everything in short, just as the people left it in the year 79 of the Christian era.

You will remember the "Last Days of Pompeii"—the Temple of Isis, which I saw, and the house of Diomedes, which must have been a very handsome, noble mansion: round the garden is a kind of cloister or cellar,—here the bodies were found. In one place the wine jars are still standing against the wall, imbedded and held up by the scoriæ of Vesuvius. The street of tombs must have been particularly fine; and outside the gate are the remains of a large hotel, where persons could stay till morning when arriving at the city after the gates were closed for the night, which practice is still continued in Italian cities; for instance, you cannot enter Rome after nine o'clock without a special permit. I mean to pay Pompeii another visit when I go to Herculaneum.

We dined at the Inn, at Pompeii, in a large open place looking over the bay: on our left hand Castel-a-Mare; on our right Vesuvius, looking very gloomy; and in front, at sea, Capri and Ischia, where we were to have gone to-day had it been fine.

Before I left Rome Father Zecchi called. I was not in, but he left for me a letter of introduction to Annibale di Gasparis here, which I shall present.

NAPLES, *May 12th*, 1851.

DEAR MAMA,

* * * * * * * * * * * * *

WE were too late to see the miracle of St. Januarius, so contented ourselves with the blood in the phial, and the tiara of the Saint, which they tell you is worth an immense amount of money.

On Monday we took a carriage and went to Baiæ. We passed through the Grotto of Posillipo, which is a much longer tunnel than I had imagined, and went along the sea shore by a most beautiful road, with unrivalled views on all sides. At Pozzuolo we saw the Temple of Jupiter Serapis; the pillars of which, three in number, indicate the rise and fall of the land, which must have been very great; the floor is some feet under water. The amphi-theatre is also sunk; so much so, that now you go down hill and enter into the second story; though so sunk, this theatre is in many respects perfect— the arches and corridors still standing—so massively have they been built to withstand the great changes produced by eruptions and earthquakes around them. We then went to the Lucrine Lake, cele-brated for its green oysters in the days of the voluptuous Romans, and passing that to the Monte Nuovo, (thrown up 500 feet in a single day during the earthquake and eruption in 1538,) which divides the Lucrine from the Lake Avernus, across which, it was said, in days of yore, no bird could fly because of the malaria, but which is now perfectly healthy. We then, with a guide, entered a dark cavern, and were carried, on men's backs, through water into the subterranean palace of the Sybil, where she uttered her oracles, but which is now nearly destroyed and closed up by the earthquake, and the lava of Monte Nuovo. We were glad to get out again, and were pretty black from the smoke of the torches which had to be carried before us. We also saw the ruined temples of Mercury and Apollo, the ruins of a palace or villa of Cicero, and then arriving at Miseno, visited another subterranean palace of Nero's, called the 100 Chambers, mostly closed by lava and ashes.

We returned by the Grotto-del-Cane : my little model at home is much *handsomer* than the reality. It is very small, and the carbonic acid gas very strong. A little dog was laid on its back ; the poor little thing rolled its eyes, panted, and soon became almost insensible. It was then taken out, and after reeling a little, came to itself again. Two great torches were instantly extinguished at some distance from the ground. In another grotto the gas exhaled appeared to me to be nitrous oxide, or laughing gas, much diluted, quite sweet to the taste. Next we visited the sulphur baths, where the hot sulphur and steam pours out of holes in the ground. The heat is very great, and soon produces perspiration.

If you stamp on the floor in any of these grottos, you hear that the ground is hollow. Near here is a lake, and in one place we saw hot water boiling up through the cold water, with a large disengagement of gas.. * * *

- On Wednesday was our grand excursion, but first, on Tuesday afternoon, I called on Annibale di Gasparis, the astronomer. Cappoli, the chief astronomer, was complicated in the revolution, and obliged to run away. Gasparis was a pupil of his and has discovered three planets; is quite a young man, and very poor. I had a long talk with him in French; he can read English, but not speak it. I was much pleased with my visit to him.

Well, now for Wednesday, the day of days. Left Naples in a carriage at eleven o'clock for Resina, and started on ponies, with a guide, to ascend Vesuvius. For some distance our route lay through a long, winding, steepish lane, gradually obtaining fine views of the bay, and ever before us the frowning summit of the mountain. We then came upon a dreary district, entirely covered with large masses of lava, it seemed as if, indeed, ploughed by thunderbolts. The lava is here and on the cone of a dusty colour. We then got into a carriage road, which leads to a villa or observatory belonging to the King, and soon arrived at the hermitage. Here we dismounted, and took a little Lachryma Christi, anything but good, after which we remounted, and continuing our course over a

similar plain of lava, reached the foot of the cone
at two o'clock. Here our labours commenced, and
we began to climb over masses of lava which are
piled up to the very top, and which constitute a
wall about as steep as a house side. One man
went before each of us, with a rope over his shoulder, by which we held on, another pushed behind,
so up we went (L—— was with us), stopping
several times to rest. Quite knocked up, we reached
the summit exactly at three o'clock, having been
one hour in ascending the cone. In a short time
we entered the old crater, such a scene of solemn
grandeur I never saw equalled; everywhere the
ground was quite hot; beneath our feet, around us,
vast masses of lava, and in front the two craters,
one of 1839, the other of last year, to which we
first went, and from which we saw the steam rising;
all around was yellow with sulphur; we walked
along the ridges at the top, and looked down on
the Monte Somma, which was the ancient crater
that destroyed Pompeii, with its steep walls
of rock, and below the vast sea of lava, which
poured down from Vesuvius in 1850. Looking
down into the new crater, we could see broken
masses of rock torn into every form, and the ashes
sloping down towards a ridge overhanging a black
pit, whence issued smoke, steam, and sulphurous
gases; we went down carefully towards this ridge,
and erected a monument on it. To look round,
and see the wonderful effects exhibited by these

stupendous forces, which are capable of rending mountains in sunder, and pouring destruction everywhere around! A man that came up with us placed some eggs in a crevice in the mountain, which were speedily roasted, even burnt.

After enjoying the splendid sight from the summit of the cone, and being half suffocated with sulphur, we went across the ancient crater, and then to the crater of 1839. This is wider than that of last year, but not so deep, and is now quite closed at the bottom, so that you could descend into it, which we did not, because of the difficulty of climbing out again over the loose ashes. Standing on the highest point of the mountain, you can form no idea of the extent and grandeur of the scene: the whole of the bay, extending to Cape Miseno; the Islands of Capri, Ischia and Procida; Sorrento with the coast down to Castel-a-Mare, and below, Pompeii; in the distance the ridges of the Appennines—altogether the most magnificent view I ever saw. When we had feasted our eyes sufficiently, we commenced the descent; plunging our heels into the loose ashes, and leaning backwards, were at the bottom in about five minutes, and when at the bottom could hardly feel our legs. Mounting our ponies we set off again, resting a short time at the Hermitage. R—— had asked L—— to get for him some blocks of lava for the Peel Park, and send them by steamer at his expense; so passing some masses we selected four blocks, which are now in Naples ready to be sent off. We arrived at our hotel at eight o'clock, having been just nine hours on our excursion.

Next day Kohn and I went to Caserta, a palace of the King's, 18 miles from Naples; his majesty is at present here. We had no permit to enter, but if you remember, a young Swiss officer I met on the Rhine steamer, gave me some introductions to Swiss officers, stationed here and at Naples. One of them, Baron S——, very politely gave us orders to go through the palace and gardens. The palace, like all other palaces, is very splendid. The Pope resided here some time, and his bust is in one of the rooms. The gardens are very fine, with large numbers of peacocks screaming,and strutting about.

On Friday I got up early, to go to Capri by the steamer, to see the Azure Grotto. Kohn was lazy, and would not get up, so I went alone. The boat was small, the sea rough, and most people, including myself, sea-sick; and when we got to the island, after three hours' sailing, we found the sea so rough that to enter the grotto was impossible; the entrance is by the sea, and through a small arch, over which the waves were dashing. We landed, and went about the island; it began to rain. I got something to eat, returned to the boat, made another attempt at the grotto, but all in vain. Saturday, G——, L——, and Julius S——, accompanied us to Herculaneum. The excavations are quite different to Pompeii, having been overwhelmed with lava, and the work is hard to effect.

The arena has been excavated completely, the seats, stage, everything. Of course it is all underground, the road to it is through a tunnel. We visited the Palace of Portici, and saw both palace and gardens. On the staircase in the palace, in one corner, is a picture of ————* to protect the inmates from the evil eye. * * * *

PALERMO, *May 20th,* 1851.

DEAR MAMA,

WE left Naples on Wednesday last, the 14th instant, at three o'clock, for Palermo. Before the steamer started, all the passengers were called over by the police, to see that none left who were not by them allowed to leave. The steamer was a good one : Kohn and I had a nice cabin on deck ; he was sick, I not, though not altogether comfortable, for the vessel rolled a great deal. There are many curious sights in the streets of Naples I never saw elsewhere : for instance, as the people generally can neither read nor write, many persons find employment as street secretaries, and sit at little tables in the streets, with their paper, pens, and ink ; and here and there an anxious face bending

* Letter torn, and name of picture obliterated.

over telling its tale, some in sorrow, some in joy, but all equally desirous that the secretary shall write what they tell him. Then there are the cook-shops, with their fires all lighted in iron stoves, in the street; and for a trifle a man can get his fill of maccaroni, which a true Neapolitan eats without knife or fork, using those supplied by nature. Most workpeople have their benches in the streets opposite their shops, and joiners, smiths, filers, all at work in the open air. Then there are the water sellers, who for a grain will sell a glass of iced water: they have a gaudy painted stand, with large buckets swinging on pivots, from which they pour the water into glasses; for two or three grains they give a glass of iced lemonade or orangeade, which they make by cutting the fruit in two, and with a pair of clams, like large nut-crackers, squeeze the juice into the glass through a strainer — and very refreshing it is. Then, everywhere are people hunting in their own shirts and heads, or their neighbours, for the small cattle so abundant in Italy. Add to these the various smells which greet you at different corners, and you will have some idea of Naples in the streets.

Whilst you are reading the above, you must imagine the night has passed away, and in the morning the rocks and mountains of Sicily are before us.

In good time we enter the Bay of Palermo, surrounded with magnificent scenery, the town close to the water, on the edge of a plain, which is on all sides shut in by mountains. We were taken to the custom-house, and for two shillings each got off any examination of luggage. We then crossed the bay to a second custom-house, where eightpence between us saved any trouble, and entered the town through a third custom-house, where the same fee was again an equivalent—three custom-houses to enter from Naples, another portion of the same kingdom. It is nothing more than official robbery, and by these shabby means a great part of the staff of the police is kept up and paid. * * * We went to the Hotel Trinacria; it is kept by a person who was for some time courier to an English family, had been often in England, and speaks English well. The rooms he had saved for us being too high up, we have instead, two bed rooms, a saloon ante-chamber, with some small rooms, in a palace next to the hotel. Our furniture is gilt, the walls covered with satin, but faded; and for all this grand accommodation we pay four shillings each a day. This palace belonged to some family exiled for political offences.

After breakfast we went to the top of Monte Pelegrino, which forms one end of the bay, and from here we had a noble view—snow-capped summits in the distance, and the mountains round tinged with the glorious colours that only an Italian atmosphere can give.

In Naples I was introduced to a young man—a Mr. P——, of Palermo. After dinner, he called

F

upon us, and took us a drive in his carriage—a very stylish turn-out. His father is the Postmaster General of Sicily, and to him we are indebted for all our pleasure here. He has placed carriages and horses at our disposal; has been with us, or rather taken us everywhere.

Our intention was to have gone on Saturday from here to Catania, but the fatigue of the journey has deterred us from it. Fifty hours in a wretched coach, on the worst roads in the world, through fine scenery, *but nothing to eat:* these considerations have, with P——'s kindness, kept us here till the 21st, when we take the steamer to Messina. P—— introduced us to his club, where we can see such papers as are admitted into Sicily. His family are at Messina, so he is alone at present.

On Friday he took us to Monreale, where there is a very fine church 1100 years old. The interior is all mosaic, and the columns are white marble. There is also some fine wood carving in it. We visited also a monastery there, with the finest cloisters I ever saw; the pillars had been nearly all in mosaic work, but that had been destroyed; the capital of each column is different from any other.

The weather is quite cool at present, but N—— says a few days ago there was a sirocco, which lasted three days, and burnt them all up. We felt it at Naples; it made us feel languid, but here it was in its fury and heat. To show you what a climate it is, there are groves of oranges, lemons, figs, and vines, all round the town; the cactus and Indian fig, with its fruit in its great leaves: strawberries and cherries are getting over, and the crops of wheat are all in, in time for a second crop, if they were not too idle.

The town of Palermo consists of two long streets, exactly crossing each other at right angles in the centre; the principal street is the Toledo, and in it are many nunneries; in the upper stories of these nunneries are grated balconies, through which you see the nuns peeping down on a world in which they cannot mingle;—it would just suit you. Outside the town are many beautiful chateaus, summer palaces, and monasteries.

On Sunday, P—— brought us donkeys, and we set off to visit San Martino, a monastery of the Benedictines, among the mountains. P—— has a friend there. It is a wealthy monastery, and has never been pillaged or interfered with. There are 17 brothers, all of rich families; 20 novices, and 30 servants; their revenue is about 40,000 crowns a year. This good Father showed us everything in the monastery (the manuscripts in the library are very valuable), the hall, the pictures, cloisters, and he took us into his own room, which is very neat, a nice bed under an alcove, a writing table, plenty of books, saintly pictures, &c. Out of a cupboard, *near his bed*, he produced some glasses and a flask of rich old wine, which we much enjoyed, and his eyes twinkled with pleasure to see that we liked it. They are noted for their hospitality to strangers, and it was with much ado we dissuaded him from giving us a dinner. *I think we should have liked it nevertheless.* We went into the chapel and heard the fine organ, and in the interval of the service were taken into the organ loft, and the organist played us a piece to show the power of the instrument, introducing drums, trumpets, and cymbals. From the windows and terraces the views are splendid on all sides; the road to it is through a valley constantly rising and winding, crossed and re-crossed by babbling currents of purest water. It was a most delightful excursion, and we parted with our kind and friendly Father with many thanks for his politeness.

We have visited most of the churches, which are very beautiful; the Cathedral is curious in its architecture. Also went to the Capuchins, out of the city; a filthy-looking friar conducted us into the vaults, where the dried bodies of monks and other people are kept; on the sides are coffins of all shapes, some with glass sides, some with glass near the head of the corpse, and you see them dressed in habits as in life. In niches above are the dried bodies of the monks for years and years, each in his gown and cowl, with a cord round his waist. On some the skin is yet hanging, some are mere skulls, on others a little hair still left, all ghastly and horrible; better to be buried out of sight at once. Children there also; one little one I noticed, features perfect, but dark coloured, dressed in silk, and on its withered hands white kid gloves, and there they will hang till bone drops from bone; it was altogether a most curious sight. In the morning P—— took us in his carriage to Bagaria, which is a small town of palaces, where, before some alteration in the laws, the Sicilian nobility resided, they are now falling into decay, none having the means to keep them up. P—— introduced us to a Prince who is still wealthy; the gardens round the palaces are very beautiful indeed.

This morning we went, about eight o'clock, in a boat to see the tunny fishing. The tunny is a large fish, caught in great quantities in the bay, each fish is worth about £4., and weighing from two to three or four hundred weight, seven or eight feet long. We were fortunate in seeing them draw the net. I don't quite understand the form of it, but it seems they are led from one to a smaller, and so on to the last. One large boat is fixed, and the men, in another, keep drawing up the net, so as to draw the fish towards the other; then you see these large monsters swimming about, splashing like whales; there were 23 in the net, the men stuck hooks into them, like boat-hooks, and pulled them into the boats, and the water, so blue a few moments before, was soon red with the blood that flowed from the terrible wounds they made in the poor fish. I have tasted them, but the flesh is very coarse, and looks not unlike poor veal when cooked.

We returned at eleven to breakfast, and then

went to the Royal Palace, to see the Observatory and the Chapel. The Directors of the Observatory are no longer there, owing to revolutions and so forth; the instruments are all English. The chapel is extremely fine, 1,000 years old, and is one mass of mosaics. We have been with P—— this evening, to the Palace at which the Emperor and Empress of Russia staid, when her imperial majesty came to Palermo for her health, and where she resided six months. It is a little gem of a place, and the gardens are luxuriantly beautiful. We then went to another garden, containing many singular contrivances: jets of water play on you suddenly, if you tread on the steps of a little summer-house, the door opens, and a figure steps out to meet you in the dress of a monk; in another is one writing, and a third nods his head, and raises his hand, being represented as reading in his cell; there is a *fourth, out of order*, but if you open it, a figure dashes water in your face. There is also a labyrinth, very difficult to thread.

Altogether we have much enjoyed Palermo; the scenery around is most beautiful, the changing hues of light and shade, the rich vegetation, all combine to produce a *tout ensemble* not to be forgotten.

Malta, *May 25th*, 1851.

Dear Mama,

You will hardly expect a line from me here, but the steamer goes to England to-morrow and I just scribble you a few lines. We left Palermo for Messina, and had a rough passage; many ill—I quite well, *and* eat my dinner. Messina is nicely situated, and the straits are very beautiful indeed, but have no time to describe them now. On our passage we had a view of Mount Etna, sublimely piercing the clouds, its summit appearing above them. It is an enormous mountain—it was smoking. Yesterday we went on board the French Government steamer, and found J—— S—— on board; at two we left, and arrived here at eleven this morning, and this evening at five we sail by the French Government steamer *Osiris*, for Constantinople, where we hope to be on the 1st of June. These steamers are commanded by officers of the French navy, and are war steamers—very good indeed. This is the first of the foreign possessions of England I ever saw. The harbour is a noble one—such forts, such tiers upon tiers of cannon, above which floats the flag of England. In the harbour are six vessels of war;—the Admiral's ship, *The Queen*, 120 guns. As soon as we dropped anchor, an English naval officer came to know all about us; where from, and what we wanted, according to custom. He looked so nice and clean, and his uniform so good; besides, he was a handsome looking fellow.

The streets of Valetta are terribly steep—in steps mostly, and strange to say, here you see policemen, with blue coats, and staffs in their hands:—great indeed is the difference between a country enjoying freedom, and under good government, and the wretched States we have been in,—for in wretchedness Sicily far goes beyond all Italy. It is Sunday, and all the ships are dressed out in flags, and look very well; all look clean, and were it not for the climate, and a few foreign indications, one would imagine one's self in England. I am only here five hours, so want to see all I can. Excuse this short scribble—look upon it as a post-script, and not a letter. Now we are going to buy a book, having none left to read. J—— S—— is going with us: in three days we shall be at Athens. * * * * * *

CONSTANTINOPLE, JUNE 1st to June 5th, 1851.
HOTEL DE BYZANCE IN PERA.

DEAR MAMA,

One letter from the City of the Mosques I must write; but, according to my usual custom,

must first write up from the last point, which was
Malta.

Being so few hours in Malta, we could not see
much beyond a general view of the harbour and
the fortifications. I should have liked to have
visited the Church of the Knights of St. John, but
it was closed. We had an English dinner at the
Hotel in Valetta, and by five o'clock were on board
the French war steamer, in which we were to go to
Constantinople. At six we started, and went to
bed in good time; the weather has been fine, sea
smooth as a lake, and our life on board very pleasant. At nine we breakfast *à la fourchette;* dinner
at five, tea at eight, all very good. On Monday we
did not see land. Tuesday, at breakfast time, were
off Cape Matapan, and during the day coasted along
the shores of the Morea, passed Cerigo, one of the
Ionian Islands, and on Wednesday morning, about
three, dropped anchor in the Piræus, the ancient
port of Athens.

I awoke when the engine stopped, and got up.
At five, Kohn, S——, and I set off together, having taken a guide, to spend the day in Athens, as
the steamer did not sail until the next morning at
six. It was curious to find yourself for the first
time surrounded by Greeks, in their handsome but
effeminate-looking dresses, scarlet or blue jackets,
white petticoats, leggings, and fancy caps. Our
guide proved honest, which does not often happen,
as the national character is anything but high in

that respect. Landing at the Piræus, we bargained with a coachman to take us to Athens, and bring us back in the evening, the distance being five miles each way. Off we went, over dirty roads, and soon came in sight of the Acropolis and Parthenon. Before entering Athens, we decided to see as much as possible before breakfast, whilst moderately cool. Went first to the Temple of Theseus, which, built 465 years before Christ, is still perfect; its just proportions, situation, &c., constitute it one of the finest monuments in the world; it is now used as a museum, and filled with statues and inscriptions. Hence we went to four caves in the rock, used as prisons—one of them is singular, and formerly the only access was by a hole in the vault above. Here the great philosopher of antiquity drank the fatal cup of hemlock. We then went to the Areopagus, where once stood the seats of justice, and all the legal state of the Republic—of which no remains now exist, beyond a few steps cut in the solid rock. Here we stood on that spot, sacred in the history of our religion, where, standing on Mars Hill, the Apostle Paul preached to the Athenians, of that unknown God in whose honour he had found an altar erected in their city. We then quietly walked to the summit of the Acropolis, and saw those architectural remains which are the wonder of the world. On entering, you wind among old walls, which formed the fortress erected by the Turks, and pass the remains of a fine theatre. At last you approach the pile of temples, which have ever been the glory of Athens—the Propylæa, with its marble stairs, and noble pillars, erected at the time of the highest power of Athens, and forming the stately entrance to the shrine of Minerva, the presiding goddess of this once proud and powerful state.

The remains of the Parthenon are familiar from the many representations of them; but no picture can give an idea of the effect produced by the perfect symmetry of all the parts. The ruins of Rome are vast in extent, but produce nothing at all when compared in effect to the Parthenon. In the Eternal City the ruins are nearly all of brick—the marble having been stripped off. Here the whole building is marble, and although much has been destroyed by the Turks, sufficient remains to give you an idea of what it must have been in its days of splendour. On one side of the Parthenon is the Erechtheum, and on the other, a Temple dedicated to Victory: it is only a small one, but very beautiful. There is a portico to the Temple of Minerva Polias or Erechtheum, supported by caryatides— very fine indeed. There is a Church in London, with a similar porch or portico, near the railway, which I dare say you will remember.

After as long a stay at the Acropolis as our time would permit, and with many a longing glance behind, we descended its time-honoured and time-worn way, and hastened to an hotel to breakfast, as it was then near ten. We passed through Athens, and a strange town it is. Wooden houses and shops, more like booths, with their masters sitting cross-legged; no pavement, all filth. In the Tower of the Winds is an ancient monument, on the old gate of the Agora, or Market Place, near which stands a pillar erected by Hadrian, on which the prices of provisions are written, and now nearly as legible as when first inscribed.

At our hotel we descended into a cool dining room, and had a good breakfast, which reconciled us considerably. After our meal, we went to see the Temple of Jupiter Olympus, of which noble structure only a few magnificent columns remain. Here is a great café, where we sat a little, and for the first time smoked the narghilley or Persian pipe. Hence we had a noble view, the Bay of Athens, with the Piræus, Salamis, where the Persian fleet was destroyed by the Athenians; Mount Hymettus, celebrated now as in times of old, for its bees and honey. * * Mount Pentelicus, in which are the quarries of white marble, whence the people drew their stone, and when brought out into form by the surpassing skill of their architects, constitute now the best proof of how great a people they must have then been. We then descended to the banks of the Ilissus, now but a small stream, easily crossed on foot over one or two stepping stones. There are the remains of a bridge over it, which led to the Stadium, where races were held; of that building very little now remains. We then went back to the hotel, well tired and exhausted by the heat, and lay down on sofas for an hour, then took a coach and went to the Observatory, which has been built and furnished by a German Baron; it is finely situated. Thence to the Pnyx, where the orators used to deliver their speeches, and from the Bema on which Demosthenes has oft thundered his denunciations. We then came back to dinner about four, and after dinner went to the palace to see the king, who generally rides out every afternoon. When we got there, we found a few shabby soldiers drawn out in parade, and the royal carriage, open, with four horses. Near the gate a *crowd* of eight old women, three boys, and two men. The women had petitions in their hands, which they gave to an officer at the gate, for presentation. In a short time the king and queen got into the carriage, he in the Greek costume, looking particularly foolish in such a fancy dress, the queen in deep mourning, rather pretty. Their majesties bowed to us *en passant*—a whirl of dust, and it was over. At a café we got some Turkish coffee; it is good, but the curiosity of it is, the grounds are not taken out; you let it stand, and then drink what remains, which is very little, as the cups are small. The cups stand in small brazen cups, similar to an egg cup. At dark we set off to the Piræus, and returned on board ship, and, after a little talk, went to bed well tired.   *   *   *   *

The next day we were sailing among the islands of the Archipelago, and early on Friday morning dropped anchor at Smyrna. Up again early, took a Smyrna Jew for a guide, and a boat soon landed us in *Asia*. The first view of an oriental town is very striking. The great number of cemeteries every where scattered about, with their cypress trees, mingled with the various coloured buildings, minarets, and mosques, tapering up on high; the wooden houses; the gay colours of Asiatic costume, all constitute a curious *tout ensemble*. But near land, grim dirt, filth, stenches, meet you on all hands; then you see that this gay scene is only lath and plaster; dogs, in countless numbers, here, in Athens, in Constantinople, even in Italy, are the only official scavengers, eating up all the offal of the streets. We went to a café, and got a little coffee, ordered breakfast for twelve o'clock, and sallied out on horseback. We went first to the place where the camels are assembled, and saw several that had arrived the day before from Persia. How they groaned and cried, and looked anything but the patient creatures we believe them to be! * *
In the course of the day we saw a great many more in a khan yard. We met some Turkish women, all veiled; the veil comes over the forehead, but not the eyes, a bandage is brought up over the mouth to the end of the nose; they are not now nearly so strict as formerly. Their slippers are yellow, with overshoes, these drop at the heel every step

they take, which gives them a clumsy, shuffling gait.
Turks in turbans, soldiers, Greeks, Armenians,
Jews, all separated in their different quarters, but
mingling in the affairs of life. We rode up a highish
hill, with the ruins of a castle on the top, whence
we had a fine view over the town and bay. Returning through the cemeteries, which are singular
enough, stones with the turban cut on the top, or
rather, I should say, the tops of the stones were in
the form of turbans; we entered the bazaars,
which are certainly the most curious and original
places of business I ever saw. Fancy a network
of streets, formed entirely of wooden booths, with
projecting roofs, sufficient to cover any person
standing in front to purchase or what not. From
each side slight rafters are thrown across, and thus
the whole street is more or less covered in—the
floor of each shop is about two feet above the road,
and covered either with a carpet or a mat, on which
the proprietor is seated. Around him, on shelves,
are his various wares. In Smyrna the bazaars are
no great things, interesting only as being the first
seen. We then went to the café or coffee-house,
and in real Turkish style, legs crossed on a raised
divan, smoked our pipes, and looked profoundly
wise; our attendants were slaves, the property, of
course, of the master of the establishment. We
wondered what they would say in Manchester, to
see us thus, in real Eastern state. In the same
place were two or three sage-looking Turks, who, in

their hearts, I doubt not, felt a proper contempt for us as Franks or infidels, and whose conversation, if it can be so called, consisted of a few wise nods, which are easily made, and do not cost the true believer any of his precious breath. After our breakfast, we visited a silk manufactory, where they wound the silk from the cocoons. In one shed there were 150 girls employed; all, or nearly so, Smyrniote Greeks, and among them some few of the most beautiful faces you can imagine, all singing, and appearing to be happy and contented.

Soon after this we returned to our floating home, and at four o'clock steamed out of Smyrna.   * * The next morning (Saturday), we entered the Dardanelles, and remained at anchor, in accordance with Turkish regulations, for some hours. No vessel is allowed to enter the Straits in the night at all. We passed the famed castles, with their big guns, but not near enough to make much out of them. We had on board an English gentleman and two young men travelling with him. His name was G——, had been private secretary to the late Dowager Queen Adelaide. He made himself extremely agreeable. Soon after dinner found us in the Sea of Marmora, which was rather rough. On Sunday morning we got up a little after four, to catch the first view of Constantinople. Gradually its minarets and mosques came in sight; about seven we cast anchor in the far-famed Golden Horn, after a pleasant voyage of eight days from Sicily.

Certainly the first view of the gorgeous capital of the East is most magnificent. As you approach, you have the Bosphorus before you, with Asia on one side and Europe on the other. The seraglio, close on your left-hand, with its palaces and gardens; rounding the extreme point of which you enter the Horn, and Constantinople presents itself to your view. On your left Stamboul; on your right Galata, Pera, and Tophanè. On each side the houses rise one above the other, intermingled with the cypress trees and gardens. The shipping, the Turkish fleet, all contribute to form a scene unrivalled in the world. When you land, the charm is broken; tumble-down wooden houses, unpaved lanes, dogs, dirt, bad smells—all this has been said a hundred times. I fear you will think I merely echo what I have read, but I assure you it is no fable to say that this is the handsomest and the most unsightly city in the universe. I have seen many bad pavements since I left England, but here the very worst is exceeded. Then the dogs; you cannot go ten yards without seeing twenty or thirty on a heap of offal. At night their noises are horrible, squealing, crying, barking, howling, and fighting, and sleeping under your feet all day. Three or four years ago 40,000 dogs were poisoned, what the numbers are now no one can tell. Each set of dogs is confined to its own quarter, and woe to the unhappy wretch that ventures on its neighbour's ground, it is fortunate if it gets back with a torn skin only. The streets give

G

you the idea that you are always going a near cut, through back lanes, and hope soon to come into the main thoroughfares, but in reality you are in the chief ways all the time. At night there are no lamps in the streets, which, being full of holes, dirt, and dogs, are dangerous enough; by law you are obliged to carry a lantern; if the police should find you without they can take you up as a thief, for they say an honest man will want to see his way, and none but a thief will go without a light. These lanterns are made of paper, and squeeze up into a small compass, and very odd it seems to walk out with them. The watchmen have sticks with iron ends, which they strike on the stones as they walk along, to warn the evil-doer of their approach. For your satisfaction, I will say our hotel is of stone, and therefore no danger of fire; the outside shutters and doors are of iron, to prevent incendiarism. Few indeed are the stone buildings except mosques; the houses are wooden frames, lined with boards, and outside covered with lath and plaster, painted.

We got our luggage through the custom-house without much trouble: S—— knew the director, who came and passed us directly. Our trunks, &c., being placed on the backs of the hamals or porters, we mounted the hill to our hotel, and got some breakfast; after which we took a servant, whom we engaged during our stay as guide and dragoman, and, going down to the sea, got into a caique,—

very light and *tickle*. Of the caiques, or boats, 80,000 ply for hire in the Golden Horn. Our boatman took us up the Horn nearly to the further extremity. We landed, and walked up a hill, passing several burial places of Sultans and great people. Looking through a window, we saw two coffins of the Sultan's two brothers, who were both kindly strangled, to prevent them troubling the succession. Some of the tombs were very handsome, the dark cypress trees giving a fine appearance to the whole. We mounted higher, till we came to another cemetery, from which we had a fine view over the town and Golden Horn. We met two funerals of women, which we followed, but were not allowed to approach the grave. The bodies were in wooden coffins :—one, the corpse of a rich, the other, that of a poor woman. The body of the latter was taken out of the coffin, and placed in the grave : the former was able to afford the luxury of a coffin. Then, a great number of Turks, who were attending the funeral, sat round, all muttering prayers, in a sing-song tone. The earth was shoveled in, and water poured over it, to settle the ground, and prevent the dogs tearing it up. Then came the Mufti to the side of the grave, and all except ourselves went away out of sight. The priest then began his prayers, standing alone, in which, I believe, he praises the dead, and says he or she is sure of Paradise. When they arrive at the gate of heaven, they must demand admission, and

give the piece of money which the corpse has in
one hand; and, if refused with that, throw at the
angel's head the stone which is in the other. We
had had a very high wind all day, which ended
in heavy rain. When we arrived at Constantinople, there had been a great drought,—no rain
for four months :—the people were suffering from
want of water; and the crops were in danger of
destruction. It rained the whole of Monday, and
such rain :—the streets became rivers, and filthy
beyond measure.

We set off this morning to the bazaars, which
are indeed curious. They are mostly vaulted buildings, and the stages of the dealers are arranged on
each side. Our entrance lay through the Egyptian
Bazaar; here they sell paints, spices, colours, nay,
in short, all that comes from Egypt. Each article
will be found in its own department, one being for
jewellery, another for shoes and slippers, one for
silks, embroidery, arms, and so on. There were
beautiful Persian shawls, scarfs, and stuffs from
India, and plenty of Manchester calico. As we
could do nothing else for rain, we stopped there
all day, and sat bargaining with Turks, sitting on
their mats. We were offered pipes and coffee.

Tuesday, still raining; in the morning we went
again to the bazaar. At one o'clock we visited the
convent of the Dancing Dervishes, to see their
performance. The entrance was through a nice
court yard, and at the porch we were made to pull

our boots off; then, entering a large room, in form
a polygon, we took our places in a gallery, which
runs all round the bottom part; over this there is
another gallery, the centre being reserved for the
dervishes, of whom there were in all twenty-one.
The chief sat on a mat facing them, and in the
upper gallery two or three more were singing or
droning out some service, in which the chief also
took part; they then marched round the enclosure,
and bowed twice to the chief's seat, and once when
opposite to it; this was done three times, and they
re-seated themselves; then a drum beat, and they
all fell flat on their faces, then got up, their
cloaks were taken off and you saw their dress, a
white petticoat and body. The extraordinary music
continued, each one walked past the superior, made
him a bow, and commenced turning round, gradually extending his arms as he became more
excited: at last all were in motion except the superior.
The second in command walked among them, so
that they did not touch him or one another. There
were also four neophytes, all twisting round and
round the room, exactly like slow waltzing. This
continued about three-quarters of an hour, with
short intervals of rest. At the end, the second in
authority made a long prayer, in which you fre-
quently heard " Allah," " Mahomet." When this
was finished, each one of them kissed the hand of
the chief and departed. Some of them looked sad
scamps. *   *   *   *

MALTA, *June 21st*, 1851.

DEAR MAMA,

     *   *   *   *   WELL, in my last letter I told you all our proceedings up to the date thereof. Fifth, in the morning still raining, we made a desperate resolve, and went to a *Turkish Bath*. Entering a large circular hall, surrounded with galleries, on which are beds and divans, we each, with a guide, were taken into a place railed off, and undressed. A person attended us, and wrapped a large cloth round us, and another over our shoulders, put us on a pair of large pattens, and then conducted us across the hall to a small door, through which we passed into a marble-floored vault, lighted from the top. The heat of this room is considerable; and, being led to couches placed on the floor, we were left to *sweat*. They brought us pipes and coffee. Various little demons hovered about, nearly naked, waiting to commence operations. In about half-an-hour we were pronounced in a proper state, and were taken into another hall,— the temperature about three times the heat of the first, and were laid down on a large marble slab. In a few minutes the perspiration was pouring off me; and then a boy began to pound my arms, and legs, and chest; then turned me over, and pounded away at my breast; tried to crack all my joints, but did not succeed. I was then conducted into a small room, opening out of this hall, where there were taps of hot and cold water, and large marble basins. I lay down, and he scrubbed me over with a *rough glove*, not any water, almost peeling my skin off, then dashed a lot of tepid water over me; and bringing a large basin, with soap, warm water, and a sort of wisp of hemp, he made an immense lather, and soaped me all over, from head to foot; then, dashing a quantity of water over me, it was finished. Our wet cloths or towels were then exchanged for dry ones. One was fitted round our heads like a turban; and then we were led back to the first room, and each placed on couches, with pillows, more clean dry cloths thrown over us, pipes brought, and then left in a dreamy, pleasant state for nearly an hour,—three hours and a half in the bath. I never was so clean in my life: I felt light, in good spirits, and altogether different.

We then went to the convent of the Howling Dervishes, a very extraordinary exhibition, impossible to describe, owing to the contortions of the body, and the movements into which they threw themselves. They howled, and sang, and shouted, and swayed backward and forward,—shook every joint for near three hours. The chief priest performed cures on poor sick people, touched their eyes, and for any disease of the body the patient lay down before him. He first passed his foot over them, and then stood upon them; even little children he treated in the same manner.

On Friday morning we crossed to Scutari again, to see the Sultan go to mosque; a guard was drawn up; and in a short time the magnificent caique, with the Sultan, came up, and he landed. The Light of the World, the Brother of the Sun, and all the rest of it, stood before us. Abdul Medjid is a young man about 28, and has the appearance of 50. He mounted a noble Arab steed, the trappings of which were entirely covered with diamonds, preceded by his great officers of state, and followed by the black eunuchs. He rode slowly past us—we had a good view of him; his horse was sent back, so we looked at the trappings closely. Ourselves and the Englishmen I before mentioned, constituted the crowd on the occasion.

After this we took our caique up the Bosphorus, to the Sweet Waters of Asia, which is a favourite fashionable resort on Friday afternoons, for the Turkish ladies. As we passed along the shore, and by the over-hanging houses, we heard many a laugh from behind the lattice-work of the women's apartments, and caught a few glances of faces quickly withdrawn. Passing up a pretty stream, we landed near a promenade, and passed many Turks smoking and chatting. We went on and saw the ladies, some sitting smoking long pipes, others walking or riding in coaches; in a short time two or three policemen told us we must remove to a greater distance, to the men's division, as the men and the women are not allowed to meet together. It was in a pretty valley; a bright day, and clear sky, all united to render it a pleasing scene. We continued our walk, and came to another part of the same general rendezvous, but by the side of the Bosphorus. The fashion is for the ladies to go at three to the first part, and at four to the other. After this we returned, having spent a very pleasant day. In walking about Stamboul, in the evening, we saw a mosque of pigeons, very curious, thousands of them fed at the expense of pious people, who believe that the souls of departed Mussulmans inhabit the bodies of these impudent birds.

Sunday, rain; but in the intervals of the showers visited two or three mosques, including that of Sulieman the Magnificent. Monday, fine; and the weather continued so during the remainder of our stay. The Seraglio and Mosque of Santa Sophia require a firman, for which you pay £10.; several persons join at one; and it is generally obtained from a valet-de-place, who makes a good profit. Perhaps twenty people go together, and he charges them £1. each. While we were there it was not the season, and few strangers in Constantinople. We, however, visited the Sultan's palace on the Bosphorus, the Sultan's general residence, but he is away at another place in Asia. It is a fine wooden building, containing fine halls; the furniture in the Eastern style; beautiful ball rooms and divans. We saw the harem, of course *empty*. The ladies having a *penchant* for musical clocks, the rooms were full of them. The gardens are laid out with great taste, the walks being covered with small sea-shells, laid on thick : your feet sink without soiling your shoes.

After this we proceeded in a three-oared caique up the Bosphorus, nine miles to Buyukdereh, and landed on the Asiatic side, and mounted the Giant's Mountain, from whence we had a magnificent view—the Bosphorus winding along at our feet, and before us its termination in the Black Sea, the waters of which stretched out on the far horizon. We dined at Buyukdereh, which is a favourite summer residence of the different ambassadors and rich people. Returning by moonlight down the Bosphorus, landed at Tophanè, when we were immediately attacked by about sixty dogs, who set on us from all sides, and with whom we had a regular battle. Being well armed with heavy sticks, sent many of our canine adversaries howling away, with damaged legs and heads :—if you show fear, they are brave; but turn on them, they are sad cowards : they only attack Franks, never any one wearing the fez.

The next day we saw some of the antiquities, the great cistern of Constantine, now called the Binderit, or the thousand-and-one columns. Beyond the outer courts of Santa Sophia, as I have said, we could not be admitted without a firman. We walked through the slave market, but did not stay

long, only a few poor black girls for sale; some
were merry, but others very, very sad.

Next day went into some mosques, and, as
Charles Matthews says, in " Used up," "nothing"
there literally; the floors covered with matting, an
immense number of large lamps, with small ones,
used for illuminations, hanging about seven feet
high from the ground. No pictures, no altars, *no
nothing*. I must say I was disappointed. Santa
Sophia is exactly the same, only larger, and the
walls have some good mosaics in them. From
here to the Sublime Porte; saw first the gardens
of the Seraglio. Nothing extraordinary. The
rooms (outside) where the slave girls belonging to
the Sultan are kept; high walls round, closed
jalousies, no right to approach. Our next visit was
to the stables. Such Arab steeds! Oh dear, I
should have liked one. There was a grey Arab
to sell, he was trotted out for us; he really was
handsome. A Circassian mounted him, one of the
most splendid riders I ever saw. If I could have
put that horse in a balloon, and sent him home, I
should have bought him. We then went to the
kitchen, where they were busy dishing up dinners
for the ladies and officers of the household, of
whom many hundreds live in the Seraglio. It is a
kitchen indeed, great furnaces full of pots and
pans! Our dragoman had a friend here in the
chief cook, who brought us some paste, of which
the moon-faced beauties devour great quantities.

It is a paste rolled out thin, on paper, drenched with pots of syrup, just baked crisp, and is most delicious: we eat a great deal of it. We then entered the gate, or Sublime Porte, which is guarded by frightful white eunuchs, and went into their apartment, close to the door leading to those secret chambers which no man except the Sultan ever enters. We bought some real pastiles of the Seraglio, which are used to perfume the royal apartments; they are too *musky* for my taste, but I thought you should have some *real*, if any.

On Thursday morning, June 12th, we took another bath, and at seven o'clock on board the French steamer Bosphorus, bid adieu to the mosques, minarets, the picturesque town of Stamboul, the Golden Horn, and the shores of the beautiful Bosphorus, after a short stay, it is true, but twelve days never to be forgotten; twelve days of new impressions, of a character entirely different to any I had before experienced.

The Turks are a dignified, courteous people, and, I doubt not, look down upon the Franks as an inferior race, represented as the latter are in Constantinople by Armenians and Greeks, than whom greater rascals or cheats do not exist in the world; but, being now active and pushing, and less scrupulous, have monopolized most part of the traffic in their own hands, and try their best to cheat both Turk and Christian!

At our hotel we had a Captain S——, who is in

the Turkish service, having been sent at the request of the Ottoman Porte by the English government, to discipline the Turkish navy. He is the second in command of the fleet and harbour, though really first, as nothing is done without his sanction; the Turkish chief admiral submits, of course, to him as the sailor. S——'s Turkish title (for he is a Pasha of three tails) is, Mushava Pasha!

At Smyrna we landed, and dined with Mr. M——. After dinner, we strolled into the slave market, and saw such a funny little black boy, in a stone trough of water, washing himself, and grinning at us :—he was the blackest lad I had ever seen: about ten years old. He put his little paw out, and I gave him a trifle.—Poor little fellow, he was delighted!—they wanted £15. for him. *I felt a fancy to buy him, as a page for you. What would you have thought about it?*

Sunday morning we arrived at Syra, where we had to perform quarantine. Here we remained twenty-two hours, in an open bay, with a heavy swell. Our steam-boat was a small one : we were knocked about immensely, which sent Kohn to bed, ill. Next morning at five, we were all summoned on deck. The doctor was in a little boat on one side, bobbing about. He looked at us all from his boat, said we looked healthy, and gave us pratique. At 10, we steamed away again, arriving here on Wednesday, the 4th, at six in the evening, and went to the Clarence Hotel again.   *   *   *

Letters from America.

LETTERS FROM AMERICA.

Saturday, August 29th, 1857.

ON BOARD THE "ASIA."

MY DEAR MAMMA,

IT is a great pleasure to be able to commence writing a letter, for after so many days almost devoid of occupation, one gladly seizes the first moment that it is really practicable to sit down and hold a pen with any chance of success. Looking forward, naturally, to an agreeable summer passage, with smooth seas, bright skies, and favouring breezes, I could scarcely expect to *enjoy* one of the worst trips, so far as weather is concerned, that has been made at this season of the year for some time. Yesterday the sea calmed down, and to-day we have but little motion. But I will not anticipate, and will therefore begin my story from the beginning. I dare say Lawrence would give you a full, true, and most particular account of our progress from the Adelphi to the Pier, and the mustering of the passengers on the tender *Satellite*, which conveyed us to the *Asia*. After the mails

H

were received, our guns were fired, and away we
went.   As we rounded the well-known light-house,
and got a mile or two out, we met the *Great Britain*
coming in from Australia, five weeks beyond her
time.   Instead of steaming along down the Welsh
coast, the usual route, we took the course called
by nautical men "north about," and in the evening came in sight, and passed pretty close to the
south end of the Isle of Man, and I have not seen
any land since then ; one eternal circle of sea and
sky has been round us ever since.   It takes a day
or two to settle down, and find people out, and make
yourself at home.   In a general way, Saturday and
Sunday were both fine days—sea increasing a little
towards Sunday evening—but two clear days enable
you to see what kind of travelling companions you
have got.   B—— and I got seats together at dinner,
and next to me I found an extremely gentlemanly
young man, named Rotherham, and Charles Matthews, who is a favourite with every one.   We next
became acquainted with a Mr. Donough, who is
going out as English Consul to Buffalo,—also a great
success.   A German gentleman introduced himself
to me, whose friends I had met in Manchester ; he
had heard that I was going out.   There is, moreover,
a representative of D——y's house, a very agreeable
man, so that we make quite a party.   We have also
a theatrical party on board, half-a-dozen ballet girls
and prima donna, with Italian dancers and singers,
going on speculation to New York and Philadelphia,

a few Americans, and some Scotchmen, who have lived long in the New World, one has travelled a good deal in Mexico, California, and such wild countries, where the rifle and revolver are necessaries of life.

We have all nations on board, but it is really astonishing how soon you find out those you think will suit you, and form a set to yourselves. We had lunch directly we got rid of the mail-boat, and were fairly on our course, about half-past twelve; at four we dinèd, tea at half-past seven, about ten broiled bones. I thought it was too good to last, but we kept on in the same way on Sunday, and I began to believe the Atlantic was a great humbug, and a voyage nothing at all. Monday wofully undeceived me; pitching and rolling, a heavy sea, and strong head-wind kept me in my berth almost all day; not sick, but all the sensations of sickness, without any relief. I got up to tea, but went down again almost immediately. Tuesday was rather better, and I managed to keep on my legs all day, but could not eat. In the afternoon we met two vessels, and made and answered some questions by means of the signal flags.

Wednesday morning I found I could not get up, and of that day I know little except the kind attempts of my bed-steward to get me something I could eat, but all in vain.

Thursday morning, I tried to get up, and with difficulty succeeded, and got a morsel of breakfast, and began to hope. Standing by the funnel, I saw ahead, the clouds driving on the water, and in five minutes we experienced a white squall;—the sea lashed up to a perfect fury, the waves dashing over the ship, drenching every one and everything. I could not stand this long, and was soon driven below to the refuge of my weary berth, where the hours dragged slowly on till Friday morning, when I found the sea subsiding, the sky clear, and I managed to eat something, for I assure you I was nearly famished, and looking ill and thin. The day was a great success, and I turned in at half-past eleven, unfortunately, for had I staid half an hour longer, I should have seen the rockets and signals made between our ship and another steamer, supposed to be the New York, from New York to Liverpool. This morning I found we were in a fog, owing to our approaching the Bank of Newfoundland, and the Gulf Stream. The whistle has been blowing nearly all day, to warn any vessels that a steamer is approaching. This is the most dangerous part of the voyage, and more accidents occur from fogs than any other cause, when the necessary precautions are neglected. The captain has been on tho bridge all day, and a very sharp look-out is kept. The sound of the whistle is unearthly and unpleasant, and we shall be glad to get away from this particular portion of our course. To-morrow we hope to see Cape Race, and then we steer south along the coast, so we expect smooth water, with a blue sky overhead. I find Captain L—— a very pleasant man; he has been very polite, but is too much occupied with his ship to have much to do with the passengers, which is as it ought to be. After all, it is monotonous work, day after day the same, and we shall all be glad, about next Thursday, to see New York. At noon each day the captain takes his observation of the sun, *and makes it noon.* You must understand that we are sailing westward, therefore losing time; *our* day, from apparent noon one day to apparent noon the next being longer, according to the rate of sailing, than if we remained fixed in one place, the total difference in time between Greenwich and New York, is five hours twenty minutes, and as we are sailing from seven to eight degrees of longitude a day, we are making our day nearly half an hour longer, that is 24½ hours to the day. From noon on Saturday, when we sailed, to noon on Sunday, we made 266 miles; to Monday, at noon, 240; noon on Tuesday, 252; Wednesday, owing to the weather, it fell to 230; Thursday, 242; noon, on Friday, only 221; and to-day, Saturday, we ran 262; that makes 1,713 miles of our 3,030. These distances are all in nautical miles, and give an average of ten miles an hour for the 24½ hours of our day. *Our* time, as I now write, is two o'clock, four bells having just struck, and as my watch is Manchester time, being quarter-past five, we have made three hours and a quarter of our westing. Now I shall close, and go on deck.

Tuesday afternoon, September 1st:—I left off writing on Saturday, and we were all glad to enjoy a really fine day in spite of the fog, which cleared in the evening, as it did on Friday evening, on both which nights we enjoyed a magnificent view of the Aurora Borealis; on Saturday evening it was most beautiful—a perfect arch across the northern sky, the brilliant light running into the most extravagant forms, ever changing in shape as well as intensity, and shooting its rays almost to the zenith; it never quite reached the horizon, but made darts down towards it, as though trying to reach the sea line. We remained watching it until midnight, and had to turn in all in the dark, all lights on board being extinguished at twelve o'clock.

Sunday, another day of dreary, wretched fog, with a heavy sea, and the whistle going all day, sounding for about five seconds every minute; the effect is most unpleasant, as it makes you perfectly nervous and irritable. I could get no breakfast, but managed to attend service in the cabin, where prayers were read very well and impressively by the surgeon of the ship, the captain being on deck owing to the fog. I got better as the day wore on, but we were all wet, our clothes soaked through with the dense and all-penetrating fog, which again cleared off about midnight; we were glad to get rid of the whistle, and have a good night's rest. During this part of the voyage, the captain's duties and anxieties are very great; he never had his clothes off for three days and nights, almost without sleep, and constantly on the bridge, looking out. To shew how alert they are, some one in the fore-cabin, without any intention of producing an effect, was imitating the sound of a horn; the captain heard it; had it been repeated the ship would have immediately been stopped, lest it might have been a signal from some vessel in our track, as we were then crossing what is called the St. Lawrence track, where so many vessels are constantly passing. In spite of the fog and the heavy sea, we ran from Saturday noon to Sunday noon 279 miles.

Monday morning commenced with some little rain, but it cleared off, and the sea began to go down, and the whole day was most delightful. In the evening, the sailors did some gymnastics, and one mounted on a donkey. This animal curiosity was covered with some kind of imitation skin, with an imitation donkey's head, and went prancing and kicking about. After this they ran steeple chases on all fours, over one another's backs, and some ropes stretched on deck. We made a collection for them, and got about £3., which no doubt they will spend in grog in New York. They then sang some sea songs and nigger melodies, very well indeed. We all then went into the forecastle, and having some singers amongst us, we kept it up with much joviality until late. People are now all getting most friendly together, and are more like a large party at some watering-place, than travellers on a long voyage. We have of course had one general row. At first, the weather was so stormy, that the fore-cabin passengers, who have no right abaft the crank hatches, were allowed to come on the saloon deck, for the benefit of the fresh air, and to sit in the capstan gallery when it rained, and as some of them were the poor ballet girls, a stern Yankee, with two most ugly and disagreeable daughters, who never went on deck, joined with three other passengers, whom we have christened " the conspirators," complained to the captain, who, of course, had no other choice than to order them to be kept forward, where they have been all stewed up in a close cabin, instead of being able to enjoy a little fresh air on deck, the portion of deck near their cabin being exposed to every sea that dashes over the ship, and in consequence they were all very seasick again—but the purity of the Yankee damsels was preserved from any contact with second-class passengers. We have all taken their part, and cut " the conspirators " dead. Some of them say they shall write to the New York papers. Let them; they will get well laughed at.

From noon on Sunday to noon yesterday we made 270 miles; it is now nearly noon again, so we must be within 500 miles of New York. We have seen no land as yet, having passed Cape Race in the fog. To-day the weather is truly magnificent,—a smooth sea, and a most brilliant sky.

We are beginning to fancy we shall be sorry to part from the ship and from one another. We have been watching shoals of porpoises rolling and jumping out of the water; B—— said he saw some flying fish, but being an Irishman, we did not believe him. You have no idea how intimate we all get together. I do not think, under all circumstances, we could have accidentally met a pleasanter party; see all at dinner, laughing and talking like a large *table d'hôte* company, and at night the candles are lighted down the tables, with parties at whist or chess, or reading or talking,—you would imagine yourself at an hotel. The table is well provided; of course the cooking is not equal to the Hotel de Prince, but it is wonderfully good; and when you consider all the difficulties on board ship in heavy weather, the wonder is that it is done at all some days, owing to the motion of the ship. The tables have ledges fixed round them, and several days cross ledges between them, to keep the plates and dishes in their places. Now and then many receive their soups in their laps, and their meat in their faces instead of their mouths. The glasses are all fixed in a species of dumb waiter, that is attached to the ceiling, and can be wound up or down. Everything is fresh—fowls, turkeys, beef, mutton, and so forth; but I must confess some of it is getting rather high, although kept in ice. Yesterday the fish was a dead failure, and the odour enough to knock you down. The supply of Wenham Lake ice is most plentiful; it is a great luxury. We expect to be in New York on Thursday, so I dare say I shall not write any more; indeed it is not very easy to write, owing to the vibration of the vessel. The Buffalo consul comes out well, we all like him. There is a New York lawyer on board; he was asking me whether we spoke of the Queen as Victoria; for instance—was Victoria at the theatre? They have queer notions, these same Yankees—but it is time enough to talk about them just yet.

Thursday, September 3rd, New York:—On Tuesday, after luncheon, we had made 279 miles. In the evening there was a good deal of singing, but about nine the fog came on heavier and denser than before, and being so much on the track of the vessels required every precaution, and the fog-whistle again commenced its doleful shriek. I, M——, and two others, sat in a place called "the fiddle," a covered room, open at both sides, commanding the capstan, which constitutes the smoking room in wet weather. We remained listening to doleful accounts of vessels run down in fogs. Captain L—— commanded the Cunard steamer *Europa*, when she ran over, literally so, the *Charles Bartlett*, emigrant ship, in three minutes and a half, only some 70 being saved out of three or four hundred: he was careful before, but as I wrote the other day, is now doubly so, and never leaves the bridge during a fog. I went to bed at two,

but in an hour more the fog cleared away, the
ship, as the captain told me, going clear out of
it, and leaving it behind, like a dense impenetrable
wall. We drank the captain's health at dinner,
and at dusk saw the revolving light on Fire Island,
close to Long Island; the distance ran from noon
on Tuesday to noon on Wednesday, being 300
miles. We were all on the look-out for the *Arabia*,
which sailed from New York on Wednesday, at
twelve noon. It was dark when she came in sight,
and we all felt the most lively interest, something
quite exciting, to see her coming steadily along.
Both ships being at good speed we drew together
fast, but our good captain announced his presence
by sending up rockets and burning blue lights—
these signals were returned, and the effect was
most beautiful. The sea had been all day as
smooth as a mirror, and the full moonlight sparkled
on the water. We gave them a good hearty cheer,
which the crew and passengers of the *Arabia*
as heartily returned. We could see them clustering
on the ship, and we all wished God speed their
voyage—that as early as possible they might arrive
at Liverpool, and announce that the good ship *Asia*
had, by God's mercy, passed safely through all the
difficulties and dangers of the mighty ocean, and was
within a few hours of its destined harbour. The
lights on the Neversink were now visible, and a
dark ridge in the outline ahead, indicated our
proximity to the New World.

We soon came up with the entrance to the Narrows, leading up to New York. I should have said that about four or five o'clock we took the pilot on board; and all looked with great interest on a real live Yankee pilot. Being full moon, and quite light, they decided to go in, and not wait for daylight. Coming up to Sandy Hook, we fired a gun or two, by which I mean metal guns of small weight, perhaps nine-pounders; the report rolled on the water, and reverberated from the land. In due time this had an effect, and a small boat came bobbing up to us; the purser then threw him a can containing telegraphic despatches. He then told us that the *Vanderbilt*, which left Southampton when we left Liverpool, had arrived at twelve that day, and so anticipated our despatches. We scarcely hoped to beat her, as she is a new and very large vessel, much exceeding the *Asia* in tonnage and power. After passing the Hook we had to fire away again for the doctor to come on board, and give us permission to pass. It took several guns to awake him, and after his arrival we steamed quietly along, and soon had the lights of New York and Brooklyn before us. Again our rockets went up, and we fired enough to arouse the whole continent of America. As we did not see the signal at the Cunard Wharf that all was right, and as our arrival was at an unusual hour, we had to wait awhile. We passed the Battery, and therefore arrived at a quarter-past three on Thursday morning, September 3rd. It was an evening of great excitement and much interest; in the interval we had the sailors singing, and various bits of fun going on; the time seemed short, we were safely moored, and then went to bed about four. Of course there was music in the ship, rattling of chains, and so forth—not much rest to be got; we were all up again about five. We then had our last breakfast on the *Asia*, got our luggage on shore, and with the greatest regret bade farewell to the good ship that had carried us so well and comfortably. All felt the parting with one another, we had been so agreeable together, had become well acquainted, and naturally were very sorry our pleasant intercourse was at an end.

I am sorry my first American impressions were not *the thing*. We landed in a black, dirty shed in Jersey City, called a custom-house; my things thrown about in a most blackguard manner; every little thing opened, my stud cases, in fact *every thing*. I had great difficulty in keeping my temper. After the man had finished my dressing bag, "Well," he exclaimed, "that *air* bag is the completest thing I ever saw in my life." Two or three of my fellow-voyagers and myself went together in one coach with our luggage; the man charged us six dollars, that is about twenty-six shillings. We first went on board a river ferry-boat, driving on board in the carriage, and so far as appearance went might have been in a street, with a quantity of vehicles in line, and foot passengers on the sides. It put me in mind of our crossing the Ticino, only in this case we went by steam power. We crossed the North River, and landed in New York, driving over a rough pavement, in a filthy condition, and very soon found ourselves in the vaunted Broadway, which is not near so broad as the Boulevards. We drove to the St. Nicholas, and found it crammed full; then to the Metropolitan, then to La Farge, then the New York, then the Astor House, and at last got taken in at the Union, in Union Square, where, in the fourth storey, we got some bedrooms about as large as dog kennels. * * * Yesterday we were dead beat, and thoroughly tired, so just strolled about. * * I am very well, as brown as a berry, in tolerable appetite, and sleep like a top. Rotherham, whom I mentioned to you, is a very gentlemanly young man, well educated, and thoroughly good-natured; and is arranging to accompany me to Canada.

* * * * * * * * * * * * *

NEW YORK, *September 6th,* 1857.

MY DEAR MAMMA,

I THINK I finished my last letter by saying that on our arrival we had a very strict, and in fact

almost rudely inquisitive examination of our luggage,
so much so that the prying Yankee even opened my
little stud cases, to see what they contained, lest I
might have brought a king in one of them, in order
to deprive the great United States of their Republican constitution. B—— was even more closely
examined, and after the ordeal was over we were
permitted to strap up our trunks, and they were borne
away to the gate, where we became the prey of sundry
drivers, who sought the favour of carrying us to our
destination. Meeting a raw-boned, lantern-jawed
individual, in a straw hat and blouse, who gave us
to understand that he was the proprietor of one of
these attendant vehicles, we proceeded to make a
bargain for the conveyance of our two selves, Mr.
C——, and Mr. M——, with all our luggage, to
the St. Nicholas. This we arranged with the pro-
viso, that if there should be no room at the St.
Nicholas, he must drive on until we found accommodation. A rough road brought us to the water's
edge, as we had to cross the North River, which
separates the state of New Jersey, where the *Asia*
lay, from New York. We were driven, as I told
you, on to a steam floating bridge, the engine in
the centre, and a roadway on each side, bounded
again by covered cabins, the one side for ladies, the
other for gentlemen. The steersman has a glass
house to himself, on the top of the vessel. Loaded
with many vehicles, and a large crowd of busy
eager-looking men, we soon crossed the river, and

were driven into New York itself. Close to the edge of the wharf we saw crowds of those extraordinary river boats for which America is so celebrated, with the great engine-beam towering above all. The first roll of our carriage told us that the pavement was not first-rate, and our olfactory nerves that the smells were more akin to those of Cologne than anything or place else. Passing up one street, we passed a handsome brown sandstone church, and turning round to the left were in the famous Broadway, and soon arrived at a splendid white marble building, thirty windows long, and six storeys high, which we found to be the St. Nicholas. I went in to see if there was room for us, and walked up a splendid hall, with a floor of black and white marble, and entered an immense hall, filled with luggage and people, where, at a counter, I found the clerk of the place. "We have no room," was the reply, and so back I went, and reported the fact. We then crossed the street, a little higher up, to the Metropolitan Hotel. "No room," again the reply, and so on to Prescott's, La Farge, the Astor House Hotel, New York Hotel, with the same result. We then entered Union Square, and tried the Union Hotel. Here we were taken in, and obtained the small kennels I mentioned before. I looked out on some wooden sheds, and I must honestly confess that I experienced one of those sad feelings of utter loneliness and desolation that is part of *your* constitution and mine, under similar circumstances. * * *

I joined the rest of the party, and sallied forth, and found the temperature much higher than was at all agreeable. The first impressions of New York are not by any means satisfactory; I do not intend to compare it, as a city, with our European capitals, because we must remember how much has been done in, comparatively speaking, a very few years; but still, owing to the state of the pavement, the place appears worse than it really is. There seems to be no order of any kind; people put casks, boxes, in fact all sorts of lumber, on the footpath, which is thus greatly encumbered. Broadway is, from the height of the buildings, a narrow street, and possesses here and there a few trees, that produce a species of Boulevard impression. Passing, as it is, through a stage of transition, in which old buildings of mean appearance are giving way to splendid structures of marble and sandstone, a very great irregularity is apparent, and the general good effect of handsome edifices is much detracted from. There is one very large stone one, evidently a copy of a Venetian palace, something like the Palazzo Pesara. Marble is largely used, and the handsome brown stone which, although I believe not so durable, is very effective in street architecture.

We found the temperature very high, in fact, for the first three days almost unbearable, and I had some idea of going away at once, but the effect of the sea voyage, which has produced some lassitude,

I

rendered it unadvisable to proceed at once; besides, after being so long confined on ship-board, I found walking excessively fatiguing. The first day my legs ached fearfully when I got in at night, so that I scarcely knew where to put myself. In the course of the day we called at the Metropolitan, being thoroughly disgusted with the Union House, and obtained a sitting-room and two bedrooms, opening *en suite* with the saloon, and removed here on Friday morning, immediately after breakfast.

On Thursday evening we went with M—— to a very pretty theatre, called Niblo's, which occupies the site of an old garden, has been gradually covered in, and forms a part of the Metropolitan. We were placed in an excellent box, and witnessed a ballet and a pantomime, the latter of the poorest possible order.

Friday Morning;—Metropolitan, which is a large brown stone building, 29 windows long, 18 deep, and six stories high, and contains within itself not merely an American hotel, (with bar, smoking-room, billiard-room, magnificently decorated public rooms, for ladies and gentlemen, with newsroom, telegraph office,) but also a theatre, garden, and shops of different kinds, the most prominent being the barber's, which is entered from the hall. It is the custom here for every one to be shaved, and not shave himself; hence a great demand for New York Gadsbys. After *fixing* ourselves in our rooms, a black man came in, and notified to us the important fact that he was Sam. " Oh, very well, Sam, mind

you come smart whenever we ring." "Ees, massa."
All the men-servants in this vast hotel are free
negroes—if not absolute negroes, only a step or
two removed—they are very civil, and a smile, or a
good-natured word will make them fly, and do anything for you.

The hotels are all replete with notices warning
you against thieves, who get into the rooms and cut
open luggage; so you are requested to leave all
valuables in the bar, where they are locked up in
an iron safe, and the proprietor is answerable to
you for them by law.

In the course of Friday I presented some of my
letters. In the evening I dined with ——'s partner, at the New York Club. On Saturday, B——
and I dined with the Buffalo consul, at the Brevoort
House, which is conducted on the English system,
where you order what you want, and are charged
for your rooms. Here it is so much a-day, whether
you eat or not, which is the only system possible
where such vast crowds pour into a house, and
pass in and out every minute. I wonder, in fact,
how they know whether a person is staying at the
house or not, for it seems as if any one might walk
in, eat his dinner, and walk out unchallenged by
any one.

On Saturday evening we saw many processions
of firemen, soldiers, militia, &c. They are exceed-
ingly fond of military display. * * * In the
middle of Saturday night we were awoke by a tre-

mendous shouting and drumming; a company of the firemen had been contending for some prize with another company at a distance, and had returned victorious. I believe their engine had squirted the farthest. These engines are a great source of pride to them, and are most highly decorated; they are undoubtedly well got up, and the fire brigade a most useful body of men.

On Sunday, we made a call on the *Asia*, to see our friends the officers, and spent an hour with them. We then went on a river steamer as far as Staten Island. Sunday is a quiet day in New York; no omnibuses running, nor anything of that kind. Yesterday I made some calls, and got put in the way of seeing some of the Institutions of the place, and who should I see but my friend W——G——. He was very much astonished to see me; he said I was about the last person he should have thought of seeing in America. He showed me about a good deal; we went to see the *Adriatic*, the new Collins steamer, which is the most magnificent vessel afloat, and is intended to beat us all. The cabins are superb, everything that can please the eye, and at the same time every convenience is carefully studied. They are far a-head of us in fitting up steamers, but I prefer the plain solidity and careful management of the Cunard line.

I then called upon General Webb, whom I found a very nice and gentlemanly man: he is the editor and proprietor of the *Courier* and *Inquirer* newspapers; he was very polite indeed, wished me to go out and stay with him a day or two, but I cannot manage it just now. He is sending a person with me to-day, to shew me some of the places I most wish to see.

This rather hurried letter I have been obliged to close hastily, that it may go by the steamer leaving Boston to-morrow. I shall write again so that my next letter will go by the *Asia*. *   *   *   *

SARATOGA SPRINGS,

Sunday, Sept. 15th, 1857.

My Dear Mamma,

I FINISHED my last letter on Tuesday, to be in time for the *America*, from Boston.

In the evening I dined with D——, at the New York Club, and was introduced to many people, all very kind, and particularly anxious to show me every attention, and do all in their power to make my visit agreeable, as they certainly succeeded in doing. New York is so decidedly a business-place that we cannot expect to see much of the people in the day, during which time they are closely engaged in their various avocations, but after business they will do anything they can to oblige you. I met at the club several to whom I had letters. A Mr. S——, cousin to W—— G——, invited me to dinner for Thursday. I also made an engagement to sail with Colonel Johnson, in his yacht, on Wednesday. He is the owner of the largest yacht in America, 250 tons, called the *Wanderer*. So, on the Wednesday afternoon, I joined a party, and we went down the New York Bay, which gave me a very good view of the splendid harbour, and of this Empire City. Charles Matthews went with me; B—— somehow missed us; I got them both included, and very much we enjoyed our sail, though, of course, the wind dropped when we got some way out, according to my usual fortune, so that we did not manage to reach Sandy Hook, as we intended. We returned to New York about ten at night, after having a capital supper of spatched woodcocks on board. The cabin was extremely handsome, and fitted-up with satin and rosewood, the berths as roomy as an ordinary French bed.

We have found New York passing through a severe financial crisis; money extremely scarce, and people failing on all sides. The best bills are discounting at from two to three per cent. per month, and I was told if any one had money to invest, it could be done with perfect security at 18 or 20 per cent. premium. * * *

On Thursday I dined with Mr. and Mrs. S——, who live in the Fifth Avenue, and spent a pleasant evening. The dinner was excellent. They use a great profusion of vegetables, tomatos, Indian corn, squash, Lima beans, yams (sweet potatoes), but, above all, the Cantaleup melons. At the hotels you get them to breakfast, dinner, and tea, half a melon at a time, much larger than our hothouse fruit. The large water melon I do not like. * * * My host and hostess had travelled a good deal in the old world. I was astonished at the uncon-cerned manner in which they regard a voyage to Europe, they think much less of it than we do of a trip to Italy. The fact is, travelling with us is much more agreeable ; the Republican principle is so fully carried out in the States, that all sorts of people sit cheek-by-jowl in the railway carriages, and it certainly is not very pleasant.

Fifth Avenue is the fashionable part of New York, and contains some very handsome mansions, quite equal to the great London houses in their propor-tion and style ; the door handles, and bell handles, and the door mountings, are all plated with silver, and look extremely well, in fact every thing is ready for an aristocracy. * * * At six o'clock on Friday morning young Rotherham joined me at the hotel, and we set off, bag and baggage, for the Hudson, or North river steamer, which sailed at seven for Albany, a distance of 145 miles : fare, one dollar and a half, about six shillings. Of all the beautiful sails in the world there are few to surpass the Hudson : a fine, wide stream, double that of the Rhine, flowing between wooded and rocky highlands, with ever-changing scenery, winding from side to side, so that you have the course of the river, often shut out from view, expanding into splendid bays and forming beautiful lakes. I must say, that our European rivers are, indeed, poor in comparison. On one side the railway runs the whole way from New York to Albany, but we preferred the steamboat, in order to obtain the best views of the river.

Soon after leaving New York, we reached a part of the river where the high rocks are of basaltic formation, called from their appearance the " Palisades." West Point is the place where a large military school is established for cadets, and here there is a fort, and on the landing step we actually saw a Yankee soldier. The largest town on the river is Newburgh, with some extensive mills close to the stream. On each side we had views of beautiful glades, extending far into the hilly country; the most beautiful were on the left, or west bank going up; the part where the rocks were bolder, and encroached more on the stream, put me a little in mind of the Lurleiberg, but on a grander scale. After passing through the highland district, the immediate shore becomes rather more level; and there we came in sight of the Catskill mountains— the general country being rather flat, much smaller elevations are called mountains than with us—and certainly the Catskill mountains are not very high.

I am sorry to say I did not hear either little Rip Van Winkle, or any of his ghostly friends, playing at bowls; but the light fell gloriously upon the hills, and partly illuminated, and partly hidden in mist, they had a sufficiently mysterious appearance. I must not forget to mention that we passed Spuyten Devil Creek, where Anthony, the Trumpeter, blew his last blast, as he sunk beneath the waves,—a story connected with the old Dutch legends of the Hudson. About five o'clock in the evening, we reached Albany, not tired, but rather hungry, as the food obtainable on board was not eatable. The day-steamers are but poor ; whereas the night-boats on the Hudson are magnificent floating palaces. We got into the railway car, and went on to a place called Troy, and stayed there all night, at a very fair hotel called Troy House. We should have remained at Albany, but it did not look inviting; and then we should have been fixed on Sunday, as no trains run on that day on the railways about here.

On Saturday morning, we went over Burder's Iron Works, where we found one of the sons. I gave him our cards,—had no introduction to him, but he at once showed us all over his place, and gave us much interesting information. They have the largest water-wheel in the world, 60 feet diameter, and 22 feet wide, equal to 1000 horse power, but they can only use 500 horse ;—they have puddling furnaces, rolling mills, foundry, and everything complete. Their principal work is making horse-shoes, nails, and spikes, by machinery; the machine turns out 60 shoes a-minute; and each machine makes twenty tons weight a-day!—It is their own patent. He told us their power costs them 700 dollars a year, being the wages of two men, to attend day and night, regulating the supply of water; and they have 70 feet fall above them to spare, that would give about 1200 horse-power more,—such is the enormous scale of water-power in this country. Mr. Burder was quite delighted to see us; took us over his grounds, and up a rough wooden tower, open at the sides, to have a view over the surrounding country; and if we had been staying, he wished to have seen us at his house. He remembered Mr. Ashworth visiting his works. When we arrived at Troy, we thought it looked like the end of the world,—such a poor, lost-looking place.

The railway stopped in a street, a man and a boy being the only people visible. On saying we would go into the office, and make some enquiries of the station-master, he said, "Wall, I guess, you will jist have to ask me, for, I calculate, I am station-master Sam Hall, and jist everything, *Sirree.*" The one boy put our traps on a wheel-barrow, and on we marched to the Troy House. After crossing the Hudson, in a dilapidated ferry boat, and passing lines of warehouses, and some un-pleasant odours, the town gradually improved. In the course of our rambles that evening and the next day, we found handsome houses, marble churches, Town Hall, courts, &c.; and had a good specimen of a thriving New York town, built partly on one side, partly on the other, of the Hudson, with some other connecting townships. Troy contains 100,000 inhabitants, although Troy proper contains only 40,000, and is a large manufacturing place. There are some mills in the neighbourhood, but having determined to spend Sunday at Saratoga did not visit them.

The railway at Troy, on the east side of the Hudson, has a station of which they are rather proud, but the great difficulty is, that you do not see a soul that looks like a station-master or porter, or anything else; and, for a stranger, it is difficult. At last, a man came to give checks for the luggage. He fastened a piece of brass, stamped with a number, attached by a strap to each article, and gave us another piece with a corresponding number, which I gave to the hotel porter on arriving here, and soon after reaching the hotel, the baggage follows.

When I left for Saratoga I put a bag and a coat on a seat in a carriage, thinking, in the innocence of my heart, that by so doing I had secured two places. On entering the carriage, I found two females had put them off, and taken the seats. Each carriage is a long affair, with rows of seats down both sides, so that the conductor marches through the train, and takes or sells tickets. One woman came in, and said to a young man near me, " Guess I want a seat," and the young man got up, and she took it, without so much as thank you !

We passed through a half-cultivated country, and at dusk reached Saratoga, and went at once to the United States Hotel, which we found an immense place, built round a large planted garden, with vast covered corridors for the guests to promenade in; they accommodate 1,200 people here in the season, and have houses, with gardens, separate from the hotel, which are let to families. The season is now over, and on the 1st of October they shut up the hotels, of which there are several : the corridors extend round both sides of the hotel, or perhaps I might better call it an assemblage of buildings, some brick, some wood. Most of the houses about here are frame-houses, plastered inside, and must be insufferably hot in summer, and cold in winter. There are now, perhaps, 100 people in the house, and it is of course deserted in appearance. This morning we walked down to the Empire Spring, and tasted the water, which is a pleasant tonic, not at all disagreeable to take. Then we visited the rock spring, the first known there, discovered originally by the Indians, when it silently poured forth in the midst of an unknown forest. They brought some English general there, who was wounded about 200 years ago, and bathed him, and cured him there, and from that period it has been celebrated.

It is a small conical hill of lime-stone, with a round hole at the summit, out of which the water used formerly to pour, but now there is some crack in it, and it runs away. The hill is only about five feet high, and has been undoubtedly formed by the water itself pouring over and petrifying. It was an extremely interesting object, and carried our minds back to the time when the red man alone ruled the land; and this spot, now the centre of attraction to the American fashionables, was the great medicine-water of the solitary Mohawk. It is situated in a dell; but the trees have all disappeared, and the ugly, unpainted, wooden frame-house, covers the sides of the dell.

Saratoga is situated prettily; the ground is undulating, and there are pleasant drives in the neighbourhood. We took one to the Saratoga Lake, called by the Mohawks the Lake of the Great Spirit, from its over-powering silence. It is about three miles wide and nine miles long, beautifully wooded. The Indians never spoke in crossing it, as they believed if they did, it would offend the Great Spirit. There is a large hotel near it, and, I must say, I would far prefer to stay there, amid the beauties of the lake, than at the springs themselves. The banks are well wooded; and the shapes of the hills about very pleasing. On the road, we passed many of the old clearings, with the tree stumps sticking up out of the ground. We met two young men carrying two small animals, and asking the driver what they were, " Wall, I guess, that air Injian has killed them with his bow and arrow." Oh, dreadful shock ! The Indian was a dirty-looking lad, in a white shirt and shabby trowsers; perhaps a descendant of some stately Mohawk sadly degenerated !

The country is alive with the chirrup of grass-hoppers that sound loud now, whilst I am writing, among the grass, in the centre of the court of the hotel, and to-day we heard the shrill cry of the locusts; in the evening another insect joins the concert, called the Katadid, from the peculiar noise it makes, " Katadid, katadid."

It would amuse you to see the black waiters. At dinner they all enter in procession, each bearing two dishes; one man claps his hands, the dishes are suspended over the table, clap two, and down they come into their places. I enclose you a bill of fare of to-day, and when I tell you it was got through in fifty minutes, I think even Lawrence must admit that neither he nor his men could do anything of the kind. They are very civil to English people, I think it is because we treat them better. An American never says, " If you please," or " Thank you," to a poor darky, and I think they feel the difference of manners. At Troy House I got a whiff from a fat negro that took my appetite away. To-morrow we start for Montreal.   *   *   *

I find my young travelling companion most agreeable. I have taken a great liking to him, which I think is mutual, and we shall get on capitally together; it is much pleasanter having company.   *   *   *

Toronto, Canada West,

Sept. 21st, 1857.

My dear Mamma,

My last letter from Saratoga would give you the history of our proceedings up to that date; and on the Monday morning, at eight, we started for Whitehall. The line passed through a beautiful country, very much undulated, and in some places rocky; always well-wooded, and supplied with streams of water. At Whitehall, we found a steamer ready to take us up Lake Champlain. At first the lake is extremely narrow, being more like a river than any part of a lake. The ground was level to the borders of the lake; but fine wood-covered hills bounded the plain land, and, gradually approaching nearer, we entered the lake through the hills, after sailing 20 or 30 miles down the river. However much we admired the Hudson, we found the scenery of Lake Champlain much finer; a succession of splendid woodland views, with retiring glades, penetrating the hills. Imagine a fine, broad sheet of water, now narrowed by the land and then expanding, dotted with islands:— the entire sail was one to be remembered for life. The boat stopped at several places, the largest being Burlington, a fine town in Vermont. We passed several localities rendered famous in the

War of Independence, and in the late war with America, among the principal being Fort Ticonderoga, which was first taken from the French by the English, and afterwards taken by the Americans. After dark, we landed at Rouse's Point, and stepped on shore in the English possessions, being the frontier of Canada. Here we got into the railway again; and, after some long delay, waiting for the direct train from New York, we proceeded on our way to Montreal. The train came to a stand, we got out, and stepped into a ferry-boat, and found ourselves on the mighty St. Lawrence! Crossing over, we were received by an accumulation of cab-drivers, omnibus cads, and so forth; and getting into an omnibus, were driven to the Donegana Hotel, where we had supper and went to bed, pretty well tired with a journey of 15 hours. The next morning we sallied forth to have our first view, and receive our first impression of a Canadian town; and were really surprised with the solid substantial appearance of every place. The buildings appear as if intended to stand, and not merely put up as make-shifts.

Montreal boasts of some really fine public edifices. The Catholic Cathedral would, from its exterior, have induced you to rush in at once. We went in, and found the pillars all wood, tho floor the same, and filled with pews; nevertheless, it is a fine, well-built church, and possesses a very imposing façade. The post-office, bank, law courts, and so forth, are handsome buildings; and the quays on the St. Lawrence, here a mile-and-a-half wide, are well-constructed. * * * Mr. Ogilvie, to whom I had a letter from Mr. Wilde, told us what to see in the town; and in the afternoon took us in his carriage a very pleasant drive round the mountain, as it is called, which is to Montreal what the Superga is to Turin. * * *

In the evening we took a river steamer for Quebec. The scenery on the St. Lawrence between Montreal and Quebec, is not particularly interesting,—the shores flat and tame; still, it is a magnificent stream of water. St. Peter's Lake, which is a part of the river, is nine miles across. We had a good steamer, and a cabin to ourselves, and at seven the next morning found ourselves at Quebec. Taking the hotel omnibus, we were jolted up a tremendously steep hill, to Russell's Hotel, which is the best there, but a wretched hole. Rotherham had taken a severe cold, and I found him very feverish, so gave him some quinine, which set him all right in a few hours.

I then called on Mr. Forsyth, to whom I had a letter from Sir John Pakington; he very kindly called upon us at half-past three, and invited us both to dinner. In the meantime I took a survey of the town, and although it does not contain anything very striking, yet it is a curious and interesting place; built on a steep hill, surrounded with strong fortifications, crowned with a citadel,

K

overlooking the grand river below, it cannot fail to strike the visitor. I found my way to a kind of plateau, on which some guns were mounted, and then I had a view of the St. Lawrence, the island of Orleans, which divides the river into two streams; and, on the other hand, the upward stream of the small river St. Charles, which empties itself into the St. Lawrence. The steep sides of the river are clothed with trees, and far away you see the higher mountains.

At half-past three Mr. Forsyth came, and we walked first to the citadel, and had a good view of the river, and the large timber depôts, where the rafts floated down the river are broken up, and the timber shipped for England and other parts. We then walked past the citadel, and called upon a partner of Mr. Forsyth, a sporting man; he has a large collection of horses, and so forth. Among his curiosities we saw an immense wild cat, killed in his garden the day before, a creature as tall as Bevis, with extraordinary long feet, and altogether especially ugly. After this visit we proceeded a little further, and stood on the Plains of Abraham, and after tracing the course taken by General Wolfe and his troops, we stood by a small pillar, with this inscription :—

"HERE DIED WOLFE, VICTORIOUS."

A spot sacred in history, where the true hero died at the moment of victory, his skill and bravery having given a new province to England. We then returned to our hotel, and after dressing went to dine with Mr. Forsyth, and met some seven or eight gentlemen, all very kindly asked to meet us, and spent a very agreeable evening.

There is a striking peculiarity about the Canadian buildings; almost all their roofs are covered with tin plate, and as the climate is dry, the tin retains its brightness for years, and their roofs glitter in the sun in the most extraordinary way, giving a curious effect to the landscape, and rendering the towns visible at a great distance, from the reflection of light on the domes and spires of the churches.

In the morning we got a carriage, and drove out to see the falls of Montmorencie: the drive was extremely pleasant, passing through a beautiful country, with a succession of views of the river, overlooked by the Citadel of Quebec. The falls are very fine, but I presume their impression is soon to be effaced by the mighty Niagara. Still, being the first really large falls I ever saw, they were particularly interesting; an immense volume of water, 50 or 60 feet wide, and two or three feet deep, pours over several rocky interruptions in its channel, for some distance gradually descending, until at last it falls over a precipice 250 feet in height; the effect is very sublime, and the roar of the water perfectly musical. The fall is close to the St. Lawrence river, and the stream at once runs into it.

The season for visitors in Quebec is about over, and in November the river freezes up, and so remains until May; the cold is then intense; at times the last winter it was 34 or 40 degrees below zero, that would be about 72 below freezing point. The mixture of races and language is extremely interesting. The signs and the notices are all repeated in French and English, and the people generally speak both tongues, though I rather fancy Paris would have some difficulty in comprehending the French of the *habitans;* still, the money, the energy, the commercial skill and activity are here, as elsewhere, with the English residents, and they seem, so far as I have talked with them, attached to the land of their adoption; but "the old country," as they endearingly call England, is always spoken of as "home." Neither time nor distance can obliterate the feelings that draw men with affection to the land of their birth, and the home of their childhood, and I am glad to see these feelings so prevalent in Canada, which must do more to keep this splendid province an English possession than anything else: they do not like their Yankee neighbours; they are too fast for them, and they look down upon their luxury and excitement with contempt. Still, they may take lessons from John Bull's younger son, more particularly in the matter of hotels, which, in Montreal and Quebec, are truly wretched, Quebec the worst; in fact, I was thinking the other day, what would Papa do here;

he could not sleep in the beds, nor could he eat the meat. The flesh meat is coarse, the cooking bad; here at Toronto, however, there is an excellent hotel, on the American plan, with really good living. We meet a vast predominance of Irish everywhere, but, somehow, here they settle down into useful people, and supply all the domestic servants including waiters, which are either Irish or negroes. I am getting quite accustomed to see a delicate black paw at the edge of my plate, or else taking a block of ice, and putting it in my glass or jug; as I told you, in another letter, the use of ice-water is the greatest luxury here possible, and it is most abundant. I have just arrived at the conclusion that an abundant supply of pure iced water is not only the greatest luxury, but also is, of all things, most conducive to temperance; we rarely drink anything else at dinner, and the majority of people at the table are satisfied with the pure element, though many, certainly, take a drink at the bar after dinner is over. There is little spitting or chewing among the Canadians, and it is really something dreadful whenever you meet a Yankee.

At Montreal we met a young man with a furious moustache; he had come over recently, and had lost his voice; he told me, in a faint whisper, that having heard there were no good saddles in Canada, he had brought one with him in a box. He was staying, and we found him there on our return from Quebec, the saddle in the box, and the man still apparently not knowing what to do with himself.

We left Quebec by railway, and passed through what will some day be a fine country. It has been cleared, but is clothed anew with a fresh growth of timber, and so, for miles, in a straight line, the train rushes on, passing nothing but wood and tree stumps, sticking up out of the ground. The Grand Trunk Railway is a fine work, vastly superior in its construction to the States Railway; it is on the broad gauge, and the carriages are pretty comfortable; they are open through, and you have perfect liberty to walk from one end of the train to the other.

We arrived at Montreal about ten, and left next morning at seven, arriving at Toronto at half-past nine in the evening; the total distance from Quebec to Toronto being 513 miles, run in twenty hours' absolute travelling. The great tubular bridge over the St. Lawrence at Montreal is in progress, but some three years must elapse ere it is completed.

The nature of the country is still the same eternal forest; and I am glad to say I saw some real log huts, which I was anxious to meet with: at Kingston, we came in sight of Lake Ontario, and ran for some distance by the side of this magnificent inland sea! The water was blue, and the waves beat on the shore, so that you could not really detect any difference between the lake and the ocean itself. At Toronto, we found an excellent hotel, and met Mr. C—— and M——, who came over with us in the *Asia;* they had been to Niagara and Chicago, and have set off this morning for Quebec.

Toronto seems a very fine rising town; the streets are all wide, and laid out at right angles; the roads are rough and dirty; the foot-paths are all well planked :—in most other towns the side-walks are planked, and, in many instances, the road itself also :—wood is so superabundant, it is burned in vast quantities in the locomotives, steamboats, &c.

Yesterday I called at the barracks, and found that Haliburton was there, but happened to be out at the time.   I want some information for our route : I am anxious to go to the Sault St. Marie, at the head of Lake Michigan, and into Lake Superior if possible.   *   *   *   *

You would be perfectly astonished at the grandeur and magnitude of the shops in this new town; they are quite equal to any we have; and the price of land is fabulous, considering the locality; and it must be some years before the property can be worth its present nominal price. There are many handsome public edifices which I have not yet had time to see, as I must finish this letter early, to catch the English mail; and have had no time nor opportunity to put pen to paper since I left Saratoga.

We shall leave here to-morrow or Wednesday for Niagara.

I met a man last night who left England on the 26th of August, and has been a little way further than Toronto, to a place called London, turned back, then saw Niagara in five minutes, and leaves next Saturday for Liverpool. How curiously people do travel!

Rotherham is a capital companion, and we get on well together. He told me he had put his card down on the table of the *Asia* (the way you mark your dinner seat), but changed it when he saw me, to *sit next me*, and we just seem to have known each other a dozen years. I see there has been a fearful wreck in a great storm on the Atlantic; off Cape Hatteras, the *Central America* foundered with 500 passengers on board, only 40 being saved. The weather here is delightfully cool and bracing; in fact quite cold morning and evening, and much more healthy than the heat we had at New York.

I must now close this rather short letter, but was determined not to miss a mail if possible. I opened the Bible last night at the 25th Psalm, which I read and went to bed. * * *

CLIFTON HOUSE, NIAGARA,

September 23rd, 1857.

MY DEAR MAMMA,

I FINISHED my last letter rather hastily; in fact I had but little time to write at all, owing to so much travelling, and the fatigue consequent thereon. After I had dispatched the letter, I received a telegram from Mr. Ogilvie, informing me that a letter had arrived at Montreal, and that I should receive it the next day; this cheered me up considerably, and I sallied forth to the Government House to find Mr. Ashworth's friend, Captain R——; but he was absent. I met Colonel Irvine, Aide-de-Camp to his Excellency, to whom I delivered the letters I had for Sir William Eyre; he took the letter to Sir William, who hoped I would call upon him the next morning.

I took Rotherham with me, to see the Toronto Observatory, which is entirely devoted to terrestrial magnetism; it is very well conducted, and the results have been of much importance to science generally. After dinner, the hour for which is two o'clock, I found Haliburton waiting to see me; he is a very good-looking fellow, and we went

out for a walk : we visited the House of Assembly,
which is a small copy of our Houses of Parliament,
having a House of Commons and Senate Chamber;
they are neatly fitted up. The Government of Canada
is peripatetic, and is now at Toronto, at Montreal,
and Quebec; the Houses of Parliament have
been burnt down, I think by Canadian mobs. At
present there is a motion before the English Government, to decide on one town, which is for the
future to be the fixed capital of Canada. I fancy
it will be Quebec, but of course the people in the
different towns, Montreal and Toronto, hope it
may be theirs, and there is a fourth claimant in
the city of Ottawa. There is an excellent library
attached to the Parliament-house, almost new, as
two libraries were destroyed at the same time the
houses were burnt in the other towns. In the
evening we went up to the old barracks, and
smoked a cigar with Haliburton; he lives in an
old wooden house, one story high, within the fort,
which is of no use now as a fort, being one of the
old stockades used in the wars with the Indians,
and is defended by mud walls, supported by strong
beams placed upright in the ground, very close to
each other, and contains several block-houses,
pierced for rifles. Though ruined and dilapidated,
it gives you a very good idea of the kind of forts
they used in that half-civilised warfare. Colonel
Irvine came during the evening, and told us many
amusing stories, principally local. I received a

card from Sir William and Lady Eyre, inviting me
to dine at Government House next Friday; but of
course I could not stay so long, and had to decline
it. Colonel Irvine gave me a note to Mr. Chessly,
the head of the Indian department, in order that
I might get some information relative to the Sault
St. Marie route, and on Tuesday morning I called
on him, and he gave me a letter to the collector of
customs. Afterwards I called on Sir William Eyre,
who was extremely kind, and offered to do anything
for me, and would not be satisfied until he had hit
on the idea that a circular letter from himself to all
English government officers on or in my route, would
be useful, which he sent me in the course of the next
day. I then went to the model school and normal
establishment, which is the Committee of Privy
Council on Education for Canada. A person came
to show me round, I wrote my name in a book, he
looked at it, and when he saw the place I came
from, " Oh, are you from Manchester?" I said
" Yes; do you know that city?" " Oh, yes; I
have a brother-in-law there, the Rev. Mr. D——."
So I told him I knew Mr. D—— slightly, and I think
I might have carried the whole place away; I did
think he was going to embrace me. It is a splendid
establishment, and is the great depôt for teaching
materials for the province, and books for the public
libraries, and so forth. He gave me a copy of their
last report, and promised to send me the new one
as soon as published.

When I got back to the hotel I found a packet containing two of your letters; the letter you refer to I have not received. I was glad to get your letters, it seemed so long a time to me to have been without a word from those so dear to me.

On Tuesday afternoon we left Toronto with real regret. It is a fine place, and with prudence will be an important seat of commerce some day. At present it is a little over-built; at least so I thought. I had not time to call on Mr. L——; I could not find exactly where he lived, York-street being 30 miles long; so I gave it up as an undertaking requiring more time than I had at my disposal.

We started in a steamer on Lake Ontario, at half-past four, and had a rough swell on the lake, which you could not in the least tell from a thorough cross sea in the ocean itself; and, I must tell the truth, I was much nearer being sick than any day during the voyage out. At the village of Niagara we got into the railway, and about half-past nine arrived at the Clifton House, close to the falls.

At this moment I am writing alone in my room, the window is open, it is past ten at night, and the roar of that mighty cataract resounds in my ears to the exclusion of every other sound except the constant tremor and vibration of the hotel itself. I feel that I am attempting a subject far beyond my power. No human language can convey any idea of the sublimity of Niagara. We arrived at

dark, and could only discover the faint light
reflected from the spray; the sound alone told us
where we were, and I lay down last night in bed,
listening to its mighty voice for long ere I could
feel any want of sleep. The sound gave the idea
of falling water, but there arose from it a deep,
hollow, bass note, which produces an indescribable
effect, not unlike the continued rolling of distant
thunder. Mamma, did you ever try and imagine
what was meant by eternity? If so, I can only
say that the ceaseless voice of Niagara gives me the
only idea, so to speak, of anything eternal. One's
mind is carried back through the countless ages
that those waters have hurried down that terrible
abyss, when the silence of the forest, and the awe
of the red man were the only witnesses of its
grandeur. It has no historic legends connected
with it; its associations with man are but few and
brief; it belongs to God alone, and speaks with
His voice, and tells of His power. That I longed
to look at those waters, yet almost dreaded daylight,
you may well believe. Shall I be disappointed?
Will Niagara equal my expectations? And then I
listened again, and felt how deep was the rebuke
for so vain a thought; the reality, the cause of
that solemn voice, must be in itself far too grand
and majestic to be associated, in any degree, with so
meagre and trivial an idea as human disappointment. When, at last, I summoned courage to
break the spell that had been on me the whole

night, I opened the window, threw back the Venetian windows, and looked forth upon the Falls. Before me, almost opposite, was the smaller, or American Fall, separated by Goat Island from the Canadian, or Great Horse Shoe Fall. I can't tell you how deep, or how broad, or how high; I dare say it is all in print somewhere. I could not stop to ask the question, or care about it one straw. There, before me, was the mighty torrent, tossed and vexed in its course, until it finally plunged into the depth below, and from that depth arose a mist of spray that hid from view the bottom of the fall, and rising, at times shut out the greater part of the fall itself. Looking to the right from Goat Island, I saw the Horse Shoe Fall, which is much larger and grander than the other one; it forms a rather acute angle, more than the round form you would imagine from its being called Horse Shoe; and the enormous amount and depth of water falling over is evidenced by the green colour it takes at the edge, and for a short way down, ere it breaks into spray. The sunlight, playing on the spray, creates beautiful rainbows, ever changing in their brightness and forms, and down below the waters boil and foam, and then appear as if they were stunned, and seem to move away sluggishly. I noticed the same effect at the falls of Montmorencie. It struck Rotherham precisely the same.

After breakfast we took a carriage, to go round

and see the different points of view; we went first to the side of the Horse Shoe Falls, and stood close to the rushing waters, where, on the 11th of this month, an Englishman, named Allen, after waving his hat, jumped into the water, and was seen no more. He staid at the Clifton Arms, and in the book he wrote his name as usual, and appended to it is, in another hand, "Jumped off Table Rock on the 11th." Brief record of an act surely of insanity, and yet I can assure you these waters have the most fascinating appearance. Our guide, to-day, said this Allen's bones might be found in the winter, jammed in the rocks.

We then put on waterproof garments, and descending a staircase, went along a ledge of rock, keeping close to the rocks, until we had proceeded some distance beneath the falls themselves. The spray beat up against us so much that I could hardly keep my breath, and was glad to get back. I have got my certificate of having been under these falls as far as Termination Rock; but, I confess, I would not go again for a good deal. I am sure it is dangerous; if we made a false step, no power could keep us from being dashed to pieces. I also found that the rock gave way at times, and pieces fell down upon the narrow path; had I known that sooner I would not have gone. I shall enclose the certificate, and have it framed and hung up, as an instance of what people will do.

NIAGARA FALLS, C. W.

TABLE ROCK HOUSE.

THIS IS TO CERTIFY THAT

MR. JOHN A. NICHOLLS

HAS THIS DAY BEEN

UNDER THE GREAT SHEET OF WATER!

The distance of two hundred and forty feet from the commencement of
the Falls to the termination of Table Rock:

WITH A COMPETENT GUIDE IN THE EMPLOY OF THE SUBSCRIBER.

Sept. 23rd, 1857.   J. DAVIS, *Proprietor.*

We then went up the stream to see the rapids, and
if Niagara did not exist, those rapids alone would be
enough to attract attention.   For more than a mile
the foaming waters leap, and toss, and fret themselves over the rocky obstructions that prevent
their easy descent; of course they are quite impassable, and at times vessels get down into them, and
are carried helplessly over the falls.   It is, I believe,
a grand sight to see vessels carried down.   Our
driver told us he saw one two years ago, that had
broken loose from the steamer that was towing it
across to Navy Island, it had sheep, horses, and
cows on board; all went over.   Just as it reached
the edge of the fall it broke in two, and only a few·
scattered timbers were ever seen again, although
boats went as near to the lower part of the fall as
possible, in order to pick up some of the dead
cattle.   We saw a burning spring, not unlike the
Harrogate water; the gas is inflammable that

comes from the spring, and the man set it on fire for our benefit.

After a long sojourn by the side of the rapids, we returned to the hotel to dinner, and then went across the suspension bridge, which is a magnificent work; the railway runs on the upper part, below which is a road for carriages and foot passengers. We then crossed a small bridge over the American rapids, and went to Goat Island, and enjoyed the view of the falls from there, and from a small tower built at the extreme point of the island, with a gallery hanging over the falls, from which the view is indeed sublime. We saw the three small islands called "The Three Sisters." It seems an old hermit found out the Indian way of crossing to Goat Island: and when the red men were away went over and destroyed the ropes by which they kept up their communication with the main land, and lived on the island the remainder of his life. Finding three little girls upon it, he placed one on each of the small islands, and there maintained them,—hence the name of "The Three Sisters."

Our man told us many stories of people being carried over the falls. After staying a long time on Goat Island we returned, calling on the way at a kind of shop kept by Indians, for the sale of their moose hair work, and I bought some things from the daughter of the chief Black Hawk. Returning by the bridge to the hotel in time for tea, I then sat down to begin this letter, after spending a day of

L

perfect enjoyment. Before I came up stairs I went out to the edge of the river, and saw the effect of the moon on the water; it is but a crescent, yet the faint light caught the spray with a very good effect. I wished, then, I could just transport you over here, without a sea voyage, to see Niagara. If I saw nothing else, and returned at once, I should consider the voyage amply repaid.

BUFFALO, *Sept. 25th.*

BEFORE I wrote, on the 23rd, and the following day, I spent in quiet contemplation of the falls, feeling, as I did, that I could never gaze long enough upon them. It was a real relief to know that the usual round of sights was completed, that the things to be done were done, and no one could challenge my right to sit and watch the mighty waters, ever rolling over the vast abyss, and casting up their clouds of mist and spray that rose far above the level of the falls themselves. I sat on a log of wood, on the Canada side, close to the edge of the great Horse Shoe Fall, about two hours, in a species of trance, and afterwards on the balcony of the hotel for some time longer. The more you look the longer you wish to stay; it was with deep regret we left Niagara, and took our places in the cars for Chippewa Creek, and then

on by the steamer up Niagara River, to Buffalo.
The sail is exquisitely lovely, the stream strong
and deep, both immediately above the rapids that
break just below Chippewa, and form the great
rapids of Niagara, rendering the navigation rather
dangerous; and again close to Buffalo, where the
stream, near a mile wide, runs at the rate of seven
miles an hour, the banks are clothed with trees
almost level with the water, presenting that closely
wooded scenery so peculiar to the American continent, and terminating in the broad water of Lake
Erie. The sun was setting in gorgeous splendour
as we arrived, gilding the sky with the deepest
golden light. On landing, we drove to the American Hotel, through a fine, wide, well-lighted
street, and after tea we found our travelling friend
Donohoe, the consul at Buffalo, was staying at
the American. He was very glad to see us, and
introduced us to a Mr. H——, a lawyer here,
with whom we went to the theatre, and were surprised to find a very handsome, well-arranged
house, and a motley audience. The dress part
was occupied with respectable people, and up stairs
were many wild-looking far-West men, with a few
negroes in the gallery.

To-day we walked about with Donohoe, and were
indeed astonished with the magnitude and busy
aspect of the place. This evening Mr. H—— took
us a drive, and showed us the splendid houses of
the richer people; from him I received a deal of

information relative to the place. In 1804 it contained about 500 inhabitants; and in 1813, the wooden town of Buffalo was burnt by the English troops, leaving one house only, which still exists. In 1833 it contained about 5,000 inhabitants, and now numbers quite 100,000. Main-street is three miles long, and Franklin and Washington-streets, running parallel with it, are fine wide streets, with footways twenty or thirty feet wide. Main-street is the principal thoroughfare, and is wider than Portland-street, containing the principal shops and two of the chief hotels. Our hotel contains 200 bed-rooms, and there are two more, equally large. The buildings are fine and handsome, and I can safely say there are shops Manchester cannot equal. It depends to a great extent on the transit trade of the far west, and its harbour is crowded with shipping. We went on board a steamer that runs to Toledo, one of the most splendid I ever saw, 335 feet long, which cost 700,000 dollars. There are three or four other boats almost equal, engaged in the passage trade to Detroit and Chicago. Buffalo is also the great place for the corn trade; the grain is there warehoused, and either sent by rail or by the Welland and Erie canals, to New York. The streets are well made, and they are going to a great expense with the levels, so as to have one system of gradients for the whole town, instead of letting people do as they please, on the good principle that the first expense is the least.

Mr. H—— seems extremely proud of Buffalo. He says, "the Americans are a people without history, without association, and devoid of all *reverence*." They have no past, and do not care about it; in fact, here it is each man for himself. A man goes into business, fails, starts something else immediately, and if that fails, tries again on fresh ground. He pointed out some people at the theatre, who, five years ago, were hardly above working men, or clerks at the highest, now rich merchants and bankers. All are in hot haste to get rich, and they feel that so large an extent of country still remaining unoccupied, affords opportunities for amassing wealth that do not exist in Europe.

I am perfectly astounded with Buffalo. I expected to see a decent country town, at most all makeshifts;—I find a city, laid out on a magnificent scale, an infant, it is true, but one of Hercules' kind, and bidding fair, in thirty years, to be as large as Manchester. Land is sold in lots, measuring frontage, and extending back 120 feet. The price in Main-street runs from 800 and 900 dollars to 1,000 and 1,200 *per foot* of frontage, and equalling about 30 dollars a square yard; nearly £7. per square yard; so much have they anticipated the future greatness of their promising city. There are large manufactories, stores, and those articles required by settlers in the distant West. I saw a large manufactory of piano fortes, nearly as large as our mill. Their hotels would surprise you; the business they do is immense, and crowds are ever coming and departing from all parts. They begin breakfast at half-past four, and supper till twelve, and during nearly the whole time people are eating.

Donohoe has been well received; resolutions passed at meetings, congratulating him on his arrival. He is the first consul ever appointed here from England, and I suppose the people are gratified to have a representative of Her Britannic Majesty in Buffalo.

SATURDAY MORNING, 26*th*.

So far last night. I have received your letter: I am glad you looked in at the school, and approve of our new Master. When you call again give him my kind regards, and tell the staff I am quite well, and getting on capitally; indeed, the same information will do for all enquiring friends.

I can truly say that I have met on all hands with the greatest politeness; they have their peculiarities, like the rest of the world; they are vain of their country; they are proud of what they have done. They have great reason to be proud, and I don't mind telling them so; it is the truth, and at the same time it pleases them. It is wonderful how far a little "soft sawder" will go. Donohoe and I were comparing notes; we perfectly agreed, that once having kissed the Blarney-stone, a man may travel through America in the most agreeable manner possible. He lays it on thick, I only gently butter,—the result is much the same, the people will do anything for you. No one can understand American peculiarities who has not travelled in the States; of that I am quite certain.

Last evening the sunset far exceeded any I ever saw before; the western sky was gorgeous in its golden glory, the deep orange tints extended round the entire horizon, and as there is hardly any twilight, ere the colour departed the stars shone out, the golden circlet gradually mellowing down, until the deep blue sky absorbed its fainting rays, and the crescent moon and bright stars formed a sky of unrivalled splendour. Our favourite reminiscence of Turin was nothing to it; and these are the ordinary sunsets of this favoured climate. It is now as warm as August in England, and we may have it so for near two months, till the end of the Indian summer. * * *

Madison City, State of Wisconsin,

October 1st, 1857.

My Dear Mamma,

My last letter I finished at Buffalo; after its completion I called on the Hon. Mr. Fillmore, ex-President of the United States, but like Cincinnatus, returned to his quiet domestic life. He is a lawyer by profession and an Unitarian by faith; he resides in a small wooden house in Franklin Street, in the greatest simplicity of style. We had a long and interesting conversation for about an hour on the general state of the country; he has lately spent a year in Europe, for the first time in his life, and was delighted with the old country, as they all call England; he regretted my stay was so short in Buffalo. I told him I was extremely glad that I had been favoured with an interview with him, which I should always remember with pleasure.

According to the plan I told you I had laid down for our route, in the evening we went on board the *Louisiana,* bound for Mackinac and Green Bay. Mr. H—— went with us, and when he saw the steamer, dissuaded us from going by her, being an old, dirty freight boat, so we at once changed our plans and route, and went on board a magnificent steamer, the *Mississippi*, bound for Detroit in Michigan. To give you some idea of these boats, the one just named is 350 feet long, 2,500 tons burden, carries 2,000 passengers, and the engineer told me the engine was 1,250 horse-power; this, however, I doubted, as I could not see that there was sufficient strength of metal to transmit so much power. We started at ten o'clock at night, and bid adieu to Donohoe and H——, from both of whom we had received all the kindness and attention they could bestow upon us. Rotherham and I had a state-room to ourselves, and soon went to bed, after making the disagreeable discovery that it was a temperance boat, and therefore we could not get a glass of brandy and water before retiring; however, my good flask supplied the means, and so to sleep. Awakened early on Sunday morning, by some horrid children in the next state-room, elevating their voices and weeping. Going out after breakfast, we found we were quite out of sight of land, and so far as appearance went, might have been on the Atlantic. The steamer is magnificently got up: the cabin is 300 feet long, all white and gold, with velvet-covered seats, marble-topped tables, and a sheet of plate-glass, with a rail before it, so placed, that you can see the engine at work. We had dinner on board, and about three o'clock drew into the land; we passed the Canada coast near, and saw the dear old flag of England waving there, and about four or half-past, landed at Detroit, and took ourselves and traps to the Biddle House, which we found pretty fair.

Detroit is an old town, and is situated on the river between Lakes Erie and St. Clair, Buffalo being at the other end of Lake Erie. Originally founded by the French, it is now progressing rapidly, and laid out with that same future expectation of greatness, which so peculiarly distinguishes this western country, streets extending for miles, and I must also say, containing some really handsome houses.

It came on to rain heavily, and so, being nearly dark, we returned to the hotel, resolved to depart the next morning, there being nothing much more to see. We found the pillars in the front of the hotel cased with strong iron, and on enquiring the reason were told that the people are so much in the habit of putting their feet up that they had worn six inches into the pillars, which, being only brick, stuccoed over, would not stand such wear and tear.

We got up at half-past five the next morning, and at half-past seven started by the Michigan Central Railway for Chicago. The road runs through a wild country, for the most part primeval forests, without a house or erection visible for miles; it was the Lightning Express, as they term their fast trains, and did the 282 miles in thirteen hours and a half. For some distance we ran along the shores of Lake Michigan, which being excessively sandy, thrown up into hillocks, had much the appearance of old Southport, with the tide in. The waves broke on the coast, and again we could have believed it was not a lake, but the great ocean itself that was before us. We then came out on the prairie, and saw a level country for miles around, richly clothed with grass, and clumps of small trees here and there, little islands in the grassy ocean, and at six ran on a kind of breakwater, on piles, into the station at Chicago, and soon found ourselves at an excellent hotel, the Richmond House, almost new. After tea we sallied out for a walk, and found a town in process of construction on a stupendous scale.

Chicago was at first built too low on the swampy plain, and now they are absolutely raising the whole town seven feet at the least, in some places more than that, making the gradients of the streets all new and repaving; instead of the old plank side-walks, constructing them of splendid blocks of granite. The evenings are now short, so we returned to our hotel after a short stroll, which proved to us there was something to see here, and then had our first game at billiards, in the room attached to the hotel. We went to bed, and were nearly devoured by mosquitoes, and suffered very much from the irritation of the bite.

After breakfast we called upon Mr. W——, the English consul, to whom A—— D—— gave me a note, and very kind and attentive he has been to us.

I told you that money matters were queer here, but since I first came out they have gone from bad to worse. Gold has almost disappeared from circulation; the banks are breaking, or bursting, as they call it, so that the ordinary paper currency is very unsafe to hold, requiring great circumspection.

Mr. W—— is in the corn and lumber trade, and told me one of their oldest bankers had stopped that day, being the first proof that the pressure had reached them so far West. He took us a good deal about the town, and in the evening we went to his house, and took tea with him.

In the course of the next morning there was a run upon another bank, and we went to see the crowds going in to draw out their deposits. This was a Mr. Swift's bank, and that did not re-open the next day.

Chicago is, without exception, the most magnificent in its plan of any western city. In 1830 its population was 0; in 1840, 4,400; in 1850, 28,200; and now, in 1857, it is quite 110,000. I was very fortunate in meeting with so excellent a cicerone as Mr. W——. In the course of the afternoon we went about the town, and saw some very splendid new churches in course of construction, and met, driving in a dirty little buggy, a man who came up to see one of the Presbyterian churches. Mr. W—— introduced me to him; fifteen years ago he was a labouring man; he has just given 100,000 dollars, more than £20,000., towards the foundation of a new

university for the State of Illinois, in which Chicago
is situated. Going along the same street, Wabash
Avenue, we found what you and I have often talked
about, a house going quietly down the middle of
the street on rollers, to be removed from some
valuable site to one less costly. The house was
wooden, with brick chimneys, two stories high,
moving along as composedly as possible, and nobody
thinking it anything of a curiosity except Rotherham and myself. We then went to some of the
large corn warehouses, Chicago being the great
centre of the trade in cereals. The cars on the
railways run into the warehouses full of grain; a
man goes in, and shovels out the wheat or corn into
a kind of funnel, where there is a tube containing a
number of small buckets fixed on a strap, and
passing over pulleys at the top of the building.
These take up the grain, and without any expenditure of human labour, convey it to the top story,
where it is emptied into large bins. The action of
the elevator, as it is called, is similar to the dredg-
ing machine. The large bins are gauged, and hold
certain quantities, and from them the grain drops
into other bins, where it is weighed, and in connection with them are large tubes, so that as soon as
say 500 bushels are weighed, the tube can be
directed into the hold of a ship, lying by the side
of the warehouse, and the grain at once shot in.
In this way vast quantities of grain are handled
without employing many people, (wages being high,)

and therefore at much less cost than with us. The cars that have brought the grain are then loaded with lumber, and dispatched through the unwooded prairie country of Illinois. The great part of the timber comes from the pineries of Canada, and these to some extent furnish the return cargo for the wheat exported to the provinces.

We also visited a new elevator warehouse, in course of erection. I pointed out to Mr. W—— a circumstance that has much struck me here. The Irish labourers with us at home insist on many absurd regulations, in order, as they imagine, to secure their own employment. Among the rest, they will have all bricks carried up in hods, and, therefore, demand so many men to be engaged for so many stories. Here, however, they are quite content to have the materials drawn up in buckets by a windlass; and, moreover, when they do carry the hod, use a much larger one than they will in England.

We then walked through some other parts of the town, and then went to Mr. W——'s to tea, where we had a roasted prairie hen. I wish you could taste them; they are like pheasants in flavour, but the flesh is the colour of grouse, and they partake more of the grouse nature; they are most excellent. We had some at the hotel the first night we arrived, but they were broiled and burnt, a very different affair to those we had at our friend's. We sat till near twelve, and went into the position and statistics of Chicago to some extent. It is the Malines of America (as to being the central point for railways), and is the centre of some 3,000 miles of railway. The railway system, the Mississippi canal, and the consequent rapid opening of the country in the vicinity, have combined to produce as their effect, the apparently miraculous development of Chicago. The warehouses and stores are already splendid buildings — rising up on every side with cast-iron fronts, or else faced with Athens marble—*(Athens being not in Greece, but Illinois:)* the streets of immense width, all being paved and well-sewered at once, so that with the labour going on everywhere in building houses, churches, stores, paving streets, and so forth, Chicago seems like a town being made to order at once. Owing to the alterations of the levels, you are always going up and down wooden steps on the side-walks from one level to another.

When we left in the evening the fire-bells were ringing, and after trying to discover where it was, found at last that it was a steamer out on the lake, the light of which we could distinctly see. I be-believe one man was lost, all the rest saved. The fire system is good: there are men always stationed at different points, and if they see a fire, ring a bell which alarms the town, and then tolling it so many times, indicates the number of the ward as a guide to the fire engines, which are also manned by volunteer fire companies. The system is well carried out, but leads to much drinking and dissipation amongst the young men. I cannot help thinking that paid fire-brigades would be better; however, this is the genius of the country.

When we arrived at Chicago, we found that the only reliable steamer for the Sault St. Marie sailed the Saturday before; also learned that we were rather late in the season for going so far north, and therefore with much regret, but yielding to good advice and sound reason, abandoned the idea. The journey to the Sault St. Marie should be made about July or August.

On Wednesday morning I went with Mr. W—— to see the land register system, with which I was much gratified. The whole states are divided into towns, each thirty-six square miles, six miles each way; and the towns are divided into thirty-six square mile divisions, each of these into four, and these again subdivided, and by commencing from the base line of the states, the whole district can be laid out more accurately; and each purchaser finds and obtains his own plot of ground by the description given. The purchase is duly registered in the land office, and that constitutes an undisputed title, even if the original be lost. Each sale of the land is registered in the same way, and thus a purchaser can, on reference, at once see through what hands the plot has passed, and its exact condition with reference to mortgages, for any mortgage not registered is not legal.

In each town one square mile is appropriated for school purposes, and the proceeds of its sale set aside as a fund to pay masters, and so forth. In Chicago the school lands have been sold for 1,000,000 dollars, still retaining a good price. It so happens that the town itself stands on the school lands, thus making them much more valuable. Mr. C—— showed us all the books, maps, and registers, and even the description of the first plot sold in Illinois, at least in Cork County, in which Chicago is situated. After dinner we went to visit one of the common schools, and a Mr. H——, one of the local school managers, went round with us. We found a well ordered, quiet, clean school, containing children of all classes, from little negroes to the children, boys and girls, of the wealthier inhabitants. The teachers were females, except one male, who took the highest division of all. We heard some of the classes read, and they read well. Such a system would fail utterly with us. The middle classes would not send their children to the same school and class as the children of the operatives, and unless a high degree of moral training exists through all classes, enforced by home example, such a system must be productive of a general lowering of the standard of morality and civilization. The lower and poorer classes are the most numerous here, as elsewhere, and the influence of their children must exceed the influence of the better class, and these must

M

suffer more or less by close contact with those who have not good examples at home. *Every human being is equal,*—that is the social doctrine of the United States. It is not true; and in establishing this principle, society does and must suffer. I do not wish so soon to form a hasty judgment, but I feel certain that America is deficient in the refined society we enjoy. In fact it is a half civilised country. This they will not acknowledge, yet their ordinary life proves it; take, for instance, the social ordinance about ladies. At every table seats are reserved for them, rooms at hotels specially set apart for them, in railways they can command any seat they fancy. * * * It does not appear to be seen that a reference to history would prove that in all semi-civilised states women were surrounded with special ordinances for their protection, because without that they would have been subject to all kinds of bad treatment; and, by similar reasoning, that unless places were set apart for ladies, in their rough condition, they could not get places for themselves,—and at public *table d'hôtes*, we, being unaccompanied with ladies, have to sit below a lot of women, ignorant, vain, over-dressed, not an idea beyond hoops, and as for the men, coarse, dirty, chewing, spitting, dollar-worshippers. They have a deal of energy, but they are a selfish, unattached, unloveable people, without local associations. I do not mean to say that this is entirely the result of their institutions. Undoubtedly, in this great western country they are necessarily rough. The men are the pioneers of future grandeur, but most conceited ones; and whilst you are willing to acknowledge all that is good and great, you are indisposed to knock under, and say further that they are the greatest people on "airth." The time to try their institutions is not come yet. The vast regions of unoccupied, unowned land, afford a vent for the numbers of people, and until these are taken up, and the real struggle for life commences, their institutions may exist. Even in our short journey, we can see the multitudes pressing to the West, and on the roads meet with vast numbers who are looking for a home in the new states of Minnesota and Nebraska, certainly different to the settlers in the East. It is something to be the leaders in cultivating these vast regions, but so full are they of dollars, so eager to get rich in a hurry, so selfish in their calculations, that all poetry, all romance is driven away, and one merely looks upon them as so many land speculators.

Mr. H—— thought our classes ought to mix at schools; I told him I should be sorry to see it. On this subject I will not say any more at present, but leave it until I have seen more of the country.

I give you my impressions as they arise; and thus, at first, they may seem contradictory, until I am able to regard the state of society as a whole. Whilst they have in this part of the country no refined society, they have plenty of rough, and the whole tone is lower than I expected, so that I am the more convinced that they owe their position to-day, not to any mental, physical, or moral superiority, but to the mere chance of possessing a vast extent of territory.

On Wednesday evening we had a very heavy thunder shower, and evidence that there would be some broken weather, and were not so sorry then that we were not at the Sault St. Marie. We intended all along to go to St. Paul's, the capital of Minnesota, and on Thursday morning we set out for Madison, on our way there, taking the steamer on the Mississippi, at Prairie du Chien. For the most part the railroad passed through a pretty country, not heavily but picturesquely timbered, with but few evidences of population on the route. Janesville is the largest town; and then a forty-five miles more brought us to Madison, which is considered, in point of situation, the most beautiful town in the States. It rained heavily when we arrived, October 2nd; but this morning, though dark and gloomy, we have seen something of the place: wide roads deep in mud, being unpaved; plank walks, scattered buildings, a State Hall, and other public edifices, though grand and unfinished, yet constitute the town. It is situated by four Lakes, Mendota and Mennona being the largest, the town standing on the neck of land between them. The silent woods cover their shores, as yet untainted by man's struggles for gain; in fine weather it must be beautiful. There is a large infusion of the German element, and their gutturals are heard all over the place :—the population about 11,000. In 1837 there was only one log hut here ; for the first nine years they reached 281 ; the second nine to 4,000 ; now, in two years, have added 7,000, making the total 11,000. This afternoon we start to Prairie du Chien, and meet the steamer.

On board the steamer " Milwaukee,"

Saturday, *October 3rd.*

I am trying to spend an hour chatting with you, but I am almost afraid the quivering table will scarcely allow of any feats of penmanship. We left for Prairie du Chien at half-past four, the country in appearance much the same as from Chicago to Madison ; but, as we approached the Mississippi, the land became more thrown up in mounds, and appeared more sandy ; no thick wood, but a fair growth of shrub. About ten we arrived at Prairie du Chien, and immediately went on board the steamer, which we found waiting for us. It did not, however, start until seven o'clock this morning ; but being no hotel there, of course we were glad to pass the night on board, and a most extraordinary boat she is, consisting of a flat-bottomed construction, about level with the water, on which is built a deck, perhaps ten feet above the lower one, supported on pillars, and open all round. This space is occupied by the boilers, which are small, high-pressure ones, with a donkey engine to pump the water in; and then, at some distance, close to each paddle-wheel, there is a separate engine, one drives the starboard, the other the port paddle, perfectly unconnected with each other, so that, in some of the rapid *bends*, one engine can stop and the other keep on, so as to turn the boat in a *short space*. The rest of the space is occupied with cargo and fuel, the latter being entirely wood. The second deck contains the cabin, which I am sure must be at least 200 feet long, with a row of state rooms on each side, containing two or four berths each. The grand saloon is very pretty, — painted enameled white, with paneled ceiling, and gothic pendants, slightly gilt: the perspective effect is extremely good. At eight we had breakfast, dinner at one, tea at six; and I wish you could have seen the darkies set the cloth: it was a rich treat. They seem to have an idea of the curve of beauty. One had a measure, a small staff, and placed each glass by rule, actually measuring its place, and putting each successive glass an inch farther than its neighbour, until the centre of the table was reached, and then drawn in again to the other end, a curve of regular shape was formed: the knives, forks, and spoons were somehow fastened together by the prongs of the forks, and then artistically fixed in the tumblers. After this each dish was, by measure again, placed in its position, and, when the whole was completed, the darkies collected together at one end, and, with heads leaning aside in an excited manner, stood to enjoy the sight of their own skill and ingenuity. One then rings a bell, and the *ladies* take their seats. As *soon as they* are seated, another hits a gong a tremendous blow, as a signal that the *male* crowd may sit down to feed. Oh dear! it is beyond measure amusing; and the stuff we eat, heaven only knows what it is; however, we must eat, and down it goes without question. How English ladies could travel here, I do not know: I know at least *one* that would decidedly starve; and as for my dear governor, the very idea of seeing him at such a table, would make one split with laughing.

I have met several very intelligent people on board, and as you know I usually make friends, we are sociable enough. At all events, it is no use travelling in a country without you can be " Hail, fellow, well met!" and least of all in America. Reserve begets reserve, and you learn nothing; whereas by throwing off our English reserve, I have had everything of importance pointed out to me, and every information given me.

As soon as breakfast was over, I went out to look at the Mississippi, and if I were to tell you the grandeur of the scenery through which we have passed to-day, you would think I was romancing. This majestic river, grand even here, 2,000 miles from the sea, flows through a valley of varying width, from four to six or seven miles across; bounded by swelling hills, clothed with trees, or bare rocky bluffs, with a scantier growth of wood upon them. The stream crosses the valley now on one side, now on the other, and its entire course is varied by numberless small islands, consisting entirely of the alluvial deposit brought down by the river, which is thick and turbid, from the large amount of earthy matter mixed with its waters. The scenery is ever changing, and you have glimpses from time to time, up lovely valleys, extending into the country beyond; fine wooded amphitheatres; and then again a succession of magnificent bluffs— some towering high in the air, with their summits part bare and rocky, often assuming the shape of old castles, keeps, and towers; all around savage, wild, and lonely; no town, no sign of life, as though we were the first on these mysterious waters, and then coming suddenly on a log hut close to the river's edge, miles away from any visible human abode, inhabited by a family of lumberers, who cut firewood to supply the steamers;—a life that must be, I should imagine, desolate and lonely, to a degree insupportable. We met several large rafts of timber floating down stream, with perhaps twenty men on each, with their huts, cooking apparatus, and so forth, going down to St. Louis, or even perhaps New Orleans, where they break up the rafts and sell the timber, returning by the steamers. The territories of Iowa, which we skirted, and Minnesota, where we are now, are almost unsettled, although towns are laid out and railways planned, with all the speed of Yankeeism. A person pointed out to me a beautiful site for a town, which is called Dacotah, consisting of a small wooden warehouse and four wooden houses, yet, in point of situation, the most lovely I ever saw : the noble stream in front; a nearly level plain, extending about seven miles into the country, backed by a magnificent amphitheatre of wooded hills, rounding to the river with a wide and effective sweep in the middle; the hills came, as though intending to reach the river, and suddenly falling back form a second semicircle, broken in the middle by a valley apparently running into the back country; and then the hills again, continuing until they terminated in a fine bluff, a sheltered spot, which some day may be the site of a large and thriving city.

The names and the associations here are all Indian. We are near the battle grounds of the Sioux and the Chippewas, and I am told I may chance to see Hole-in-the-Day, the Chippewa chief, at St. Paul's, who, I believe, is a splendid specimen of the Indian, six feet six inches high; he was so named because at the moment of his birth the sun suddenly broke out of a dense cloud; he is believed to bear a charmed life, and when a party of Sioux came to a house in which he was, intending to kill him, they covered their heads with their blankets, and pressed their faces to the windows, to make sure he was there; he noticed something, and rising, went calmly to the window, and placed his face close to theirs in the inside, and they were so terrified at his steady and determined glance that they turned and fled.

Unfortunately the day has been gloomy and misty; I should like to see the river in all the glory of a brilliant day. The leaves are touched with autumn tints, and the scarlet ivy and other gaudy-coloured plants mingle well with the dark green of the trees yet unaffected by approaching winter. We shall arrive at St. Paul's about two o'clock to-morrow afternoon, Sunday, the distance being 302 miles from Prairie du Chien, and then ninety-one miles from Madison makes a pretty long journey.

This Upper Mississippi far exceeds my expectations; I did not conceive anything so fine as the reality, and I believe this magnificent scenery extends for 600 miles. There is now the charm of nature on it; we see it as it is, fresh from the hand of God, untouched by man, for the few scattered abodes are as nothing in a distance of 302 miles, what I have always longed to see—real, wild, untamed nature, and it is grand, and fills the soul with feelings of awe and reverence.

I am in a good hotel, floating on these great waters, which, twenty years ago, knew only the birch canoe of the Indian; civilization and wild, savage life

thus close together, side by side. It is wonderful,
and I feel it to be so. I wish you could see this
scenery, it would fill your mind with thoughts and
images that could never be lost; I know no one
that would and could so thoroughly enjoy it, but it
is too far away, at least 5,000 miles from home. I
feel, however, that I am as much under the care
and protection of God here as at home; here I see
His works in their natural grandeur, where I can
feel their influence on my heart and mind.

SUNDAY EVENING, ST. PAUL'S, MINNESOTA.

So far I wrote last night, before retiring to our narrow and small state-room, just space enough for one
person to stand, not containing any of the ordinary
conveniences of a bed-room. After dressing, every
passenger had to go into a room with four marble
wash basins, and scrub in common, wiping ourselves on towels (round towels) provided for all,—
republican equality with a vengeance, rather too
much for one!

When I got up this morning, I found that in the
night, at one of the stopping places, a small steam
engine was landed, and in taking the fly-wheel off
the steamer the gangway plank broke; the men
jumped off, but one poor fellow slipped, and the

wheel crashed upon him, cut one leg clean off at the ancle, and smashed the other one most fearfully. There was a young M.D. on board, going up country, to settle, and he attended him, but having no means at hand, and no help, the poor creature was relieved from his intense sufferings by death, in about four hours. We brought the dead body on to St. Paul's; his wife and children live a few miles from here. The deck was stained with his blood. I saw the body, covered with a piece of sailcloth, but did not see the injured limb. I was shocked to see how little notice, or even care, was taken of the occurrence; it seemed forgotten long before we got to St. Paul's; so little do they heed life in this country.

St. Paul's stands on a bluff, overhanging the Mississippi, and in point of situation is truly magnificent; at present it consists of scattered wooden houses, with some few brick and stone buildings. One hotel, the Fuller House, is on the grand scale of other places in this country. Fancy a town four years old, with an hotel larger than the Queen's, full of people. I believe the population is about 12,000, and is to be one of the greatest places in the States. It has a theatre, several churches, and a large cathedral—Catholic, I think,—in process of erection. Oliphant's description of the place would not do now, although I recognised his sketch of the place as it was, in approaching up the river. We landed to-day about one o'clock. The river is

beautiful, but there was not the same amount of
fine scenery that we passed through yesterday; we
had on one side more prairie country, but for the
greater part of the way the banks are most densely
wooded. You cannot imagine any navigation more
difficult than that of the Upper Mississippi; in
addition to multitudes of small islands, the river
bends about a great deal, and is full of shallow
places, we were aground twice to-day, and our
steamer only draws thirty inches of water, so you
may easily imagine how shallow it is, when such a
boat has not sufficient water to float in. The
pilots are highly paid, 400 or 500 dollars a month,
during the seven months navigation is open. I
have been highly delighted with the sail, which is
the most interesting in point of scenery I ever saw
in my life. There is one wide part of the river
called Lake Pepin, which is I believe very beautiful;
this we unfortunately passed in the night, but we
must try and see it going down again. We have
now travelled, including the sea voyage, about
5,867 miles since leaving Liverpool.

We shall visit the falls of St. Anthony, Minneapolis, and Minnehaha, or the "Laughing Waters,"
and then turn our backs on this rough western
country. I am glad I have seen it; it well repays a
visit: no one without this could form any idea of what
is doing by the vast expansion going on, the uncommon extent of country becoming gradually settled.
But for those who prefer the pleasures of civilized

society, and the comforts of a more settled and less excitable condition, this part would be to them a most dreary exile. There is no conversation but of dollars, town-lots, pre-empting, driving bargains, and fast trotting horses. They say St. Paul's is founded by broken-down eastern men—that is from the Atlantic States—and as I think I have said in a former letter, no man is thought the worse of for failing. I was told that if a man fails, unless he has put aside enough to start with again, he is considered a fool, so low is the standard of commercial morality; people say St. Paul's is the fastest, the most dissipated, and most immoral place in the States. I suppose it is like a young man sowing his wild oats. The amount of gambling is fearful; but, I understand, is done less publicly than it was a year or two ago.

Ourselves, and an English nobleman with two friends, are the only real English at present *en route;* in this part of the world it is almost untrodden ground, but I fancy it will attract many sporting men, as there is bear, buffalo, and deer shooting in the neighbourhood. Minnesotian life is rather curious.

ON BOARD THE " GALENA,"

SATURDAY, *October 7th.*

MY DEAR MAMMA,

My last letter I dispatched from St. Paul's, I hope in time for the steamer: I ended by saying Minnesotian life was curious. On Sunday evening I went down to the bar of the hotel to get some whiskey and water. I must tell you that the bar of the hotel in America is a separate institution; literally a bar fitted up like an English gin shop, with a counter, at which people stand up to drink: and here everything not drank at table, such as wine, &c. is taken, and to which people have access from the street. A young man, a gentleman, (all are gentlemen here,) asked me if I was English, I said yes; he then enquired my name, I told him; he then told me his, and at once introduced me to about a dozen men, all of whom cordially shook hands: then my introducer said, "Drinks for the crowd," and politely requested me to drink with them; of course refusal would be considered bad manners, and I joined them; I wished them to drink with me, but they would not allow me to pay for anything. I got afraid at last of taking my cigar case out, for if I was not smoking I had a dozen thrust in my hand from as many of my new acquaintance, not one of whose names I have the least recollection of. Everybody that entered the bar was immediately introduced, and asked me to drink, so I was at last compelled as politely as I could, to decline such repeated overtures. This mania for introducing is an extraordinary feature in this western country, everyone introduces everyone else, and really means a species of hospitable kindness, which no one can take amiss.

There is an American and his friend staying at the hotel, who came with us on board the steamer. Mr. D—— is a good-natured fellow, resides at —— and is very wealthy, has perhaps £30,000. a year, a great sporting man, the owner of the fastest horses in the States; he is lately married, and made a tour in Europe for his wedding-trip, he is a regular fast fellow. They afforded us the greatest fun imaginable, and introduced us to quantities of people; giving us an interesting specimen of the wealthy youth of America. I have promised to visit him at ——; they had so many friends that the drinks became overpowering, and Mr. D—— and his friend Jack S—— swayed about on their legs in a very suggestive manner. One of their friends was an Indian trader, who when he became a little elevated, danced the great medicine dance, and otherwise comported himself in a somewhat curious manner.

I think these bars very injurious places; I am sure there is engendered a great habit of tippling, in short, I fear I must rescind the opinion I expressed that Americans were very temperate; it is true they drink but little, at dinner you rarely see a bottle of wine on the table, only the bar is their great resort, and drink after drink must leave many of them intoxicated, and get them into such habits. All classes mingle here, and a man of education and property may be taking his cocktail, mint julep, brandy smash, sherry cobbler, or whiskey straight, side by side with the roughest of the rough.

St. Louis, Missouri,
Sunday, *October 11th.*

I FOUND myself obliged to abandon the idea of writing on board the steamer *Galena,* and when I look back at the two pages I have written, I almost fear they will prove an interesting puzzle. The vibration of the boat was most excessive, and so I gave up in despair.

The amusing manners of a western city gave us plenty of occupation, and we were compelled to acknowledge the hotel at St. Paul's the very worst we have stayed in; large and pretentious, the table was filthy, and the food execrable, but the Fuller House having a monopoly in this town, being the one large hotel, the proprietors seek not their visitors' comfort, but to make as much money as they can in the least time.

Monday proving a splendid day, we took a car-

N

riage, and drove over the lovely undulating open prairie to St. Anthony, which is a thriving town at the extreme head of the navigation of the Mississippi, which here pours from a higher level, over the Falls of St. Anthony. These falls have been pretty some time, but the town being a great place for the timber trade, the water power is taken advantage of, and a large number of saw-mills are erected there, which, being rough wooden sheds, surrounded with split wood, sawdust, and shavings, don't add to the beauty of the scene. The main fall is so filled and choked with logs of wood which have floated down the river, strayed from rafts, that all the attractive features are lost, and you see water pouring over and amongst large upright and *slant right* pieces and trees in all directions. The volume of water is, however, considerable, and in any other country would be thought grand; but of course the idea of Niagara renders all others small and insignificant. We went into several saw mills, and saw the trees drawn up out of the water and cut up into deals, in a very short time, the stouter and rougher pieces being made into shingles for roofing houses, and clap-boards for outside weather boarding; planing and tenoning machines were also at work, so that in one place we saw the rough tree, just as felled in the solitary forest, and panel doors and window frames, with the other house timber, all ready to put a frame-house together at the shortest notice. St. Anthony will be a large, wealthy, and important place; it has the elements of prosperity, and with that vast water power must in a few years be one of the most thriving towns in the north west. Crossing a suspension bridge over the Mississippi (this was the extreme north-western part of our route) we came to another town, Minneapolis, why built, or what for, I cannot imagine, except by speculators in town lots; perhaps they intend to make it the capital of Minnesota, as they seem to fix on capital towns in the most arbitrary manner possible. They may have a share of the falls, being on the opposite side of the river from St. Anthony, but the formation of the land, and their position relative to the falls, are not so favourable as in the other town. Driving along the prairie (for we did not stop at Minneapolis), we came to a small and lonely gorge, formed by a stream of water, which here falls down some forty feet in one beautiful sheet, almost a mass of spray, ere it strikes the ground. This fall retains its Indian name of Minnehaha, or the Laughing Waters, and very bright and sunny is their smile. I thought I should like to see them from the bottom, and so commenced the descent of the gorge. I had not, however, gone far, before I met a young rattlesnake, which flattened its head, and put out its tongue. I gave the youth a blow on the head with a small stick I had in my hand, and killed him at once, but thinking his mother might know her son was out, and be sitting up for him to come home, I deferred my descent until some other time, as I had no wish to meet the stern " parient," who might not be so easily disposed of. I might have romanced; I fear I have thrown away a splendid opportunity of describing a fierce combat with a rattlesnake, and final overthrow of the monster! * * *

Leaving this lovely scene with regret, we drove on to Fort Snelling, an old fort, built in the days of the Indian warfare, commanding the junction of the river Minnesota with the Great Father of Waters. The land is sold, and in a short time the fort will be pulled down, and all memorial of it lost. I saw some dirty German soldiers on duty, and all wore a mean and slovenly aspect. From thence we went down to see a curious cave, formed by a stream of clear pure water, flowing through a bed of rocky white sand, perfectly clean, and free from all impurity; it would make the best glass possible. We went some distance, but the guide said he had been a mile and a half up the stream without reaching the end of the cave. We then crossed the Mississippi in a ferry boat, on the same principle we crossed the Ticino, and reached St. Paul's at dark, having spent a most delightful and interesting day. Just before sunset we saw an immense flight of black birds, about three miles long, and about six to ten birds abreast, all flying in the most orderly manner after their leader. In twenty minutes after sunset it is quite dusk, and in half an hour dark, as there is little twilight. In the evening we met our liquoring friends, and saw some more specimens of the Far West, all of whom amused us greatly. Their toast is " Ho." I could not make it out, every man that drank shouted it out. On enquiry I found it was merely the Indian " *Ugh*," meaning " How are you ?" They add the peculiar elongation to the word " Sir," when they wish to be emphatic, and say " Ho, Sirree."

On Tuesday we found our long sought bear, pronounced *bar*-skins, and purchased a couple of fine ones. We got them from an Indian trader, who deals with the Winebago and Sioux; these we have were purchased from the Indians on the Red River, 800 miles from St. Paul's. * * * We saw some real genuine Indians, in blankets, leggings, and moccassins; but dismiss all romance,— a more filthy, beggarly, inane-looking set I never saw in my life. We met some fine-looking half-breeds, on horseback, and saw some of the Indian wooden carts, which travel immense distances, and have not a single morsel of iron about them. Oxen are the principal draught cattle, and in case of accident the flesh is valuable, whereas the horse is more expensive, and useless when dead.

St. Paul's is a most interesting place, but I feel sure it has been forced into too hasty a growth; there is too much of the hot-house about it,— speculation has gone mad; but, situated as it is at the head of the river navigation, it must be the great port of the North West; and although it may ruin hundreds, even when things get into their proper healthy state, it will become, with legitimate trade, a wealthy and important city. I should have much liked to have penetrated farther into the country, and gone to the Indian settlement, the nearest point of which is ninety miles from St. Paul's, but my time would not permit; and I confess, it was with feelings of regret that I looked for the last time on the city of the bluffs.

On Wednesday morning we went on the *Galena*, which sailed at ten, and arrived at Dunleith at six the next afternoon. The day was glorious: the scenery of the river really magnificent. We passed Lake Pepin and the Maiden's Rock, so called from some Indian girl named Winona converting it into a western lover's leap. Before sunset I was much gratified with the scenery,—quiet, calm, unruffled: there is a majesty in nature which far transcends all human genius; and its greatest majesty is seen when man and his works are the furthest removed! Solitude becomes it best; and I can only repeat and strengthen from a second view, favoured with splendid weather, what I said of the sail up the Mississippi!

The river is rapidly falling; and though our steamer only draws twenty-six inches of water, we stuck fast several times. On putting out two huge masts, one on each bow, which, resting on the bottom, formed a purchase, and then men hauling ropes running from the deck through blocks in the masts, and driving the engines as hard as they could go, we were forced, grating, over the obstacle. They are high-pressure boats, and I was really glad to get on shore. Our room was over the boiler, carry-ing from 150 to 200 pounds on the inch : they are not more than three feet in diameter, and, if sound, will stand the pressure; but you never know how long they have been at work. When we were a-ground over the principal bar we met, the darkies were piling the wood on the fire at a tremendous rate, and every joint was blowing like fury, till the jimcrack boat quivered again. We passed, coming down, a boat that had been run into between Sunday and Wednesday, cut down, and sunk, and some five persons (German emi-grants, I believe,) drowned whilst asleep. We had excellent fare on the *Galena*. I told the steward, a negro, that he beat the Fuller House and the other steamer, whereat he seemed much pleased. Afterwards, I had a deal of talk with him. He was born a slave, bought himself free, found it necessary to read and write: worked at this needful instruction for a year after he was twenty-one, and now receives 75 dollars a-month, more than £15. and his keep. He bought his mother and sisters, whom he left in slavery. " Got 'em cheap, Massa, paid leben hunnerd dolla for 'em, Sar !" He has a number of black lads as waiters, whose wages run from 20 dollars a-month and upwards. I had much conversation with him about the condition of the free negroes. He said that, for the most part, they were house, personal, and favourite servants, whom their masters manumitted, and, having been accustomed to the luxuries of a wealthy household, spent their money too freely, and did not do as well as they might. He said when one of the banks stopped just now, he and his boys (his black waiters) had 1500 dollars deposited there. The great difficulty of the free coloured men appears to be that no white artizan will work with them, so that they are driven to other employments than mechanical ones, hence the reason such numbers become waiters, servants, and so forth. He named some instances to me of real good mechanics among them, which I was glad to hear. I said, "Well, I am an Englishman, and in our land no man can be the property of another, be he white or coloured." "Ah!" he said, "but for Canada, I don't know what many of our people would do :"—(the provinces containing a great number of runaway slaves.) He said that the planters think no more of selling a man or his child away to a distance, than if he were a horse, often not so much :—that side of the question I have to see. This much I can say, that I never met a more intelligent, humble-minded creature, in his sphere of life, than the black steward of the *Galena*. They want to be left alone. In many of

the States, their oath is not taken against a white
man; and, therefore, he said, we wish only for
quiet, and to keep out of all legal troubles. Quiet
submission is the only chance for a peaceful life,
and this in a country that boasts itself the "land
of the free and the brave."

At Dunleith we took the railway, and it being
dark immediately, we ran on all night. At nine
the next morning, stopped at a small wooden
village, called Pana, where we found we had to
wait till three in the afternoon, for the train to St.
Louis. A more tiresome six hours I never passed.
At a wretched village, out on the boundless prairie,
and a burning hot day,—you may imagine our
delight when we got off at three; and at seven,
crossing the Mississippi in a ferry-boat, were
driven to the Planters' House, an immense hotel,
which we found crammed full. Still they took us
in; and then we discovered that we were to sleep
in a large dining-room, with sixteen beds in it;
and to add to the inducement, there were notices
stuck up, "Persons sleeping in this room, are
requested to beware of pick-pockets!" Pleasant,
very. Rotherham and I were very much down in
the mouth. I had made up my mind what to do;
and, after having some supper, I told him to come
with me, and we went off to another hotel, of which
I had heard, and engaged rooms; went back to the
Planters' House, paid for our supper, and took ourselves and traps to Barnum's Hotel, where I am

now writing. I must say at the Planters' they were extremely polite, and regretted their position, and at first declined to allow me to pay anything, but I, of course, insisted on paying for our supper, so he said, " Well, then, say one dollar; and I guess you will come in as you please, and use the news-room, or any part of the house when you like." So we parted quite in a friendly manner. This is a quieter, and, I think, better hotel. They are extremely attentive.

St. Louis is an old town, standing on the Mississippi, founded by the early French settlers; it is in the State of Missouri, twenty miles from the mouth of the river of that name, and has a large trade both up and down the rivers Missouri, Mississippi, and Ohio, commanding a river navigation of 8,000 miles. I had a letter here to a firm, but I heard at St. Paul's that in consequence of a sudden call of 150,000 dollars for railway shares, they had suspended, simply from want of ready cash, being immensely rich people. I did not, therefore, feel myself justified in troubling them; and their time would be sufficiently occupied without being bothered with strangers.

I fear for our Manchester houses. This American suspension is fearful throughout the country, all from over speculation and extravagance as a nation, importing more than they could pay for; and, perhaps, above all, making railways faster than they could afford. They have not the capital to

lock up in earth-works; and from what I have seen
of their lines and management, I should prefer
other investments. They are robbed right and
left: every servant gets rich; and the poor shareholders are left in the lurch. One fact alone shews
the system. People seldom take tickets, but get
them from the conductor or guard, who goes with
the train. For the money he gives a check, and
this check he receives back again before the
passengers get out, so that it is all left to his
honesty as to what account he pleases to render of
the receipts.

To-day I went to the Unitarian Church, which
I found at the corner of Olive and Ninth Streets,
(called the Church of the Messiah) a splendid
stone structure, with a most aspiring spire. A
broad lobby across the width of the Church, gave
access to three doors, one leading down the centre,
the others to the side aisles, which were covered with
handsome carpets, not our common cocoa-nut matting. A door-keeper put me in a comfortable pew;
and on looking round, I found it was a fine gothic
building, with lancet and mullioned windows on
each side, filled with stained glass, and a small
Catherine wheel over the pulpit end : the roof was
in dark oak panels : a gallery ran round, supported
on pillars, forming gothic arches over the gallery,
the same as St. Andrew's : the pulpit was something like the one in Brook Street, only one desk
as wide as two. There was a large and most

respectable congregation; the minister a Mr. Eliott. They have a form of service, but it is departed from at the minister's pleasure: the singing was good, but the congregation don't join. We had an excellent sermon on faith in Christ. I felt not a little affected to hear some of our old chapel hymns so far away from home, on the banks of the Mississippi, and to find there the simple form of worship which is most accordant to my own views and feelings! After the service, I stayed, and introduced myself to Mr. Eliott. He had been in Manchester in 1852, and regretted he had not seen me sooner, and that I was leaving so early. He is rather like Mr. H.——might be taken for his brother. By the way, you must tell Mrs. C——, with my kind remembrances, that I can speak most favourably of Unitarianism in Missouri.

Rotherham went to the Episcopalian Church, and a Bishop preached. He said he could not make out the voluntaries they played; he thought he knew them, and at last he found out they were airs from the opera of "Trovatore." The Bishop was ordaining a Deacon, and I asked Rotherham if he had had a good sermon. "Well, you see, I thought it would be about the duties of a Deacon, and as I am not going to be one, I did not listen." St. Louis had been visited with a severe shock of earthquake, the day before we arrived here, which frightened all the good people from their propriety. It seems to have been extremely terrible.

It occurred in the night during which we were in the railway car, travelling from Dunleith here. This is the first slave State we have entered ; and on enquiring, I found that the black porter and black servants, fifteen or sixteen, were all slaves :— the property of the house. I had some talk with one of the proprietors, and he said they could not be induced to run away : they were all well off, and satisfied, much better cared for than the white boys (the waiters were white); and they never heard of any discontent, unless some d——d aboli- tionist came talking with them. They allow them 15 dollars each a-month spending money. Some are married ; and, on pressing him, he said, of course, their children are the property of the hotel, and are *sometimes* sold. This conversation took place at tea one evening ; and just opposite sat a gentleman, who inquired from Mr. F—— what the old man would take for Paris; guessed 1000 dollars,—Paris being one of the house servants,—as he had a good mind to buy him. This was the first time I ever heard a man seriously ask the price of another; for although I have asked the price of slaves in the East, and more especially the small boy at Smyrna, I do not consider that until then I had really heard the query as a matter of business. This I must say, that apparently the boys were merry enough, and seemed to have a vast deal of fun among themselves. Sunday appeared to be a holiday, as I did not see any of them about the hotel during the entire day, which I was glad to think might even be a day of rest to the poor slave.

There is not much to interest in a town like St. Louis: it is a mere common-place business city, not unlike some third-rate French provincial town, but inferior to such because devoid of the fine old buildings that give such places a gilding and a glory reflected from the sunlight of past ages; and again, there is not the perfect charm of novelty such as we meet with in a perfectly new place, like Chicago or St. Paul's. * * * * The Upper Mississippi is an extraordinary river, receiving such vast streams, and yet not apparently undergoing much enlargement. The river is not more than half-a-mile wide, and yet here it has received the waters of the mighty Missouri, which joins about twenty miles above St. Louis. In the upper portion the colour of the water is peaty, and rather dark: the sheet falling over at St. Anthony, reflects a strong yellow colour, but here it has the appearance of a stream of liquid mud, the discoloration being occasioned by the water of the Missouri. I am sorry not to see the Missouri; but there is no practical object in travelling forty miles merely to see the junction. I had thought of visiting Kansas city, but the elections are going on there, under the supervision of the United States' troops: difficulties occurring, and the town full of rowdies and scamps from all quarters, so that it is, although perhaps not absolutely unsafe, still risky; and, therefore, I did not feel justified either in going myself or taking Rotherham, as the lad goes and does just what I tell him, or where I take him, without a word of question. * * * *

TUESDAY EVENING, *October* 13*th*,

GALT HOUSE, LOUISVILLE.

AT half-past nine yesterday (Monday morning), we left the hotel, and crossing the river, embarked in the railway cars for Louisville,—I say embarked, because the word *here* for every sort of conveyance, railway, steam-boat, and omnibus. When about to start, "is all aboard?" and after a long, tedious, and most uninteresting journey, arrived here at half-past four this morning. The distance is only 274 miles, so that our speed was not great. We got a capital bed-room, the best we have had, and were glad to turn in at five o'clock, thoroughly done up. The day has been dull, and now it is raining heavily; but there is nothing to see, except the river, which we went to look at, and found the Ohio a muddy, dirty-looking stream, about from a quarter to half-a-mile wide. The Falls of the Ohio are close to the town, but being only two feet high, are not very imposing. Louisville is a thoroughly uninteresting town, and we only stay here as the point of departure for the Mammoth Cave. We expected to have got on this afternoon, but find we must start in the morning; get up at half-past four for fifty miles of rail, and then fifty-five by stage-coach; the journey only taking from six a.m. to eight p.m. : the stage appears to go about four miles an hour, and at the most five. As I knew you would be anxious about *that same cave*, I shall finish this letter when I have been, and so not leave you in any suspense, waiting for another mail, though, if I do so, I must keep it back a little, but shall post it from Cincinnati.   *   *   *   *

We went to the theatre this evening, for a little amusement, and *heard* an Irish actor, who seems a favourite. The audience make horrible noises. There is one gallery for the negroes, where they sit by themselves.

The commercial crisis seems extending here, and several New York bankers are down. The whole conversation is the state of the money market:— gold is at an immense premium; and many hotels refuse currency, that is paper money. I feel glad to find the Canadian Banks so well esteemed in Chicago; they considered Canadian notes as good as specie. I have one five-dollar note, but that won't go here in Kentucky, because they have no trade with Canada, but it will be paid in New York or Boston.   *   *   *   *   From Cincinnati I go by Wheeling, Pittsburg, Harrisburg, Philadelphia, through New York to Boston, and the places thereabout, before the cold weather sets in; thence to Philadelphia, Baltimore, Richmond, Washington, &c. At Philadelphia, Rotherham and I separate, but expect to meet in Boston, as he must go to Washington direct, because he leaves for home about the first week in December. I must now close for the night, having to be up so early, but I like an hour's chat with you. How fearful these Indian accounts are; I see extracts from our papers in the American ones, but I cannot bear to read them: the day of retribution will be a fearful one.

BELL'S TAVERN,

WEDNESDAY EVENING, *October 14th.*

NEVER was I so much rejoiced as to arrive at this place. At half-past four this morning, the darkies kept up an incessant clamour at the door, until quite sure we were thoroughly wide awake, and then visited us each three minutes to keep up the irritation, and ask if our luggage was ready. Breakfasted at five, and took our seats in the omnibus for the railway, which took us through a dense forest to Newhaven, where we arrived about

o

eight, and then were transferred into an American stage. Can I describe it?—let me try. Imagine an old Manchester two-horse coach, made a trifle wider in the body, and lengthened out eighteen inches, with the usual seats back and front; then place another seat between the two, with a strap slung from the top, and fixed to each side as a back, and then cram in nine people, three on each side, and you will be near the idea. Sling the entire machine on great leather springs, put six people more outside, a large quantity of luggage on a shelf behind, and some more on the top; splash the whole well with mud, and you may not be far from a comprehension of the thing. We started—our two selves, two Americans, four German Jew pedlars, and a big old negro, as the inside complement. One of the Americans was a pleasant, chatty man. The pedlars insufferable, impudent scamps, far inferior to the poor negro. Jolt, toss, roll, tumble, the whole of them together, from eight in the morning till eight in the evening, doing fifty-five miles, and you will admit that I might be glad to escape such purgatory. The road was rough to a degree, but passed through some pretty scenery; mostly untouched forest, with scattered clearings and log huts.

Well, here we are, seven miles from the cave, at a primitive inn in the midst of a Kentucky forest, with a hard day's work before us to-morrow. Our room opens on a verandah, and as it is cool, having rained heavily last night, and much of to-day, we have a bright warm log fire, by which I am writing. The old negro man interested me very much. I found he had been manumitted by his master, having been born a slave, and had emigrated to Liberia, on the coast of Africa, which is a settlement of free blacks, and where the emancipated slave is introducing civilization to the African native tribes. He had been out three years, and had returned all that way to see if he could buy two of his sons, and take them back with him to Africa, the paternal affection showing itself in such a clear and expressive form in the acts of this poor old black. I doubt whether many of the Yankees, who so despise the coloured people, would do as much. He gave a good account of their prospects in Liberia, and apparently its position, as a real *bonâ fide* settlement, seems secured. They have sometimes to fight with the native tribes, but having cannon and guns they manage to hold their own. Each settler has ten acres of land, which he is bound to improve, and when he has built a substantial dwelling, has a vote, the constitution being a copy of the United States. He had with him his voting ticket, being a supporter of the Republican ticket, which he was proud to exhibit to us. They don't grow much cotton; principally corn, sugar, rice, coffee, and palm oil. So much for the idea that the coloured races are incapable of improvement.

In this house the servants are all slaves, men

and women, and it is amusing to hear their remarks. They chat and laugh at their own dark jokes, whilst waiting at table, where they hover about like so many dusky spirits from a lower world.

Our travelling companions went on in the stage, which goes to Nashville, eighty miles further, and having in our place two women and a drunken Kentuckian, who turned the blacky out, and the last we heard of them, as the stage drove away, was the same intoxicated fellow threatening the German Jews that he would shoot two or three of them if they did not mind their p's and q's, as no man should travel with him that was not a true downright full-blooded Republican and Democrat.

Cincinnati, Saturday Morning.

Being well fatigued, on Wednesday, I wrote up to our arrival at Bell's Tavern. On the following morning, the pertinacious darkies knocked away at an early hour, and after breakfast, at seven, we took our seats in the stage that runs through the forest to the cave, nine miles distant from Bell's, or to call it by its local name, Three Forks. We had four horses, and the stage to ourselves, nevertheless the journey occupied two hours and a half, so rough

is the road; you may imagine how rough when I
tell you that our exemplar, the road from Inver-
snaid, of old recollections, is a perfect Macàdam
pet in comparison. Our ponderous vehicle
swayed, and jumped and jolted over rocks, through
ruts, jerking us fairly off our seats; now dashing
over a stone as big as a house, and then varying it
by driving over a prostrate tree. Forest on all
sides, with but few clearings, in one of which was
a small log-hut school, full of gaping little Ken-
tuckians.

The waste of timber is very striking: trees are
felled and tossed rotting on the ground, or if in too
great a hurry, either barked round the bottom and
thus slowly killed, or simply burnt down by lighting
a fire round the roots. The farmers want their
crops free from the shade of trees, and by this means
they effect their object, at a less cost than by cutting
down and removing. It is melancholy to see them
rotten and rotting, falling about on all sides, or
standing like blighted pillars, intermingled with the
charred trunks of those which have been burnt
down; fortunately the day was fine, and in spite of
sore bones, we much enjoyed the ride; certainly
the jolting came rather hard upon us after our long
journey of the previous day. We passed several
tobacco fields, with the log barns filled with the
drying leaves of the *noxious weed.* About half-past
nine we reached the hotel at the cave, and taking
a guide, at once commenced our underground

pilgrimage, each with a large open lamp in hand. The season and rush of visitors is over, so we had a guide quietly to ourselves, and told him we must see all in one day—the route is two days—but it can be done in one if you are determined, and a well-spent tip to the guide will, as usual, ensure it.

Descending an inclined road, we turned suddenly to the right, and then down below us yawned the mouth of the tremendous abyss; not unlike the entrance to the Peak cavern. This was the main gallery, which runs four miles under ground, with a width of from forty to eighty feet, and a height of from sixty to near a hundred. At the entrance are some old pits, used by the people during the war in 1812, to make saltpetre. We soon left daylight behind, and turning suddenly round, about a mile from the entrance, ascended a flight of wooden stairs, and proceeding through some long galleries, entered a series of immense chambers, containing a large number of enormous stalactites, which are named from the forms they have assumed, as "The Tree," which presents the exact similitude of a tree, with rough bark and broken branches; "The Elephant's Head," "The Arm Chair," "The Gothic Chamber," "The Altar," and so forth. Most extraordinary is the tracery, which has been formed by the slow dropping of water, charged with carbonate of lime. I believe some geologists calculate thirty years, to form the thickness of a wafer; and, therefore, these pillars must represent the slow processes of nature during millions of years. On one I watched a drop of water hanging at the end, and was almost lost in contemplating the wonderful continuity and perseverance displayed in every act of the Creator. The guide carried with him a number of Bengal lights, which he fired now and then, to exhibit by illumination the size of the chambers. The dome of one is very grand from its vast proportions. In another, there is a natural pulpit and gallery, which was used twenty years ago by the Methodists. The ground is strewed with the enormous slabs of limestone-rock, which at times have fallen from the roof, until the arch form was fully completed and thus stability ensured. On all sides the marks of water are visible, so that, no doubt, some time or other, a river has flowed through these galleries and halls.

After a sufficient view of these stalactitic wonders, we retraced our steps, and re-entered the grand avenue. The guide pointed out an enormous block of rock, weighing thousands of tons, which had fallen sometime, in shape like a coffin, hence called "The Giant's Coffin." We passed immediately behind it, and stooping low, proceeded along a gallery into another immense vault, which we traversed entirely, and then ascended a hill covered with loose stones, very steep, called "The Hill of Difficulty" —and then crossed a level tract, very wide, (we could not with our lamps see the sides,) called "The Wry-necked Passage," since you have to put your head on one side * * * then a higer vault, called "The Valley of Relief." The guide told us to be careful and follow him close, for there were chasms sixty or a hundred feet deep, down which we might fall; no real danger, but if alone, you might easily be killed. We came to the edge of one called "The Bottomless Pit," and crossed a portion of it on "The Bridge of Sighs." On through more streets of rocks, and then we entered "The Fat Man's Difficulty," being a most extraordinary passage through the rock, having the precise appearance of being cut out with a miner's pick, even to the marks of the pick. It is eighteen inches wide, and winds about considerably; each projection has its corresponding recess; the height is about four feet, and then it expands to a much greater width. We forced through it, and then entered "The Tall Man's Difficulty;" which was, as you may suppose, a case of stoop. We must have gone a mile through these narrow places, when we descended into another "Valley of Relief," and found ourselves on the edge of a silent river, solemn in its eternal night. This we crossed in a boat, and then traversing a long passage, about the proportions of the Medlock at Ardwick, the bottom covered with moist sand, and the arched roof at least sixty feet overhead, we came to another hill, which we mounted, and looked down into the "Dead Sea," which we skirted, and crossed some portion on a ladder; the

walk is protected by an iron rail, but a footslip
would be destruction. On again, and then we
came to " the River," as it is called, and entering
a boat, we passed along its dark waters; stooping
low, to pass through the low arch-way, we went
along some distance, and listened to the echoes
that died away among the rocks. We were now
four miles from the entrance of the cave, and
might go five miles more, the length being nine
miles; but had seen the objects of most interest.
We sat a long time in the boat, quiet and silent,
and then tried the echoes again. The guide sang
in a deep tone, and the notes seemed prolonged by
some sweet organ, in the far recesses of the cave.
Here live the eyeless fishes—creatures that never
have the light near them, and who are thus
fitted by a wise providence for their drear abode.
They are difficult to catch, for, like blind people,
their other senses are wonderfully acute, and the
first touch of an oar is felt by them to an immense
distance, and they seek their places of safety. There
are, also, small lobsters, that appear to have a small
eye, but really are quite blind. I got from the
guide one of each preserved in spirits; the fish
has no mark even where the eye could be. I do
not know whether they have a specimen in our
Museum,* if not, I will give them this one; but, if
they have, I will give it to the Free Library
Museum.

* The fish were presented to the Museum, Peter Street, by Dr. Ashton.

We now retraced our steps, and re-crossing the sandy road, which is often overflowed by the river, re-entered our various purgatories. I asked the guide when passing in the boat through the low arch, if it was ever impassable. He said very often people could not enter, and once, when he was in, the waters rose so suddenly and rapidly, that he lay flat in the boat in the wet, and with his hands and feet pushing the boat through, resting them against the roof, and only just escaped. This river was first discovered by the celebrated guide Stephen, who died this year of consumption, only thirty-five; he had unfortunately taken to drinking. What strange feelings, to be the first to look on this silent, dark, and apparently motionless stream! It is presumed that it flows into the Green river. It is three hundred and sixty feet below the surface of the earth. Diverging from our route we entered a narrow staircase, over which hangs an enormous slab of rock, resting on a small point, and crossing several narrow bridges, and going up and down wooden steps, we were shown "Moran's Dome," a fearful chasm. Our position was about half-way up and we looked through a kind of window naturally formed; the guide went up to some height above, and then fired a Bengal light, and illuminated the profound abyss from top to bottom, near four hundred feet sheer straight down, with a magnificent arched dome roof. The light soon died, and the unbroken night again wrapped it in darkness and mystery.

Returning, we again entered the main avenue, from behind "The Giant's Coffin," and went along some distance farther to "The Angle Hall," where the cave turns off to the left at an acute angle, and then we entered the part called "The Star Chamber." The ceiling of the cave in many places is marked with an incrustation of ferruginous lime-stone, and most fantastic are the forms assumed. Men, women, children, Indians, horses, ant-eater on a tree, all there as distinct as if purposely sketched out. I noticed one, and said, "There is an Indian with the feather on his head; he ought to be Black Hawk." The guide said, "That is exactly the name we give it." So you see from that the appearances are real, and not distorted fancies.

The ceiling of "The Star Chamber" is seventy feet above the ground, and completely covered with this dark deposit. We sat down on a bench, and the guide took our lamps, and in some nook shaded the light from the ceiling, and told us to look steadily up. He then allowed the light to steal gently over the roof, and in the apparently dark sky, the stars came out, one after the other, large and small, glittering precisely as the heavens on a frosty night. One group has a hazy appearance, and is called the "The Comet;" and, in another place, an enormous number give a perfect representation of the milky way. The deception is most com-plete. The sky assumes a deep blue, and you cannot really tell that it is not the true sky on which you are gazing. Our guide then left us, and took away the light, so that we might, whilst sitting quiet and safely, realise the darkness of the cave. Words can give no idea of its intensity. No ray, however feeble, finds its way there. I bared my shirt sleeve, to see if any reflection came from it, but all was black. It was a darkness that might be felt. I have been in the dark cells in the gaol, but there you can put out your hand and feel the walls; here the space around you and above you is vast, and you feel as if returned to chaos. The intensity of this eternal night soon became most painful; and we were glad when our conductor reappeared with his light, and informed us that we had seen all the principal objects in the cave. To see it all you must give weeks, but then you see a repetition of the same kind of general effect.

"The Grand Halls" we had seen, "The Ball Room," "The Hall of Revellers," "The Church," "The Grand Dome," and so forth, and "The River;" so we felt very well satisfied, and were surprised when told that we had, in the bowels of the earth, walked twelve miles. One of the passages is arched in a most extraordinary manner, as though chiselled out by the hand of a mason. So far as is known, there are two hundred and twenty distinct galleries.

Near "The Star Chamber" there were fifteen houses built some twelve years ago, with the idea that the air and temperature of the cave were favourable for consumptive patients. One poor fellow lived four months in one of the houses. Imagine such a life, in eternal gloom, night, and silence, for the silence is as overpowering as the darkness. But it was of no avail—he died. The temperature is uniform, all the year 59° of Fahrenheit. The ventilation is perfect and most delicious. The day was warm and bright, and a gentle air seemed breathing from the most distant recesses towards the mouth of the cave. Between five and six hours soon went, and after a most gratifying sojourn we re-ascended to daylight, not so much tired as might have been expected. Dined at the hotel, and then returned along the forest road, which Rotherham described to be a road made by cutting down the trees, and leaving the stumps above ground, which is exactly the fact. We got back to Bell's safely, and sat quietly watching a heavy storm that swept over with great fury and suddenness, just as we returned. It made us rather anxious, for as we were to take the stage back to Louisville, we had to depend on what vacant seats there were when it arrived, and feared that we might have to go outside in the cold and rain. It arrived at ten, and I found there was room inside, which was a great relief—so then went and laid down till two, when I was woke again, and at half-past we started to retrace our weary journey. We had rather better company back, and at six o'clock p.m. reached Louisville, got supper, and started at eight from the hotel to the railway; the train left at nine, and soon after five this morning we reached Cincinnati, as you may suppose well tired.

This week we have travelled,—Monday, from nine morning to five next morning; Wednesday, from five a.m. to nine p.m.; Friday, from 2 30 a.m. to five a.m. Saturday; in all 628 miles. Here we shall stay a few days; it seems a nice town.

I was glad to find your letter of the 18th September here, (some one named John A. Nicholls had opened it at Chicago,) and thank you for the scrap of paper, which told me my first per the *North Star* had duly been received, it seemed like the first re-establishment of the link with home again. Tell Lawrence I am very much pleased and gratified with his letter, in every way a very good letter, not only on account of the writing and the expression, but the goodness of heart that shines through all.

Rotherham is one of the best lads I ever knew in my life, always merry, singing, and whistling. He has none of the awkwardness of most lads of twenty, and none of the vice of many of that age. He is coming to see me when I get home; he is just a lad you will like. I am glad to see the Heron testimonial. Tell Papa to put my name down. I should like it to appear among his friends.

We intend to go to the theatre this evening, as I see that Mr. and Mrs. John Wood, formerly in

Manchester are acting here. I knew the fact
that the *Arabia* met us going into New York,
would be a great relief to your mind; you may
imagine how grateful I was when her light came in
sight, since by her you must know of our safety,
some days before you would receive a letter. Give
my love to them in Mosley Street and Ludlow; tell
Mary I really have not yet had time to write to
her. Papa may tell them at the mill that I am
quite well. We seem to be in an excellent hotel,
the Burnet House, very large, clean, and comfortable, and good food, which is most desirable, for
such rubbish as we have eaten cannot be good for
any one. So far from the passage making me ill, I
never was better in my life.

BURNET HOUSE, CINCINNATI,

October 18*th*, 1857.

MY DEAR MAMMA,

So soon as I have finished one letter, I
generally lay the keel of another, so that my diary
is in your hands. I have written several letters
to-day. On my arrival here I found yours, one
from Mr. Ferguson, and a telegraphic despatch from
Charles Matthews. I therefore wrote Matthews
and Mr. Ferguson each a long epistle, giving them

some of my impressions on America and American things in general. * * * *

I also wrote to Mary Staley, giving her an account of the darkies, and Mississippi steam-boat life. This one I have commenced on a sheet of the hotel paper, which is abundantly supplied to the guests of the house, free of charge. I do so because it has a picture of the house upon it, and you may thus form an idea of the grandeur of the principal hotel in a town not half so large as Manchester.

I have told you before something of the way these immense establishments are managed, but I think this the most perfect I have seen: you enter a large square hall, the roof supported by pillars, the floor paved with alternate squares of black and white marble; facing the entrance is a large marble counter, behind which stands the clerk; on this counter there is a book, in which each guest writes his name on arrival, and then the number of the room is written in another column; a third part is left, in which the clerk puts the time of your arrival, thus: B., D., T., or S. stands for an arrival in time for Breakfast, Dinner, Tea, or Supper, and L., if too late for any meal. Your key is then given to you, your luggage pointed out, carried up, and you are free of the house; the general charge is two dollars and a half per day, some places three; no extras.

The rack that holds the keys has a number of

pigeon holes, each of which corresponds to the number of a room, and any letters, cards, small parcels, &c., are placed therein for you. Near the clerk is a large frame, with a number of small plates; if any one rings a bell, the corresponding plate falls down, and uncovers the number, so that although in this house there are near four hundred rooms, there is only one bell for them all. On the right of the office is a washing-room, provided with basins, mirrors, and plenty of clean towels; on the left, a telegraphic office, so that without leaving the house you may send and receive a message from any part of the States or Canada. There is a large magnificent drawing-room, luxuriously furnished, and two comfortable smoking and writing rooms, an immense dining-room completes the public part of the house. On the ground floor are tailor's, haberdasher's, barber's, and cigar shops, with a bar, hot and cold baths, and in the hall a small marble stand for the sale of cigars. Attached to the house are some three or four boys, who sell newspapers, and these little urchins, precocious beyond their years, board there, and eat and drink at the public table. There used to be a great number of hotel robberies. No one knows anything about the guests, who or what they are, and hotel thieves were in the habit of frequenting the large houses, and in the absence of people, entering their rooms, with false keys, and cutting and breaking open their trunks for money, &c. The hotel

P

keepers are liable, but by an act of Congress each hotel keeper is authorized to put up a notice in each room, that he provides a fire and fraud-proof safe, in which all valuables can be stored belonging to the guests, and if such a provision be made, he is no longer responsible for any loss from robbery. If you miss the proper meal-time you must go without till the next, and so long as you hold the key you are considered a guest, and whether you take a meal or not in the house are charged just the same. So the bookkeeping is very simple indeed. Wines of course are extra, and any meals served in private; there is no bowing and scraping or cringing to rich people, all are on exactly the same footing—great civility, but nothing more. When the system is well carried out it is an excellent one; when it is not it is execrable, for you have no appeal. "Don't like it; well then, leave it." I consider this, and the Metropolitan in New York, the best I have seen in America, but of course we must expect them to be better in the older and more settled country.

We have walked about here something like country gapers at Whitsuntide, for we have not seen a regular orderly city for some five weeks, and it really appears strange, after plank walks and wooden houses, intermingled with log huts. This country is the real paradise of pigs; they are allowed the free run of the streets, and grunt and root about everywhere.   *   *   *   It is

a handsome town, built on the Ohio river, which is
a sad muddy stream, and is the largest town in
the State of Ohio, called the "Buckeye State."
Columbus is the capital, which we shall visit as we
go hence to Pittsburg; the streets are on the usual
plan, all laid out quite square, and at right angles
with each other, a plan which renders it extremely
easy to find your way about. The streets leading
up from the river are named after trees, as chestnut, walnut, sycamore, and the cross streets simply
by number; thus our hotel is corner of *Third and
Chestnut*, and so they go on, Third, Fourth, &c.;
in giving or writing an address they never add the
word "street," but put it just as I have done.

The police do not wear any uniform, but as they
usually look the idlest men about, you may thus
detect them. On close inspection they wear a star
on their waistcoat, but you must be near to see it;
they are badly managed, and are a most inefficient
force,—in fact, all their municipal matters are
villainously managed, and there is great peculation.
I see that from the treasury of the New York corporation, ten or twelve millions of dollars have
disappeared in three or four years, of which no one
knows anything, there being no vouchers to account
for the expenditure. What would Mr. Clark say
to such a state of things? Cabs are also sadly
wanting in proper control. I don't often enter
one, if you do you must bargain, &c. On arrival
at a town a few miles out, a person goes through

the train, asks you for your luggage ticket, which you give him, each piece being numbered. He then gives you a receipt and an omnibus check, you pay him a quarter, twenty-five cents, about one shilling, you take your seat in the 'bus, are set down at your hotel, and in a few minutes your luggage arrives there too, quite safe, so you need not hire coaches, and have no trouble with porters; it saves your time, your pocket, and your temper. The luggage checks are pieces of brass, stamped with a number, the initials of the railway company, and the destination, and a similar piece is fastened on the piece of luggage by a small strap, so that no mistake can occur; a system that deserves imitation.

I have filled this sheet with general, and I think you will say not uninteresting items,—short episodes,—and proceed again as usual.

STEUBENVILLE, *October* 22.

Mr. T—— J—— being still from home, we had to confine our knowledge of Cincinnati to what we could pick up, wandering about alone. It delights in the title of " Porkopolis," from the large number of hogs killed and the meat preserved here during the season, and certainly that swinish multitude is allowed considerable license, and is permitted to wander unquestioned throughout the principal streets. In the course of our wanderings we saw all of interest that we knew of; visited one of the large upholstery stores and manufactories for which Cincinnati is celebrated, and which constitutes a large portion of its trade. We also saw one of the immense steam fire-engines, of which there are nine in the city; they are drawn by four horses, and the pumps are worked by steam-engines, throwing a jet of water one inch and a quarter in diameter to a height of two hundred and fifty feet. On an alarm of fire the steam can be got up in eight minutes; the whole of the machinery is in beautiful order, and regularly worked, so that any defect may be discovered in time.

The telegraph system through the States is that known as Morse's, in which a metallic point ticks upon a plate, the point can make either a tick or a dash; a piece of paper run under the point by clock-work receives a series of dots and dashes, which constitute the telegraphic alphabet. At our hotel there was a station, and the operator is a very nice, civil, intelligent young man; being a practised operator he did not use the slip of paper, but merely sat and listened to the ticking of the instrument, and then read off the message, so that in sending despatches it was really a conversation; a good ear, and some practice, is required to enable a person to work on this system. But he said so accustomed was he, that he could tell what operator was at work sending him a message at a distant station, exactly as he could distinguish any one's voice.

On Wednesday morning we left Cincinnati with regret; should have left a day sooner, but had made an arrangement, expecting to meet Mr. J—— * * * * and had much matter requiring time and no little fatigue to get over. The weather has entirely changed, the evenings are frosty and the mid-day warm, the leaves have changed their tints, and are rapidly falling, so that I fear the Indian summer is a myth. Leaving Cincinnati by railway, we had a rather pretty ride of one hundred and twenty miles to Columbus, the capital of Ohio; boasting an imposing Capitol, to my taste heavy and ugly, Grecian in its architecture, and one or two public buildings, but in the main a dull and uninteresting place, still, one to be seen as the specimen of a capital of a state so important as Ohio. We left the next morning without much regret, and took our places for Pittsburg—two hundred and seventeen miles further. We started late from some train delay, and on arriving at Steubenville junction, our train with which we should have connected had passed, and we were compelled to remain all night in Steubenville. We asked about hotels; a gentleman in the car said "Well, there are two, the 'United States House'

and the ' Washington Hall ; ' whichever you go to,
you will wish you had gone to the other." Our luggage being checked through, was taken in charge by
the railway people, carrying only what was absolutely
necessary. We were directed on our way, and
reached the " United States," entered a filthy room,
full of loafish-looking fellows, " Can we have beds?"
" Yes, sir." But on pressing the landlord, we
found the bedrooms contained three or four, or
even more beds, and we declined. " Then I can't
accommodate you." " Very well," and off we set
to the other, entered a similar dirty hole, full of
rowdy fellows, betting and boasting. " Is this the
Washington House?" I enquired from a dirty-looking
youth behind a counter. " It is the Washington
Hall, Sir!" " Oh, can we have bedrooms?" " I
will tell you when the old man comes in," being
the landlord that he meant. Luck would have it
he found us a room, two beds, a small washstand,
and a hole in the ceiling, from which the plaster
had fallen. We had some supper served in a large
dirty back room, by a disgustingly filthy negro,
and I presume cooked by such another. I cannot
describe the beds ; I suggested that they were
made of the stalks of Indian corn, with just a sheet
between us and the stems. " No," said Rotherham,
" they are made of a cord of firewood, with the
ends sticking up." I laughed and went to sleep,
got up at six, not much refreshed. Our breakfast
was almost a repetition of the supper, except that

the landlord waited upon us *two*, and got us everything fresh and hot, and would not let us eat what
the rest were consuming. I suppose two English
gentlemen were rarities in his house. How relieved we were to get away!

PITTSBURG.

WE started from Steubenville at 9 20, passing
through a wild and beautiful country alongside the
river Ohio, arriving at the smoky American Birmingham, at 12 30. It is situated at the junction
of the rivers Alleghany and Monongahela, which,
when united, form the Ohio. The town is a very
dirty place, containing large iron and glass works,
and as this is a coal district, we have lost our
charming log fires, and return to coal and smuts.

We have been about the town; it does not
contain any very fine buildings, but has some
handsome bridges across the river. It is a busy,
bustling place, but I fear will suffer from the
general depression. To-morrow morning we start
at seven, and arrive, I hope, at Philadelphia, at
12 50 night, nearly eighteen hours rail. I have
been the last few days writing the accompanying
letter, which you can send to the " Guardian"
office; if they like to publish it they can. * * *

They talk of a general suspension; many persons I have casually met and conversed with say, "We must all suspend, wipe off our debts, and begin again." I suggested that such a course might ruin the creditors. "Well, I am not going to ruin myself." There's morality for you! I have not alluded to such a state of things in my letter, it would be injudicious. In fact I have not said half I know. I consider the whole railway property gone; lines are suspending one after another, entirely from wretched management. What do you think of paying the President of a small line the sum of 25,000 dollars a year, equal to £5,000., not to do anything, but because he is respectable, and can raise money for them in an easy manner; the officials eat up the whole receipts, leaving the bones for the shareholders to pick if they like. I assure you it is a sad state of things altogether. By the way, I must not forget to tell you that Rotherham and I got photographed together at Cincinnati.

PHILADELPHIA, SUNDAY MORNING.

RISING at half-past five yesterday morning we went to the station, and started punctually at seven. The train ran some distance through the town, crossing streets, the engine bell ringing all the time. For the first two or three hours the road passed through a fine settled country, but about ten we came to the Alleghany Mountains, and commenced a long, steep incline for many miles, with the heaviest cuttings and works I have seen in the States. Our route lay along a wild and magnificent country—winding round in the most extraordinary manner, by the side of mountain gorges, crossing streams, the largest the Juniata. At one point we went completely round one of the gorges, the line winding as sharply as the road over the hills to Buxton. At the top of the incline we went through a tunnel, which runs through the highest point of the mountains on our route, and were then 2,500 feet above the sea. We stopped at a place called Altoona, to dine, where there was an excellent refreshment-room, more like our own at Birmingham or Derby. Although not so wild, the scenery was still fine, and continued so until dusk. We had tea at Harrisburg, where the train ran through the principal streets; imagine a train running down some of our streets! About half-past eleven we reached the outskirts of the " Quaker City," the engine then left us, and horses were harnessed to each car, and we were drawn in this way into the town, through the streets to the station; our luggage tickets were given up, we took a coach, and arrived at the Girard House, an excellent first-class hotel; our luggage came soon after, and taking supper, we went to bed, well tired with

our journey of 353 miles. Buying a newspaper on
the way, we found Charles Matthews begins here
to-morrow night, so that in all probability he will
arrive at the hotel to-day, from Boston, and I mean
to stay over to-morow to see him, and leave on
Tuesday for New York, so that I may spend a quiet
day with Rotherham before we part. I expect to
see him in Boston, but it is just a chance. We
also found the opera company here who crossed in
the *Asia* with us. They are leaving to-night, *en
route* to Havana. It commenced raining heavily at
Harrisburg last evening, and still continues, so we
are home-bound, but glad that we are in good
quarters, for to be so fixed in some places we have
visited would be fearful.   *   *   *

The ensuing winter will be the severest trial the
United States ever experienced, and I think it will
go hard with their institutions. There is no deny-
ing the fact that mob-law is the only law here. It
may be a good country for the poor, but it is the
opposite for the rich. The grossest corruption
pervades the whole state, everything is political,
and even in the administration of justice party
feeling runs so high that the judges are not exempt
from influence. They are poorly paid, and politically appointed, and on such a system cannot be
fair and impartial. I have before said that municipal affairs are most wretchedly managed. At
Cincinnati, the other day, Rotherham, I, and the
telegraph young man were walking together, and I

pointed to a man asleep in a doorway, and said,
"He is drunk, I suppose." "Oh no; it is only a
policeman, taking a nap." Fancy one of ours
reposing during the time he is on duty, in a doorway, in a most public street!

In New York they have just discovered a further
defalcation of eight million dollars in the public
funds—gone, no one knows where or how. The
plunder obtainable is the great inducement for
taking office, and I do believe that even
Russian officials are pure compared with the bulk
of the American. I regret it should be so; but
the fact is the suffrage is too low, and obtained
with too great ease. Unless a more stringent law
be introduced, and put in execution, the political
future of the States is dark indeed. Don't imagine,
however, that my radicalism is affected—not a bit
of it; I only deplore the evils of indiscriminate
universal suffrage. With us the suffrage is too
high,—here it is much too low, and, as a consequence, the worst men get into power. I see at
New York the Corporation wants to do something
during the winter for the working classes, simply
because they fear their dangerous classes, just
as Louis Napoleon does those of Paris. Most of
the bankers have paid the smaller depositors but
refused the cheques of their large customers, because
they fear the consequences if the mob should
become enraged and jealous. They have the power
in their own hands, not only politically by their

majority, but also physically by their numbers, as there is no military force to keep them in order, and virtually no police. If, therefore, a want of food should follow the present crisis, what may be the consequences no one can tell. There are crowds of demagogues, all selfish in their aims, who will seek to rise on the general prostration, and can lead the masses as they please. I see in some places they have formed committees to watch the banks, and prevent merchants and others from drawing out gold; if they attempt to do so they will risk their lives. Give me the true, equal liberty of England. There is more talk of it here, but less reality. American equality is that which drags all down to the lowest level. I trust I may see in the large towns some society that may at least give me the idea, that the well-dressed mobs I meet in travelling are not their upper classes. *   *   *   *

Rotherham and I have travelled together in the States 4,307 miles, by steamboat and railway, and, I thank God, without the least accident of any kind, for which I feel truly grateful in my heart. I never had a better travelling companion except yourself. We have not had a moment's difference of any sort, even the slightest, and are sorry we cannot go farther together. He returns by the *Arabia*, sailing on the 25th November, and goes at once to Washington, and then, I hope, will meet me for a day or two at Boston. *   *   *   *

I got up at half-past five this (Tuesday) morning,

took the train for New York, and went to my old hotel, the Metropolitan; there I found two letters from you, and one from Sebastian. New York looks strange; every shop is selling off at or below prime cost. I believe the ladies have rushed in crowds, so much so that the proprietors had to put up barriers, to keep off the excessive pressure. The whole place has a panic-struck look. They imagine the Bank of England will suspend cash payments, on the receipt of the last or present mail; the drain of bullion will be very great.   *   *   *

[*The following is the communication to the "Manchester Guardian," which is referred to in the preceding letter.*]

THE AMERICAN CRISIS.

To the Editor of the Manchester Guardian.

CINCINNATI, *October 22*, 1857.

SIR,

IT may not be uninteresting to your readers at this particular juncture, to receive some few remarks bearing on the present crisis in the United States. Having arrived here from a tour in what is now the Far West, I have had a favourable opportunity of investigating some of the social

causes which have led to the general suspension,
and the severe commercial depression through
which the people of the States are now passing.
For those who have not witnessed the extent of
the rapid territorial expansion which is now, and
has been taking place for the last four or five years,
it is a matter of difficulty, nay, almost of impossibility, to realise the amount of speculation which
has tended to diffuse an already scanty population
over an enormous extent of country, whilst the
Eastern States were concentrating on a sufficiently
large, but still manageable and accessible territory,
an industrious and thrifty people, absorbing, as
their wants and means warranted them in doing,
more and more land, and thus creating new states,
in accordance with the natural law of supply and
demand, the progress of the country in wealth and
sound material prosperity was placed on an unas-
sailable basis. The tendency of the last few years
has entirely reversed the operation of this natural
law; and, leaving behind vast tracts of fertile and
productive land in the middle states, the tide of
human life has flowed with unceasing rapidity to
those far regions in the West, where the white man
has again been brought into immediate contact
with the aboriginal owners of the soil. Towns and
cities have sprung up in those distant regions, with
all the wants and requirements of civilisation, yet
compelled to draw their supplies from the southern
and eastern seaboard, at a great cost for freight,

and all other incidental charges, and owing their existence solely to a furious spirit of speculation, and a mad desire for the rapid achievement of wealth. In their turn they have, if not created, at least fostered, the unparalleled growth of their intermediate cities, which rank as the gates of the West, through which their supplies must be drawn. In anticipation of future commercial greatness, the price of real estate in such places as Chicago, has touched a fabulous height. As an immediate result, rents in that town are extravagantly great, leading to a corresponding increase in the expenses connected with all business transactions. Your readers will hardly credit this statement, yet I can vouch for the fact, that land in good business sites in Chicago was selling in lots of 120 to 130 feet deep, at prices ranging between 700 and 1,500 dollars per lineal foot of frontage, and a friend pointed out to me a small wooden four-roomed house, in a poorly-built street, which he inhabited for a year or two, at an annual rental of £150. sterling, a house which, if tenantable at all in England, would be thought dear at £20. per annum. So fictitious is the value assigned to property in perhaps one of the most prosperous cities of the West. Not content, however, with the immense outlay required for the purchase of land, the merchants of Chicago have vied with each other in the erection of the most magnificent and imposing warehouses to be met with in any city in the world.

We are inclined to regard Manchester as essentially distinguished for its splendid mercantile edifices; but the Queen City of the Prairies boasts of structures equalling, if not exceeding ours in the beauty and chasteness of their architecture, and the costliness of their materials. For the most part, the fronts are constructed of cast-iron, or faced with white marble, and in mere decoration have locked up for ever an enormous amount of money that can be ill spared in a new country. The owner of a magnificent warehouse must possess a residence to correspond; and we find in the immediate vicinity of Chicago, Buffalo, and even the less known Detroit, mansions that would do no discredit to Belgravia itself; and hence a generally expensive style of living becomes the fashion among those classes who, with us, are carefully husbanding their resources, to enable them to carry on their ordinary business with the greater ease, derivable alone from ampler means. Nevertheless, there are elements of prosperity in Chicago, which must enrich its future merchants, be the fate of the present race what it may. Situated on Lake Michigan, it has an uninterrupted communication by means of the chain of inland seas and the mighty St. Lawrence with the Atlantic ocean, except during the extreme severity of the winter; and vessels laden with grain have successfully completed the voyage between Chicago and Liverpool. Its proximity to the Canadian frontier has made it the chief point of

Q

communication between the provinces and the west, sharing with Buffalo the greater portion of the trade which has been largely augmented by the treaty of reciprocity. By the Sault St. Marie and Lake Superior its sea-going vessels can penetrate to the far west, and the construction of a few auxiliary canals in connection with that lake would place it in communication with the Mississippi, and the enormous inland navigation associated with that river. Under such favourable natural circumstances, can we feel astonished that so great a field for the wildest speculation should excite the cupidity of our American brethren? Few nations could resist a temptation so magnificent.

Although the growth of Chicago has been unprecedented, and its increase of population beyond credit, there were peculiar circumstances that favoured this sudden developement, namely, the almost simultaneous completion of the network of railways centering here, and the boat canal joining the Mississippi, for the carriage of grain, of which I need not say Chicago promises to be the largest emporium in the world. With these commercial facilities thoroughly sound in themselves, the population has increased from about 20,000 in 1850 to 110,000 in 1857. Receiving the produce of the rich prairie land, it returns to these vast, open, and rolling tracts, cargoes of lumber for the construction of houses and farm buildings, and the various supplies needed by the population, but depending

for the maintenance of its position on the steady
settlement and improvement of the surrounding
country. But the cry is still "To the west;"
and, instead of bringing into cultivation the
prairies of Illinois, traversed by railways—the
directors of which are unable to dispose, even at
low prices, of the land in the vicinity of their
lines—the stream of emigration is losing itself on
the banks of the Mississippi, and the vast, and as
yet almost unknown tracts of Kansas, Nebraska,
Iowa, and Minnesota. One of these lines, the
Illinois Central, has become bankrupt, from the
fact principally that the directors have been unable
to sell their lands, through which the line passes,
so as to enable them to meet their engagements as
they became due.

Leaving Chicago, by a railway of which its
English shareholders, if there be any such, know
nothing, either with reference to the county of
Winsconsin, through which it passes, or the actual
state of the road itself, I visited the new city of
Madison, the capital of the state, most beautiful in
point of situation, but passing the understanding
of man to know why it was built, except that a
thinly peopled country, numbering, at the largest
and most liberal computation, one million souls,
inhabiting an area of thirty millions of acres, must
have immediately a capital city, laid out in metropolitan style, and boasting metropolitan edifices,
with an existence depending alone on the sessions

of the state legislature. Again taking the railway, which runs through an entirely unsettled country, I reached the Mississippi at Prairie du Chien, and thence proceeded by a steamboat 400 miles up the river, through a magnificent forest wilderness, with here and there a few wooden houses, dignified by the name of cities, bringing forcibly to mind Dickens's description of Eden. Arriving at the city of St. Paul, at the head of the river navigation, I found there perhaps the best exemplar of the present rage for land speculations. Four years ago its name was almost unknown, except to the comparatively few engaged in trading with the Indians, who number some 60,000 in the state of Minnesota. At that period a few wooden houses and log huts, with some 300 residents at the most, constituted the entire town, which now contains upwards of 10,000 inhabitants. Situated on one of those bold and commanding bluffs, which constitute a peculiar feature in the scenery of the upper Mississippi, with an almost unlimited extent of fertile prairie land on every side, awaiting the plough and the hand of the husbandman, to yield its abundant harvests, and standing at the head of the river navigation, which is interrupted a few miles higher up by the shallows and the falls of St. Anthony, St. Paul has within itself the seeds of future prosperity, which cannot, however, be realised, until the surrounding territory is brought into play; the work, I may say, of centuries.

Nevertheless, again in anticipation of what at some future and distant period may be the value of the land, building lots in the town are selling at the most exaggerated prices, and the city laid out on the scale of some European capital. Yet its sole dependence for years must be the supply of the scattered settlers inhabiting the open country and one or two small towns in its immediate vicinity, together with its old Indian trade, becoming more and more limited as years pass away. On this, to our notion, slender basis, a vast speculative super-structure is erected. So long as eager multitudes pressed to the western El Dorado, and blindly purchased land at any price, paying down in cash a certain proportion of the purchase money, and leaving the rest on mortgage, for a shorter or longer term of years, at a high rate of interest, the original proprietors were well satisfied, and believing in the durability of their position, lived accordingly, and to such a degree, that St. Paul's bore the distinction of being the " fastest" city in the States. I need hardly say that such are not the men required to settle a new country, are unfit to cope with the difficulties and privations of such a position, or to follow in the footsteps of the hardy pioneers of American greatness.

In founding these western cities, the projectors appear to have no conception of waiting and per-mitting the due course of events to develope addi-tional building when required; but call forth, as by an enchanted wand, a vast collection of structures, far removed from the settled country, and exceeding, in a great degree, the possible wants of the people, leaving their support to depend on the after settlement of the surrounding districts. So long as the money or credit could be found this system might endure; but the day of reckoning was certain to arrive, being merely a question of time and the extent of individual credulity. The line must run out—the limit has been reached—and now the certain re-action has commenced. At the price of two months ago land is unsaleable in St. Paul's, and its value is descending with the utmost rapidity, although it may not yet have reached the state of complete collapse which I see, from the latest reports, has befallen the still newer city of Superior, situated on the lake of the same name, whose merchants, being unable to meet the expenses of freight on one or two steamboat cargoes recently arrived, the captains declined to discharge, and have returned them to the shippers.

In addition to the vast amounts expended in building new cities and erecting splendid edifices, we must also bear in mind the rapid manner in which the people of the States have constructed an immense network of railways, extending from the Atlantic Ocean beyond the Mississippi, and from Canada to the Gulf of Mexico, covering the country in every direction with numerous competing lines, actually employing agents to tout for passengers. In the east these lines follow the course and increase of population, and adapt themselves to the service of towns in existence. In the west, however, they precede population and its possible wants for years to come, and pursue their way from one terminal point to another, distant two, three, or four hundred miles, totally devoid of any wayside traffic, and dependent alone on the through business from one of their distant points to the other. Through boundless and silent forests, over vast prairies, they make their solitary way, and, from the facility and apparent cheapness with which they have been constructed, have contributed largely to increase the mania for distant settlements, by affording, at absurdly low fares, a means of ready access to these remote regions, at the cost of the unfortunate shareholders. Not content with the great highways which nature has so bountifully provided, railways run alongside the rivers, competing for the traffic, thus needlessly incurring large expenses, and encouraging an unnecessary rivalry. Whilst in Virginia and Kentucky, and other middle and fertile States, enormous tracts of country lie in total neglect, covered with valuable timber, and inviting settlers, the system of excessive railroad extension has carried the pioneers of civilisation into less promising regions, where the value of the land has been raised artificially, in place of encouraging that gradual and really useful extension which, taking its departure from the seaboard, would cover the surface with its surges of living water, each succeeding wave passing a little in advance of its predecessor, instead of those spasmodic efforts which may force some small portions into narrow and distant channels, there to stagnate until the refreshing tide can absorb them into its vaster and purer mass. Of the management of these railways I will not venture to speak; but I feel certain that many of them will require vast outlays of money to render them permanently available. Built cheaply, badly laid, and imperfectly ballasted, a few years will render their reconstruction in a great degree absolutely necessary, and if, by any accident, the means should not be forthcoming when wanted, the insecure position of western property becomes at once clearly manifest. To many of the eastern roads these remarks do not apply; they refer to those extended lines which intersect the western States.

With so rapid a conversion of the floating and available capital of the nation into a fixed, and, I fear, to a great extent, unremunerative form, it would be impossible to expect any other effect than the present existing prostration; and when, in addition, we call to mind the large importation of expensive manufactures which has been taking place for some time, exhibiting a taste for lavish individual expenditure, we are compelled to draw the inference, that the people have been living far beyond their means, at the same time that they have extended their commercial undertakings, without reference to their power of successfully carrying them on when completed. Among a certain party there is a tendency to refer the present disaster to the changes in the tariff. A little consideration of the simple laws of political economy will convince even the most sceptical, that the evils arise from the causes to which I have referred. There is, however, no ground for despondency; the material resources of this country are too vast, and its population, in the main, too industrious, to admit of any doubt of a speedy return to more prosperous days. To arrive at that result, however, the present over-reaching policy of rapid extension must be abandoned, and greater efforts made for the concentration of the population. A wandering and an unsettled spirit has been encouraged; and, without local attachments, the people pass from place to place, trying here, trying there; and thus fritter away their time and their energy in unmeaning and useless changes. It was not thus that the early settlers succeeded in their struggles, and founded a mighty empire; and it is only by a return to a mode of procedure similar to theirs, and in accordance with the improved opportunities of modern times, that a permanent condition of prosperity can be induced.

An Englishman must ever feel a deep and sincere interest, apart from all selfish considerations, in the progress and welfare of the United

States.   Connected by every tie that is held most
sacred   among men,—speaking a common language—recognising the same great principles of
liberty—acknowledging the same laws,—England
and America have too many points of sympathy to
render the one country indifferent to the prosperity
of the other, and when a season of adversity arrives,
from whatever cause, the suffering induced is felt
with a greater or less intensity on both sides of the
Atlantic.   It is impossible to travel over any
considerable portion of this western world, and to
mingle freely with its people, without being deeply
impressed by the strong affection for what is
fondly termed the " old country," manifested on all
sides, and their anxiety to show that, in spite of
ephemeral political differences, they are one with
us in everything that constitutes the unity of a
nation, except the mere name, and I esteem it
essentially a duty to reciprocate this feeling on
every possible occasion.

The very difficulties of the present crisis arise
from an excess of that spirit, which springs from
the innate energy of the Anglo-Saxon race, and
the temporary adversity will serve, I sincerely
believe, to direct it into other and more remunerative channels, and be the precursor of a long
and unbroken career of prosperity.

Truly yours,

JOHN A. NICHOLLS.

Revere House, Boston,

Sunday Evening, November 1, 1857.

My Dear Mamma,

I TOLD you at the end of my last letter
that I might miss a mail, but I cannot refrain from
sending you a few lines, although I tell you at the
outset this will be a meagre epistle. After I posted
my last Bristow came in, looking ill and thin; he
was delighted to see me, and begged so hard that I
consented to remain in New York until Friday
morning, a day longer than I had resolved to do.
Up to Thursday evening it rained in torrents, and
was extremely cold, so that after all, my sacrifice of
a day really cost me nothing. On Wednesday
afternoon the *Persia* arrived, and that evening,
through Mr. Ferguson's great kindness in sending
up his clerk on purpose, I received your welcome
letters; it seemed almost like a return by post,
instead of the long anxious waiting I have had
before. Finding from your letter that Lewis Young
and Henry Shawcross were coming by the *Persia*, I
looked over the passenger list, and meeting their
names duly inscribed, Bristow and I set off to search

for them, and in ten minutes' time, discovered
them both at the New York Hotel. We were all
much pleased to meet, and enjoyed a good long
chat together. * * * * Our good old ship
duly sailed out, and I should have gone and seen
them off, but intending to leave the next day, I
wished to see Mr. Ferguson. He quite laughed at
the idea of the Bank of England suspending, but
I do think some of these Yankees would feel
proud if their panic should have had so severe
an effect.

I don't much like New York, there is just one
street, the Broadway, to which the whole population
flock, rendered all but impassable by the women's
hoops, empty boxes, packages, &c.

I was glad when Friday came. I got up at six,
and started at eight, by railway, for Boston. The
cars were drawn out of the station by horses, and
the train formed in the street, just as though our
carriages for London were all on Bank Top,
with the engine waiting to take them on. The
train ran through the town, with a good view of
the extensions taking place, which must in time
make Manhattan Island one vast city, crossing the
Harlem river on a drawbridge, where some years
ago a frightful accident occurred, from a train
rushing over when the bridge was open, pre-
cipitating the unfortunate people in the deep water,
and drowning a vast number. The road runs by
the side of Long Island Sound, and is extremely

beautiful, from the lovely glimpses of the bright water. The country had all day a more settled appearance, good cultivation, and although many wooden houses, still possessing a substantial look. After passing through the pretty town of New-haven, we turned from the sea, and ran by the Connecticut river to Springfield, then on to Worcester, and finally reached Boston, about a quarter-past five, 236 miles. We had one little accident on the road between Springfield and Worcester, the train suddenly stopped, and then ran back some distance—people all looked out, and crowded the platforms of the cars, so I got out with the rest, when the train stood still, and found that the cow catcher, a large iron frame attached to the front of the engine, had struck a calf that had strayed on the line, and smashed one of its hind legs. I did pity the poor creature, and so did all the passengers—they wanted the conductor to kill it; some one brought him an axe, but he said he knew better, and so pushed it through the fence, to wait until the owner came. There were several cows in the field, and they all stood still, looking at the calf in the most extraordinary manner, as though quite aware that something had happened, their looks were perfectly indescribable; several persons noticed the circumstance with astonish-ment.

Entering Boston, we came over a species of causeway constructed in the water, and arriving at the station, the Revere House coach took me to the hotel. The town is built on a peninsula, and is much elevated toward the centre,—there the State House is built, towering over the rest of the city. When I got in, I felt very unwell, I had got cold from the change of climate, and had a pain in my side, so, at half-past seven I took a hot bath, and went to bed; next morning I was much better, but did not feel disposed for much exertion.

I called on Mr. B——, to whom I had a letter from Mr. Wildes. I am to see him again to-morrow, when he will introduce me to the Mayor. I then walked to the common, the docks, and made out some of the localities. Boston is not built on the modern American plan, all square streets, but on the old system, streets running about as they please. I saw the outside of the Faneuil Hall, so celebrated in the revolution. I did no more that day, but sat quietly in the evening, and went to bed early. This morning I went to the Federal Street Church, where Channing used to preach, and heard an excellent discourse by Dr. Gannett. It is a nice, clean-looking, old-fashioned place. The gentleman I sat with kindly said I could come to his pew when I wished. The pulpit was very wide, and the minister sat down, quite away from the desk, during the singing, performed by the choir, and not joined in by the congregation, who all sat still and listened. I do not like that way; I prefer to hear the voices of all united.

Three or four times during the sermon the minister coughed, cleared his throat, and leaning to one side, gave a good genuine spit out, so I presume, must have been furnished with a spittoon, which article I saw was in all the pews; fancy, at the end of a beautiful passage, a climax in the divisions of the sermon, the preacher spitting out, and then wiping his mouth with his handkerchief? What should we say if Mr. Gaskell did so? I will ask him, when I see him, how he would feel under similar circumstances. It disgusted me, and I hoped, in my mind, that Dr. Channing did not spit in the pulpit, yet I fear the practice is universal in places of worship. There are nearly twenty Unitarian churches here, our body being the largest and most influential in this city.

To-morrow my work will begin with a thorough investigation of the school system of Massachusetts, the best in the world. I shall visit Lowell, Lawrence, Cambridge, and Providence, and if I can, Plymouth, where the Pilgrim fathers landed. The weather is taking up again; I feel better, though not quite well, so must be careful for a few days.

TUESDAY EVENING.

YESTERDAY Mr. B—— introduced me to the Mayor of Boston, the Hon. Mr. Rice, who devoted five hours to me, and took me nearly all over the town, showing me all that it was possible to do in the time; but a special description of what I saw I shall leave till my next letter, which must be written more quietly than the one I am now sending.

This morning Rotherham and Bristow woke me up at seven, having arrived from New York by the Fall River boat and rail. I had a letter from Rotherham, saying he was so very dull by himself, and was running on, to be here as to-morrow morning, but it seems the lad got so much duller that he came on at once.

To-morrow Bristow leaves for England, by the Europa, a very fine ship; we went on board her to-day, and could almost have fancied ourselves on our beloved *Asia*. I shall not be able, I am sorry to say, to see him off, because I have an appointment with the Inspector of Schools at nine, to go round with him and visit some of the schools in Boston; he is giving the day to me for that purpose, at the request of the Mayor, to whom I am under great obligations.

There has been an election to-day for State

Governor, and other officers. We have just heard the new Governor make a speech. I went with the Mayor into one of the polling booths.

I shall write by the next steamer, the *Persia*, from New York, and I think even now I have materials for a most interesting letter, but I could not possibly do justice to it at present. I have seen some things which have given me more pleasure than anything I have met with in the States, so I shall leave you in suspense for one short week.

I have quite got over my cold, and am perfectly well again. * * * *

Boston,

November 8th, 1857.

My Dear Mamma,

I despatched my last letter per Bristow, which no doubt will arrive as soon as if duly posted. I told you but little therein, as my time had been too much occupied to have left any space for letter writing.

On Wednesday morning, the Mayor went out with me to show me the arrangements connected

R

with the fire department. The city is divided into wards as usual, and each ward into several fire districts, at each of which there is a means of communicating with a central office by telegraphic wires. To this central office we went, and ascending a flight of stairs in a house close to the City Hall, we came to a room on one side of which the telegraphic apparatus was arranged. When a fire takes place, whoever discovers it runs to one of the stations,—say No. 1 Ward, No. 5 Station. The station is an iron box fastened to a wall, with the telegraphic wire carried from it over the house to the central office. Obtaining the key, a handle inside the box is turned, which rings a bell in the principal office, and records on a strip of paper the number of the ward and station; and the apparatus is so contrived that that particular handle can only be turned so as to make one particular sign.

The person in charge of the office at once sets in motion an apparatus communicating with every church bell in the city, which tolls one for the number of the ward, or whatever the number of this may be, and at the same time, a second, which ticks in these iron boxes the number of the district. Thus, hearing the bells toll the number of the ward, the firemen know at once which to make their way to, and passing any of the iron boxes, and placing their ears pretty close, can hear the number of the district by the ticking sound, and thus go directly to the seat of the fire. I certainly never saw anything more perfect and complete. It saves a great loss of time, and all uncertainty, because the signals are not sent, unless some one known to the holder of the key brings the information, preventing false alarms at the central office.

After spending some time in examining the apparatus and the working details, we visited the police department and prison cells. There was a large collection of people awaiting their turn to go before the Justices. In the office of the head of the police, is a curious collection of criminal curiosities, such as knives with which murders had been committed, and the rope with which the Professor Dr. Webster was hung for the murder of Dr. Parkman,—a crime which produced a terrible effect in Boston society some few years ago. We then took a coach, and drove to the city prisons. The cells are different to ours; the windows are large, and to the outside, and the cells receive their light by barred windows, and opened barred doors looking on to the galleries running round, and through the outside windows. They seemed pretty full; among the prisoners I saw two condemned to death for murder, each chained by the leg.

The law allows a condemned criminal one year between sentence and execution, and as the execution depends on the will of the State Governor, there is a good deal of uncertainty as to whether the law be permitted to take its course or not.

From this prison we went to the State Room, and finding the Sergeant-at-Arms, he sent a person with us, who showed us the Senate House and Chamber of Representatives.

In the Senate House are several of the pictures of early Colonial Governors of Massachusetts, and opposite the President, on the wall above the entrance, are a drum, musket, and sword, taken, I regret to say, from the British during the War of Independence, and hung up as a warning to all British drummers for future ages. It is a handsome chamber, and each member has his own seat and desk: in the lower houses the seats are benches. We went through the Governor's office to see him, but he was not in; and then ascended to the lantern at the top of the dome, from which we had a magnificent view over the city, the harbour, the ocean beyond, and the suburbs, the towns of Cambridge, Charleytown, and Roxbury, and South and East Boston. The State House stands on the old Beacon Hill, and the gilded top of the cupola, seen far out at sea, is hailed by the mariners as the first indication of making the land. Down stairs are some tablets which were placed round the base of an old pillar that stood there, erected in honour of the heroes of the Revolution. In the entrance hall there is a statue of Washington by Chantrey, —a very fine work indeed. We visited the adjutant general commanding the troops in the States, to whom the Mayor introduced me, and he showed me specimens of their military arms, and also two old American drums, that had been beaten at Bunker's Hill and Lexington.

Close to the State House stands an old stone house—I presume one of the oldest in the city—celebrated as having been the residence of John Hancock, the first signer of the Declaration of Independence. From the State House we went to the Athenæum, which is an excellent library; and where I was introduced to the librarian. He took me into a small room, and showed me Washington's private library, each volume having " G. Washington " written in it by his own hand, and in one the names of his father and mother, also autographs. I assure you I looked on the hand-writing of Washington with the greatest respect. In their collection, they have the first book printed in America—a copy of the New Testament, translated into some Indian dialect now unknown and unreadable. In the same build- ing there is a collection of pictures, many certainly not art treasures : but there is the original unfin- ished picture of Washington by Stuart, of which only the face is completed, and is the standard from which all others have been taken. Near here is an old cemetery containing an obelisk, placed over the remains of Franklin's father and mother. In this way we spent five hours, and I felt much indebted to the Mayor for giving me more than half the day.

I told you that on Tuesday morning I went with

the Mayor into the voting booths, to see the mode of voting. The different parties print tickets, containing the name they have decided upon, and each voter places the ticket he selects in a box, and his name is checked as having voted; for here there is a proper registration, fully carried out, so as to render duplicate or illegal voting impossible. Every man of twenty-one, paying a dollar and a half a year, has a vote. This poll-tax is the qualification, so that there is not absolutely universal suffrage—a tax must be paid, or there is no vote. The next morning I bid Bristow good-bye, and leaving Rotherham to see him off joined the School Superintendent, with whom I went to the High School, consisting of two departments: the English, or commencing, and the Latin, or collegiate. In all the details I was convinced that the boys were thoroughly well grounded. I do not think I ever saw greater accuracy of information, especially in the Latin school. By means of excellent maps and photographs, the boys are as familiar with the topography of Rome and Athens as if they had been there. Each boy has a separate desk and chair, and stands out to answer his question or read his part, with his hand resting on the desk, in the most self-possessed manner possible. I remained till two (from nine) in the schools, and when I was leaving I told the head-master and superintendent that I was very much pleased with the mental attainments displayed, but, I said " they are not boys; I have not seen a boy in your country, and have with me a real specimen of an English lad that would thrash your whole school." Never did I see such a collection of anxious faces in my life : pale, sallow, nerveless-looking creatures. I do believe not a row among the lot. The next day I spent the same time in inspecting two other schools and one grammar school, and there I saw the boys at play. I looked into a large yard where they were, walking about, talking politics, perhaps chewing, not a jump or a bit of a lark going on among them. I pointed this out to the master, and told him however much I might admire the mental exercise, and the excellence of the scholastic training, there was a want of physical training that would nullify the whole. The superintendent and the head master had read " Arnold's Life," from which they had obtained an insight into English public school life they had never before met with, and agreed with me that they had a very great deficiency in this respect.

I was much pleased with the common primary schools I visited. The teachers are mostly females, and the system decidedly good. The superintendent is a very superior man, and is doing a great work in improving the elementary modes of teaching.

Whilst I was with the Mayor, a person came in, and gave him a paper; he told me this was " a truant officer," whose duty it is to visit the scholars in his district, and search out all truants, and compel their parents to send them. All children found in the street are taken to school; all schools are perfectly free—no payment whatever, and, if they are unable to find their own books, the State pays for them. Thus, in Boston, more than one-fourth of the total taxation of the city is expended on education. I got a large number of documents from the superintendent. He gave me reports for several years back, and the State report, as well as some specimens of their school books. After completing my visits, I took Rotherham with me, and introduced him to the Mayor. His honor and I had then a long talk about city matters, and my impressions of what I had seen. I said I disapproved of the want of physical training, and, in fact, the entire management of children in the States, in which he entirely agrees with me.

I told the Mayor I should much like to have a copy of their Corporation Manual, and to my surprise he gave me one, handsomely bound—two more large volumes, full bound, gilt edged, being copies of the proceedings of the Boston Council for the year 1856, and a large volume, being a copy of all acts and documents relating to the government of the city. From these I can complete my information relative to Boston.

A friend of Rotherham's invited us to dine at Parker's, a capital *restaurant* here ; our fourth was a Mr. Gilman, whom Charles Matthews wishes to meet; he is an architect, and a most amusing man.

We dined with them on Thursday and Friday; we also took a walk with them, and met Everett, and Prescott, the author of " The Lives of Ferdinand and Isabella." Gilman amused us very much; he has been in Europe, and thinks there is no place like England; never lowered himself by giving a vote in his life, but considers himself as an unfortunate subject of Queen Victoria's, living here in exile.

Rotherham left me on Saturday, and I think would meet Gilman, who went by the same train to Buffalo, where he is going to give a lecture on " Characteristics of New England humour," which I should much like to hear; he has a fund of good stories, and is an excellent mimic.

I saw Mr. Lawrence, and he will have tickets for me to go on Monday to Lawrence, and, if I can, Lowell; one is exactly the same as the other, Lawrence being the new town. I then visited the State Courts, and must say I prefer the state and pomp of our judicial bench. A judge in a black coat and dirty collar does not look well, and the barrister, standing with his back to him, talks to the jury. In the Police Court, the police and magistrates were talking a case all over together, but quite devoid of all respect of any kind.

Mr. J—— has very kindly put my name down at the club, so that I have admission for a month. On Thursday morning I met another of our *Asia* friends, a young man Matthews christened Ovidius Naso. The *Asia*, you will begin to think, is a widow's cruse, inexhaustible in its resources and reminiscensos.

I had intended visiting Plymouth on Saturday, but supposing there were plenty of trains, found only one suitable, 8 10 in the morning, and as I made the discovery at half-past eight, it was too late. I went off to Bunker's Hill, and passing the State prison in my way, applied for leave to visit it, which was granted, and a warder took me through. The system is a self-supporting one. The prisoners are not allowed to speak to each other; they wear a curious dress, half red, half white, like Touchstone's motley. Their labour is let out to contractors. Thus, a large upholsterer has made a contract with the state, he pays for each prisoner's labour from thirty-five to fifty-two cents per day, which pays for the prisoner's support; he finds tools, materials, power, and teachers, and keeps the prisoners busily employed in making chairs, tables, &c. Another set are engaged in shoemaking, another in brushmaking, another in the manufacture of whips, and sundry others in the various departments of smith work, and also in dressing stone. There is a good deal to be said on both sides of the question, and this system has some advantages. Their cells are very comfortless, merely a mattrass, no furniture. I saw the kitchen, and their food is decidedly inferior to ours, but they have as much black bread allowed them as they can eat.

Hence I made a painful pilgrimage to Bunker's Hill, and lamented to see a place where my country was defeated, though I more regretted the folly of stupid old George Rex and our Tory rulers. There is no shame from such a defeat,—the shame would have been in victory. The monument is an obelisk, quite plain, and no inscription to offend an Englishman. From here I went to the navy yard, and saw one of their fine new men-of-war, the *Roanoake*, built two years ago, and so rotten now they are cutting off her outside planking, I presume to put it all on again new. She has the dry rot in her timber; her armament is large; I saw all her guns on the wharf. I then got back into Boston, and saw and really walked through the Faneuil Hall Market, and thought of you. This reminds me that I omitted saying that I went into Faneuil Hall, the great focus of revolution. It was built and given to the town by Mr. Faneuil, a rich merchant; his picture is on one side, and Washington's on the other, of the platform.

On Thursday I went to Harvard, and presented my letter to the Professor Bond. His son shewed me the Observatory, which contains one of the most magnificent equatorials in the world, similar to the one at Pultowa, in Russia; he also showed me their mode of transit, observing of telegraphs, and was very polite indeed.

On Saturday, after dinner, I revisited Cambridge, and called on Mr. Longfellow, who resides at the house that was Washington's head quarters. Unfortunately Mr. Longfellow was not at home, so I went on a little farther, and visited the beautiful cemetery of Mount Auburn, filled with handsome monuments, a provincial Père la Chaise; all the tombs are white marble; I found Spurzheim's and Abbot Lawrence's—a cenotaph to Franklin, who was born at Boston. The ground undulates a great deal, and therefore the effect is more beautiful.

This morning I went to hear Theodore Parker; he lectured in the Music Hall, and I heard a splendid discourse. I presume he does not belong to any body of a sectarian character, but is more Unitarian than anything else. His sermon was from the text, " Glory to God in the highest, and on earth peace, goodwill toward men." He dwelt largely on the importance of education, and compared New England with South Carolina, visiting severely the sin of slave-holding. He divided his discourse into three true ideas in religion. First, the recognition of a higher law of action; second, the duties of charity; third, the importance of education. In some remarks on the Roman Catholic religion, and its contrast with the Protestant, he dwelt on the remaining feudalism in England, but still could not help calling it " that dear old island." The service commenced with a hymn, then a prayer, after which he read some scattered passages from the Bible, then a hymn, then his sermon, and I presume it lasted an hour, which appeared but as a few minutes; it seemed to be a written discourse, or, certainly, he had copious notes.

In the afternoon I went to the Melodeon to hear Mrs. Cora Hatch preach. I paid ten cents admission, 5d., and found myself one of a large audience. The service began by four women singing a hymn, and then Mrs. Cora Hatch stepped up to a desk. She is seventeen, and preaches or lectures on any subject at a moment's notice, by means of Spiritualism—that is to say, she is inspired, and the medium uses her tongue to utter its spiritual lessons to the world. She is a pale, flaxen-haired looking mortal ; and, folding her hands, in a rather agreeable tone of voice, began a prayer, and when that was ended, informed us that she should have preferred some of the audience to have given her a subject, but that her medium was not quite well. In the evening, however, at seven, a committee of the audience was to be appointed to fix on the subject. She would, therefore, preach " On the Internal and External Beauty," and commenced a flow of such rubbish as I think I never heard before ; not one single idea, but, no doubt, a great command of mere words. I thought of Dickens's description of a woman commencing an address to Martin Chuzzlewit, " Howls the sublime." She talked about *etarnal* melodies, and harmonies, and vibrations, and astronomy, geology, botany, painting, sculpture, everything. Her definition of beauty was very fine, "Beauty is that which strikes our minds and souls with *the* idea of the beautiful." Memory was *spontaneous*, and arose from spontaneity of nature, and so on. I thought it dear at five-pence. After she had finished, she regretted it was not so good, but her medium was ill, and folding her hands on her face, her husband took her in his arms, and replaced her on her seat, and then the four women howled another hymn, but I escaped before its completion, thoroughly well tired of Spiritualism. I wish Plymouth was done, and as it is a day's affair to see a bit of rock the Pilgrim Fathers landed on, I almost think I shall shirk it, having so much more of importance to see here; and now my time draws on apace. We have changeable weather: last evening Nowlan and I sat in the hotel porch till after nine, quite warm; to-day, a Scotch mist, damp and cold.

I had no idea that Boston would have taken so much time to see properly. There, I must stop; I have been writing over three hours. I am glad to have so much information, and documents, from which I can fully inform myself on the education question. Of course I do not fill up my letters, as I could easily do, with an account of school organization, and so forth, that would not interest you, but rather give a sketch of what I have seen. Had it not been for the Mayor's great kindness, I could not have seen or learned so much as I have.

MONDAY.—This morning I have been to Lawrence, but really that is all, the mills are all standing. Not meeting with Mr. Lawrence, according to promise, I could not see what I wished—it is all coarse work, and I can see just the same at home. The rooms are beautifully clean, and are arranged more like show places than real hardworking shops.   *   *   *   *

PHILADELPHIA,

November 16th, 1857.

MY DEAR MAMMA,

MY letter by the *Persia* would inform you of my proceedings up to Monday. Last Tuesday the Mayor of Boston almost entirely devoted to me. We visited the House of Correction, and the City Lunatic Asylum, both well-conducted establishments. In the latter I saw one poor old woman, who believed herself to be the Queen of England, Queen Joanna, married to Charlemagne, who resided in Boston. I never visited a mad-house before, and was most painfully impressed with poor humanity divested of the godlike power of reason. The patients are kept clean, and, with some few exceptions, have little restraint. The

House of Correction is on the same principle as
the State prison, namely, the remunerative labour
system. The Mayor gave me a number of addi-
tional documents he obtained from the Governor
for me, and begged my acceptance of a large
handsome volume, containing an account of the
proceedings connected with the inauguration of
the fine statue of Franklin, which stands behind
the State House, in Boston. I then dined with
the Mayor, at Parker's *restaurant*, and attended a
meeting of the Public School Committee, and had
an opportunity of seeing how their public business
is conducted.

Mr. Rice gave me a kind and special letter of
introduction to Mr. Vaux, the Mayor of Philadelphia, and then, with deep regret, I said good
bye, and expressed my sincere gratitude for all his
kindness.

Wednesday, I returned by rail to New York, and
went to my old quarters at the Metropolitan, where,
and here at the Girard House, I feel quite at home.
My darkies welcomed me, and I had the same
rooms again. Did not stir out of the hotel that
evening, being thoroughly well tired.

Thursday, I was very busy all day; bought a new
trunk, which I completely filled. The operation
took me some time. The spare trunk I left at the
hotel, in the baggage room. They will take care
of anything for me, which saves me a deal of
trouble.

The *Arabia* having arrived, I went on Friday morning to see if Mr. Robert Gourdin had come, but did not meet with him. I met a newspaper boy, "Want an extra, Sir; *Arabia's* news?" I said "No," but casting my eyes on the paper, I saw "Capture of Delhi!" I seized the lad by the arm. "Give me that paper," and then I gave a shout, I could not have kept it in for the life of me. Here the people rejoice just as much as though it were a pure American victory.

On Saturday morning I called upon the Mayor of Philadelphia; he was not in. When I returned to the hotel I found a card from Mr. C——; he called three times on that day, and again on Sunday morning, very early. I did not see him, but called up about one, and found it was ————'s brother, who had seen my name in the list of arrivals at the Girard, and called upon me. He has been ten years in America, and was glad to see some one who knew Manchester. I then went to the club, and left a letter of introduction to Mr. Barclay, from whom, in the evening, I received a circular, telling me my name was down at the club, and inviting me to use it whilst in town, the invitation being good for a month. On Sunday evening I went to C——'s rooms; he lives at a boarding house, and I was glad to see what they were like, and had tea with him and the rest of the inmates.   *   *   *   *

This morning I called upon the Mayor, and had a long chat with him, "*he will put me through, and*

s

show me the elephants" (these are genuine Yankee phrases). He calls for me in the morning at nine, and will give some time to me each day. I then called upon Mr. Gilpin, Mr. Ashworth's friend; I was shown into a large and splendid library, and found Mr. Gilpin, who was (but really it is one story, and I can only keep repeating it over and over again) very kind and cordial. He was Attorney General during Van Buren's Presidency. I do believe I shall have as many friends on this side of the Atlantic as I have at home.

Philadelphia is laid out perfectly square, and the streets contain some very handsome marble buildings; white marble is used in profusion. Not far from the hotel, which is a most perfectly conducted establishment, there is a pretty square, like ours in London, (called parks in this country), which is overrun with tame squirrels, that will feed out of your hands, and run up your body to get a bit to eat; I never saw such pretty little creatures. The old State House, in which the Declaration of Independence was signed, still stands in the same street in which the Girard House is situated, Chestnut street. As I told you of Cincinnati, the streets from the river are named after trees, and the cross streets by numbers. To-morrow I begin my proper sight-seeing, under mayoral superintendence. The weather keeps unsettled; rather cold on Saturday, and yesterday quite a frost. I was amused at your idea that I must rest a week at New York. Please

how am I to get along, if I rest a week at a time?
I have a long journey before me, from here to
Charleston : I shall break it at Baltimore, Washington, Richmond, and then there is a long, hard pull
to Charleston. I can assure you of one thing,
I am getting more and more pleased with America
every day. I said in a former letter I might contradict myself sometimes; let that be so, but a
correct opinion is, and must be, a corrected one.
At first one's information is limited; gradually
extending, fresh facts come to your knowledge, and
enable you to correct previous opinions; and so,
by a slow, but certain chain of circumstances, you
may eliminate opinions that will serve for your own
satisfaction, and stand the test of trial. * * *

GIRARD HOUSE, PHILADELPHIA,

November 20th, 1857.

MY DEAR MAMMA,

AT dinner I was called out by my friend
Chadwick to see Mr. Barclay, who had come to the
hotel to see me. I found him a kindly looking old
gentleman ; he had called to become personally
acquainted with me, and to invite me to dine at the

Club Dinner on Tuesday, to meet some dozen who dine together now and then and ask a friend, not unlike our own club, the difference being that the hour is four. At night it rained in torrents, but C—— and his young friend came down to see me and have a chat; they sat till about nine. * * *

On Tuesday morning the Mayor called upon me, and gave me some letters of introduction to the Principals of the Girard College and the High School. I went first to the Girard College, but Professor Allen, the President, was not in, so deferred visiting the Institution until I could meet with him. I went thence to the High School, where the Head Master, Dr. Hart, showed me the working of one of the best collegiate academies I ever saw. I staid till after two o'clock, and then walked about the town until time to return to the hotel, and dress for dinner. On entering the hall I met Mr. Gilpin, who had very kindly called and brought a note to leave in case I should be out, asking me to take tea, and spend Wednesday evening at his house, which invitation I most gladly accepted. He also said he would send me some letters to people in the town, who could assist me in seeing the different places in which I felt an interest. I then dressed, and went to the club, where I found Mr. Barclay waiting for me, and going up stairs we entered the dining room, and found I made the twelfth when all had assembled. I was introduced to each one,—— the English Consul among the number,——we sat down to dinner. We had first, oysters in the shell; but I don't remember whether I have said anything about American oysters: they are an uncommon size, and have a most delicate flavour, I think far superior to ours;—then white soup, and a long pause which we occupied with eating celery, and drinking most excellent wine,—Madeira and Sherry. Then came four dishes, each containing a pair of real—what? canvass back ducks. I cannot describe them; no poet in his highest imaginative flight ever reached so high; delicious creatures, done not to ——'s taste, but to mine; the gravy just following the knife. I thought what would Sir J—— or Mr. —— have done, had such a treat been theirs? Well, you did not eat them; there was no occasion for the ordinary human process of mastication and deglutition, — they just melted and disappeared. The four pair left but a few bony relics behind, to show that something had been that was not; another pause,—and Mr. Barclay said "some more hot ducks coming," and some three more pair came, just from the fire, and shared the fate of their predecessors. I felt ashamed to eat more, but I said, apologetically, " I never tasted them before," and the whole party looked on me with deep fatherly interest, perhaps longing for so new a sensation, and assured me I might eat till I felt the meat as high as my throat. Still though it seemed to me that the quantity I consumed was large, I was only on about a par with the rest.

The dinner concluded with a dozen woodcocks, one for each, and so they disappeared. No sweets,—no pudding, but some good Champagne, and excellent Hock. I can honestly say, I never enjoyed the mere animal gastronomic part of a dinner so much before. The flavour of the canvass back is derived from the wild celery on which they feed at this season, and they are only met with in the Chesapeake Bay.

They were all cultivated men, and decidedly English in their predilections, and the most Tory or Conservative set I have met on this side. All had, I think, been in England, and liked to talk about the old country and its associations; we smoked our cigars, and about ten I went home, well pleased with my evening, and gratified with the cordial and hospitable manner in which I had been treated.

On Wednesday, I called on the Mayor; he has not so much time on his hands as my good friend Mr. Rice, having more onerous duties, but gives me as much as he can. I then went to the Board of Controllers of Public Schools, and had a long conversation with the Secretary, and one of the Board. They have sent me a large number of reports and books, as well as some of the various forms for carrying on their school management.

I then visited the Normal School, for the instruction of teachers, with which I was very much pleased, and then went to the Refuge for Criminals and Neglected Children. This institution is of a valuable character, but I do not approve of the arrangement and management; the children are mixed together, and the already vicious have the power to contaminate the others; they work at trades, as in the Boston prisons, and are locked up at night in cells, arranged the same in construction as those in our jail. This terminated my day's work. I dined, as usual, at the ladies' ordinary, at four o'clock, which is an excellent *table d'hôte*.

In the evening I went to Mr. Gilpin's, and was introduced to the family, also to a lady whose sister married Colonel Fremont, so well known in connection with California, and who was a candidate for the Presidency, at the last election, in opposition to Mr. Buchanan. Major Wagner, of the United States army, should have been there; he has been engaged in an interesting experiment for the government, in bringing over camels from the East, and trying, I understand with success, to introduce their use on the prairies; also a Professor Bache, the head of the United States' survey department, the President's physician, and many others. I had a deal of talk with Mrs. Fremont's sister, and I am to have a letter to her father; they are a Virginian family, most bitter against Mrs. Stowe, who, I find, does not occupy any position in American society, and is considered exactly what I judged her to be, a vulgar, vain, strong-minded woman. *   *   *   *

The whole of the party consisted of most highly cultivated, refined, and intelligent people, giving me an elevated idea of the best American society, which, in Philadelphia, is always to be met with at Mr. Gilpin's. I was treated with the greatest kindness, and assure you I spent a most delightful evening. Mr. Gilpin is going to give me a letter to the President, and I do think has taken a bit of a fancy to me; to Mr. Ashworth I am indebted for so valuable an introduction. The next day Major Wagner left his card for me, and I found one from Newhall, who crossed with me; (*Asia* again !)

On Thursday morning I went to see the Mayor, and sat in his office a couple of hours talking politics; he is a regular politician, was secretary of legation in London before he was twenty, was Recorder of Philadelphia seven years, and has been Mayor two; he is in his forty-sixth year. He made as short work of his business yesterday as he could, as he intended to devote the rest of it to me, and so we went first to the Old Independence Hall, where the Declaration was signed, in which there are some relics of those most interesting days; the large bell is there, which tolled out the announcement to the people that the Convention had agreed to the Declaration. Then we proceeded in Mr. Vaux's buggy, which is a light, four-wheeled gig, drawn by two fast-trotting horses, to the Penitentiary, a large jail, on the solitary and separate system, in which the prisoners never can see each other; they work in their cells; and have each a small exercising yard, one to each cell. On Sundays the cell doors are partly opened, perhaps six inches, and so fastened, each opening towards the centre, and a minister stands in the gallery and conducts a service, which, I was told, could be heard distinctly by each prisoner.

As a visitor with the Mayor, who is the President of the Jail Commission, I was permitted to go about as I pleased, and open the cell doors, and ask the prisoners anything I liked. I talked to one who had been ten years there, and had two more to remain, being sentenced for burglary and arson. I dare say I spoke to twenty. I found two darkies in one cell, and I said "what are you boys here for?" at which they grinned and showed their white teeth. "Well, Massa, I spec we're in for manslaughter!" whereupon I left them to their work again. I do not know why the two were together, but I fancy they don't mind the niggers so much, although in the Refuge I could see no difference in their treatment from the white boys, except that they were in a separate building.* I staid as long as I could decently keep the Mayor, perhaps two hours, and came away quite convinced that my views of the Refuge were correct, from the fact that so large a number of its inmates find their way to prison. Of the prisoners only ten per

* On after onquiry, I find it is done sometimes by order of the Medical Supervisors, but only for medical reasons.

cent. ever return on their hands, which is a satisfactory result of the system.

The Mayor then drove me about twelve miles, passing over the Schuylkill river twice; once on a suspension, and secondly on a railway and road bridge, the railway being the one I had come over from Pittsburg. Returning from the West, we went nearly to the junction of the Schuylkill with the Delaware, and then drove through what Mr. Vaux called the worst part of the town, where the negroes and Irish live pigging together, which I suppose accounts for the number of mulatto children. He said he was determined I should see all parts of the town, and not go away with the idea that the aristocratic quarters were all Philadelphia. He told me that the municipal arrangements have been recently altered, and the whole district consolidated, so that the town contains nearly 200 square miles,—of course not all built upon. I am going with him again on Sunday, and go to his house; to-morrow evening I accompany him to the Whister Party, which is a species of club, meeting at the houses of the members alternately, so called from his great uncle, who was an eminent physician in large practice, and having only Sunday evening at liberty, expected his friends to come to him then; since his death it has been kept up. It is held at Governor Coles's house on Saturday: he was the first Governor of Illinois, when it was formed into a State.

I was very much pleased with my ride, and all

the information I obtained. The Mayor is quite
independent of the Council, does not sit with them,
is elected by the people, and has a veto power on
the ordinance of the council, unless there has been
a clear majority of two-thirds, then the ordinance
is put in force in spite of the veto. At night it
began to sleet, and snow, and freeze most keenly,
and to-day has been bitter cold. Newhall called
again this morning; I went with him to their
large sugar refinery, and saw the process of purify-
ing the dark sugar that is brought from Cuba;
they use charcoal made from animal bones. I
saw all the kinds, white and brown, and the
intermediate kinds; they cast some sugar loaves,
to show me, and the mode of drawing off the
treacle and golden syrup. In their office he
introduced me to his father, and a Mr. R——,
from Manchester, who said he knew my father.
Newhall then showed me some of the business
parts of the town, and will fetch me in the morning
for a drive. Afterwards I visited the Girard College,
and President Allen took me through the institution. It is founded for fatherless boys. The central
building is a fine white marble copy of the Made-
line, and contains the school, and so forth, and
in two buildings of white marble on each side are
the offices, teachers' houses, and boys' living rooms.
Of course you know it was founded by Stephen
Girard, and by his will no minister of any deno-
mination may ever set foot within its walls, even

as a visitor, so afraid was he of spiritual tyranny and domination.

After my return from the club last night, whom should I meet at the hotel but my St. Paul friend, B. W—— D——, who was delighted to see me. He was on his way to New York, but should be at home in Baltimore about Sunday. He will give me some shooting of canvass backs, wild geese and swans, in the Chesapeake. I was considerably amused at the idea. Then I am to see his fast-trotting horses, and all the rest. He is a strange mortal.

I think I predicted in one of my letters that the Bank discount would be up to nine or ten per cent., they did not know how bad things really were on this side. The news of the *Arabia* improved the tone here very much, but as I said, Delhi won't pay American debts; still things are decidedly on the improvement, and if there be no further bad news from Europe will rapidly progress to a sounder state; such is the expansive power of this country and its unequalled elasticity, it is rich in everything, and has been only too rich in speculation. * * *

SUNDAY.

FIRST let me say I duly received your letters. I was sure the Cave would interest you very much, but no description is equal to giving a proper idea of its magnitude and wonders. * * *

MONDAY, 23rd.

IN conversation with Mr. Gilpin the other day,
I found that the Professor Bache I met at his house,
is a grandson of Benjamin Franklin's; and an
extremely nice young fellow, living where C——
boards, named Dallas Bache, is a great grandson
of the same illustrious man.

I told Mr. Gilpin I thought I should tire him
with so many questions; he said, " Oh dear, no!
ask me anything you wish to know. I like to be
questioned, and some years ago, a good many now,
a friend of mine used to come every morning with
a string of questions written down, and catechize
me upon them, and that friend was De Tocqueville."
Mr. Gilpin speaks exactly like Mr. Newman, is full
of information, an excellent classic, and in all
respects a most admirable and instructive friend.

On Saturday evening I went with the Mayor to
Governor Coles's, to the Whister party, and met a
large number of gentlemen, including the Bishop,
the Judges, several Colonels, Professors, and so
forth, to most of whom I was introduced, and spent
a very agreeable evening. We had a stand-up
supper, the rule being that no member must give
any dish that requires a knife, to keep them from
needless expense and rivalry in their entertain-
ments. Governor Coles was secretary to Jefferson

at the time of the treaty of Ghent. On Sunday morning the Mayor called for me at the hotel, with his buggy, and drove me at once to see the vicinity of the city. We started at eleven, and went as far as Chestnut Hill, passing by the scenes of some of the battles of the revolution, where we got licked. From Chestnut Hill we had a splendid view over a wide extent of country, terminating in the skirts of the Alleghanies, which I crossed coming from the west. The day was lovely, cool, not unlike a bright Christmas-day—the night before, it was snowing when we left Governor Coles's, and whilst I am writing now it is warm, and rains fast,—so variable is this most extraordinary climate.

The Mayor showed me many splendid houses by the road side, and beguiled the way with an account of his London adventures. He was Secretary of Legation, under Stevenson, at the time of the Queen's coronation, and was present at the ceremony. We got back at two o'clock, to dinner, after a drive of thirty-nine miles.

After dinner, the Mayor showed me several interesting relics which had belonged to Penn: his family came over with Penn. * *   I left between seven and eight, and went to Mr. Gilpin's, where I found a good many people calling, as it is understood they are at home on Sunday evening. I staid till after ten, discussing many things, and then I went to C——'s.

This morning, by appointment with Colonel

Snowdon, the Director of the Mint of the United States, which is in Philadelphia, I visited this interesting establishment, and was shown all over it by the Colonel himself; I met him at Governor Coles's. I never saw money coined before; the whole process was shown me, from casting the ingots to the final counting of the finished coin— both gold and silver. Unfortunately I could not bring any of the specimens of this manufacture away with me.

Afterwards I went to the hotel, and met Mr. Warde, the Curator of the Historical Society, who called on me by appointment. I met him at Mr. Gilpin's. He took me first to the Philosophical Society, where he showed me the original draft of the Declaration of Independence, in the handwriting of Jefferson, with all the erasures and corrections, and the clause about slavery, which was struck out when the full and perfect deed was drawn up. I looked at it with much interest, as it no doubt is the only document of such a nature in the world, not only existing, but that ever did exist, for nations were not originally founded by the drawing up of an unanswerable paper of this kind, which at once produced a powerful people, and a complete constitution and perfect form of government. Thence we went to the Public Library, where they have four volumes of James the First's letters and papers, relating principally to Irish affairs, all in manuscript, with Jemmy's signature. I thought how papa would have looked at it, and chuckled inwardly while so doing.

After this we visited the Historical Society's rooms. They have a portrait of Penn, in armour, and have just had given them by Mr. Granville Penn the original wampum belt which the Indians gave Penn in exchange for the treaty by which Pennsylvania was founded; it consists of eighteen rows of white beads, with three black beads running obliquely across, and in the centre, in black beads, a figure of an Indian, holding by the hand a stout man, with a broad-brimmed hat, meant, of course, to represent Penn himself; it is a singular piece of work, and really the title of the people to the State of Pennsylvania. They have also Penn's razor and shaving bowl. I scraped my chin with the razor, much to Mr. Warde's amusement. They have a ring with his hair in it, and also another relic of interest, Franklin's reading magnifying glass.

I then called upon the Mayor at his house, but he was out, so left my card; also left a note at the club for Mr. Barclay, and then went to say good bye to Mr. Gilpin; he has done everything possible for me, and just sent some letters to the President, Colonel Bealer, Senator Douglas, and the Judge of the Supreme Court,—also to Baltimore, New Orleans. He has given me some pamphlets, and some in charge for Mr. Ashworth, Mr. Cobden, and Mr. Bright; two of the pamphlets

I have received, are copies of addresses delivered by Mr. Gilpin on " The American Missionaries in Greece," where he has travelled a good deal, and another on " The Character of Franklin."

Now have I not been kindly treated, and do you wonder at my liking America? At first I did not understand the people, but I have had so many opportunities for information, that I have seen reason partly to modify my first impressions, and I feel every day more satisfied with the course I took at the last election. It was painful to oppose a friend, but there are duties in life far higher than mere personal likes and dislikes; and there are great principles, which I felt must be maintained at all hazards, and under all circumstances, and I hope, wherever I see the finger of honest conviction pointing, that I shall never swerve from that course for any considerations whatever. * * There is much to find fault with, no doubt, but for the most part the evils result from that reckless spirit which is fostered by a love of adventure and change, and in the eastern cities from the large influx of our own ignorant emigrants.

I miss Rotherham very much, and should have done so still more had I not met with such kind friends. Tell Lawrence I want him just to come over and straighten my trunks; their present condition is not bad, but the ties and stockings are mixed up in most inextricable confusion; can't tell which is which. *   *   *   *

T

BALTIMORE,

November 27th, 1857.

MY DEAR MAMMA,

ON Tuesday morning, after my packing-up labour, I called on my kind friend, the Mayor, and sat with him as long as I could, thanked him for all his kindness to me, and expressed my hope of seeing him in England. He said he should be glad to see me anywhere; and when we parted he said, " God bless you!" He is a fine, genuine-hearted fellow; and had I known him twenty years, he could not have treated me better: C—— came to the station to see me off, and I really left Philadelphia with much regret. The railway is interrupted at one point in passing the river Susquehanna. We left the cars, and went over on a very curious steam-boat, on the top deck of which were two or three lines of rails, for the mail and baggage wagons, which are thus taken over without being unpacked: afterwards we skirted the Chesapeake Bay, and arrived about five at Baltimore,—ninety-nine miles in four hours. I drove direct to Barnum's. After tea, who should I meet but H—— P—— and W. J. H——, just arrived from Washington: they have been much the same route, including St. Paul's. I noticed a person walking backwards and forwards for some time after H—— and P—— left me. He came to me, and said, "I think you are Mr. Nicholls, of Manchester." I looked at him, and found it was Blakeway, a friend of mine, Sebastian Bazley's, and George Ashworth's; he had just come from South America. I had not seen him for four years;—a most extraordinary meeting. (Am I not an extraordinary person for meeting friends everywhere?) Well, we talked till late, and I happened to say, "I have some introductions in Baltimore," and showed him my letters. He was very glad to find I had one to Mr. Latrobe (it was from Mr. Gilpin); he knew the family most intimately. Mr. Latrobe is an eminent lawyer here, and is at present in Europe.

On Wednesday morning we called on Ferdinand Latrobe, and I found him one of the finest young men I ever met. He said at once, "You must come out to our country house this evening, and spend it with us." We then called on his brother Osman, who repeated the invitation, and fixed for us to dine with him, at half-past two, and go with them to Fairy Knowe. Whilst talking, Mrs. Latrobe came, and kindly seconded her son's invitation, and invited us to spend Saturday and Sunday with them, which we were glad to do. She then said good bye, but returned in a few minutes to say that her friend, who was in the carriage at the door, wished us to dine at her house the day following, being Thanksgiving Day, the one great family holiday in America, which invitation we also accepted. At half-past two we met again; and, after dining on canvass-back ducks, we took the train, and went out to Fairy Knowe, which is a handsome country house, situated, as its name imports, on an elevation, overlooking a fine extent of country. * * * * The night was intensely cold; but good fires in all parts of the house, kept us warm;—a dry still cold we never feel in England, but which makes all metal-work stick to your hand as though it were red hot;—bright moon and glittering stars; no wind, and the temperature near zero !

Next day, about noon, we returned to Baltimore, and walked about the town, which they were anxious to show me. Baltimore is not so handsome as Philadelphia, but contains some splendid houses, particularly about Monument Square, in the centre of which is a handsome white marble column, with a statue of Washington on the top. We then dressed, and went to dine at Mr. Winan's. On Thanksgiving Day people expect their friends to visit them almost uninvited.

We staid till after midnight, and arranged to call to-day to see the studio, in which Mr. Winan takes great delight, being himself an excellent artist. Mrs. Latrobe has been very kind to me, and is giving me a letter to her brother, who is a large planter, on the Mississippi. She told me frankly she knew only of one difficulty in my going there, and that was to get away again. The more South I go, the kinder and more hospitable people are. They are anxious that I should become acquainted with the Baltimore families, in order that I may see Mrs. Stowe is not a real specimen of American ladies. They quite hate her name, and declare her statements are untrue; she has never even been in a slave state. Mr. Latrobe is President of the Liberian Emigration Society. I told Ferdinand of my meeting the returned darkies in the stage, and how well they were doing there, which he was glad to hear. So far from taking offence at any discussion on the slavery question they introduce it themselves, admit its evils, but do not see how any one can point out, at present, the proper remedy.

I have just received a letter from Rotherham, who sailed on Wednesday. I was sorry to part with the lad, for he has a most affectionate disposition, and was excellent company for me, when I should have been very lonely in that western country. There is only one part of my letter to the "Guardian" I wish I could alter, and that is to express more strongly the good feeling of Americans for everything English, and their kindness to Englishmen. I could never have anticipated such kindness from perfect strangers.

SATURDAY.

JUST received your letter. I did hope the *Africa* would have beaten the *Vanderbilt*, but her news was telegraphed from Cape Race, and so anticipated the *Africa's*. Mr. Gourdin has no need to fear my not liking both American *fair* and *fare*—good Mr. Bazley's joke. You must remember me to him, and say I had a good laugh at both the jokes, and rather expect I shall have to knock under to his puns when I get home again.

Congress meets on Monday next, the 7th of December, and I expect to be in Washington this time next week.

———————

BALTIMORE,

December 2nd, 1857.

MY DEAR MAMMA,

I BELIEVE it was last Friday that I completed and despatched a letter, but the days pass away so rapidly that I can hardly keep them in mind, for I am going through a perfect round of hospitality of every kind. A few weeks ago I felt much regret that Congress did not meet till the first Monday in the month, which left me a week that I thought I should have some difficulty in filling up. Instead of that being the case, I find the period only comes too soon, as I might stay here a month, and have more invitations than I should know what to do with.

On Saturday afternoon we went to Fairy Knowe, and remained until Monday morning. Saturday evening was spent very pleasantly; there was a large party staying in the house, and after supper the slave lad brought in his banjo, and played some plaintive negro songs.

Sunday was a magnificent day, as bright as the finest summer weather, without its heat. We took a walk, and then went to their private gas works for the house, which is lighted all through with gas made on the premises. In the evening we had a stroll, by the light of a splendid moon, through the grounds, as they wanted me to see a good view of the Railway Viaduct, by the quiet light of the moon. We returned to Baltimore on Monday morning.

WASHINGTON, FRIDAY EVENING.

I WROTE so far at Baltimore, but having a quiet evening, I wish to spend it in the way most agreeable to myself, that is, *chatting with you.*

On Saturday, I gave Ferdinand one of the copies of my letter to the "Guardian" that you sent me. He considered it to be a perfectly correct account of the causes that have induced so much disaster in the States, and he was also gratified with the remarks at the end, relative to the feelings between the two countries, and the expression I had given to them, as an Englishman. On Monday morning I called at a Mr. Webster's office, who is Mr. R——D——'s lawyer, and there I found the gentleman himself, whom I at once recognised by his likeness to Mr. Denison, whom he resembles somewhat in appearance, but most particularly so in the tone of his voice and laugh. He was very glad to see me; we went to his club, which I had an invitation to use as long as I remained in town. Mr. R——D—— said candidly he did nothing, lived quietly some miles from Baltimore, and never liked the idea of work in his life. He asked me to go out with him that evening or the next; but on the Tuesday I was already engaged, and it so happened there was an invitation from a committee of a new club, just established, to the members of the old and their friends, to take supper at the house-warming of the new establishment that evening. I saw by the twinkle of his eyes he wanted to go, and he asked me if I should like it? I told him I should, and that as I considered him as an old friend, I should also like my friend Blakeway to go with me. He jumped at it at once, and as we

took a walk together, we met Blakeway; I introduced them, and the matter was immediately
arranged. I had seen, at Mr. Webster's office, a
Mr. Birkhead, who married a cousin of Mr. R——
D——. We had promised to take tea with him before
going to the club, so in the evening we went to Mr.
Birkhead's, who was also a friend of Blakeway's.

About nine we went to the club, where I was
introduced to more people than I can remember,
but still they all remembered me. We had an
excellent supper, and made acquaintance for the
first time with terrapins—small land turtle, most
delicious eating—a kind of cross between turtle
soup and turtle fins. We had apple toddy, unlimited whiskey punch, and cigars. A Mr. Smith
talked to me a long time; he had been over to
England, had gone with endless prejudices about
the country and people; was perfectly astonished
to find all his pre-conceived notions false; was
treated with the greatest kindness, and makes it a
point to show his appreciation of England by
paying every attention to the English he meets in
America. We thought to leave about eleven, but
found Mr. D—— in a lower room (we had supper
up stairs), and in company with some twenty men,
to whom I was formally introduced, drinking toddy,
and getting decidedly drunk (I shirked the drink,
and enjoyed the scene). They sang and joked, and
when they all got to putting their hats on the floor,
and sitting down upon them, between one and

two, we thought it about time to disappear. They had locked the doors to keep us there, but we slipped down some stairs into the kitchen, and up some others into the area, and so got out. We thought Mr. D—— would have gone away then, but, no thank you, he returned to the revels within. It was a wet night; we got home much amused with the variety we had seen there. I cannot say that there is much to see in Baltimore, but I had every opportunity of seeing their social life, of which I was very glad. I generally spend two or three hours every day with Ferdinand Latrobe, who is an extremely intelligent fellow.

On Tuesday evening we dined at Mr. Thomas's, a cousin of Blakeway's. Osman Latrobe drove out home, but Ferdinand came with us, and staid at the hotel. Mrs. Latrobe asked me to spend one more evening at Fairy Knowe; it was to have been Wednesday, but as we were dining with ——, and Mrs. Winan had invited us to come to a small dance at her house in the evening, we fixed Thursday night, my last in Baltimore.

On Wednesday, Mr. D—— and I had a long walk about the town; he is quite a middle-aged beau, an old bachelor. We made some calls on friends of his, and as he has a large acquaintance, my introductions were pretty numerous. In the evening we dined at Mr. ——'s, and had a pleasant party, some ten ladies and gentlemen, the former all great talkers, one a rich young widow on whom I

think Mr. D—— cast tender glances, a Mrs. ——,
with 150,000 dollars. After dinner they were all
going to a concert. Blakeway and I went to Mrs.
Winan's, where we found a small party dancing,—
so ending the day very pleasantly.

On Thursday afternoon, after packing up, always
a sad bore, I went out by the cars to Fairy Knowe,
and spent a most agreeable evening; some of the
young ladies came out also, a coloured fiddler was
found, and some little dancing varied our amuse-
ments. The days were splendid, the nights lovely,
the moon clear and bright,—and as I went to bed
last night, I opened the casement and looked out
over the wooded hills, and the dancing waters of
the river Patapsco, above which the house almost
hangs, and thought how the same clear light had a
few hours before shone on my own dear home.
This weather is the Indian summer.

They were all sorry to part with me this morning, but I have promised on my way home, to go
straight to their house, and stay two or three days
with them. Now, my dear Mamma, can you wonder
if I left Baltimore with real regret? I told them I
felt as if I had known them twenty years.

I left at half-past ten for Washington, and I
could not help casting a lingering look at Fairy
Knowe, as our train passed it. I arrived soon
after five, and found the hotel crammed. I
had written for a room, and so got one, but pretty
high up in the world. The place is crowded with

people attracted by Congress. I can hear them on all sides, discussing the merits of the various candidates for the innumerable offices connected with the Chambers. I forgot to say that there is a Mr. Buonaparte, son of Jerome, residing at Baltimore, married to Miss Patterson. He was away from home, so I did not meet him; but I was told his facial likeness to the First Napoleon was wonderful. He leads a very quiet life. It must seem strange to you when you read this letter, to see names of persons you never heard of in this world before, mentioned so familiarly by me; but as they interest me, I know they will you.

SUNDAY.

A WET, miserable, soaking day, in the house all the time.

Yesterday morning, I went out to find and present my letter to Lord Napier, and on leaving the hotel found myself in a vast wide street, called Pennsylvania Avenue, which comes from the Capitol to the Treasury, almost straight, and then turns round and passes the White House, the residence of the President. The houses are poor on each side, and the immense width of the street makes them appear still shabbier. Washington is called the " City of Magnificent Distances," which fact is strongly impressed upon you in walking about, for the distances are indeed immense. The Treasury is a splendid marble edifice, with a row of imposing columns in front. The President's house is also marble.

I found Lord Napier's house in H. Street, a large, but not particularly handsome-looking place. Several people were calling, and the servant said his Lordship could not see any one but diplomatic people that day. However, I gave him the letter, and my card, and said it was a letter of introduction from Lord Stanley, so he showed me into a small waiting room, and said his Excellency would be with me immediately. Lord Napier then came in; he is a very good-looking man, most courteous in his behaviour. We had a longish chat. I told him I had been interested in the educational institutions, about which he asked me a good deal, and said he and Lady Napier were disengaged that evening, and were dining quite alone, and he should be glad, if I had no engagement, if I would dine with them, which invitation I accepted. I told his Lordship I had letters to the President, but did not know the most proper manner of presenting them. He laughed, and said they were so very unceremonious about it here that he hardly knew himself, but would write to the President's Private Secretary, and enquire; but told me in the meantime to leave my letters and card at the White House; so on my way back I called there,

where I found a great many people going in, to see
the President, and gave my letters and card to the
servant, or gentleman, at the door, as he would
expect to be called. He told me to go right up,
but I declined for the present. I then walked
through the Patent Office; I mean to go thoroughly
through it, and will say then what it is. Thence
to the Capitol, which is really a magnificent building of white marble, but still unfinished; they are
erecting an immense dome on the top. I went
into the Chambers of Representatives and Senators,
which are quite handsome rooms. They are pre-
paring a new room for the meeting of Representatives, which is gaudy, ugly, and in bad taste, quite
unworthy of the building it is in.

In looking over the register of names at the
hotel, I found that the Hon. Mr. Miles, Senator for
South Carolina, was there, so sent my letters
and card up to him. Soon after, Blakeway came,
I had succeeded in keeping him a room. I then
dressed and called on Mr. Miles, whom I found a
youngish, most agreeable, and gentlemanly man.

I then set off to the British Embassy. I should
have said, as I left in the morning, Lord Napier
introduced me to Lady Napier.

The only guests at dinner were a Mr. Manly and
myself. Lady Napier is a very pleasant person,
not absolutely handsome, but good features. She
gave me a great deal of information respecting the
social manner of life amongst the American ladies.

Lord Napier told me they always received on a Tuesday evening, and should be glad to see me.

I left about a quarter to ten, having spent a very pleasant evening; Blakeway was waiting for me, and we had a chat and a cigar before going to bed. I am quite well now, so you need not be anxious; shall decide about my trip to the Havanna at Charleston, taking advice there upon the subject. If I don't go to Cuba, I shall always regret it, since I shall never retrace my steps in this country again, in all human probability.

By the bye, I forgot to tell you that by Western and Kentucky law I am a Colonel, because I have killed a rattlesnake.—I had written so far when Mr. Miles came into my room, as we had agreed to dine together; he asked me to call with him on one of his colleagues, Colonel Orr, who is to be Speaker of the House, it having been agreed upon at a democratic caucus held on Saturday evening, at which 114 members were present, so that it may be considered decided upon.

In Colonel Orr's room I was introduced to General Bonhem, another South Carolinian, and the successor of the Mr. Brooks who assaulted Sumner, and several others. I intend to go to the House this morning, but I do not suppose much of interest will be going on, as no real business is done till after January. There is no Directory published, so that I have great difficulty in finding out the people my letters are directed to. * * *

WASHINGTON,

December 11*th*, 1857.

MY DEAR MAMMA,

My time has been so much occupied whilst in the American capital, that I have not really been able to sit down and write a line in advance, and as the steamer sails next from Boston, I am anxious not to miss a post, lest you should be at all uneasy on my account. I expect to have time at Richmond to write up all my Washington experiences, which I cannot do to-night; it is now near nine, and I start at five in the morning for Richmond. I have been dining with the Speaker, and a number of members of Congress. I told you in my last that Colonel Orr was to be Speaker, and he was duly elected on Monday, and I was present in the House at the time. I sent Papa a copy of the President's Message, so that he might read the financial statement for himself, in full.

Mr. Miles has just been with some letters for me; he is a very fine fellow, and has been a very kind friend to me. The weather has been most charming all the week; a heavy storm on Wednesday night, but quite late in the night only; not cold nor hot since the storm. Last Monday was most oppressive, like an August day in England. The sky is clear and bright, with an Italian look and effect, so that I really believe we have now the true Indian summer, though late. The nights are frosty, and the air pure, clear, and bracing. I feel its effects immediately, and never felt better in my whole life.

I have not presented all my letters here. I had not time to do so, and saw no especial advantage in it after I knew sufficient people to get along with comfortably, which you will trust me for doing, I know. I shall not apologise for so short a note, as you know the reason of its being so ; *and you have told me not to write too much.*

BALLARD'S HOTEL, RICHMOND, VIRGINIA,

December 12th, 1857.

MY DEAR MAMMA,

INSTEAD of the dreadfully shabby letter I sent you last, I must now endeavour to give you some proper account of my doings in Washington, and first, before stating what I did, I will tell you whom I have met. First stands Mr. Miles, a perfect Carolinian gentleman, a man of first-rate

W

education; was Professor of Mathematics in the University of South Carolina, and invited to be its President, but declined the office; was then elected Mayor of Charleston; and now makes his first appearance in Congress. He introduced me to his five colleagues—Colonel Orr, the new Speaker; General Bonham, Colonel Keitt, General M'Queen, and one more, whose name I have forgotten, as I only saw him once; also Mr. Edmondson, of Virginia; Mr. Russell, of New York, and several others; in all some twenty Representatives of his own and other States, of the present or thirty-fifth Congress.

On Monday, Blakeway and I breakfasted with Miles, and then went down to the House of Representatives. Great crowds were streaming down Pennsylvanian Avenue on their way to the Capitol; we found the best places in the galleries all filled, and not liking the heat and steam, we went down to the entrance of the House itself, and as the session was not declared then open, we got in, and remained in a kind of carpeted lobby, running round the chamber immediately behind the seats of the members. This part was also full of people, both members and others; and, in fact, the whole room was a living, chattering mass of persons. Precisely at twelve, noon, the Clerk of the House, the one, that is, who held the post last session, rose at the desk, and said, "It is now twelve o'clock, and according to the rules, the House of Representatives will come to order immediately." A great commotion took place, the crowd separated, the members remained within the legislative enclosure, and those who had no right there withdrew. Each member then took his seat, having an armchair to sit in, and a desk in front, furnished with lock-up drawer, inkstand, &c., and to each two seats, the invariable spittoon. The outside gallery was now crammed,—we had found a sofa in one recess, and sat quietly down, an official proceeded to clear away all strangers. Well, I thought and said, " Sit still, keep quiet, look as if we had business, and they will take us for members of the diplomatic corps." They looked at us, but never spoke a word; and we thus, by sheer impudence, and perhaps being recognised as strangers, managed to remain. The Clerk then began to read the list of members by States, and each one present answered to the roll call; out of 234 members, not more than a dozen were then absent. After the reading was over, which occupied more than an hour, he again read over the names of all that had replied, so as to make any requisite corrections; and when all was completed to his satisfaction, he said,—" The House will now come to order, and elect a Speaker to preside over the present Thirty-fifth Congress of the United States of America." Some one then rose and proposed Colonel Orr, of South Carolina. I think it was Mr. Banks, who, I told you, was elected Governor of Massachusetts, when I was in Boston, and was himself the last Speaker, who got up and proposed some one else. The Clerk then demanded how the House would vote, and according to its decision, the names of all the members were again read over, and each called out the name for which he desired to record his vote. When this was completed, the names voting for each candidate were read over again, and then I found the explanation of some sounds I had heard, but could not catch their meaning where I sat, as it appeared there were some five candidates, of whom one received only one vote. Colonel Orr was then declared duly elected Speaker, by a considerable majority, and was conducted to his seat by the former Speaker, and the oldest member of the House. He sat down, and immediately a silver-mounted staff, with a globe, and eagle with outstretched wings, also in silver, was placed upright in a socket by the chair, acting, I presume, as the mace in our House. The Speaker then rose, and in a few appropriate sentences, expressed his gratitude for the great honour the House had done him, and his intention to act with the strictest impartiality; so to conduct the proceedings, that they might redound to the honour and prosperity of their great country. The oldest member then swore him in, and he, calling the House to order, proceeded to swear in the members by States. This was a long affair, and took up the rest of the day, as the House seldom sits later than three or half-past. We then looked into the Senate Chamber, but here could only get into the gallery. There is very little difference in the appearance of the two rooms; but the members of that body are older, and perhaps more sedate-looking persons. They were busy electing their various paid officers, and their proceedings had no interest for us. We then returned to the hotel; after dinner I went into Mr. Miles's room, and had a talk over the day's proceedings and various subjects of interest to me, not without the solace of a quiet cigar; he has some excellent ones, won in a bet from Robert Gourdin.

The election of Colonel Orr is a triumph for the Democratic party. Last session they were eight weeks before they chose a Speaker, and ballotted some hundred times. Now what is the Democratic party, you will ask? It is the party of conservatism and State rights, as opposed to the Republican, who aim at a greater centralization of government at Washington, and to obtain a control over the actions of the State Legislatures.

For myself, I candidly confess, that before I came to the States, I had no definite idea how completely the separate States are sovereign in their own territories, and how little, really, is the influence of Congress. Each State has its own House of Representatives, its own Governor and officers, elected immediately by the vote of the people, its own magistrates, judges, and supreme courts of appeal. It forms its own constitution, makes and administers its own laws, levies and expends its own taxes,—but that constitution, and those laws, must be in accordance with the constitution of the United States, as defined by the Act forming the Federal Government, founded on the Declaration of Independence. This is the only tie they have, and as the original constitution provides that only white people can be citizens, or are citizens in its eye, and also recognises the institution of slavery, each State can, if it so please, decree, by the voice of a majority, that slavery shall or shall not exist. This is the great doctrine upheld by the Democrats, that each State shall decide on *all* its domestic institutions for itself and itself alone.

The Republicans say we will grant all that, except slavery, and will not allow its extension to new States, about to be admitted into Union as States, and sending representatives to Congress.

The Ultra-Republicans or Black-Republicans, as they are called, go the whole ticket for the abolition of slavery altogether. There is a third, but a falling party, that of the Americans or Know-nothings, whose doctrine is, that only Americans shall govern America, and that no foreign-born citizen shall hold any office. This strikes a blow at the large infusion of Irish and German element in the Government. Some modify it, and demand twenty-one years' residence before full citizenship can be obtained. They hate the Irish and all

Catholics. Their doctrine in its extreme, is wrong; for after all each State can decide for itself, what shall be the nature and claims for the exercise of the suffrage, and a share in the government; but it is not altogether wrong, for in many places, especially New York, men land from emigrant ships and vote almost immediately, which is the great cause why New York is such a "rowdy," badly-governed city. They ought to reside at least five or seven years before voting, so as to know something about the country and the people. I told ——, who is an American, that if I was a citizen, I should embrace Democratic Americanism. Their party has done good, it has ventilated the question and shown its importance; but it is powerless to carry out any extended measure. The South is, to a man, Democratic, of course, on account of the doctrine of States rights, and without which they could not maintain slavery for a day; if I may use the expression, they are Aristocratic Democrats; in fact, I told Miles he was far more an Aristocrat than myself. He wished to persuade me I was not a Radical, but that would not go down.

The duty of Congress is to make all laws having reference to the States, as a whole; the foreign relations, the army, navy, the regulations of customs, general post-office, Indian and territorial affairs, to decide on the admission of New States, and all questions of a Federal, as distinguished from a State character. The duties levied at the post constitute the revenue, which the Federal Government expend for Federal purposes; each member of Congress is paid 3,000 dollars per annum and mileage; formerly their pay was so much *per diem*, but they dragged out the session so long, that the present system has been adopted.

The great bore of members is the patronage. They are followed by a crowd of hungry aspirants for some office or other; and Miles told me it was even then, so early, a decided nuisance. I saw one impudent chap with him that didn't want a small, mean office, but some attachéship! and he told me of one poor, humble being, that perfectly haunted him. When he came down in the morning, he met him on the stairs, and he meekly bowed, and looked piteous and plaintive like, but never spoke: if he looked up from reading a newspaper, he was humbly bowing at his elbow: at the Capitol, wherever his eye fell, it lighted on this poor but persistent beggar; and he said, "I shall really try and do something for him, if I can, if only to get rid of such meek importunity." It is perfectly astounding to see the numbers that congregate about the members on all sides, to beg some favour from them.

On Tuesday, I essayed a visit to the White House, to call upon President Buchanan. I had on Saturday left my letters of introduction, and the door-keeper told me to step into the rooms. I went into a large, handsome apartment, furnished with chairs and sofas, covered with silk damask; mirrors on the walls; several people sitting down, some with their hats on. Out of that, a handsome room opened, and a suite of smaller rooms:—from the window there was a fine view of the Potomac. Whilst waiting in the large room, one free and independent citizen pulled off his hat, took out his pocket-comb, and combed his hair: when he had finished, he looked at the points, and then carefully wiped them on the silk sofa-cover, and returned the animal killer to his pocket! I thought I should have burst out laughing. After sitting till I got tired, a man came and said we had better go up stairs. So, thinks I, he doesn't receive here, after all; I had expected him to come into the room. Up stairs we went, and all sat some time in a small, rather shabby-looking room, and then his attendant or messenger, said, "Any gentleman wishing to see the President, can come in." I marched out first, crossed a small library, and entered the President's writing and business room. At a desk, writing, sat a white-headed old man, who immediately rose. I told him my name, and that I had sent him some letters, naming from whom. He shook hands with me, and said he was very glad to see me. He then went round, and did and said the same to all the rest. He wore a white tie, an old-fashioned coat, with broad laps, out of the pocket of which stuck a silk handkerchief, and he

had on an old pair of carpet slippers; still he is a
fine, dignified, yet simple-looking old man, and put
me somehow in mind of my dear old grandfather!
He then came back to me, and asked me how long
I had been in the States, when I left England, and
so forth; and then, which way was I going? I told
him to the South. He said, "I am very glad to
hear it," and then raising his voice, continued, "I
wish more of your countrymen would come and do
so, and observe that particular institution of the
South they so little understand, for themselves;
this would disabuse their minds of the impression
that 'Uncle Tom's Cabin' is a correct, or even any
picture of slavery." I was taken aback at such an
unexpected outburst from the President. I replied
that I should certainly avail myself of every possible
opportunity of making my own observations, and
forming my own independent judgment, but said
nothing more than that. He then expressed a
hope to see me again some evening, and introduce
me to his family, put out his hand, and so our
interview ended. I did not, however, avail myself
of the invitation; for, in the first place, I did not
know when to go, and I don't think I cared much
about going again. That was my visit to the White
House. Still, I have done all I cared for. * *

I called afterwards on Colonel Benton, an old
Senator, who has been long engaged in writing a
history of the Senate; and when nearly completed,
his house, in that part containing his books and

papers, was burnt to the ground. I had a longish
chat with him. He is the father of Mrs. ——, I
met at Mr. Gilpin's, and of Mrs. Colonel Fremont.
I expressed my regret at the loss he had had. He
said,—" For a long time after he could do nothing,
but sat for hours at a time, unable to collect a thought
or express an idea; but he had endeavoured and
mastered himself." I thought it, and I did not
hesitate to tell him so, the finest instance of perseverance and application, under overwhelming
difficulty and trouble, I had ever known or heard
of. He is a very fine old man, but quite absorbed
in his work, and I could see, that whilst talking
even, his mind was busy with other things.

We all dined together again: Miles, Blakeway,
and myself, went to the Speaker's room, and sat
some time with him; afterwards we went down
stairs, and I met the St. Paul's Indian trader, Ebury,
who danced the Medicine Dance for us. He introduced me to Mr. Kingsbury, the delegate from Minnesota, which is not yet a State, only a territory,
but will be admitted soon. The delegates only vote
in Congress on questions relating to their own
territories, and not on Federal questions.

On Wednesday morning, Blakeway returned to
Baltimore; we were mutually sorry to part; he is a
good fellow, and circumstances have made me
much indebted to him.

I went down to the Senate that day, but found
the galleries fearfully hot, so having a letter to

Senator Douglas, I asked the doorkeeper if he were in : he said " Yes," and took the letter and my card. Mr. Douglas came out immediately, expressed his pleasure at seeing me, but said he was very busy just then, but would I like to come into the body of the House?—exactly what I wanted. I thanked him, and said how much I should be obliged,—he passed me in and went to his seat, and I stood by the side of an old gentleman I thought I knew. I said to him, have I not the pleasure of seeing General Watson Webb, of New York? I was introduced to him by a letter from Mr. Stell. He immediately remembered me, and was very glad to see me. Having already, whilst talking, looked round the House, I fixed in my mind on one person, and I said, " Is Senator Sumner in the House ?" " There he sits, quite close to us," Webb said, " That is Burlingame talking to him; he was the member that challenged Brook, for assaulting him." " Oh ! " I said, "I have a letter of introduction to him in my portmanteau." Webb called Burlingame, and introduced me, and he then introduced me to Sumner. I said my father had had the pleasure of meeting him in Manchester. We had a little talk. He is a large man, and put me in mind of Mr. Dombey. Just then Douglas got the floor, and began to speak on the Kansas question, explaining in a speech of great power, but sophistical, his opposition to the President's message. Touching that point, as he is the most powerful debater in the Chamber, I was glad to hear him :—he spoke for more than an hour, accounting for the fact of his being busy, and made me feel all the more obliged to him for his kindness in coming out to me at such a moment. At the conclusion of his speech, the people in the crowded galleries cheered and clapped their hands, whereupon Senator Mason moved that the House be cleared of all strangers ; and read them a merited lecture on the impropriety of their conduct. Several others expressed most strongly their disapproval, but begged him to withdraw his motion, as it arose from ignorance on their part. He consented at last, and so they remained. Nothing much of interest followed Senator Douglas's speech, so I paid a visit to the Supreme Court of the United States, also situated in the Capitol, where I saw some eight respectable, staid-looking old judges, in black gowns, presiding over the quietest court I ever saw in my life.

I then looked into the Lower House, where the members were balloting for their seats, taking choice by rotation, as their names were drawn out of a box. Miles and I then walked back to the hotel, and dined with some half-dozen new members. Afterwards I got into conversation with a young officer of the United States Army, named Putnam, descended from the Revolutionary family, a general of which distinguished himself greatly in the Indian fights; and there is a celebrated leap he made to escape from them when almost made captive. Putnam wanted to arrange and go with me to Mount Vernon, but was under orders for the West, and left the next day.

On Thursday, after breakfast, I went down to the House. I wanted to go in, but could not get; I sent my card therefore to Miles, but before he could come out, I met the Minnesota delegate, who passed me in. Miles then found me, and there being a vacant seat next him within the bar, I took it, and sat beside him, and heard a deal of discussion, whether they should have a paid Chaplain to open their proceedings with prayer, or whether they should accept an offer from several clergymen to do it alternately, free gratis for nothing. It amused me a good deal, especially when one of them agreed it would save them 10,000 dollars a year, to accept the offer of gratuitous services. At two o'clock the House adjourned until Monday next, when the Speaker will name the various Committees. Just before adjourning, a message was sent from the Superintendent of Public Works, to say that the New Hall was quite ready for the use of the House. I then bid adieu to the House of Representatives, and intended to look a last look at the Senate, but they were in secret session with closed doors, and all strangers excluded. I don't know what they could be doing, so I left and visited the Patent Office, where I was interested in examining some of the models. All persons who take out patents are compelled to deposit a correct model of their invention, and these models are kept in glass cases, in a large hall. Mr. Miles kindly got me a copy of the last report of the Patent Office. In another portion of the same building, are preserved some most interesting historical relics; transcendant beyond all, is the original Declaration of Independence, with the signatures, which, alas, are rapidly fading away! John Hancock's is still visible, but that is about all now legible. In the same case are Washington's coat and trowsers, sword, camp equipage, writing desk, and some interesting documents:—the original treaties with Louis the XVI., Napoleon, and other European powers, with their signatures. The rest of the room is an ordinary museum. I then visited the Smithsonian Institute, which is founded by the will of a Mr. Smithson, for public lectures, library, &c. The building is very handsome, but still unfinished. I did not call it particularly interesting, except a collection of Indian portraits, nearly all of whom my cicerone knew, and had something to say about each. At dinner I met our usual Congressional party; and having the usual sit with Miles after, I went down stairs, and when I was in the bar, a gentleman introduced himself to me, and said he was a friend of Putnam's, and was a Captain Bryant, of the United States Army. He asked me if I was alone, if I would come to his room, and spend an hour with him and a friend. I

did so, and found the Captain a pleasant fellow :—
had been in the wars with the Sioux, and all the
North Western Indians ; and told me all about
their trails and their fights, so two or three hours
passed pleasantly. They drank the health of Queen
Victoria, and then I proposed the United States
Army, which pleased them a good deal. A gentleman stopped me one day in Washington, and
recalled himself to my mind as having been in the
stage with me from the Mammoth Cave to Louisville :—he was ill, and I had the power of rendering
him some little service, for which he seems eternally
grateful. He is a medical student ; but what his
name is, I have no idea, though he knew mine pat
enough.

On Friday morning I rose early, and set off,
about eight, to the steam-boat, to go down and pay
a visit to Mount Vernon, the residence and birth-
place of General Washington! The sail down
was very beautiful, the day magnificent; we stopped
at Fort Washington going down, and landed to
look at it. It is well built, but neither garrisoned
nor armed; some cannon, but not complete. Shortly
after leaving the Fort, the bell of the steamer
began to toll a funeral knell, which told me we were
close to Mount Vernon. It is the honoured custom
of all steamers passing the burial place of Washington
to toll their bells, and has been long the practice.
I liked the thought—the continued expression of
regret, that such a man could not live for ever—the

mark of national respect and gratitude, that no time can efface.

On a hill stood the old wooden house, overlooking the river; we drew up at a small wooden pier, and went ashore, having an hour and a half to stay. The distance from the Capital is about twenty miles. Walking up the path we came to the tomb, which is an ugly brick arch, with an iron grate, containing two stone sarcophagi—one of the General, the other of his wife. On his is an eagle, and this inscription,—" Washington,"—simple and sufficient. But what can I say of one right before the spectator, cut on the end of his coffin? I copied it, and here it is,—

BY THE PERMISSION OF

LAWRENCE LEWIS,

THE SURVIVING EXECUTOR OF

GENERAL WASHINGTON,

THIS SARCOPHAGUS WAS PRESENTED

BY JOHN STRUTHERS,

OF PHILADELPHIA, *Marble Mason.*

A.D. 1837.

As a specimen of an advertisement, it beats the "disconsolate widow" in Père la Chaise. It staggered, it disgusted me, and I turned away sadly chagrined. I took a twig from a tree that hung over the vault: I then visited the spot which he himself selected, and where he was interred, but removed to the new place. It is on the summit of a wooded knoll, and commands a lovely view up and down the Potomac.

x

How they dared to change the place, I cannot
imagine. His wish should have been law to the
end of time; but the people are so fond of change.
The house is a dilapidated wooden edifice, planned
by the General; the outbuildings are in ruins, and
the ground neglected. The owner, John A.
Washington, is poor; they say he keeps it so that
the nation may buy it. From a negro woman I
bought a hickory stick, cut in the woods; she was
inside the gate, which is not open for strangers, as
they pick and cut everything. Lots of little black
children toddling about. I went into one hut, and
saw two black babies, under the care of two little
darkies not much bigger themselves.

I hope, for the credit of the country, they will do
something to rescue this interesting spot from absolute decay. They are erecting an immense obelisk
at Washington in his honour, as ugly as anything can
be conceived. The money so spent, might have
been better employed in finding a fit resting-place,
for the remains of the greatest and purest of men,
the Founder of American Independence. They are
too busy speculating, and in too great a hurry to
give one thought to times gone by, or even to
services rendered. I gave one parting look at the
ugly advertising stone chest that contains his
remains, and went on board our little steamer;
got back at three, and dined again as usual. In
the evening, a band came to the hotel, and sere-
naded the Speaker. He made them a short speech,

expressing his gratitude for the unexpected compliment.

In talking with my Minnesotian friends, they quite endorsed my opinion about St. Paul's, and the impossibility of its maintaining its present forced position, and the high price of its land and building lots; mine was an opinion formed independently, from what I saw myself; theirs from a long acquaintance with the place, and an interest in that section of the country.

———————

MONDAY, *December* 14*th.*

I WROTE so far on Saturday night. To resume. On Friday night I bid all friends adieu, and arose at five on Saturday morning, to catch the Potomac steamer, *en route* to Richmond. The railway commences at a bend in the river, called Acquia Creek, about fifty miles from Washington. The boat was a large swift steamer, and the trip very pleasant; the day lovely and warm, and the scenery on the river showed to great advantage. In passing Mount Vernon the bell tolls, and I caught a glimpse of the old house *en passant.* The sweeps of the river are very pretty; it is extremely wide, and flocks of sea gulls followed us, to pick up the waifs and strays, in the form of bits of bread, as we had breakfasted on board.

At breakfast, an extremely gentlemanly young man, with some ladies, sat next me; we got into a chat, and afterwards, when I went on deck to smoke a cigar, he joined me. In the course of conversation he said he had met an Englishman at Baltimore, that he had known at the Virginia Springs, in the summer. I said, "Do you mean Blakeway?" "Yes," he replied; "Is your name Nicholls?" I replied that it was. His name is Allan, and he belongs to one of the oldest Virginian families. At Acquia Creek we took the cars. The road passes through a fine country, and it seemed strange to see nothing but darkies working in the fields. We reached Richmond about three, and on arriving at the Hotel Ballard, got an excellent room in the part always kept for ladies and married people. I have a capital negro man to wait upon me, who talks to me, and amuses me greatly; he is a big, fine young man, named Henry Watkins, of course a slave, belongs to some Mr. Tinsley. All the servants in the house, some hundred and thirty-five, are slaves, so now I am in full contact with the "domestic institution." I had a fire in my room, and sat writing till near two in the morning. Henry made up my fire in the morning, and soon after some one came and thundered at the door, and called out my name. Who can this be? thinks I. It proved to be young

Newhall, of Philadelphia, who had been a week in Richmond, and had seen my name in the book. "Well," says he, "how do you manage to get such capital rooms? I never can." I told him my *appearance* was sufficient to account for all that, and more; he had seen my rooms at the Girard.

After breakfast I went to the Coloured Church, where I saw some hundreds of coloured people, from black to nearly white, most attentive to the service. I believe it is a Methodist chapel; the preacher was a white man, niggers not being allowed to preach, or even to learn to read or write. I don't like that. Their singing was excellent, and when the parson was more earnest than usual, you could hear the old negroes groan out quite loud. The men all sat on one side, the women on the other. But who shall describe their toilets or their hoops, or their crinolines even? and for colours and small bonnets, white, pink, blue and black lace, gorgeously trimmed—the hues of the rainbow were poor in comparison to the glories of a coloured congregation. It was a very interesting sight; except myself and the parson, there was not a pure-blood white man there, and perhaps not ten free blacks—all slaves. I made my arrangements to be in Richmond on Sunday, on purpose to go to this church, and am glad I did so. It was a little close, but I did not perceive any unpleasant odour from them; in fact, though I have had so many near me, I have only once perceived anything

unpleasant, and that was from a fat, greasy old
black, at Troy. They had a collection after service, and one old darkey offered up a prayer; they
are allowed to pray to the God of all colours, black
or white. In the afternoon Mr. Allan called upon
me, and introduced me to a young Englishman,
who is going South; he wishes to go on with me.
I shall cut him as soon as I can; he is a regular
ass. He was half a day in Philadelphia, half a day
in Baltimore, one day in Washington, and then on
here. The evening I spent with Mr. Allan. His
mother is a very fine old lady; she was at the ball
at the Hotel de Ville, at which Papa was. I
was introduced to a queer fish, a Mr. Ward, a
member of the legislature of Virginia, which is now
in session here, and which I shall see to-morrow.

When I came down this morning, the office-
keeper gave me a card which a gentleman left for
me, to my great surprise and pleasure: a gentleman
to whom you and I owe a deal of gratification,
amusement, and also instruction,—I wish I could
keep you in suspense, but it was by G. P. R. James,
who is Consul at Richmond. I knew he was here,
and intended to call upon him, but was the more
pleased that he called first. His secretary lives at
the hotel, and had told Mr. James that I was here,
and so he called.   *   *   *   *   Mr. Allan,
according to promise, brought his buggy and pair,
and drove me about the town, to see the views and
so forth; the town is prettily situated on several

hills, and is divided by the James River from the town of Manchester, a small place on the other side. We looked over Pow-hattan, where the Indian Chief, the father of Pow-hattan, is buried.

We then went to a tobacco factory, and saw the process of pressing the chewing tobacco : horrid, dirty stuff, for a man to put into his mouth. We also visited an immense flour mill, where they grind some 1,500 barrels a day,—an enormous establishment.

I afterwards called on Mr. James; he is an old man, with a fine head, and takes a large amount of snuff: he asked after Sir John Potter, but it proved to be Sir Thomas he meant; he invited me to dine with him on Wednesday at five o'clock, which I promised to do. On my return, I found Mr. H——'s card, and several others, so you see I am getting on middling well, though I did not expect to know a soul. I have some letters for here, but have had no occasion to present them.

Among the servants are two so nearly white, that I asked about them, and to my surprise was told they were slaves. One, to my eye, is as white as I am; has straight, rather light brown hair, and looks for all the world like an English, or at the farthest, an Irish lad; the other is not quite so clear a white, and has black hair, not wool like the true negro. I told Ballard I could not stand that. No white slavery! It is running too close to the wind, to keep in that condition those who have so

large an admixture of pure blood in their veins;
perhaps not more than 1-16th or 1-32nd part is black
blood. When that point is reached, they ought to
be free, and possess the rights of freedom, for they
must certainly be as capable of taking care of
themselves as necessary—unlike the negroes, who
are as so many children.

WEDNESDAY.

YESTERDAY morning, I went down the street in
which the hotel is situated, to two dirty-looking
empty rooms, except for a few forms, and a stone
block: from their doors hung out red flags, on which
were affixed notices that so many negroes would
be sold at ten o'clock.

Imagine a dirty apartment, with a row of forms
against the wall; in the centre a raised platform,
and a lower one on one side; a little behind,
another form, on which three girls were sitting, and
a woman and child, a little boy, and a little girl,
and leaning against a pillar, one man. These
were all for sale; and as the room filled with men
chewing and smoking, those who thought of pur-
chasing, "went to the cattle" and examined them,
feeling their arms and hands, turning back their
fingers and thumbs to see that the joints worked

freely, opening their mouths to look at their teeth, and treating them generally as you would in buying a horse or a dog. Whilst watching this, some one came in and announced that he was just about to sell two boys, and would be glad if the company would step up to his auction room. I went with the crowd, and found two young men about to be disposed of. They were taken behind a screen and stripped, so that the purchasers could see whether they were sound, and free from all blemishes of any kind. One was then ordered to mount the block, his feet bared, and his trowsers turned up, that his limbs might be perfectly seen. The bidding commenced, and ran up to about 800 dollars. He was then ordered to go down, and walk quickly once or twice the length of the room, that people might see he had no lameness: put on the stand again, and finally knocked down for 905 dollars. The other one took his place, and being a likely, strong youth, the bidding ran up, and he was sold for 1,020 dollars. We then adjourned to the auction rooms, and the girls were put up; one went for 820, but a mulatto girl only brought about 620. The man was then put up, but he did not seem to suit the market, and was withdrawn: a little girl about 13 was then sold, but it was found on examination she had a burn, or some mark on her stomach,—she brought but a low price, as damaged goods. The little boy was bid for so poorly, that the auctioneer withdrew him, and declared the sale over for the day. The mulattoes are not so valuable as the pure blacks,—the admixture of white blood weakens the race, and in time they die out. This morning I saw a mulatto sold; he was said to be a good coachman, but only brought 430 dollars. Then there were two more young men for sale; but I had had enough, my very soul was sickened with what I had seen. Yet I cannot say there was any cruelty practised, or that the slaves appeared in the least to feel their position; but still there was the naked fact, in all its hideousness, of one human being disposing of another by public auction, and evidently considering that the human cattle were no more worth than dogs or horses. " Now, gentlemen, give me a bid;—anything to start with. Here is a likely young negro, right and tight and sound?"—that was his expression ; and between bids he kept repeating it,—" Right and tight and sound." I find that this sale of slaves is looked upon by the respectable classes with the greatest abhorrence, and the office of slave auctioneer esteemed about parallel with that of hangman. I afterwards walked with Mr. H—— about the town, who showed me some parts I had not seen before. We went to the Capitol, and walked into the Chambers, which adjourned soon after. Each state has its two houses, one of delegates, one for the Senate, arranged much the same as those at Washington; we went to the Library, and saw Washington's cane and telescope, which I had in my own hand.

This morning, after the sale, I went to the Capitol, and found one of the delegates to whom Allan had introduced me; an extraordinary creature, named Ward, from the wild back woods of Western Virginia, for the old dominions contain primeval forests of immense extent, mountain ranges, and splendid scenery, including the natural bridge; then, there are the springs, and the Weir's Cave, which I should like to have seen; but remember the State of Virginia is as large as all England; and to see the natural bridge from here, would consume five days.

I got a seat inside the House, and listened for nearly three hours to an interminable discussion on the appointment of a public printer, during which members shook their fists in each other's faces, whilst some sat with their feet on desks in front of them; certainly not a dignified assembly by any means. The beauty of it was, that when all was done, they were not one bit nearer the solution of their question than when they commenced, and on their adjournment had not decided whether they would proceed to the election, or postpone it until Monday next. It was an amusing exhibition taken as a whole, but left a query in my mind unsatisfied—How does legislation get on at all, in such a body? In truth, as I have often observed, this country gets on without being governed at all, in our sense of the word. The time to try their institutions has not arrived, but when the country is more fully peopled, then will be the real test. I went to Mr. James's, where I met a pleasant party, and spent a delightful evening. Mr. James is a genial, jovial, and amusing man, full of anecdotes and stories; he is well off, and owns a deal of land in Wisconsin, where one of his sons is settled, who is a civil engineer, and in that capacity has constructed several railroads. The present Duke of —— lays out 5,000 dollars a year in land in that State, leaving young James to select it for him. Mr. James is about sixty, and takes enormous quantities of snuff; has given up smoking, he used to smoke twenty-eight cigars a day, but nevertheless gave us some excellent ones after dinner. He was anxious to have had Governor Win to meet me, but he could not come.

I got your letter by the *Europa* last evening; she was sixteen days in crossing. Bless your dear heart, there is no more danger from wars than if I were at home. I dare say you are dull without me, and I shall be glad to get to my own dear home again, but still, now that I am so far, I must see all I can. I cannot yet make up my mind about The Havana. To-morrow I start for Charleston, twenty-six or thirty hours' journey, and hope to see some of the plantations, and negro labour as it really is.

MILLS HOUSE, CHARLESTON,

December 19*th.*

ON Thursday morning I paid one more visit to
the slave auction room, and saw several more
negroes disposed of as before, and although the
keen edge of disgust may to some extent wear off
on seeing more of it, that is because of its really
hardening influence on the mind, and not that it
has one redeeming point about it. " Here is a fine
young man, good field-hand, can drive and plough,
warranted sound and healthy, right and tight and
good." There he stands on a stool, looked at,
pulled, examined, made to walk or run, to show
his paces, his eye wandering anxiously round, to
see who may be his next master, and what his future
lot and destiny; and the hardened wretch stands
by his side, and knocks him down to the highest
bidder, as he has done some hundreds before,
making them of no more account than so many
cattle. Such an exhibition is a crying shame to
the country, and can never produce good; its evil
effects sink deep in the social heart of the South,
and yield the most baleful fruit. I then called
upon Mr. James; he was not in. His new novel
is called "Lord Montague's Page, a Tale of the

Seventeenth Century," and begins, " On a dark and stormy night." I saw it in the manuscript.

I started at three o'clock for Charleston; the rail crosses the James river, close to the falls, which are rapids, extending some distance, filled with islands, from a square foot to near an acre in size, and on through the forest, to Petersburg. Here we changed cars, and went on to Weldon, where we arrived about half-past eight, and had tea.

At nine, we left in other cars for Wilmington, and arrived there about half-past four in the morning. Here we staid an hour and a half, and had breakfast. We then crossed Cape Fear river in a steamboat, and taking the cars on the other side, went on to Florence, the road passing through a pine forest the whole 107 miles, not a town or village to be seen, only a few log huts for stations. In many places the swamps are large and deep, and the road carried over on piles, the water below discoloured with decaying vegetable matter, and vast trunks of trees rotting in the swamp: the trees are hung with a peculiar moss, that gives the appearance of hair, producing a singular effect. Florence proved to be a wooden station, and a wooden eating-room, where we had dinner; and at one o'clock started in another railway for Charleston. The road from Florence is equally through forest; in some places the line runs for miles, as straight as an arrow, without the slightest bend in it. On the road you see the pine trees cut and tapped, to allow the turpentine to run out, being one great staple of the district. We also passed some cotton fields; the plants looked black and uninteresting, the crops being gathered. I only saw one field that still retained a sufficient quantity to give some faint idea of what the appearance must be, when the ripened pods burst, and their white films cover the whole, as though with the purest snow. Curiously enough, the engine that brought our train from Florence, was named after my good friend Wm. Porcher Miles, which I took for a good omen. We arrived at Charleston about eight. I came straight to the Mills House, and got excellent accommodation, pretty well tired as you may suppose. I woke this morning, and felt a considerable shaking of the room, which I supposed to be an earthquake : when it was over, I went to sleep again as composedly as ever, and I find it has been a very sharp shock.

The morning mild and beautiful, I sallied forth to take a look at Charleston, which bears the appearance of being a good age. The houses of the better class are all surrounded with gardens, and have terraces and verandahs, which make them look well, and conduce to their comfort in the extreme heats of the summer. I walked straight down Meeting Street, and came to a fine open public part, right upon the sea, with the fresh Atlantic breeze, and the water dancing and sparkling in the sun. The harbour is a fine one, not very deep. At the corner of the street I saw a coloured man, and asked him if he knew where Mr. Gourdin lived? "Exactly." This was his answer. "Well, can you tell me where his office is?" "No one better; I waits on him." So I had accidentally hit upon his own servant. Following his direction, I turned down a street, and met Lewis Young, who took me straight to Mr. Gourdin's. Mr. Matthiessen joined us directly; Mr. Robert Gourdin was at Savannah. They were extremely glad to see me. I expect to visit some plantations this next week; it will be the darkies' holiday, and they give themselves up to fun for three days, so that if I get on some out-of-the-way plantation, I shall not be able to send you a letter per the Boston steamer; in fact I have now the difficulty I had in the West, not knowing when I ought to post a letter to ensure its catching the steamer; you won't, however, be uneasy, now you know the reason, should I miss a post. This is indeed a glorious climate; to-day, the 19th of December, I am sitting with my coat off, and the window open, writing to you;—not too hot, but that agreeable, temperate heat, which is not difficult to endure with plenty of exercise.

[The second letter from Charleston, containing a long and minute description of the cotton plantation, and addressed to Mr. Nicholls, was unaccountably and unfortunately lost.]

HAVANA, *January 7th*, 1858.

MY DEAR MAMMA,

As I find there is a chance of catching the next steamer from Boston, if I write to-day, I shall content myself with a few lines to say that I have arrived safe in Her Spanish Majesty's dominions of Cuba.

We left Charleston on Monday morning, and arrived here this morning about nine—seventy-three hours' sailing. Mr. Gourdin introduced me to a young Englishman from Liverpool, named Forwood, so we managed to come on together, which has made it much pleasanter for me. On board the *Isabel*, Forwood met a German he knew, named Weiss, so we three made a party to ourselves. Mr. Gourdin gave me a letter to the captain of the *Isabel*, who was extremely polite to us. The weather was charming, very little swell. We coasted along to Edisto, one of the Sea Islands, and at three stopped off Savannah, to leave mails, &c., and a small

Y

steamer came to fetch them on shore. Tuesday, saw but little land. Wednesday, ran all day along the coast of Florida, seeing nothing but the barren coral reefs, which render this shore so extremely dangerous; sometimes we were not two hundred yards from the reefs, which rise almost perpendicularly from the bottom of the ocean, with deep water quite close to them. Plenty of porpoises played about us, with shoals of small fish almost springing out of the sea, to escape from the dolphins. In the course of the afternoon, we saw an immense turtle quietly swimming along, and lazily raising his head to look at us as we passed. I wonder if he knew what an alderman is? Man-of-war birds, pelicans, were busy sailing about in search of the poor little fish, which are thus surrounded with enemies in the air, as well as the sea. The only vessels we saw, were small schooners belonging to wreckers, it being their principal occupation: as, owing to the dangerous navigation, shipwrecks are of constant occurrence. About half-past eight at night, we arrived at Key West, in Florida, where we stopped for half-an hour, to land cargo, mails, and passengers; so took a walk on shore, and, for the first time, saw cocoa-nut trees, palms, and so forth, in the streets and gardens. Tropical vegetation is a new wonder to me; and most luxuriant it appears. Soon as we left Key West, where we took on board a bride and bridegroom, who had gone there from Havana to be married, as there is no Protestant place of

worship in Cuba,—and, by the way, the gentleman, a Mr. Wills, a very nice young German,
proved to be the agent in Havana both of Forwood
and Weiss, and made himself useful to us at
once,—we passed some more coral reefs, and then
entered the great Gulf Stream, where there was a
good deal of motion. The night was hot, and the
state-rooms close. I saw some immense cock-
roaches walking about the sides and ceiling, at least
from two to three inches long, some of which I
killed; but as so many more came to the funeral,
I soon desisted, and fell asleep. I dressed, and
came on deck about six, and found the Island of
Cuba, bathed in the golden light of early morning,
lay before us,—the mountains dim and hazy; and
right a-head the Mora, the castle and lighthouse,
and the white dwellings of Havana! Close to the
ship whole myriads of flying-fish darted from the
water, and skimmed along its surface :—they do
not seem to rise high, but fly along on the top of
the sea; and every now and then, we saw a
beautiful nautilus, sailing about in its stately shell!
Hot was the morning, hotter was the day; and
when we rounded into the harbour, and dropped
anchor, we found what a West Indian January is.
We breakfasted on board, and found the place
quite full. At last one of the hotel agents said he
could give us a room with three beds in it, which
we were fain to take, at the Gardiner's House.
The room is high up and airy, and removed from

the close smells of the lower part of the houses, which are not unlike those of the Croce di Malta. This is the healthy season, but still very hot; no sickness about. I shall not attempt any description of the town till I have seen more of it. Mr. Wills took me to Mr. Crawford, to whom he is related by marriage. The old gentleman was very polite, and invited me to go there to-morrow evening, when they are at home. I also saw Mr. Bell, who crossed over with me in the *Asia*. Last Sunday, I dined and spent the day with Mr. Gourdin. They have indeed been kind to me; and all of them quite sorry to part with me: the lads have done all they possibly could,—far more than I could have expected:— Mr. Robert wished me to go to Savannah with him, and see the rice plantation, but I had not time.

HAVANA,

January 29th, 1858.

My Dear Mamma,

I REALLY have been most fortunate in always meeting with some agreeable companions to travel with, which, after all, is a great comfort, more especially in a place like this, where the language is one you are totally unacquainted with.

It is of less consequence in the United States, particularly when your letters of introduction turn out well, which mine certainly have done, in every instance.

My last letter I had finished before I had seen anything of this curious and interesting city, and was an account of the voyage itself.

After our arrival we got such accommodation as we could at the Gardiner's House; but I imagine it would be quite impossible to find worse hotels in any part of the world than are to be met with in Havana. The city stands in a fine harbour, with two extensive arms running into the land, at almost right angles to each other. The entrance from the ocean is rather narrow, and is commanded by a fine fort, called the Mora, on which is an excellent light-house, with revolving light. On landing at the shed, which serves the purpose of a custom-house, our luggage was very slightly examined, and on payment of two dollars we received permissive passports to remain one month in the island, our passports themselves being retained at the Police Office. I took mine with me, in case I should need one, which was *viséd* by the Spanish Consul at Charleston.

We followed the hotel proprietor (who had come on board to look for game) through narrow streets, until we reached the Calle del Oreille, in which this lovely mansion is situated, and, as I told you, met those delicious odours which brought back

reminiscences of other places. We had breakfasted on board, but found a second repast prepared, and sat down at table, on which were dishes
quite unknown to me, and which will so remain,
for of all messes I never saw their equal before.
Among them were baked bananas, which showed
how far South we were. After dressing, we ven-
tured forth, and endeavoured to find the office
and warehouse of Mr. Wills, who had been our
fellow-passenger. As there is no Directory, and
none of the large merchants have their names
affixed to their doors, and moreover, as we did not
possess three words of Spanish among us, it was a
work of some difficulty, and we had to proceed as
people do who cannot read, but have a direction
written down for them; this we had, and showing
it first at one shop and then another, we gradually
succeeded in finding the place we wanted. Not
more than two vehicles can pass in the street, and
only one in the narrow ones. The footpaths, less
than a yard wide, will give you some idea of the
magnitude of the streets. The shops, for the most
part, are open to the footpaths, without any windows, merely a large open doorway, or more than
one, if the establishment be extensive, so that
there may be a free circulation of air. Very few
buidings are more than two storeys high, and the
moment you leave the denser parts of the city,
have only one lofty storey. We passed the Governor's palace, in front of which is a handsome

square, laid out as a garden, a statue of the Queen
in the centre, which is a gravelled area, at each
corner of which there stands a magnificent palm
tree.   The style of architecture throughout is no
doubt derived from old Spain, and would recall
that country to mind more than any other.   The
population contains a large amount of negroes,
mulattos, some Chinese coolies, and various grades
of half-breeds, from purely black to nearly white.
The labourers and servants are mostly negroes, the
better class of workpeople being Cubans or Spaniards.
These are an indolent race.   Among the young
men you may see very many extremely handsome
faces, their striking paleness being rendered more
apparent by contrast with their black hair and
eyes; but all appearance of beauty is lost when
they grow older.   Mr. Wills took me to see Mr.
Crawford, the English Consul, and though an introduction to him may be necessary, I don't expect much
in that quarter; he invited me to come to his house
next evening, which I accepted.   Forwood and I
then strolled about the city, along by the harbour,
where several Spanish ships of war are stationed,
more than usual, as it is expected they will soon
be at war with Mexico.

We were much amused with the vehicles in
common use here, called "volantes," which consist
of a body like half a phæton, with a large splash-
board, two enormous wheels, and immense shafts,
which place the horse far in advance of the

carriage; the driver rides as postilion; and in these vehicles you see ladies driving about without bonnets, quite in evening dress. Sometimes there are two horses, the one being in the shafts; the other, ridden by the driver, is harnessed at one side; the whole affair bears a strong resemblance to the Maltese calèche. I have not seen a single bonnet in the place; the ladies go about with a veil thrown over their heads. We found it so excessively hot, that we got light hats; and I could not help smiling when I thought how astonished you would be if you could see your son, with his waistcoat open, his collar turned down, bronzed face and hands, a very handsome moustache, and a large Spanish sombrero on his head! We then returned to our hotel, and had what they called dinner, which I cannot pretend to describe. I had some turkey, with a species of dirt for stuffing, which I did not attempt to touch: the best part was some capital oranges. The temperature was 82 all day, and about 76 at night. The stars shine with a brilliancy we are not accustomed to; and the want of twilight is very striking to one from a northern latitude :—in ten or fifteen minutes from sunset it is quite dark. In the evening we went to hear the band play, in front of the palace, and met some of our fellow-passengers. We had to put up with cots to sleep in, which are mere canvass stretchers, with a sheet over; and were most miserably bitten by mosquitos. Fortunately, my face escaped; but the irritation in my hands and legs, is intolerable. We got up about half-past six, to have a walk, before the great heat of the day, and strolled to the outside of the city:—it is quite impossible to take any exercise in the middle of the day, the heat is so great; and it is not advisable for new comers to be too much exposed to the noonday sun. After dinner, Forwood and I went out in another direction, and visited another hotel, but found it no better than our own. We walked as far as a large barrack, in front of which a number of soldiers were being drilled. We walked on as far as the shore, where the wild Atlantic dashes on the coral rocks that surround this part of the island: then we passed a large building, and heard a great clanking of chains, which proceeded from several gangs of convicts, who were returning to this place, which we found was the prison, from their various labours. They were all chained by the legs, some two and two; others, merely from their ankles to their waists. They were accompanied by armed men, and drivers, who carried immense whips, which, no doubt, are often used. While we stood there, at least from two to three hundred passed in; and a person near, to whom I spoke in French, told me there were about 10,000 in the prisons. I thought there were more blacks than whites; but a more ferocious-looking set of beings I never saw: I could not help feeling a strong pity for them;—such treatment must convert men into wild animals. I returned to the hotel, dressed, and went to Mr. Crawford's, where I found some twenty people. We had tea, and talked, and I left at half-past ten, quite tired.

Their houses are well suited to the climate: this is one storey high. The entrance hall is the principal central room, with a marble floor; a room at each end forming a suite of three apartments; the windows are merely large openings, with iron bars running longitudinally; no glass, and Venetian shutters, all open and lighted up; any passer-by can see everything going on. As you pass down the street, you see into all the houses at night, in the same way. I called at Le Grand Hotel, outside the city, as I returned, and found Weiss, Forwood, and Mr. Getty (Wills' senior partner) having some supper, of which I gladly partook, being really hungry. As we returned through the gates, the sentinel challenged us, and Mr. Getty replied that we were for Spain, and friends *(Amigos)*.

This morning, after a few more mosquitoes, Forwood and I got up early, and had a walk. About half-past eight, went to Mr. Getty's, and had breakfast. He was amused at our hunger, as we cannot really eat the stuff at the hotel, and so invited us from absolute charity. Before breakfast we visited some half-dozen churches, all poor and shabby in the extreme. In the course of the day, we got better rooms, which had been promised us when the late occupiers (a young Russian prince

and his tutor) left, which they did to-day. After
dinner, we took a carriage, and drove out to the
Serro, a suburb of the city, containing very many
handsome dwellings, all in the same style, with
their verandahs and exposed rooms surrounded with
beautiful gardens, filled with the wild luxuriance of
tropical vegetation! We drove under avenues of
almond trees,—the oleander blossoming at the road
side, the stately palms, palmettos, and cocoa-nut
trees varied the larger growth; and as for the multitude of beautiful shrubs, my botanical knowledge is
too limited to describe them at all! We went on as
far as the old Bishop's Palace and Gardens, which
is now a desolate ruin, but has been a splendid
garden sometime. Here we saw the banana, the
palm, the bamboo canes growing in large clusters,
making a singular creaking noise in the wind, not
unlike the straining of a ship's masts. One tree
we could not make out, but it proved to be the
bread-fruit tree, with the fruit hanging on it: the
large cactus plant, fuschias, roses, all growing in a
wild, uncultivated state;—plants requiring the
greatest hot-house care with us! I think the palm
the most beautiful tree I ever saw, with its long,
peculiar-shaped trunk, without a single rough
branch, and the tuft of magnificent leaves at the
top, gracefully hanging, like feathers, from its lofty
head! For garden beauties, I never had a more
delightful drive in my life anywhere; and the
pleasure vastly increased by the natural productions

of this fair West Indian Isle! It seems strange to me to think I am really in the West Indies, where I never expected to be in my life:—I am glad to have seen the tropics; but I would not live here for anything in the world.

Tuesday.

On Sunday morning, early, we went down to the principal church, attended by the military, but it was really nothing particular; and after breakfast, just as we were going out for a walk, we found a large funeral passing the door, of the Intendant's wife. The body was carried by four persons, on a sort of bier, with a pall thrown over, but no coffin; and you could see the form of the corpse, and even the feet, which had on a new pair of boots, so, I presume, she was dressed out in very fine clothes:—we counted 140 carriages in the procession. We then crossed the harbour, in a small boat, and went up a flight of stairs, which brought us between the lines of fortifications, on the heights opposite the city. The forts are of great strength and size, and it took us a good while to pass over. The road brought us finally to the sea-shore, where we wandered for some time, picking up pieces of coral. The reefs are all coral;

but, of course, not like the beautiful coloured productions of the Mediterranean. It was dreadfully hot, and we returned to the hotel very much fatigued. After dinner, we took a "volante," and drove to the Amphitheatre, to see a bull-fight. The Queen of Spain has had a son lately; and, therefore, there have been sundry rejoicings—among them, this bull-fight.

You can imagine the arena at Verona, built of wood, and hence have a good idea of the circus here; it is very large, and I should say would hold 10,000 persons, or thereabouts. At half-past four the picadores, bandellieros, and matadores, all entered the arena, and bowed to the Captain General's box, in which the director of the fight sat, with a trumpeter by his side. He threw down a key, which a man tried to catch in his hat; if he succeeded he received half an ounce, if not he went without; this time he missed.

The picadores were two in number, and rode on horseback, with thick spears in their hands. The bandellieros shake the coloured cloths, to enrage the bull, the matadores finish the contest. As soon as the key was received it was applied to a door, just below where I sat; the man threw it open, and got behind it, when out rushed a magnificent black bull, with a small ribbon fastened in his back, which is done with a sharp iron, to enrage him. He flew round, glared wildly about, when one or two of the bandellieros ran to him, and shook a coloured cloth in his face, at which he immediately charged. At four points round the arena were double shields, behind which the men could get if hard pressed, and too strong to be broken down by the bull. The picadores attacked him with their spears; he flew at the horse, and gored his legs, which bled profusely, and turning suddenly on the other, before the man could protect it with his spear, plunged his horns into the poor thing's belly, and tore it so much that its bowels hung out. Again he charged, and quite ripped it open; the horse fell, the man was got off, the bull being attracted by the other men, in order to save him; he again turned, and finding the horse on the ground, gored it fearfully. The trumpeter then sounded his horn, and each bandelliera took two small darts in his hand, ornamented with paper, and ran about the bull until they had an opportunity of thrusting them into his neck. The maddened creature roared and dashed at the men, but they, springing nimbly aside, got behind the shields for protection. When the horn blew again, the matador made his appearance, and bowing to the box, took a red mantle in one hand and a sword in the other; the mantle he shook in the bull's face, nimbly leaping aside when the infuriated beast was about to charge; at last, seeing his chance, he plunged the sword in the animal, just above the shoulder. Its bellowings were the most loud and terrible, as it rushed about in mortal agony. The sword at last fell out, and the matador took it again, and again drove it into the back of its neck; the bull dropped on its knees, the blood pouring from its mouth, and then a man stepped up, and drove a small sharp dagger into the back of the neck, I presume into the spine, when it fell dead. Then three mules, gaily caparisoned, came in, and drew its body away, and dragged off the carcase of the horse.

The activity of the men is most wonderful; and their escapes hair-breadth at times:—running, jumping, shaking the cloths in the bulls' faces, springing on one side to avoid the charge, and often driven to shelter behind the screens,—they carry their lives in their hands. The gate opened again, and out rushed another bull, which immediately attacked a horseman ; and, plunging its horns in the horse's side, threw horse and man to the ground. They got up, only to receive another attack, until the horse was killed, although the other rider tried to divert its attention, which ended in this man being badly hurt before the trumpet sounded, and the attack with darts commenced:— the matador took two thrusts before that bull was killed. After this, Forwood said he had had enough ; I thought he would have fainted. I felt very queer, but got over it; and was resolved to see it out, as I had come for the purpose. The next bull had long sharp horns, like the first. He soon finished one horse, by breaking his leg; and,

turning on another, ran his horns straight into its
chest. The blood spurted from the large wound;
the horse began to quiver and stagger, and then
fell, and got up, and fell again; but before it was
quite dead, the bull charged it again, and tore it
dreadfully, when they attacked this one with darts.
They had fireworks somehow attached to them,
which went off, burning the animal's back, and
driving it into a perfect fury. The matador stood
in front a few minutes, exciting the beast still
more. He dodged it a few times, and then, standing steady, plunged his sword close to the spine:
the animal fell on his knees, then over on his side,
and was dead immediately! This is the highest
achievement of the matador, to kill at one thrust,
and it was received with loud cheers. The fourth
bull was also killed with one blow; the fifth had
two sword thrusts; and the sixth escaped with his
life as it had got dusk, and his death could not
have been properly witnessed. In all, eight horses
were killed; six of them in the arena, and two
must have died soon after.

The excitement of the people is most extraordinary; they shout and scream, clap their hands,
and almost dance, so much do they enter into the
sport, which, to my mind, is a most cruel exhibition. If men like to fight bulls, let them do so,
but not bring poor horses to be miserably torn to
pieces for no purpose, for of course the horse has
no means of defence against such a formidable

opponent as a bull. I am glad I have seen one, but have no curiosity to repeat a visit. I expected one man to have been killed; the bull threw his horse down, and he went with great force against the wooden hoarding round the circle, and the bull charged the horse several times as it lay down, without, however, injuring him; he was dragged from under, and seemed quite stunned.

On Monday, Mr. Crawford gave me a letter to a Signor Arrieta, at Flor de Cuba, beyond Cardenas, for which plantation we start in the morning. Forwood accompanies me, but as he has business here, we cannot leave until to-morrow; having, therefore, one spare day, I took it easily, for I find the climate very enervating. I went to the opera in the evening, where I found —— and —— who came over with us, and went behind the scenes, where I smoked a cigar, and was introduced to Tagliafico, Amodeo, and some others. I had planned to leave Havana to-morrow, but found the steamer *Quaker City* belonged to a broken company, and is seized for debt at New York, so I must wait for the regular United States mail, of which there is only one in a fortnight, and shall leave on Sunday, by the *Cahawba*, for New Orleans. Weiss and Forwood's friends, Gettig and Wills, have been very kind to us; this evening we dine with them, and go to Mr. Schneidler's afterwards, to a wedding party, Wills having married a Miss Schneidler.

z

This is a horridly dear place, three-and-a-half dollars a-day for miserable rooms, and nothing to eat. I am nearly famished; and we are quite grateful to any one to give us a meal's meat. I am reminded of old Baker's acting; instead of eating, we are eaten, by mosquitoes, fleas, &c. I can easily understand yellow-fever making such ravages here in the summer and autumn :—the people are not as cleanly even as in Italy. On Tuesday evening, we dined with our friends Gettig and Wills, and had a really good dinner, which we thoroughly enjoyed, and afterwards set off in a carriage to Mr. Schneidler's, where we found a moderate-sized party prepared for a dance. The house is constructed on the usual plan of the houses here,— no proper windows, but the space filled with iron bars, too close to admit any small child being put through; lofty rooms, a good verandah in front, all well lighted, and as open to the street as though it were a ball at Belle-Vue. The parties being early, all the carriages waited, and the street was soon quite filled with them. The drivers, and all the black population round about, thronged the rails of the balcony, to see the dancing, and hear the music. The gentlemen smoked about the room, and sat in the balcony, when not dancing. That part of the ball suited me very well. I had one quadrille with a lady I met at Mr. Crawford's. We had tea, lemonade, with a little wine, or brandy and water for the gentlemen; quite sufficient for the climate, but a poor support for real hard dancing. We left about half-past eleven, and got to bed a little after twelve.

WEDNESDAY MORNING.

I AWOKE exactly at half-past four, we put a few things together, got a cup of milk and a poached egg, and set off to the railway station for Tinguaro. Fortunately for us the ticket clerk was an Englishman; he warned us to take care our pockets were not picked. We took our seat in the carriage, which was exactly on the American plan, except that the seats were all cane-bottomed and sided, cool, but confoundedly hard to travel 180 miles upon. We started at six, at eight were detained till ten by a train of cars loaded with produce having got off the line a-head of our train, arrived at Guines, where we breakfasted about eleven. We met in the car a Cuban, who spoke English, and who showed us where to change cars, and what cars to take. He went with us to breakfast, ordered for us, and to our vexation paid for us too. At Union we changed cars, and again at Navajas, finally at Bemba, as the line branches first to Matanzas, then to Cardenas, and finally to Isabel.

We passed through a lovely country, groaning

with a profuse vegetation, groves of orange trees, loaded with fruit, bananas or plantains, bread-fruit trees, cocoa-nut palms, acres and acres of sugar canes, fields of pine apples, mangos, guavas, and towering above all the graceful but monotonous palm.

The country is rolling, and our horizon for many miles was bounded by a chain of mountains. After changing at Union we found another young Cuban, who spoke English, named Fernandez; he was also going to Tinguaro to his plantation close there, and he kindly offered to help us all he could. The Flor de Cuba being about five miles from the station, we did not know how to get over the distance. At five we reached Tinguaro, and our friend said, " There are some of the Flor de Cuba horses." They were, however, for an overseer and two slaves, one of them was manacled, having run away and kept away three years. The overseer was rather a surly fellow, by him we sent our traps to Flor de Cuba, and then walked rather more than a mile to the Tinguaro estate, belonging to the brother-in-law of Signor Arrieta, Don Diego; Fernandez went with us, but it so happened the owner was away, and the chief superintendent, so that we could not get any horses. The engineer came to us, and being an Irishman, was glad to have a talk; as it began to get dark, being close on sun-down, he said that he would put us on the road to the Flor; he walked some distance, and showed us the light of the place, as they make and use gas for themselves,

and then left us. We walked on and came to a bend
in the road, which turned off to the right hand,
the light being straight before us. It was then
quite dark, not a soul to be seen, and fixed as we
were we did not want to see any one, as we had no
pistols with us, every one going armed about here.
We tried a large cane-brake, but could make nothing
of it; then went down the road, but it appeared
so bad and rough that we could make nothing of
it, and so returned again; still without success, we
then went further along the road, and at last I said,
let us try this narrow passage between the canes,
as I saw a light through it; this we did, and came
suddenly on a wide track with the Flor de Cuba
lights on our left; we had been wandering in the
dark more than an hour, and arrived at seven at
the estate, quite tired. A person took us into the
works, and we found Signor Arrieta, to whom I
gave Mr. Crawford's letter. He received us most
kindly, and sent us to the house close to the works,
which he keeps entirely for visitors, having so many
in the course of the year, and ordered some dinner
for us; our luggage had arrived, and we found a neat
bedroom ready.

After a very good dinner, the Signor came to us,
told us to do just as we liked,—the only law he
enforced was, that we must be ready to go up to his
house at nine in the morning, to breakfast, and at
four, to dinner. He told us he had 800 slaves, including 200 Chinese coolies, who are slaves for

eight years,—called, however, apprentices. The
Chinese are treacherous, and he always wears a
sword, not knowing when or how they might be troublesome. He bid us good evening; and afterwards
we went into the works, where all the processes are
conducted, from the sugar cane to the finished
sugar. The head engineer is a Scotchman,—he
walked about with us, and told us a good deal relative to the condition of the slaves. From the top
of the boilers we looked down into the fire-hole,
where they were feeding the furnaces with crushed
cane; several men were working there in chains,
among them, the man we had seen manacled at the
station, and a big negro, with a whip, was lashing
it about their legs and backs every now and then.
All those who have misbehaved are set to work in the
fire-hole,—it is the penal labour of this plantation,
—both blacks and coolies. We then saw the immense
rollers, crushing the cane, and the sweet juice running down, and along a canal, to the place where
it is forced up into the vat. In this state it is called
waràpo—I drank some, but did not like it. Our
Scotch friend took us to his rooms, and said, he
would " gie us a gude drink." He sent a nigger for
some waràpo from the first boiling, broke into it
some eggs, and put some rum into it, which made
a most superlative drink, and was not only good,
but did us good. We then went to bed about half-
past ten, well fatigued; our room was on the second
floor, and under was the young nigger nursery.

Up at six the next morning, and into the works again, where we interested ourselves for some time in looking at the different processes, and admiring the beautiful machinery, attended by the two curious and distinct races of Africa and China, superintended by Spaniards, Cubans, Germans, and French, with a Scotchman, to keep the moving power in order, having several steam-engines under his care. A little before nine, a carriage came down for us, and took us to the house, a mile from the works. We were introduced to Signora Arrieta and her two sisters, all speaking English, having been educated at New York. Signor Arrieta also speaks English, and his brother a little, with whom I spoke French, as also with Signora Diego, the mother-in-law. They were all most kind, quiet, unaffected, and simple in their ways. They only come to this estate at the boiling season, when Signor Arrieta is in his works, generally from four in the morning until twelve at night,—rather long hours. About noon, the carriage took us down to the works, when Signor Arrieta's brother went round with us, and explained all the processes, from the crushing mill to the completion of the white sugar. They make about 10,000 boxes a year, besides the Muscavado sugar and molasses; the Muscavado is dried in centrifugal machines, and the treacle runs out into a trough at the bottom. The negroes live in a large square, formed by their houses, with a gate at each end, and a cookhouse in the centre. The Chinese are separated from them, as there is great antipathy between the races. A medical man lives on the premises, and great care is taken of them. The Chinese will try and get opium to smoke, and are much more difficult to manage than the blacks; they run away often, commit suicide, maim themselves, but are far more intelligent, and can be made good workmen, with great care.

The negroes are true Africans, retaining their language as the Chinese do theirs, but all knowing some Spanish. I told Signor Arrieta I thought it must be a difficult thing to manage such a combination of elements, which he said was the case. To the one slavery has no terrors, to the other it is thoroughly obnoxious, and though called apprentices for a time, they are slaves in reality. In their case the owner has no interest beyond the term of eight years, during which he must get all the work out of them possible; they cost him a high price, and he pays them each four dollars a month, besides their food and clothes. The negro is his for life, and therefore is not so hardly worked, since, if he falls ill he must be kept, and if prematurely old has to be relieved from toil.

I have not yet said anything to you about slavery in the States; it is very different here, and in some plantations exists in all its greatest horrors and abuse, but at Flor de Cuba punishment is rare, and they are all alike well treated. We had a

walk in the garden, where all the splendid productions of these tropical regions flourish in wild
abundance. What do you think of green peas
ready in January, in the open air? I saw one
negro there, whose back was terribly marked with
the lash, quite in long streaked wounds, which had
healed, but left life-long marks behind; I noticed
it, and pointed it out to Forwood, but made no
remark. At four the carriage came and took us
to dinner; after dinner we had horses, and rode
over the plantation till quite dark, having only
been over about a third of it, we then returned to
the works and sat with Signor Arrieta; he is much
opposed to the slave trade, says it is entirely carried
on by the Spaniards, not Cubans, between whom
there is no love lost, and in fact the Cubans appear
to sympathise with the Americans. This estate,
so far as its arrangements are concerned, is the
best, and the best managed in the island, and
therefore the one most interesting to strangers.
We expressed our gratiude to Signor Arrieta, and
retired early, having to rise at half-past four, which
we succeeded in doing; and at five, horses came
down, which took us to the Tinguaro Station,
arriving half an hour before the train left. It is a very
different mode of arriving at a station from what we
are accustomed to; every one comes on horseback,
with pistols in the holsters in front of his saddle,
and the effect is decidedly picturesque. Of course
the road was the same we had travelled before,

therefore nothing new; after all, the palm tree becomes monotonous. We got safely back about half-past three, choked with the red dust, which rose from the fields, the soil being of that colour.

On Saturday, I went on board the *Wabash*, an American frigate, a magnificent screw steamer, 6,000 tons. I introduced myself to the officer on deck, who presented me to the first-lieutenant, by whom I was conducted over the ship, and shown everything with great politeness. On board the *Wabash* were a large number of Fillibusters, who had been seized by the ship, and were being carried to New York. The first lieutenant expressed himself to me very strongly on the subject of such piratical expeditions, and I was gratified at the high tone he took, showing that, although the rowdyism of America may support such expeditions, the sensible people are quite opposed to them. We spent Sunday, literally hanging about, watching for the steamer, for they remain only a few hours, and unless you are on the *qui vive*, you might miss them. We dined with Mr. Gettig, at five, being then too late for her to come in. During the afternoon, I saw another splendid funeral of a Count Villa Nuova, who died of smallpox in the morning—buried in the afternoon;—short work that.

On Monday morning I got up early, and had the felicity of seeing the *Cahawba's* ship masts, as she came in about six. I was on board at half-past ten, and at one we sailed.

New Orleans, Friday,

January 22nd.

NEVER in my life was I so glad as to quit Havana.
It is a dirty, disgusting, plundering hole, and now
that I am safe, I will tell you that my anxiety to
escape was great, for not only had yellow-fever
broken out, but the most virulent kind of smallpox
was raging as an epidemic in one quarter of the
town,—not where we were, fortunately, but how
soon it might reach, who can tell? I was, indeed,
thankful, as we placed mile after mile between us
and that place. The weather had been unusually
hot and close, for the season; hence disease was so
rife. Nearly all the people who came with us from
Charleston, left by the *Cahawba*, including Mr.
King, of Washington, Attorney-General for the district of Columbia, all alike glad to escape. The
captain and purser were both officers in the navy,
and most agreeable and polite. The sea was rough,
but I did not miss a meal on board,—but few
managed that.
On Tuesday night one of the sailors died; he had
been ill when the ship left New York, and on Wednesday morning at ten, I witnessed that sad and
impressive scene, a funeral at sea. The flags were

hoisted half-mast high, the bell tolled, the engine stopped, and the body, fastened up in sail-cloth, with a heavy weight attached to the feet, the whole covered with the ship's colour, was borne to the after-deck, and placed by the paddle-box; the crew followed, the passengers all assembled, and with uncovered heads, listened to that solemn service which separates the dead from the living. The captain read the service with great earnestness and emotion, and at the words, "We commit his body to the deep," the corpse was slid down the board on which it was carried, and plunged into the blue waters, the eddies curled round it for a few passing moments—and then no trace remained of the sailor's grave. Afterwards, at New Orleans, in a paper called the "Picayune," I found the following lines, written by a passenger on board :—

THE BURIAL OF THE DANE.

Blue Gulf all around us,
　Blue sky overhead;
Muster all on the quarter,
　We must bury our dead!

It is but a Danish sailor,
　Rugged in front and form;
A common son of the forecastle,
　Grizzled with sun and storm.

His name, and the spot he hailed from,
　We know—and there's nothing more!
But perhaps his mother is waiting
　In the lonely island of Fohr.

Still as he lay there dying,
  Reason drifting a wreck,
" Tis my watch," he would mutter,
  " I must go upon deck."

Aye, on deck—by the foremast!—
  But watch and look-out are done;
The Union Jack laid o'er him,
  How quiet he lies in the sun!

Slow the ponderous engine,
  Stay the hurrying shaft!
Let the roll of the ocean
  Cradle our giant craft!
Gather around the grating,
  Carry your messmate aft!

Stand in order, and listen
  To the holiest page of prayer;
Let every foot be quiet,
  Every head be bare,
While the soft trade-wind is lifting
  A hundred locks of hair.

Our captain reads the service,
  (A little spray on his cheeks)
The grand old words of burial,
  And the trust a true heart seeks;
" We therefore commit his body
  To the deep"—and as he speaks,

Launched from the weather railing,
  Swift as the eye can mark,
The ghastly, shotted hammock
  Plunges, away from the shark,
Down, a thousand fathoms,
  Down into the dark!

A thousand summers and winters
  The stormy Gulf shall roll
High o'er his canvas coffin—
  But silence to doubt and dole!
There's a quiet harbour somewhere
  For the poor aweary soul.

Free the straining engine;
  Speed the tireless shaft;
Loose to' gallant and top-sail,
  The breeze is fair abaft!

Blue sea all around us,
  Blue sky bright o'er head;
Every man to his duty,
  We have buried our dead!

On Wednesday evening, January 20, we reached the bar of the Mississippi, but for miles we had been sailing in a sea of liquid mud; the point of the junction of the river and the tide is marked by a white streak, and after that no more blue water. We found the steamer, *Empire City*, fast on the bar of the south-west pass, with several ships near her, all in the same predicament, among which it was a matter of great difficulty to steer; at last, a shout and a crash informed us we had run into one, broken our bowsprit off, and damaged the starboard quarters; we swung round, and nearly carried away the *Empire City's* bowsprit, and then almost into a third. The captain then gave it up, and stood for the Pass à l'Outre, which we reached about twelve, and anchored for the night.

At six, on Thursday morning, we crossed the bar,

and found ourselves in a sort of canal, between
rushes, covered with water, so that no ground was
visible. A little further, driftwood appeared; next,
attached to the rushes, gradually banking up, a little
sand; until by degrees, there showed some real firm-
looking land, and a few miles more being passed,
we found a hut here and there, a few acres cleared
and planted, the river being excluded by means of
banks or levées, as they are called here. On our
right hand we could still see the ocean, the land
forming merely a sort of bank between us and it,
not more than a hundred yards across in some
places. So it goes on, step by step, becoming
larger and larger as you sail up, until you meet
plantations, houses, roads, and everything apper-
taining to *terra firma*. But the whole gradation
from muddy water to sugar plantations, is very
curious and interesting to see. The whole land is
formed by the deposits of this mighty river, which
reaches the sea by means of several mouths, les-
sening the effect of entering very much indeed,
but which forms land with greater rapidity. Nevertheless, it is a serious pity that so noble a stream,—
more than 3,000 miles long,—should be thus choked
at its *embouchures*, rendering its navigation to the
ocean so difficult, as well as dangerous. We came
at last to the junction of all the mouths with the
main stream, a mile and a half wide. There had
been a strong freshet in the river, and the captain
said he had never seen it so high before. The cur-

rent was strong against us, and we did not fairly arrive at New Orleans until Thursday night, at half-past ten, having been more than sixteen hours in sailing up the river, 118 miles. We had brought with us, from Charleston, a Mr. and Mrs. O——, of Washington; he was in a consumption, intending to stay some time in Havana, but the sickness drove him away; he looked dreadfully wearied; I felt quite grieved for him; he did not leave the ship that night, it being damp and foggy. I went to the St. Charles Hotel, where I found Herbert Shawcross had engaged me a room.

———————

SATURDAY.

THE first person I saw yesterday was Herbert. I went down to the steamer to get my traps, as it was too late the night before to pass them through the Custom House.

I called on Mr. Connor, to whom I had a letter from Mr. Gourdin, and found two letters from you, and two or three others: I was glad to have some news about home; I was sadly wanting to hear, but the time draws near when I hope to be at our dear home. Don't imagine I am not as much an Englishman as ever, but I am not a prejudiced

Englishman; after all, what is the difference between an American and an Englishman? They live on two sides of a great ocean, that is all. New Orleans is a queer place, very dirty; not so handsome by a great deal as I expected to find it, but it feels quite cool and agreeable after that horrid Havana. This hotel is a monster, accommodates 1,000 people; not any very striking buildings in the city; the greatest curiosity is the Levee, covered with cotton and merchandise, crowded with all the bustle of a sea-port, the sides lined with a cloud of steamers, those famous Mississippi boats. I could not help laughing to think your fears for the Havana trip all ran on pirates and so forth; how much more anxious you would have been had you known the real danger, but believe me had I known it I should most certainly not have gone there, for you must not think I would knowingly run such risks: I thank God I am safe and well here. This morning I was told our poor invalid passenger, Mr. O——, died in the night at this hotel;—what misery to die away from home, but it must be a relief that he lived to reach America, and had not died in that wretched Cuba, where the very existence of a Protestant is ignored.

A A

New Orleans,

January 27th, 1858.

My Dear Mamma,

* * * * This New Orleans is the dirtiest place I ever saw in my life, and as the weather has been wet, the streets are all but impassable from mud. Mr. Connor has been very kind to me, but I have been unfortunate in not meeting Mr. Claiborne until to-day, and as we leave to-morrow, I cannot avail myself of his good offices most kindly offered. Colonel Claiborne is attending the Legislature at Baton Rouge, and, therefore, away from his plantation at Point Coupeé, and the Hamptons are all absent owing to the wedding of a son, who is married to-day, therefore I shall not see any more plantations. I have, however, been so fortunate all along that I cannot complain, though just at one place I am not so lucky. Forwood and I start together to-morrow afternoon up the river, the steamer goes to Louisville and we shall get on to Cincinnati, and take the Baltimore and Ohio line to Baltimore. Louisville is 1,500 miles distant, and I presume we shall be seven days getting there— a long and tedious journey—but there is no other practical way of going. There will be only one

part of the country I shall not have seen—Georgia
and Alabama—but it is quite impossible to do it
all, and I am beginning to feel that I want my own
dear home again, and my usual occupations. New
Orleans stands, or, perhaps, more correctly speaking, floats on a swamp; dig down two feet and
all is water. The buildings are erected on planks
and piles sunk in the slime, and nothing but the
Levee prevents the city from being utterly destroyed, as the level of the water is twelve feet above
the lowest part of the place. The streets are wide
but wretchedly paved, and a ride over them is like a
jolt over a newly-ploughed field, splashing and
floundering in oceans of mud; the gutters are
open, the green slime festers in them, and the
effluvia nearly as bad as in Havana.

On Tuesday Mr. Connor took me a drive to Lake
Pontchartrain: after leaving the town the road is a
good one, being made entirely of shells, beaten
down by the traffic into the consistence of good
Macadam; the swamp surrounds it, rotting trees
of stunted growth; nothing can be conceived more
truly dismal. We stopped to look at a steam engine
turning a large wheel with floats like a steamer's
paddles, which forces the water from a lower to a
higher level, and this is the way the city is drained,
all the drainage running into canals, and being
forced from one level to another till it finally
reaches the lake.

We visited the old cemetery, which is Catholic,

and quite French, but few English graves. Even the dead they cannot bury, but build places not unlike ovens, in which the coffins are placed, and then the fronts cemented up, as there is literally no land in which they can dig a grave,—so that the dead are kept above ground. The appearance of such a cemetery is most singular, putting one somewhat in mind of the Columbaria of Rome. We also saw one of the great cotton presses, in which the bales are compressed, before sending them on board ship. Of all parts of the city the most extraordinary is the Levee, where all the merchandise is collected together. A line of these curious river-steamers, heads on to the Levee, are discharging their various cargoes, some loaded with cotton, so that the form of the ship is scarcely discernible; others bringing sugar, flour, Indian corn, all the varied products of the thousands of miles that form the water navigation of the Mississippi, Missouri, and Ohio rivers.

Herbert Shawcross has been very attentive to me, and has done all in his power to show me anything he could. We called to-day to see the Mayor, he was not in, being unwell, but we saw his Secretary; to-morrow morning we shall see him, and have a police-officer at our disposal, to show us the prison which I am anxious to visit. I should have been glad to have left here sooner, but it is always advisable to get a good boat up, and worth waiting a day for; I am glad I shall have company.

I shall not stop at any place on the river, but keep steadily on, and shall be glad to feel my face is at last turned homewards. I have not felt very energetic here; I attribute it to the re-laxing climate of Cuba, and shall feel different when I get, as I hope soon to do, into a colder and more bracing atmosphere. The people are listless, no one likes the place, but they live here to make money and get away. The city is quite healthy now, I believe, but I can easily understand why yellow fever is so constant a visitor in this city of swamps. The river is very high at present, so that I have no doubt its level above the lower point of the city will be more than twelve feet, which is the ordinary grade.

ON BOARD THE " ROBERT J. WARD,"

MISSISSIPPI RIVER,

January 31*st*, 1858.

MY DEAR MAMMA,

ON Thursday morning, by appointment, Shawcross and I went to the City Hall, where we saw the Mayor's Secretary, and from him received a letter to the Sheriff, in order to enable us to visit the prison. He also put up for me several pamphlets, and reports relating to city affairs, which he kindly sent to the hotel. One of his clerks went with us, to the Sheriff's Officer. This great official placed us in charge of a policeman, who took us to the prison. On entering, the turnkey said, " I cannot be answerable for your watches or pocket books, in going through." I thought this a somewhat singular statement, not reflecting much credit on the discipline of the establishment. We entered, and found all the prisoners living indiscriminately together, walking about in a large yard, just a kind of place that might have represented a prison a century ago, but totally subversive of our ideas of prison management. Four men were playing a game of whist. "What are they in for ?" "Waiting their trial for murder." Two most respectable looking young men were pointed out to me, as in on the same charge. I was relieved to get out of such a den of iniquity and wretchedness—I felt it was a disgrace to the country, to allow such holes to exist. There is no question that the administration of the law and of justice is not what it ought to be in some of the States, more especially in those which possess large seaports, receiving every year a great number of emigrants. After leaving the prisons, we visited some slave-auction rooms, and saw some 200 negroes for sale. Slave dealers are ever looked upon with feelings of aversion, and no respectable person will associate with a regular trafficker in human beings, although they may avail themselves of their services when required. I think I made the same observation before, and I find the fact universal. In this place was a very intelligent, free coloured man, who gave me a good deal of information with reference to the individuals for sale, and also of their treatment by some owners. It is most difficult to get at the truth. I believe, however, that the high-minded, educated and humane South Carolinian, would consider any ill-treatment of his negroes as a slur and a stain on his character. I believe that this same feeling prevails, to a vast extent, among slave-holders; that, moreover, just as on our side of the Atlantic, a more proper estimate of the value and dignity of labour prevails than formerly used to be the case, so here a change has taken place in the condition of the slave, and no person who ill-uses one, would be regarded in any other light than a brute, regardless of all human feeling, and would be treated accordingly. Yet it is possible there may be men callous to public opinion—men who will disregard all the instincts of human nature, and if such as these become slave-holders, they will, in all probability, abuse and over-tax their negroes. Everywhere, the laws for the protection of the slave are stringent, and neighbours can become informers. If a case of cruelty be proved, the master is punished, and the slave taken away from him, and sold to some other master, so that his former owner may not wreak his vengeance upon him. On the other hand, there are slaves who will not be amenable to any management, who rob and steal, who, in a word, constitute the criminals of the black population. I believe that a large proportion of those who are disposed of by auction are of the above class, except only in those cases where the master has been overtaken with misfortune, and compelled to sell his slaves to pay his debts.

The separation of families is of rare occurrence, and no child under ten can by law be disposed of separated from its mother. The free negroes in the North are a miserable and degraded race, gradually dying out; they have no care, no forethought, but exist on, as so many children, becoming paupers and criminals; they do not possess the energy which enables them to provide for themselves and their families. In the South the slaves are multiplying fast; they are free from all care and all anxieties; their work is laid down for them, and when completed they are free to do as they please, certain that when old and incapable there is a home provided for them, on the estate to which they have always been attached, and among those with whom their lives have been spent. That their condition in the North is not owing to the severity of climate, we need only call to mind that in the West Indian Islands, in a tropical climate, they are even worse off than in the free states, and that these fertile regions have gone almost entirely out of cultivation, because the need of labour is withdrawn. It is a position of high and serious responsibility, to feel that you hold in your own hand the destinies, the welfare, and the happiness of some hundreds of human beings, whether black or white; that their future depends on you; and above all, that there is another and a higher Power than your own, or any in this world, to which you must give an account of your stewardship. The stewardship of human life, of human souls, is a far more serious, a far higher and weightier duty than the administration of goods and chattels, and I can well enter into the feelings of the worthy and the excellent men who, in that position, striving to do as they would be done by, when taunted and upbraided by pseudo-philanthropists, recoil upon themselves, and exhibit the most intense hatred for the whole abolition North. Firmness and kindness are the two great principles on which the government of all good estates is based, and so completely is the negro character one of passive reflection, that from the character of the negroes you can tell that of the master, and from that of the master you may predict the disposition and conduct of his negroes. Hence the greater the responsibility, and I cannot help thinking that after all, the question of slavery is one that concerns the white man even more than it does the negro. The affections of the negro, if cultivated, are strong, and those affections are stronger towards the white master, when well treated, than to his own people; nay, even stronger than his animal instinctive love of life. Signor Arrieta told me an instance—that once his boiler valves were out of order; he was standing on the boiler at the time, expecting every moment a fearful explosion ; he ordered a negro standing near him to go away to a place of safety, as he felt compelled to stay and do all in his power to prevent an accident. " No, sar," was the reply, "if you die I will die with you." When this love is cultivated by judicious treatment, and the elements of a religious belief, the African becomes one of the happiest beings, in a condition which a white man would hold to be one of absolute degradation, and from which death would be hailed as a release. Unless this particular temperament be properly understood, it is difficult for any person to begin and be a slave-owner.

When with Mr. Townsend,* we discussed this point together; I had noticed numbers of little darkies going about and after his son, wherever he went. He said, " can any but good feeling spring up between them?" and then added, " I have negroes on my own plantation, brought up with me in the same way, who would lay down their lives for me; what must be my feelings towards them?" He never locks a door in his house; his slaves

---

* Mr. Townsend, of Bleak Hall, Edisto Island, at whose residence Mr. John Nicholls spent the last four or five days of 1857.

could have free access to him, if they wished, at any hour, day or night; and yet the Northern abolitionists persist in saying, that the planters are in such fear of their slaves that they lock them in their houses at night, and bolt and bar their own doors, and sleep with revolvers under their pillows. Now, do you wonder at my intense hatred of these liars? Wherever white labour can be employed it will drive out slavery, so that before many years are over the institution will practically be confined to the extreme South, and the cotton, sugar, and rice plantations; climate itself will form the impassable boundary line, on the temperate side white, on the tropical, negro labour. I see by the papers there is some discussion about introducing coolies into the West Indies; surely the English people will not be so utterly blind as not to perceive, that this would be the revival of the slave-trade in its worst phase. The Asiatics are to be brought over and apprenticed for a term of years; during that period they will be to all intents and purposes slaves. The interest of their temporary owners will be to get as much out of them in the time as possible; their future con-dition is no question for them. If they complete their term, it matters not how wretched, how debased they may be, how unable to continue to labour for their own support. If exhausted by toil they will be turned adrift, as there can be no obligation for their future maintenance; in a word, the machine called a coolie will cost £100, and that capital must produce, in the given time, its maximum amount. Contrast that with the condition of the African slave; wear him out early in life by undue labour, and he remains a burden for the rest of his days; whereas, by judicious management, his period of usefulness will be greatly prolonged. This was exactly what I saw in Cuba. The coolies had to do work which the negroes were exempt from; the consequences were manifest, the latter appeared happier and more comfortable: among the former suicides were frequent, many ran away, and all were more or less discontented.

February 1st.

AT five o'clock on Thursday evening we went on board the steamer, *Robert J. Ward,* which is a fine specimen of the truly magnificent Mississippi boat; she is 310 feet long over all ; her saloon is 256 feet in length, and her width about 50 feet; height from keel to the top of the pilot-house 60 feet. The fare is excellent, the management more in the restaurant style, one or two long tables, and several small ones. Forwood and I, with a young New Yorker, named Hunter, made a party together, got a table to ourselves, and one man to wait upon us. Herbert Shawcross came to see me off. Before I left,

I saw Mr. Connor, who introduced me to Colonel
Preston, brother-in-law of Colonel Hampton, to
whom I have a letter. Christopher Hampton is at
the plantation. Colonel Preston advised me to stop
at Skipwith's Landing, 495 miles above New Orleans,
As the boat started off, the darkies on board set up
a vigorous song, in chorus; and another steamer,
the *Vicksburg*, came after, she had evidently been
waiting to have a race with us. She was a smaller
and lighter boat than ours, and in time passed us.
But for a little while it was an exciting race—we
could see them piling the wood on to their fires,
and no doubt the same was taking place on our
boat, and all steam she could be made to bear was
carried. For my own part, I was glad when the race
was decided by our rival passing us. As it was just
dark, the glare of the fire, the shouts, the hoarse
puffing of the steam from the vent pipes, the rapid
rush through the water, all contributed to give a
good picture of life on this great river. Before tea,
I went to wash my hands, when a young man
stepped up to me, and said, " Don't you live in
Scotland?" I replied, " No." Well, " Were you
not at the Hotel des Princes, in Paris, last July?"
" Yes. Why, you are not Mr. Seymour, are
you?" " Indeed, I am." You will remember
the American we met in Paris, last summer;
this was the said American, to my surprise,
thus meeting again on a Mississippi steamer.
He was delighted to see me, and only re-

gretted we had not met in New Orleans. He joined our party, and made a comfortable fourth. He is full of fun, and helped us to pass a good time, as they say in this country;—another of my extraordinary *rencontres*. For miles and miles the banks of the Mississippi are low and flat, ever changing by the wash and wear of the great river, which averages a mile to a mile and a half in width, with a current of more than four miles an hour. The scenery is monotonous, but the most wonderful part of all is the accuracy with which the boat is steered day and night; it requires an apprenticeship of four years to learn the river, and then constant practice to be able to remember the bends, as well as to notice the changes ever occurring in the bed of the river, by the formation of new bars, islands, and fresh channels. The captain is a very kind and polite man, rather like the Duke of ———, wearing, like his Grace, a large sandy-coloured beard and whiskers. We spend a good deal of time in the Pilot House, from which we have the best view—it is a privilege not often allowed to passengers, but our captain seems quite glad to have us there. In the course of Friday, we stopped once at the river side to take in wood, and went ashore for a run. The engines are high-pressure, of course, each about 600-horse power, and the pressure carried is about 125 to 135 lbs. on the inch, burning nearly 70 cords of wood in 24 hours, at from three to four dollars a cord. Since then we

have always had a boat come along-side, and towed it
with us, until emptied, it then drops down with the
current to its own place. We passed Red River
and Natchez about nightfall, next day arrived at
Vicksburg, where Seymour left us. The captain
said he would stay for me at Skipwith's Landing,
and enquire if Mr. Hampton was at his place,
which is seven miles from the Landing. In the
course of the day we took in wood, from a person who
seemed so superior a man that I got into conversation with him; curiously enough he was a relation of
Hampton's, but did not know whether any of the
family were at the plantation or not. He had been
educated at West Point military school, had been a
fillibuster, first with the expedition of Lopez to Cuba,
where he was taken prisoner, and afterwards with
Walker, to Nicaragua. Now he has some 2,500 acres
of land, 150 hands, and is settled down on the river,
as a planter, selling his wood off to the steamers, as
he clears the land; he said he sold 12,000 dollars'
worth last year. Such is a specimen of a real
settler, a man of good education, a little wild in his
notions and habits at first, finally taking his place
and share in opening out this western country. I
found at last that we should not arrive at Skipwith's
Landing till ten at night, uncertain, perhaps, whether
Mr. Hampton was there or not; set on shore in a
pine wood, seven miles from the place, only a small
wooden hut at the Landing, so I decided, with
regret, that I would not remain, but go with the

steamer the entire route to Louisville. The weather was now much colder. Yesterday, we passed the mouth of the Arkansas river, and at night it became intensely dark, so that we thought at one time we must have lain to all night; it rained heavily, the rain turned to snow, but somehow we kept on, almost feeling our way with the lead and line.

This morning the ground was white, we stopped at Memphis, where Hunter left us, so now Forwood and I go on alone. This river rises and falls from its greatest height to its lowest water, 45 feet; imagine the quantity of water that represents a mile and a quarter wide, which will be its average width for 1,000 miles. It looks even wider now than at New Orleans, though we are about 850 miles from that city, and 1,000 from the sea. The change in the weather consoled me for not staying at Mr. Hampton's, for it would have been most miserable work in the country such weather as this. A fortnight ago I was suffering from heat in Havana, could not find cool enough things to wear, and now I have on my winter clothes, and my heavy pilot cloth suit; but the cold suits me far better than the heat. The state rooms on board are extremely comfortable, the berths large, and all very clean. It is curious how one gets accustomed to these boats and their excessive steam pressure; at first there is a feeling of complete insecurity, you feel each throb of the engines, and start at each puff of steam from the waste pipes, your sensations are those of sleeping over a powder-magazine in a storm of thunder and lightning, but by degrees it all wears off, and the last two nights I have slept as sound as in bed at home, though above the boilers, and one escape-pipe close to, making more noise than half-a-dozen locomotives puffing together.

This morning we passed a boat that had run on a sunken wreck in the river, and gone down in shallowish water; the pilot-house and part of Texas, the name given to the officers' cabin above the saloon, were above water; her back lay broken, and a more forlorn-looking thing I never saw; no lives lost, as there was so much of her out of water. We see plenty of snags, which are trees that have floated down; their roots in the water then catch fast in the mud; the stream breaks off the branches, and the sharp end of the tree sticks up, just at the right angles for catching any up-river boat, and often runs right through them, making a large leak, and sinking the unfortunate steamer. We have not many passengers, this not being the busy time. We have met a good many boats loaded with cotton, going down stream to New Orleans. On Saturday evening, we stopped to take some one on board from a plantation. On shore they lighted a pine-wood fire, and waved a torch to attract notice; we came to, and a large cresset, filled with lighted pitch-pine, was held on board, to give light; the whole scene was very picturesque, with a number of darkies round the fire on shore.

OHIO RIVER,

February 3rd.

YESTERDAY, about noon, we reached Cairo, at the mouth of the Ohio, where that river pours its great volume of water into the Mississippi, 1,000 miles above New Orleans. Before leaving the Father of Waters, I got a pint bottle, and filled it from the river, so, if no mischance occur to it, I shall bring home, I hope, a bottle of Mississippi water. The Ohio is a more picturesque stream than the greater river, the banks are more elevated. For several days, the only elevations we saw were the Chickasaw Bluffs. The islands are numerous, and well-wooded; in fact, the banks, the entire distance, have been covered with dense forests, except just where some few towns and clearings are situated. We have passed the mouths of the Tennessee and Cumberland rivers, also the Wabash and Green rivers, and expect to be at Louisville in good time to-morrow, proceeding on up the river to Cincinnati. The captain, Captain Millar, is a very agreeable and gentlemanly man, and has given me a deal of information about the river, as have the two pilots also, for we have spent most of our time in the pilot-house, for the sake of the magnificent view. The captain is the proprietor of the boat entirely, except one-eighth share. She cost 80,000 dollars, and her total receipts, last season, amounted to 67,000 dollars for passengers, and 45,000 for freight, 112,000 dollars in all. One of these steamers would be regarded with intense curiosity in Europe, as we have nothing approaching them in build. In former years, the flat boats conveyed all the goods and produce, and they were pushed up the river with poles; imagine the time and labour to push a boat, heavily loaded, 2,200 miles. The boatmen of the Mississippi were then a race peculiar to that river, having no compeers in the world. When steam-boats commenced running, they had to stop and cut their own wood, in the forests, as they went along. It is not very rapid, being seven days in doing 1,500 miles; and to-morrow will be our seventh day from New Orleans. There is, however, no doubt that, risks apart, it is one of the most comfortable modes of travelling in the world; you have plenty of room, good fare, and in the great travelling season, plenty of agreeable company.

We have only one lady on board, and she is a new-married widow, returning from her second honey-moon; she is pretty rich, and her husband is very attentive, he has never left her side all the time, and I really don't think that she has been outside the saloon during the trip. She is, moreover, an inveterate talker, and all in that cold prosaic tone that makes me think he will have enough of her before long. The captain told me he heard her descanting to her second on the merits of her dear departed first—how agreeable! There are, of course, a few gamblers on board; they have a faro table, but I don't see that any one plays, so they have been doing a little whist and all fours in the cabins, with sundry flats, though I don't think their journey a successful one.

From Cincinnati I intend to go again for a few more days to Washington, and learn a little more of party politics, then to Baltimore, one day in Philadelphia, leaving me a week in New York, before taking my departure from a country I shall much regret to leave, and which perhaps I may never have an opportunity of revisiting. Therefore it is that I am anxious to spend a few more days in the capital city, where I know so many who readily give me every information I require.

BURNET HOUSE, CINCINNATI,

February 5th.

EARLY in the morning of yesterday, the 4th, we arrived at Louisville, but did not leave the steamer until after breakfast, Captain Millar having invited us to stay and take breakfast with him, before going on shore, as he seemed quite sorry to lose us. No one could have been kinder than he was all the trip, and as we spent so much time with him and the pilots in the pilot-house, we saw all of the river that was interesting, and I have no doubt the pilots will often quote us as the two Englishmen that went up with them such a trip, and be astonished if every other Britisher they meet does not know us. We drove at once to the Cincinnati boat, and put our traps on board, having about two hours and a half to wait the sailing at noon.

We went to Captain Millar's office, and he gave me a picture of the *R. J. Ward*, the only one he had. We then went on board the Cincinnati boat, and arrived here about two this morning. The captain politely invited us to stay and breakfast with him ; we wanted, however, to get to our hotel, so, with regret, refused his kind invitation. Arriving at the Burnet-house, about six o'clock, it was like getting home again. I got an excellent room, and went to bed, for the last night had been one of considerable disturbance, owing to the frequent stoppage of the boat to land mails, and so forth.

I know you will be glad to find that I have now done with high-pressure steam boats. I have been 170 hours, and have travelled between 1,650 and 1,700 miles on the Mississippi and Ohio rivers, in that time,—no small journey,—without the slightest accident of any kind, in fact, accidents now are of extremely rare occurrence ; the engineers employed are steady, careful men, and the pilots know the river so well. I have before

remarked on the wonders of this river navigation, that a man should know 1,600 miles of
river as well as he knows the way up to bed at
night—every bend, every sand-bar and shallow,—for
the entire of that immense distance. One of these
pilots, to my surprise, said he had never seen the
sea, nor the river below New Orleans, or above St.
Louis, and has been twenty years running between
New Orleans and Louisville. He asked me, one
night, " How long, Mr. Nicholls, do you think
you could keep the boat in the river?"—meaning,
if I were steering. " How long I could keep her
up stream ?" I replied, " No longer than it would
take me to reach the nearest bank," which reply
amused him greatly.

Mr. Gourdin gave me a second letter to Mr.
Talbot Jones. I found him to-day, and he took
me to the club and the news-room. It is most
intensely cold here, and I feel it rather just now,
but a day or two will make me harder again.
When we left Havana we had a Mr. Harper
on board; he is the great New York publisher,
and last evening I found him in the river packet
again. He had come up from New Orleans a day
or two before me. Being acquainted with several
of my friends, both in England and in America,
we had a good deal in common to talk about. He
invited me to visit their large publishing and print-
ing place in New York, which I certainly shall do.
From the papers I see Mr. Douglas, in Kansas, is

quite the hero at present, and I am glad I have determined to revisit Washington for a few days, that I may see a little more of what is going on there, and get posted (as they say in the States) on this question, which is the great trial of the Buchanan administration, and I think three or four days there will amply repay me for the visit. I may then have the opportunity of attending one of the President's receptions, which had not commenced when I was there before.

I feel proud when I think that all the wonders achieved here are the result of the energy and spirit, as well as the love of freedom, derived from our own little island. I must say I think it is the only country worth visiting. I don't mean to say that all here is perfect, far from it; but the evils will be corrected, and there is that independence of character and action, which must make a great people in time.

Up to to-day, from leaving home, I have travelled exactly 12,750 miles—more than half the distance round the world. * * * *

BROWN'S HOTEL, WASHINGTON CITY.

February 13*th*, 1858.

MY DEAR MAMMA,

My last letter brought me up to Cincinnati, and on its receipt all your anxieties about
the South, and the dangers of Mississippi boats
would be at an end.

On Saturday I felt as usual after much travelling,
so determined to rest and stay quietly till Monday
morning, when I rose at half-past four, and started
in the train at six, arriving in Washington the next
day at noon, having travelled 620 miles in thirty
hours. The road is really splendid, the scenery
magnificent, especially at Harper's Ferry. I had
written for a bedroom, which was kept for me,
though the hotel was crammed full, but my friend
Stewart had taken care of me. I met a pleasant
old gentleman in the train, formerly Governor of
Minnesota, with whom I had a deal of chat. I first
went to the Capitol, and found Miles, who was glad to
see me; on my way down I met Mr. Rice, of Boston,
and was glad to meet him. Miles made an appointment with me for the evening, and I went into the
gallery of the New Hall of Representatives, where

the sittings are now being held. The new is much more commodious than the old hall, and the accommodations for the public very ample indeed. I remained till the house adjourned, and on my way back to dinner I fell in with Mr. Kingsley, of Minnesota, and went with him to his rooms. In the evening Mr. Miles called for me, and we went to the White House, to the President's reception.

I did not get an opportunity of speaking to the President, but found sufficient amusement in looking at the medley of people in the rooms. In one large apartment there was a band of music, people promenaded about, just as they pleased, and I left about half-past ten. We went late, as Miles was dining out first, and came only on my account. I met Mr. B——, of Troy, and had a little talk with him; I should not have recognised him if he had not told me who he was.

Wednesday I spent at the Capitol, and Thursday also. In the evening I dined with Miles; he and Keith, General Bonham, Mr. Garnett, of Virginia, and Banks, the printer of the house, all live together, and have a capital mess; Captain Calhoun dined there also, he is a son of the great Calhoun, one of the most distinguished men America ever produced. On Thursday morning I had a chat with General Sam Houston, of Texas; and a long and interesting conversation with General Quitman, of Mississippi, here at the hotel. I met a Captain Moore, an old Englishman, who is the despatch

agent to the Embassy, and he introduced me to
every one,—among the number, to General Blake,
an old Indian agent, who has spent almost all his life
among the tribes—he has left, to-day, for Florida,
to go among the Seminoles; he introduced me to
the head of the Indian department, and we dined
together yesterday. I asked this gentleman which
of the tribes were most true to the noble Indian
character? He told me the Dacotahs were the finest
race left on the Continent. Now, not more than
350,000 Indians exist in the States. I was also
introduced to the reporter for the official paper, the
Congressional Globe; Mr. Sutton, the head, is an
Englishman, and knew Manchester well. He has two
youths, one perhaps twenty-one, the other nine-
teen, and they do all the reporting for the " Senate;"
their organisation is most extraordinary. The
enclosed letter is for the " Guardian;" the information therein contained I have received from
members of Congress, such men as the Speaker
Orr, General Quitman, Miles, Bonham, Keith,
Kingsley, and so on. Of course I give, as I
intend, the Southern view of the subject and the
fight; I had the story from Keith himself, and
Miles, who sits close to him, so that it is perfectly
correct. I went up to-day to see them, Miles being
poorly, and Bonham and I sat a long long while
talking. Both to-day and yesterday it has been
snowing heavily, and I see plenty of sleighs already
in the streets, with the horses covered with bells,

jingling as they go along. My time has been so devoted to politics, that I have not much to tell you.

My next letter will be my last from this side of the Atlantic. I am going to say good-bye to my kind friends at Baltimore and Philadelphia; then a few days in New York, to see some of the out-skirts of the city, and then home again. I shall be glad to be at home, but I shall ever look upon this trip as the most important to me, the most momentous and interesting I have ever made. I shall leave hundreds of friends behind me; many that in all human probability I may never see again; some I do hope to see in England.

I have been very much interested in reading the account of the Princess Royal's marriage. Poor girl, her natural feelings, and those of her mother, were at last too strong for court etiquette. I like them both all the better for it, and I think the whole country will do the same; it must have been a very affecting scene indeed.

[This letter, which is alluded to in the preceding one, was sent to the " Manchester Guardian," by desire of Mr. John Nicholls, accompanied with a letter to the Editor, requesting its publication. It did not, however, appear, and the M.S. was ultimately returned.]

AMERICAN POLITICS.

WASHINGTON CITY,

February 13th, 1858.

SIR,

AMONG the great questions that have from time to time agitated the political world of the United States, few perhaps have offered subjects for more serious reflection than those which are connected with the elevation of Kansas from the position of a Territory to the dignity of a Sovereign State. The entire history of Kansas has been from the first one of constant struggle, of fierce excitement, party recrimination, and even bloodshed. After the passage of the Kansas-Nebraska Act, when it became evident that the people of those two new territories must decide on their own institutions for themselves, without any interference on the part of Congress, and must therefore decide whether slavery should or should not be a fundamental law of the new States, the Northern Abolitionists formed emigrant aid societies for the express purpose of settling the country with free-soil men, to the exclusion of slave-holders. The society of Massachusetts subscribed a capital of five million dollars to carry out these objects; and in order to counteract their influence, large numbers of persons came in from Missouri and other slave states. The resistance was thus first provoked by the Northern men; and the emigrants, in passing through Missouri, used such strong language in reference to the institutions of that State, that no other result could be expected than the antagonistic position occupied by both parties. The priority of interference, and the persistence of the Northern men, must be borne in mind when we hear the charge of "border ruffianism" brought against the Southern people.

To the delegates elected to represent the people of Kansas in the Lecompton convention, was confided the duty of drawing up a constitution for the future government of the State. It matters not now to enter into any discussion as to the mode of election of those delegates. We have heard charges of fraud and violence from the free-soil men, who, however, cannot be said to come into the contest with clean hands. The fact of their stupendous organisation was there; and if one party can be accused of violence the other is equally open to the charge; and so far as the people were concerned, their vote appointed the delegates to the Lecompton convention. If numbers refused to vote, they cannot blame those who exercised the franchise because the issue is opposed to their views. The President and his administration have acknowledged the validity of that convention; and at this moment all the influence of Government is exerted to procure the admission of Kansas into the Union, with the constitution agreed upon by the delegates in the Lecompton convention; under which constitution the new State would come in, acknowledging slavery as a legal institution.. The republican party denied the right of the convention to present a constitution to Congress, until they had referred it back to the people for their approval. The slavery clause being the great point at issue, the constitution with, or the constitution without slavery, was the test-question submitted to the people of Kansas, and their vote has pronounced in favour of the admission of their State into the Union as a slave state.

In the celebrated speech made at the commencement of the present session by Judge Douglas (a speech which I was so fortunate as to hear), the learned Senator, greatly to the surprise of his Southern Democratic friends, took exception to the mode in which the Lecompton constitution had been submitted to the people. He contended, that the several clauses of that constitution ought, one by one, to have received the ratification of a popular vote, and not merely the solitary clause relating to slavery. The Senator further denies the right of the Territorial Legislature to summon a convention, without a direct enabling act from Congress, or, in other words, that the convention, as summoned, was not legally empowered to form and offer to the people, any constitution whatever.

At the time this speech was delivered, the popular vote had not been taken, and therefore no application for admission from Kansas was before the House, further than the reference made to it in the President's message. On the second of the present month His Excellency Mr. Buchanan, delivered his message to Congress on this question, having received from the President of the " Constitutional Convention of Kansas," a copy of the constitution framed by that body. The subject is, therefore, at this moment, fairly before Congress, and its discussion excites the most serious apprehensions in the minds of the people generally.

Without entering into any lengthy statements relative to the legality of the Lecompton convention, it will be sufficient for me to refer to the celebrated Kansas-Nebraska Act, itself the offspring of Senator Douglas—an Act competent to give full authority to the people of those territories, to form and present such constitutions as may be agreed upon by a majority of the legal electors, without further action on the part of Congress. This act can hardly be considered as providing for the mere organisation of their temporary, territorial governments. It looks beyond the territorial states, it provides for the admission of a State; and in express terms pledges the faith of Government, that it shall be received into the Union, " with, or without slavery, as its constitution may prescribe, at the time of such admission." It also declares the " intent and meaning of this act" to be, " not to legislate slavery into any territory or state, nor to exclude it therefrom, but to leave the people thereof, perfectly free to form and regulate their institutions in their own way, subject only to the Constitution of the United States, and the provisions of this Act." This language is sufficiently clear. It was left to the people, whether directly or by delegations, to decide what should be the organic laws of the new State. The free-soil men in Kansas abstained from voting, therefore judgment has gone by default. It is most unreasonable on their part to expect, that under such circumstances the question shall be referred to them again, because they affirm they have a majority, and yet have declined to prove that majority at the ballot-box. The abolition party have organised their own so-called Topeka legislature, directly at variance with the laws of the United States, and the presence of Federal troops in the territory has been necessary, to restrain the violence of the free-soil men, who, in Lawrence, which is the hot-bed of all the abolition movements in the territory, were in actual insurrection, "involving an open defiance of the laws, and the establishment of an insurgent government in that city."

Thus we see that if the North accuses the South of undue and improper interference, the South may equally accuse the North of a serious breach of law, and the establishment of a state of anarchy. From the returns which have been received, it is reported that a majority of the State officers elected are free-soil men; the question, therefore, naturally arises,—Why should not the North permit the admission of Kansas, without raising any other question, since, if it be true that the anti-slavery men are in the majority, on the re-consideration of the Constitution in 1864, the State may become absolutely free? Thus it would appear to an outsider, that the contest was one of little moment. This, however, is not the case; Kansas is but the ground on which the North has decided at present to fight the abolition battle, and if there victorious will lay down as a law, that no more Slave States shall be admitted into the Union, thus over-riding the great fundamental principle of State sovereignty, that each State shall decide on its own domestic institutions for itself. We in England may not

C C

understand how rapidly the abolition party has increased in numerical strength. We regard it, perhaps, too much in the same light as we look upon the advocates of the Maine Liquor Law,—persistent, but powerless. In the Presidential contest of 1840, with James G. Birney, of Michigan, as its candidate, it polled 7,000 votes. In 1844, with the same candidate, it polled 62,140 votes. In 1848, with Martin Van Buren as its protegé, it polled 296,232 votes; and in 1856, with John C. Fremont as its Presidential candidate, it polled 1,341,812 votes. A very important element in this great accession of power, has been derived from the vast numbers of Germans who have come over and settled in the country subsequent to the revolutions of 1848-9. They were at once attracted by the word republicanism, and the idea of freedom for the slave, but at the same time perfectly ignorant of the constitutional history of the country. In addition to the actual professors and advocates of pure abolition doctrines, we must also regard the positions and platform of the republican party. In the Convention held in Philadelphia on the 18th of June, 1856, among the resolutions adopted were the two following:—" That we deny the authority of Congress, of a territorial legislature, of any individual, or association of individuals, to give legal existence to slavery in any territory of the United States, while the present Constitution shall be maintained." Resolved, " That the Constitution confers upon Congress sovereign power over the territories of the United States for their government, and that, in the exercise of this power, it is both the right and duty of Congress to prohibit in the territories those twin relics of barbarism—polygamy and slavery."

Such are the views, such the temper of the North, assuming year by year a more menacing attitude, and endeavouring to restrict the power of new States, to provide for their own internal institutions, by placing an absolute veto on slavery. The moment that a Slave State applies for admission, every difficulty that ingenuity can devise is thrown in the way; yet Free States are embraced at once, nay, dragged in without the slightest regard to law or precedent—California being a case in point. The opposition to the admission of Kansas is a great party move, to which, to the serious injury of his own future political prospects, Senator Douglas, in an evil hour, has lent himself. With a fair chance of succeeding Mr. Buchanan, the Senator, believing himself secure with the South, where, from his previous able advocacy of State sovereignty, he has been a favourite, has endeavoured, by splitting hairs on Kansas, to curry favour with the North, and now finds that between the two stools he has come to the ground, and signed the death-warrant of his own political advancement. He has most unfortunately divided the democratic party, and thrown upon that section of it which belongs to the Free States, the onus of either deserting the Southern section, or of standing forward as the advocate of slave institutions, necessarily fatal to its existence and influence on either issue. All this by-play is preparatory to the Presidential campaign of 1860. Mr. Douglas expected to be the nominee of the democratic party; his own move has broken up that party, and strengthened the hands of the republican. We may therefore expect that, at the next election, the democratic party will be defeated, and the republicans will come into power. For the present, on the Kansas question, the administration has been defeated. A proposition, made in the Lower House, to refer the question to the Committee on Territories, was lost by a majority of one only, and by a majority of three the opposition have referred the consideration of the Lecompton constitution to a special committee of fifteen. In the Senate, the subject has been referred to the Committee on Territories, and should that body agree on a bill, it may come down to the Lower House, and be voted upon before the select committee has had any opportunity of getting to work, and in all probability, so far as I can at present ascertain, may pass the House of Representatives by a bare majority, as some members now opposed may be reached through administrative influence. Under either result the democratic party will be divided, and the election of 1860 will, in all human probability, surrender the power into the hands of the North. The policy of the abolition party in relation to the admission of new States is, to throw every obstacle in the way of new Slave States, thus endeavouring to confine slavery to the localities in which it exists, by surrounding them with a cordon of Free States. After Kansas will come Arizna, and New Mexico,— each, like Kansas, to be kept " bleeding," to serve the purposes of mere party politics. To this the South is strenuously opposed, and every day the struggle in Congress becomes more and more decidedly sectional. It is no longer party, whether republican or democratic, that divides the two houses, but it is absolutely North *versus* South. Day by day the breach widens, the abuse of the North has embittered the feelings of Southern men. The constant attacks made by the abolition party on the domestic institutions of the South, have excited an intensity of hatred for the North, which becomes painfully apparent in conversing with people in the Slave States. Not only is the question of slavery a bone of contention between these two grand divisions of the country, but on questions of general policy they are widely separated. Whilst the North clings to high tariffs and protective duties, the interests of the producing South are all on the side of free trade; but, so long as it remains in a minority, it is compelled to submit to the gross injustice inflicted upon it, by the excessive duties levied on imports, to support and encourage Northern manufactures. Seeking a greater development of the Western country, as an increased market for its productions, the North desires to devote large sums of money, drawn from the Federal treasury, for the purpose of extending railroads which may afford outlets for its own commercial enterprise, at the expense of the Southern consumer. That the North is not especially scrupulous as to the means exerted to further its own ends, is apparent from the revelations consequent on the bankruptcy of a prominent firm, which at this moment are being the subjects of enquiry before a select committee of the House of Representatives. Constantly seeking a greater centralisation of government in Washington, for the sake of increased patronage, and for political purposes,—in opposition to the views of the South, which are strongly on the side of state sovereignty, of free-trade and of direct taxation,—the two separate lines of policy are becoming more and more strongly marked, and in effect, no one can witness a debate in the House without remarking the fact to which I have alluded, that all former parties are broken down, and North and South stand now fairly face to face in direct opposition. Such is the position of affairs,—a position which excites alarm in the minds of all true lovers of the Union. Should the admission of Kansas under the Lecompton constitution, with slavery, be denied by a vote of the House, so far as I can learn from conversing with many different

members, there is great danger of a serious rupture.
I cannot exactly believe in absolute disunion, but
I should not be surprised to see the Southern men
retire, in a body, from Congress, and hold a
Southern democratic convention, which, in all
human probability, would advocate the establishment of a Southern slave-holding confederacy. In
fact, I cannot avoid the conclusion, that never since
the nullification days of South Carolina, has the
union between the two irreconcileable parties of
North and South, been so fragile as at the present
moment. If, however, as I expect will be the
case, Kansas is admitted with the slave clause, the
evil day will be postponed, and it will then remain
to be seen whether, in 1860, an abolition administration shall be inaugurated, pledged to refuse
admission to all new Slave States. Should that be
the case, the South will be thoroughly united, and
separation will be inevitable. Nothing will, apparently, satisfy the North, but total abolition
doctrines, and their hostility to the South has been
ever on the increase from the date of the Missouri
compromise to the present time; and I fear that
hostility will never cease, until it has succeeded in
sundering that Union, which was effected by the
genius of Washington, and cemented in the blood
of the patriots of the American Revolution.

In the case of a Southern confederacy being
formed, we should find how strong are the feelings
of attachment to England throughout the South,

and how closely they would desire to be united with the mother country. These feelings are, moreover, strengthened by the great interests of the cotton-growing States, between which and our own district, the connection is of the closest kind. Our industries depend mainly on the cotton-crop of the Southern States,—that slave-grown crop, without which our machinery must remain idle, and our working-classes literally starve to death. To us, therefore, the questions assuming such large proportions in Congress, are of vital consequence. If, however, slavery be a gross injustice, a wrong to the African, no material interests or commercial expediences, can be permitted to outweigh the great principles of right and justice. No one, however, can calmly and dispassionately examine the workings of the " domestic institution of the South" for himself, without being convinced that by its means, the African becomes, up to a certain point, a civilised being. The influences of Christianity are brought to bear upon him. His affections are cultivated. His physical wants are amply supplied. Statistics prove that the slaves are larger consumers of animal food than any other labouring population in the world. His labour is not great, his hours of relaxation are numerous, and in sickness and old age he has a home provided for him, on the estate to which he belongs, and his declining years are passed among those who have been attached to him for life. In exchange for these realities, he gives his labour, and his freedom, the latter an unknown quantity in his native Africa, a something which he only learns by coming in contact with the white race. There are certain peculiarities about the negro race, which we do not understand at all in England. We do not realise the fact, that in a state detestable to a white man, the negro is perfectly happy, and the instances of slaves refusing their freedom, are of every-day occurrence. In fact, the African accepts the condition of servitude mainly from the fact, that he is incapable of self-control, and the exercise of the forethought necessary to enable him to provide for himself, in a free state. The most casual observer must see how degraded, lost, forlorn, is the condition of nine-tenths of the free blacks in the North, and how utterly wretched, when compared with their enslaved, but comfortable and well-fed brethren at the South. The real fact of the case is this, that negro labour, whether it be slave or free, cannot compete with white labour; and as the latter is in the ascendant at the North, the unprotected and helpless free negro soon sinks into a deplorable state. Abolitionists may talk as much as they please about negro rights, but no one can observe their treatment of the negro without feeling, that all this talk, this pretended sympathy, is put on for political purposes. The negroes are not permitted to come near a Northern man, to sit in the same car with him, or even to pray to God in the same hour, unless it be in some place set apart for the coloured race. In the South, the master and the slave take each other by the hand, and receive the sacramental elements from the same minister, and drink from the same cup. In fact, I cannot give a better or a clearer idea, to those who have never seen a well-ordered plantation, than by saying, that the term " domestic institution" most thoroughly explains the relations between the superior and inferior races. We have witnessed the results of wholesale emancipation in our West Indian Islands, and with that example before them, the Southern men cannot see much inducement to enact the same folly at home. There are two important considerations connected with this subject. In the first place, certain productions of consequence to man are met with only in tropical regions. Secondly, none but the African or Asiatic can labour in those regions, which are fatal to the white man. Hence, one of two conclusions is inevitable,—either the abandonment of these regions, or the employment of these races. Under the rule of Great Britain, the negroes were carried into America, and have prospered and grown there, until they have reached the large number of some four millions. To disturb the present position of things would be, at one blow, to destroy the producing power of those states, and to inflict the most serious injuries on the whole civilised world. Hence we can understand how bitter are the feelings evoked in the South, by the endeavours of the North to raise up, not only the hostility of other sections of the country against them, but even, at times, to seek to arouse their own slaves to actual rebellion. I am not maintaining that there have never been evils, perhaps cruelties, connected with slavery,—but from my own observation I have arrived at the conclusion, that an amelioration has taken place in the condition of the slave, similar to that which has taken place in the condition of the labouring classes all over the world. If the Americans had their hard drivers, we had our children working in coal mines, under the most degraded conditions. Whilst we have legislated for these cases, education and public opinion in America have placed a shield over the negro, which preserves him from all cruelties. In fact, the very idea of the permission of cruelties towards their slaves, is as gross an insult to the great body of planters, as the accusations of Lord Ashley were to the manufacturers of Lancashire. Two great principles are combined in protecting the slave from oppression,—interest, and humanity,—and these operate far more in the Southern States than anywhere else in the world, where capital and labour are brought into mutual relation. Since the suppression of the slave trade in 1808, the slave population has doubled every twenty-six years and four months, and we find the duration of life among the negroes equal to that of the most favoured races in the New or Old World.

These two facts alone, are a sufficient answer to the charge of cruel or improper treatment. I have not the time, nor is this the place, to enter into any examination of slavery as a principle. I merely content myself with recording what I know to be facts, derived from my own observation or from reliable sources, and I cannot avoid the conclusion, that the more thoroughly we become acquainted with the labour question of the Southern States, the more we shall sympathise with those classes, who have been unjustly abused and held up to public scorn, by the Stowes and other extreme partisans of abolition doctrines.

An incident occurred in the House of Representatives the other evening, which may produce an impression in England, that the members of Congress are somewhat fond of an appeal to force. I have not seen a fair statement of the facts of the case in any of the papers, for the general impression derivable from the reports in the journals would be, that Mr. Keith made an unprovoked assault on Mr. Grow, of Pennsylvania. The sitting had been prolonged to an unusual hour, two in the morning, and the members were all fatigued, as well as irritated by the warfare of tactics which had been going on all day with reference to questions connected with Kansas. Mr. Grow came over to the Southern side of the house, and whilst there some questions were put from the Chair, to which he said he objected. For an opposition member to speak from the administrative side is a breach of etiquette, and Mr. Keith told him, in plain terms, to leave that side and speak from his own place. Mr. Grow retorted that it was a free hall, whereupon Mr. Keith, excited as well as exasperated, sprang up, and seizing him by the throat, pushed him away. A friend seized Keith, and thrust him back on his desk, but in the meantime the confusion became general, and I believe if it had not been for the place, the scene was ludicrous in the highest degree. One Southern man, flinging up his arms, exclaimed "that the revolution had commenced," and plunged into the *melée*. The smallest member of the house, Mr. Washburn, of Maine, attacked the biggest man he could find, and fell upon Mr. Craige, who is a giant in size;—an amusing scene was the result, the dwarf not being able to strike so high as his opponent's knees, and the giant making unavailing efforts to reach down low enough to touch the little one's head. One member had his wig knocked off, which gave rise to a report that some one was scalped; altogether, whilst the scene lasted, the prevailing sound was laughter. Order was restored and the house adjourned. Mr. Keith, at the next sitting, made an ample and gentlemanly apology, which fully satisfied the house and the country, but Mr. Grow made his own position worse by the terms in which he expressed his regret for the occurrence. One fact was very apparent and suggestive during the fight,—the Southern men singled out Northern men, and the Northern men Southern men, as their opponents. The general feeling was one of regret that any exhibition of the kind should have taken place within the walls of the House of Representatives.

A bill has been introduced into the Senate to provide for an increase of the army by the addition of five new regiments. This measure has been so strongly opposed that it has dwindled down to a proposal to add two companies to fifteen regiments, and it is still very doubtful whether it can pass.

In connection with the alleged appropriation by Lawrence, Stone and Co. of 87,000 dollars for the purpose of carrying the last tariff through Congress, a constitutional question of some importance has arisen. Fifty-eight thousand dollars were traced directly to the hands of a Mr. Walcott, and when examined before a committee of the House he declined to state what he did with the money. When closely pressed he solemnly declared, that neither directly nor indirectly was any part of it devoted to the purpose of influencing the votes of members, and that the expenditure was entirely private, therefore the House had no right to insist on an inquiry which would compel him to enter into details relating to his own special affairs. The House is not satisfied, but demands a reply; in the meantime Mr. Walcott is in custody of the

Sergeant-at-Arms, and is in consultation with his counsel as to what replies he is bound to furnish,— the committee demanding that he shall make a clean breast of the whole transaction, whether it be private or not. Whilst the Kansas question occupies the field, the other suppliant territory of Minnesota awaits the conclusion of the contest, to receive her call to the Union. Her senators and representatives are now in Washington, but I am informed that on account of some rather injudicious expressions of opinion on the part of one of the members elect, with reference to their actions in the Kansas controversy, they are compelled to remain outside the walls of the Capitol, lest in this nice balance of parties a new State should practically decide on the admission of another new State to the Union. From all I can learn, the administration counts on a majority which will enable it to carry the Lecompton constitution through the house, although the majority may be but small. The question has now for so long a time monopolised public attention, that all parties throughout the country, who are really actuated by patriotic motives, desire to see it set at rest, and withdrawn from the political arena for ever. Then the *bonâ fide* settlers of the country can model their institutions to suit their own views and interests, without provoking the interference of any other sections of the country, whether belonging to the North or the South.

I cannot conclude this already lengthy communication without expressing my own sincere hope, that the clouds at present hanging over the American Union may be dissipated, and that all these perplexing questions may, by mutual concession, be decided in a conciliatory spirit, for I can conceive nothing more hostile to the developement of liberal opinions throughout the world, than any assumption of an antagonistic position between the two grand sectional divisions of the Southern and Northern States of this great Union.

    I remain, Sir,

      Yours most truly,

        JOHN A. NICHOLLS.

       FAIRY KNOWE,

         February 21st, 1858.

MY DEAR MAMMA,

    You will see from the address of this, that I am staying, according to my promise, with the Latrobes, before leaving America, and I am now writing my last letter from the New World. I could not really tear myself away, without again visiting those who have been so kind to me.

According to arrángement, I came on from Washington, and as the operatic troupe were here, all the fashionables of Baltimore were at the Theatre; so the first evening I went to Barnum's Hotel. At the Theatre, I met most of my kind friends, all so delighted to see me, that it was quite pleasant to be so welcomed. The next day, Old Uncle William looked after my traps, and brought them here by the train; I drove out with Osman, in his buggy, and was met at the door by the whole family, most happy to see me. On Saturday, and, in fact, from Thursday night, it snowed heavily, and so on Saturday morning I went into town with Osman, in his sleigh, the first time in my life I ever had a sleigh ride. He has a most comfortable one; we were all wrapped up in furs, our two horses covered with sweet-toned bells, and they jingled merrily on our way. In Baltimore we met plenty; every one that could command the service of a horse mounted something on runners, if only a basket or a box. The motion is easy and pleasant; you glide over the snow with hardly an effort, but I do not think it would be half the fun it is without the bells. I found they had all heard that Havana had been unhealthy, were in great anxiety on my account, and had written to New Orleans about me, to find out where and how I was. I sincerely hope you did not hear anything to make you uneasy.

So they have turned us all out at the Athenæum. Well, I don't care much; in fact, being so long absent, I might expect not to be re-elected, but they seem to have swept out many of the old ones.

It is quite pleasant to have a good bed to sleep in, and be kept warm and comfortable; in fact, this rest at Fairy Knowe has done me good, and I am glad that my last letter home should be written from under this kind and hospitable roof.

I have just received your letter per *Baltic*. Why so uneasy? Because you might be quite certain that there was a possibility of one of my letters missing, as well as some of yours have done. I am quite well, never better, but much disturbed at your anxiety. I declare it is a bad thing to write regularly, for then the least irregularity excites anxiety. * * * *

FINIS.

Johnson and Rawson, Printers, Manchester.

www.ingramcontent.com/pod-product-compliance
Lightning Source LLC
Chambersburg PA
CBHW021329110726
47900CB00005B/1410